Cry of the Raven

Center Point
Large Print

Also by Morgan L. Busse and available from Center Point Large Print:

Mark of the Raven
Flight of the Raven

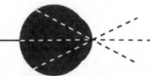

**This Large Print Book carries the
Seal of Approval of N.A.V.H.**

THE
RAVENWOOD
SAGA

BOOK THREE

Cry of
the Raven

MORGAN L. BUSSE

CENTER POINT LARGE PRINT
THORNDIKE, MAINE

This Center Point Large Print edition
is published in the year 2020 by arrangement with
Bethany House Publishers, a division of Baker
Publishing Group.

The text of this Large Print edition is unabridged.
In other aspects, this book may vary
from the original edition.
Printed in the United States of America
on permanent paper.
Set in 16-point Times New Roman type.

ISBN: 978-1-64358-567-3

The Library of Congress has cataloged this record
under Library of Congress Control Number: 2019956943

To my mother.
Thank you for life, for love,
and for your wisdom.
I love you.

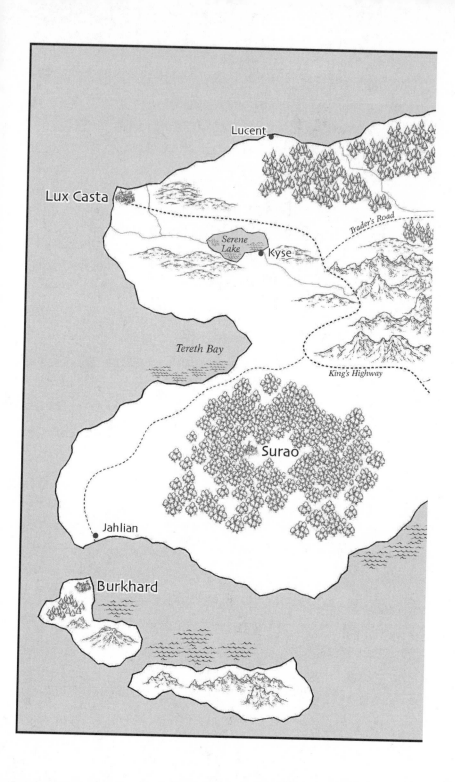

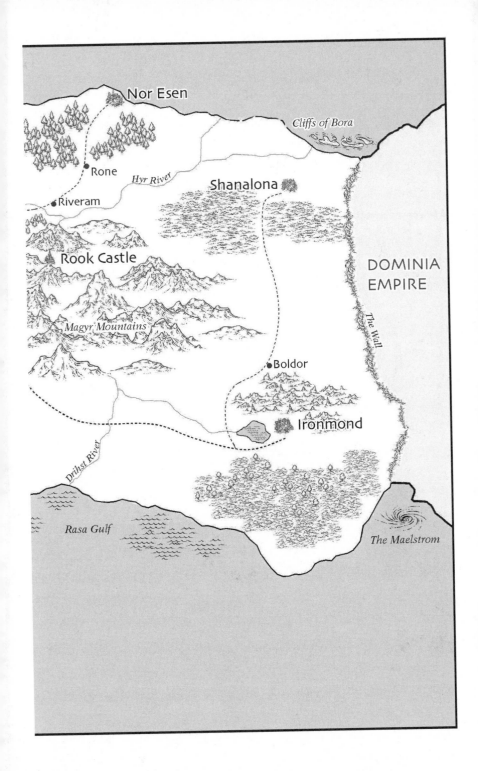

Character List

HOUSE RAVENWOOD
House of Dreamers

Grand Lady Ragna
Caiaphas (consort)
Amara (deceased)
Opheliana

HOUSE MARIS
House of Waters

Grand Lord Damien
Grand Lady Selene Ravenwood
Grand Lord Remfrey (deceased)
Serawyn (deceased)
Quinn (deceased)

HOUSE FRIERE
House of Fire and Earth

Grand Lord Ivulf
Raoul

HOUSE VIVEK

House of Wisdom

Grand Lord Rune (brother) (deceased)
Grand Lady Runa (sister) (deceased)
Renlar

HOUSE RAFEL

House of Healing

Grand Lord Haruk
Ayaka

HOUSE LUCERAS

House of Light

Grand Lord Warin (deceased)
Grand Lord Leo
Tyrn
Elric
Adalyn

HOUSE MEREK

House of Courage

Grand Lady Bryren
Reidin (consort)
Grand Lord Malrin (deceased)

Cry of the Raven

1

Numb. So numb.

The only thing Selene could feel was the dull thump of her heart beating as she sat beside the window in the guest chambers the next day.

I love you.

Damien's words echoed inside her mind as she stared outside. Her sister Amara's last words before she died in the dreamscape were not far behind: *I think I cared about you too, a little. I was just too jealous to see how much we needed each other.*

A single tear trickled down Selene's cheek. Powerful words, words she had been waiting to hear for a long time, both spoken in the same night.

And she had no answer for either.

Amara was gone now. And she had yet to answer Damien's declaration, even though she already had her response.

I love you too.

The sentence lay upon her lips, waiting to be spoken. And yet everything inside of her felt heavy. With love came grief and hurt. It would be easier to steal back behind her cold mask, back to the numbness. If she had done what she had been trained to do, she would not be grieving over Amara's death now. And she would not be feeling the euphoria of Damien's words.

"No." Selene spoke the word aloud, her hand curled over the arm of the chair. "I will not go back to who I was. No matter how hard it is to feel." She stood up and crossed the temporary bedroom she shared with Damien. He was already gone, making the inquiries of her sister on her behalf, letting the others know that she would be grieving for the rest of the day.

The blood on the floor in the other room had been cleaned, but she could still picture her sister lying there. She swallowed and paused. At least she had been able to show Amara who they were meant to be as dreamwalkers and who the Light was at the end.

A sad smile spread across Selene's lips. Her sister was at peace and free of their mother.

The pattering sound behind her announced that the rainstorm threatening Lux Casta had started. It was as if the weather was a reflection of her own grieving heart, and yet it was cleansing as well.

Selene left the bedchambers and entered the common room. The room was dark and cool, the windows filled with grey clouds outside. Karl stood by the door on guard, his dark hair brushed back, his spine straight. He glanced at her and nodded. She bowed her head in return. Sometime in the last couple days—or even weeks—Karl had finally dropped his disdain for her.

The main door opened a minute later, and Damien and Taegis walked in. The moment she locked eyes with Damien, the heaviness across her chest lifted, and her heart began to beat again.

He returned her look with an intense one of his own. "Selene." He crossed the room and took one of her hands and kissed her fingers. His lips and breath were warm across her skin. "I spoke to Lord Leo," he said as he lifted his head. "It is not their custom to burn bodies, and he was less inclined to do anything for a would-be assassin, but since Amara was your sister, and she was a member of a Great House, he will see that her body is prepared and the ashes given to you."

She curled her fingers around his. "Thank you, Damien."

"While I was with Lord Leo, we received word that Grand Lord Renlar will be arriving tomorrow."

"The son of Lord Rune Vivek?"

"I know you are grieving, but we cannot let any more time pass before signing the treaty. Would you be willing to represent House Ravenwood when he arrives?"

"Yes." There was no hesitation in her voice. Her mother might still be the figurehead for House Ravenwood, but her gift had already marked her as the new head of house. And she had a promise to keep to Amara: to protect their sister Opheliana at any cost. She would find a way back to Rook Castle. One way or another.

The rain continued to fall as Selene walked beside Damien toward the meeting hall the next afternoon. The usual gleaming white halls of Lux Casta were cool and grey in the light of the storm. Every few minutes, lightning flashed outside, followed by a hollow boom.

Servants moved from room to room, removing the mourning cloth from pictures and furniture and replacing the black banners with the standards of House Luceras once again. Lord Warin's body had been escorted to the family mausoleum that morning, but war did not allow time for grieving or for the luxury of announcing the next grand lord. Instead, Lord Leo had been named head of House Luceras in a private coronation in the Temple of Splendor, with only his siblings and the priests as his witnesses, shortly after his father was interred. Now Lord Leo would represent his people in the upcoming treaty, and Selene wondered if he would still vote the same way his father had.

A guard stood on either side of the white double doors that led into the room beyond. Both bowed to Damien and Selene before one opened the door on the right and ushered them into a long hall with white stone walls, alabaster marble floor, and tall windows along one side of the room. Rain tapped against the glass in a soothing manner.

In the middle was a beautifully carved table that filled the length of the room. Around the table were ornate chairs, almost like small thrones. A silver chandelier hung above the table, casting light across the area.

They were the first to arrive. Damien walked over to the left and pulled out the chair farthest from the door. Without a word, Selene took the seat, and he pushed the chair in before taking the one next to her.

Soon after, Lady Bryren arrived. She spotted Damien and Selene and nodded, remaining unusually quiet and reserved as she sat on the opposite side of them.

Rain ticked off the time as the three waited. Low, muffled voices echoed on the other side of the doors. When the door opened seconds later, Lord Leo entered, his white cloak fluttering behind him and his blond hair brushing his collar like threads of gold.

Right behind him came another man, with rich dark skin and thick black hair, wearing the striking colors House Vivek was known for. His tunic was deep blue and made of silk, with stars embroidered along the collar, the symbol and colors for his house. A black leather vest and pants completed his outfit. His face drew Selene's gaze, those smooth edges, that glint of intellect. There was no doubt about it. He was Lord Renlar Vivek, the son of Lord Rune.

Lord Leo approached the table. He stopped at the head and placed his fingers along the wooden surface, then looked at those gathered. There was something different about him. He seemed taller, more regal. There was an air of confidence and authority around him. Almost as if the coronation had changed him from a firstborn son to grand lord.

He motioned toward Lord Renlar, who now stood at his side. "My fellow lords and ladies, may I present to you Grand Lord Renlar of House Vivek."

Starting to the right, Lord Leo introduced each person present. Lady Bryren dipped her head at the mention of her name. Damien and Lady Selene bowed.

"Thank you, everyone," Lord Leo continued, "for agreeing to meet on such short notice, even though you just arrived"—he glanced at Lord Renlar—"and with all the events that have occurred over the last few days." His jaw tightened for a moment. Selene felt the same contraction as grief washed over her own heart.

Lord Renlar bowed. "I understand the gravity of this meeting." His voice was low and had a slight rumble to it. "But perhaps before we begin discussing the treaty, we should talk about some events that have come to light, such as my origins, Lord Damien's escape from Rook Castle, the duplicity of House Ravenwood and House Friere, amongst other things. I believe before we align our houses and people, there should be no more secrets."

Damien affirmed Lord Renlar's words with a small nod. Selene also agreed. No more hiding in the dark. It was time for the truth to come out.

Lord Leo took a seat at the head of the table and motioned for Lord Renlar to continue. "Please, Lord Renlar, go first."

Lord Renlar nodded and took a step forward toward the table. "Many of you didn't know of my existence until recently. My mother was a commoner. Her marriage to my father was a secret, and so was my birth. Because of my mother's status, it was decided that my aunt would carry on House Vivek's line, and I was sent away to study in the great libraries. It was there that I learned to use my gift of wisdom and decided to apply it toward my people in quiet, subtle ways. Even when I became an adult, very few knew of my life or my connection to House Vivek. House Maris was one of those who did."

He nodded toward Damien before continuing. "Eventually my aunt married, but no heir ever came of her union. When word reached Shanalona last harvest of Lord Rune's and Lady Runa's deaths, I was given the choice to claim the title of grand lord publicly or to remain anonymous and allow a lesser house to take over House Vivek. My study of our history—all of our histories—informed my decision. What I came to realize is the importance of the Great Houses and our gifts. The only way we will win against the empire is to combine our gifts. It was this very reason we were given these abilities." He placed a hand on his chest. "I carry the gift of wisdom through my father's bloodline. Because of that, I have a responsibility to all people to use my gift to help them. And now I stand here today as grand lord of House Vivek in place of my father." Lord Renlar bowed again before he took a seat to the left of Lord Leo.

Lord Leo folded his hands and looked around the room. "I understand your sentiments, Lord Renlar. But as you know, only six of the seven Great Houses still have their gifts. And one of those houses has chosen to align with the empire. I'm afraid this unity you speak of will never happen, even if House Friere returns to us."

"I am aware," Lord Renlar said calmly, "but even still, I believe we have a chance."

A cool sweat formed along Selene's palms. They didn't know yet that House Ravenwood still, in fact, had the gift of dreamwalking.

Damien stood. "Since we are sharing secrets, it is time to share some of my own. As you can see, I'm still alive." Lady Bryren chuckled while the others nodded. "You already know from my letters that I was a target at the Assembly, and I had to escape in order to save my life."

"Yes, but did you know that House Vivek was also a target?" Lord Leo asked.

Damien glanced at Lord Renlar. "Not until it was too late. I'm sorry I wasn't able to help your father or your aunt."

A shadow passed over Lord Renlar's face.

"How did you find out you were a target?" Lord Leo asked. "And how did you escape? Can you tell us now?"

Damien pressed his fingers against the edge of the table. "Because of house secrets, there was very little I could reveal about that night through correspondence, other than it was Lady Selene who helped me escape."

All eyes came to rest on Selene.

Before they could question her, Damien continued. "However, I know who the real assassin was, and it was not the empire—not directly—contrary to what Lady Ragna told you."

"Then who was it?"

Damien stared down at the table as he answered. "As Lord Renlar said, things have come to light over the last couple of months. There have also been subtle shifts of power amongst the Great Houses. Due to those shifts, I can now share what I know of the events surrounding the Assembly of the Great Houses that took place at Rook Castle."

"You can share who the assassin was?" Lord Leo said.

Damien raised his head. "Yes. There were two of them."

Selene's stomach tightened. She knew Damien was going to share about her family's involvement, and though she was tired of all the secrets, her heart beat rapidly, knowing that every house would learn of Ravenwood's duplicity and her own dark secret.

Damien took a deep breath. "The assassins were Lady Ragna . . . and Lady Selene."

There was a collective gasp around the room.

Lord Leo stood to his feet. "That is a grave accusation, Lord Damien. You never said any of this in your missives."

"I couldn't, because those facts were hidden within the secrets of House Ravenwood. But things have changed."

"That's not possible. House Ravenwood was wiped out centuries ago, and a lesser house took its place. When the gift of House Ravenwood disappeared, so did their secrets."

"And that's another secret of House Ravenwood's."

Lord Leo turned to Selene. "What is he saying?"

Selene drew on all her internal strength for the courage to step into the light. She placed her hand on Damien's and stood. He took that as his cue to sit. She looked around the room, at this one last time where she was regarded as a neutral party, then spoke. "Damien is telling the truth. Ravenwood has kept many secrets because we were never truly wiped out."

"Are you serious?" Lady Bryren stared at Selene. "How is that possible? The last Ravenwood died during the first razing of the Dominia Empire."

Selene noticed Lord Renlar eyeing her with a subtle fascination, almost as if he had figured out the truth. Then he looked away with a pained expression on his face.

She lifted her chin. "It is now time for me to share my own secrets."

Lord Leo sat down and crossed his arms, his face hard. "Indeed it is."

Where to begin? A whirlwind of feelings sent adrenaline coursing through her veins. The gravity of what her ancestors had put into motion all those years ago came crashing down on her. They had lied to everyone. They killed and stole from the very people they should have been working with. How could she tell them that? She opened, then closed her mouth.

"Start at the beginning," Damien said quietly, almost as if he could read her mind.

Just hearing his voice brought back a measure of control. "During the first razing, my entire house was wiped out except for one person, a young woman by the name of Rabanna. She was

23

taken to Dominia when the empire's forces were routed back to their country and the wall put in place. The empire took her as spoils of war. They had no idea who she really was. During her time in the Dominia Empire, she honed her power of dreamwalking and used it to make her way back to our lands."

Lady Bryren stared at her with wide eyes. "How?"

A huge weight settled across Selene's chest. "The gift of dreamwalking can be used in many different ways. Rabanna chose to use her gift to manipulate and slay those who stood between her and home. She found a ship willing to take her to the port town of Jahlian, then she made her way to Rook Castle, where she eventually married Grand Lord Remyl, from the lesser house that took over the mountain region. Since then, every generation of Ravenwood women have honed their gift of dreamwalking in secret."

Sharing Rabanna's trials made her realize what her forebearer had gone through to make it back. It didn't make it right, but it did show strength of spirit and a willingness to overcome great obstacles. If only Rabanna had found a better way.

Lady Bryren shook her head. "I don't understand. Why did Ravenwood keep all of this a secret?"

"Fear." Selene raised her eyes. "Fear that our

house would be razed again. And hatred for what was done to us."

The room grew uncomfortably silent.

Just as Selene went to sit, Lord Leo spoke. "If this information is bound in house secrecy, how is it that you can tell us about this? Lady Ragna is the head of your house, is she not?"

"My mother is a powerful dreamwalker in her own right. Each of my foremothers has always been powerful. However, the mark I bear on my back is different. Only recently have I come to understand what it means. The ancient power of Ravenwood has chosen me as head of House Ravenwood."

Lord Leo shook his head. "Only after the death of the grand lord or lady can a new head of house be chosen."

"Unless someone of exceptional power comes along," Lord Renlar said quietly. "I read of this happening one other time, with House Friere."

"How exactly?"

"If a member of a Great House exceeds in the power of his or her head of house, there will be an internal transfer of headship. The strongest always leads."

"You have the gift of dreamwalking, *and* you're the new head of Ravenwood?" Lord Leo looked from Lord Renlar to Selene.

"Yes, she is," Damien said in response. "I've witnessed firsthand what she can do. The

Ravenwood gift is alive and well within Lady Selene."

"By the heavens," Lady Bryren said under her breath. "A dreamwalker." She glanced over at Selene. "But Lord Damien also said you were one of the assassins. Since Lord Damien is still with us, I assume you changed your mind. How did you go from almost killing Damien to being married to him?"

Selene looked down at Damien's hand on the table near hers. "I was trained to steal secrets and take lives. But when it came time . . ." She took a deep breath. "I couldn't do it."

"Couldn't do it?" Lord Leo asked suspiciously.

Selene looked up. "I'm not a killer, and I never will be. I chose to go against my mother and my own house and save Lord Damien."

"To go against one's house is treason of the highest degree." Lady Bryren tilted her head to the side in thought. "Yet you chose to save Lord Damien. That must have taken a lot of courage."

"We know from Lord Damien's letters that House Ravenwood and Friere are in league with the empire," Lord Leo said. "Is that why you were sent to kill Lord Damien?"

"Yes. And no." Selene sighed. "My mother received a prophecy from the Dark Lady before the Assembly. It was foretold that a threat would come from the north, one that would mean the end of House Ravenwood. My mother took that to mean she needed to take out the northern houses—House Vivek and House Maris—in order to preserve her own. I was tasked to kill Lord Damien." She lowered her eyes, unable to look at Lord Renlar. "While my mother took out House Vivek."

"And your marriage?" Lady Bryren asked.

Selene glanced at Damien.

"Because she saved me, I married Lady Selene so I could safely bring her into my lands and protect her from House Ravenwood."

"Ah yes." Lady Bryren nodded. "The water barrier. So you married Lady Selene to make her a part of your people?"

"Yes."

"Fascinating," she said. "So the threat the Dark Lady spoke of wasn't House Maris?"

Selene laughed bitterly. "That's the thing about interpreting prophecies. The threat to House Ravenwood was never House Maris or House Vivek—it was me. When I chose to leave my house, I became the fulfillment of the Dark Lady's words."

Silence fell across the room.

Lord Leo rubbed the back of his neck. "This is a lot to consider, and the afternoon is growing late. I move to adjourn and reconvene in the morning."

Lord Renlar nodded. "I agree."

"And I," said Lady Bryren.

Damien and Selene also agreed. The lords and ladies stood, some moving toward the doors while others stretched. Lord Renlar made his way around the table and approached Selene as Damien went to speak to Lord Leo.

"Lady Selene, if I may, could I have a moment of your time, in private?"

"Is it important?" Selene asked, feeling drained from the meeting.

"Yes, it is something I feel I must share with the others, but now that I know a true Ravenwood exists, it is only right I tell you first."

Selene frowned.

"It is imperative that we talk."

Selene looked over at Damien, who seemed to be in deep discussion with Lord Leo, then back at Lord Renlar. "All right, we can speak."

"Good, then follow me."

2

Lord Renlar led Selene over to the corner near one of the windows, far enough away that they could speak quietly, but close enough that the remaining houses could see them.

He paused beside the window and stared outside. The storm had turned into a slow, wet drizzle. This close, she could see his father even more in his face and physique, although he wasn't as broad as Lord Rune had been. His blue tunic accented his rich, warm skin and brought out the flecks of gold in his eyes.

After a moment, he turned. "As I shared earlier, I was trained in the libraries of House Vivek before taking my father and aunt's place as grand lord of House Vivek. Studying the texts and wisdom of my people has made me privy to information not known to many. One of the secrets I discovered was the downfall of House Ravenwood."

"Downfall? You mean the razing?"

"Yes, the razing as you call it. What do you know of that time?"

Selene drew her eyebrows together, recalling her mother's words. "House Ravenwood was seen as inferior to the other houses. So when the empire marched on the Magyr Mountains, the other Great Houses did not come to our aid, which led to our annihilation. Only afterward did the other houses step in and drive the empire back, raising the wall after Dominia Empire was forced to retreat into their own country."

"Yes. Some of that is correct. But there is more."

She furrowed her brow. "More?"

He sighed and looked out the window again. "I'm telling you this because it is time House Vivek apologized to your house for our part in almost wiping out your family. It wasn't that the other houses stood back and let the Dominia Empire raze your house. . . . We—all of us—orchestrated it."

She took a step back, a thickness filling her throat. "What do you mean?"

"The empire feared your power more than any other house because your gift involves the dream world. Unfortunately, my ancestors did not understand that. During the war, all they could see was the physical power of House Maris and House Luceras and House Merek's courage during battle. And the healing and protective abilities of House Rafel and House Friere. The lords and ladies of my own house were the strategists. In our minds, what was dreamwalking compared to those gifts?"

"What indeed," Selene murmured. Had she not thought the same thing?

"There were hints that the empire wanted House Ravenwood. My ancestors saw an opportunity to win the war and push back the Dominia Empire. With the help of the other houses, they set up House Ravenwood."

Chills ran up and down her spine. Part of her wanted Lord Renlar to stop, but another part of her wanted to know exactly what happened to her family. "How?"

"My ancestors believed that by sacrificing one house, they could save the others. So they planted false information about the movement and battle plans of the Great Houses, allowing the empire an opening into the Magyr Mountains. House Ravenwood knew about this and agreed to be the bait. What your family didn't know was that the other houses chose to let the empire actually do away with you. Commander Tolrun was too shrewd to simply walk into a trap. In order to capture him and drive back the empire, it had to be real. House Ravenwood had to be given over to the empire." Lord Renlar sighed as he looked down at the windowsill and pressed his fingers against the wood. "Ravenwood never saw it coming."

Selene took another step back, a wave of cold spilling across her, as if someone had dumped a bucket of water over her head. "The other houses lied to House Ravenwood?"

There was a pause. "Yes."

Selene held a hand to her throat. "Then what I heard . . . that the other houses simply didn't step in on time . . . that was all false."

"Yes. It wasn't that the rest of the Great Houses didn't come to Ravenwood's rescue. The truth is they handed Ravenwood to the empire. On purpose."

The room began to spin. This—this couldn't be. The other Great Houses gave her family over to Commander Tolrun and his forces?

They murdered her ancestors?

Selene reached for the windowpane for support, her mind swimming. "You're sure about this?"

He let out a pained sigh. "Yes. The records of that time were buried deep within the library at Shanalona, but the true account of what happened during the first war is there. There was much shame and regret afterward, and so the history of what happened was hidden away. I don't think even my father knew what House Vivek and the other houses had done. I don't believe anyone else here does either."

A fire began to burn inside of Selene, washing away the chill, and she crushed her hand into a fist. "Why are you telling me this now?"

"Because if we are going to work together, I first need to ask for forgiveness on behalf of my house for what was done during the first war. And I need to swear to you House Vivek will protect you. We will not let House Ravenwood fall again, now that I know your house is still alive."

Selene let out her breath. He was right. She looked up. "Lord Renlar, you have apologized to my family, and now it is time I did the same. Words are not enough to say how sorry I am for what happened to your father and your aunt. My family—we were wrong." Her heart contracted. She knew in the end there was nothing she could have done. Her mother had already started her mission. But still . . .

"There have been wrongs committed on both sides."

Selene nodded slowly, her gaze moving toward the window nearby. "You know, you didn't have to tell me any of this, and I would have never known. Now . . ." She pressed a hand to her chest. "Now I'm not sure if I can trust you. Or any of the other houses."

She saw Lord Renlar's shrug from the corner of her eye. "How do we know if anyone can trust anyone else? But trust is the only way we will succeed against the empire. I had to say something because I want the relationship between our houses from this point forward to be built on truth." Lord Renlar's voice rumbled quietly. "And that starts with the past. Yours and mine."

Selene felt like she had been punched in the stomach. Her mother never knew. None of her ancestors had known, or else it would have been passed down from one daughter to the next, flaming an even brighter torch of hatred than the one that already burned.

What did she do with this information? Could she trust Lord Renlar? Then again, could he trust her? She glanced over her shoulder at the people gathered in the room. Damien was still talking with Lord Leo near the table. Lady Bryren had already left. Could she trust them?

She pressed her lips together. Had her ancestors believed their comrades? Was it that very trust that led to them being wiped out?

"I believe we should share this information with everyone," Lord Renlar said softly.

Selene looked back at Lord Renlar.

"They should know what happened, what it has cost years later. We are reaping what our forebearers sowed by their actions. But we are also in a place to understand what they apparently did not: No house is expendable. And no war can truly be won with lies and deception. We need to work together this time around—all of us—and never let another house fall again."

She couldn't help but marvel at his words, despite the emotional pain ricocheting through her body. Lord Renlar appeared to possess the wisdom his house was famous for. So how did his ancestors not see that wisdom in the past? Had the ravages of war driven them to cross a line they would have never crossed otherwise?

"My words are a blow to you. I can see it on your face."

"Yes." They were like weights on her chest, making it hard to breathe.

"However, we don't have much time. And I think for true unity, this needs to be addressed tomorrow."

"Tomorrow?"

"Yes. Hundreds of years later, this wound still festers."

He was right. She understood her mother's hatred toward the other houses—even without this new information. But hatred only begat more hatred, and her desire to break this cycle was even stronger than her current anger. For the sake of her sisters. For the sake of her future. "Tomorrow, then."

"I'm sorry to have brought pain to you, Lady Selene."

She glanced at Lord Renlar. "Thank you for saying that. It helps a little."

"Until then." He bowed toward her, then made his way to the other side of the room.

Selene remained where she was beside the window, watching the rain as it pattered against the glass.

"What were you and Lord Renlar talking

about?" Damien asked a moment later as he came to stand beside her.

Selene remained where she was and looked at his reflection in the window. She swallowed hard and pressed a hand to her chest. "I'm not ready to talk about it."

"Selene?"

"Please, Damien."

Between the death of her sister, fatigue from fighting in the dreamscape, and now this latest news, she wasn't sure she could handle any more. Even if she had wanted to speak, there were no words right now for the pain inside her heart. The hurt was too deep.

"All right. Then let us retire to our rooms. You appear as tired as I feel."

"Thank you."

He placed his arm beneath hers and led her toward the door. She had entered this room ready to share the truth of her family. Instead, she had discovered so much more than she had ever wanted to know.

Now this new truth hung around her neck like a chain forged from steel, choking her. It wasn't omission that had caused her family to be almost wiped out. It had been planned out in detail, signed off on by every other Great House.

What would stop them from doing it again? Half of the houses had proven they would do what was best for themselves before helping others. Had any of them really changed since the first razing? Or would each house act according to their own interest?

She glanced at the man at her side. Even House Maris?

3

Selene remained silent the rest of the evening. She spotted Damien's concerned gaze, and a few times he opened his mouth to speak. But she wasn't ready to talk, so she turned away. The shock and hurt from Lord Renlar's words had punched a hole through her chest. One moment she was numb, then she was angry. Anger turned to hurt, hurt to grieving. Then the cycle would start again.

Now she understood her mother's anger toward the other houses and Amara's zeal for their own. What Ravenwood did to the other houses afterward still wasn't right, but now she understood their mind-set. There was even a temptation to embrace it.

She went to bed early, her mind still in turmoil. Damien came in an hour later, quietly changed, and climbed into bed beside her. His hand briefly brushed her arm before he shifted away. Part of her wanted to sit up, tell him everything, and let him hold her, but she couldn't move. All she could do was stare ahead at the dark wall and feel the dull thumping of her heart.

Darkness came and the dreamscape beckoned. She dreamed of Amara and Ophie. They were sitting in a field, laughing together while forming crowns of daisies. Along her subconscious, she could tell she was shielding her dream so as not to bring others in. In this respect, she was becoming better at controlling her power, but she wasn't sure whether that was because the Dark Lady was no longer here or because she truly was becoming more powerful.

Daylight came, and Selene hardly spoke a word. She dressed, broke her fast, and prepared to meet with the Great Houses again.

"Selene, is everything all right?"

She turned around and found Damien studying her from the doorway. When did he appear?

"You've barely said a word to me. I thought it might be because of what you shared yesterday during the meeting, and so I chose to give you space. But now I'm really worried about you."

She opened her mouth, then closed it. Why couldn't she speak? Was it because she was afraid? Who could she trust?

She pressed two fingers to her forehead. "I'm not feeling well." It was the truth, but not all of the truth.

Damien crossed the room. "Do you need to stay here? You've been through a lot the last few days, and you haven't yet had a chance to grieve."

"No." Lord Renlar would be sharing his information with the rest of the Great Houses. As much as she wished this knowledge had never come to be, it existed, and it needed to be dealt with. Reparations made. Trust regained. On both sides.

He studied her a moment longer before offering his arm. "Let me know if there is anything I can do."

She took his arm and gripped it firmly as they walked to the meeting hall, her throat tight as she stared ahead. *I wish none of this had come to be.*

Selene could feel Damien's gaze on her as Lord Renlar shared the information he had made her privy to yesterday with those gathered in the audience hall. The lines around his mouth deepened, and his eyebrows inched closer together. He rubbed the bottom of his lip with his finger, his eyes never wavering from her face.

She shifted in her chair but didn't return his stare. She still wasn't sure what to think. She had balled up all of her emotions and locked them away deep inside in order to be here. Numb. That's what she was. But she could feel those emotions from last night pressing against the iron door she had shoved them behind, and sooner or later they would come bursting out.

Lord Leo stared down at the tabletop with a frown on his face.

Lady Bryren's gaze moved from Lord Renlar to Selene and back to Lord Renlar, her eyes widening every second. "Every house was a part of this?" she interrupted.

He looked over at her. "Yes. Every house not only knew of the plan, but they consented to it. Even House Merek. It was the wyvern riders who drove the empire through the mountain valleys after the massacre and out onto the plains, where they were funneled by the forces from the other houses across the border. Then House Maris and House Friere erected the eastern wall."

"I can't believe this," Lady Bryren murmured, her fingers touching her parted lips. "Neither my father nor my grandfather ever spoke of this."

"From what I can tell, the truth of what happened was hidden away because of shame. I stumbled upon the historic documents sealed behind a small door while helping excavate the ruins of Vade Mecum Library. I don't think any house knew about it except those involved at the time."

Lord Leo stirred. "But how could our ancestors keep such a thing secret? Surely there were more than just the grand lords and ladies who knew about this?"

"The true purpose of the attack was never shared with anyone. The military commanders and forces were led to believe the battle plan went horribly wrong and that House Ravenwood was wiped out because of that. There was no indication that House Ravenwood had been set up and given over to the empire."

Nausea swept across Selene, and she placed a hand across her middle. The blatant betrayal of the other houses hit her again, sending her emotions clamoring inside of her. She shoved her fist against her midsection. *No, I will not lose control, not here, not in front of everyone.*

Damien must have noticed her subtle movement because he straightened, placed his hands on the table, and opened his mouth, but before he could speak, Lord Leo spoke again.

"Why was the empire interested in House Ravenwood? What made the empire take the bait and go after the mountain house?"

"Because of Ravenwood's gift," Lord Renlar said calmly, but Selene sensed a storm brewing under his calm veneer.

"Their gift?" Lord Leo looked at Selene. "What threat is there in someone who can walk in dreams?"

She almost laughed. Those present knew the dreamwalking gift existed, but she had yet to reveal what the purpose had been.

Lord Renlar answered for her. "The empire understood Ravenwood's ability more than our own houses did. Even I don't fully understand what dreamwalkers are capable of. But what I read said that those of Ravenwood have the power to enter the hearts, minds, and memories of not just one person, but many people, and influence them or inspire them."

Lord Leo looked at her. "The dreamwalking gift can work with more than one person?"

Selene lifted her chin. "Yes."

"Then why is this coming to our attention now?"

Her nostrils flared. "As I shared yesterday, my ancestors kept our gift a secret, fearing that what happened during the first razing would happen again." Even though it seemed even Rabanna didn't realize the full extent of the treachery wrought against her house, she had been right to fear.

Lord Leo crossed his arms. "It seems to me that your gift—although you can influence people—is still not as powerful as the others'."

Selene stared at Lord Leo, her anger giving her courage. "Have you ever noticed when waking up from a dream how powerful your emotions are? If you dreamed about the death of a loved one, you cry. If you dreamed about something happy, you feel full and satisfied. Dreams tear down walls and open your heart up to your feelings. Dreams are when you are most vulnerable. Because of that, my family has been able to use dreams to find your most private secrets—and even take your lives."

His eyes narrowed. "What do you mean?"

The rest of the houses were silent as they turned their attention to her. Damien's stare became more intense, whether to warn her about what she was about to share or something more. She didn't care either way. She was sick of the lies, the misunderstandings, and there was a recklessness inside of her now that wanted to prove her house was just as valid as theirs.

"When I walk in your dreams, your mind is open to me. I see your memories, your secrets, your fears. I have the power to manipulate those, to either bring peace and light to your soul or to snuff out your existence."

"Wait, what are you saying?" Lady Bryren asked. "Yesterday when you said you were sent to kill Lord Damien, I took that to mean with your swords. Are you saying you were going to kill him with your gift?"

Selene swallowed. "Yes."

The room grew even more silent.

"I can make you relive your greatest fear until your heart gives out. We were once known as the dreamwalkers. But after the razing, my family became dreamkillers. Many have died by our gift. And many of your own houses"—she looked around—"have employed our services at one point or another over the centuries. To underestimate my mother or my house is to invite death."

"Are you threatening us?" Lord Leo asked.

"No. I want you to be aware of what House Ravenwood is capable of. What my mother is capable of. What my house became when we were given over to the empire!"

Lady Bryren raised her chin and her eyes flashed. "Have you done this before? You were sent to kill Lord Damien, but chose not to. Did you kill others before him?"

Selene looked around the room. "Have I killed someone with my gift? No. Was I trained to kill? Yes. Have I hurt someone with my power?" She paused. "Yes." Her chest constricted at her last answer.

Lord Renlar eyed her shrewdly. "I've heard of these services you speak of. I know my aunt employed them once years ago. But never did she suspect it was your house."

Lord Leo made a strange noise in his throat and looked away. Selene gritted her teeth. She knew even House Luceras had used their services. Every house here had, save House Maris, even if the current lord or lady didn't know about it.

"How did it come to this?" Lady Bryren asked, her eyes flashing. "How did the gifts of our houses become so perverted?"

"Hatred," Damien said quietly. "It's a poison that seeps into the very soul of a person. It can turn the light into darkness."

"And what do we do now?"

Lord Renlar looked around the room. "First, we acknowledge what our forebearers did. They thought one family was dispensable. Perhaps it was the war that brought them to that decision. Or maybe that thought was always there. But in the eyes of the Light, every house, every nation, every *person* is valuable. The first step in winning this war is to remember that. Yes, we are going to lose some of those valuable lives. There will be death. It is inevitable. But that doesn't mean we throw them away. Rather, we recognize every sacrifice and mourn when those lives are lost, and do everything we can so we don't lose any more."

"What about House Ravenwood and Friere?" Lord Leo asked darkly.

Lord Renlar turned toward him. "They are still a part of this land. I have already pledged my protection to Lady Selene so that House Ravenwood does not die out."

"Even though her mother sided with the empire?"

"Yes."

"So we give no thought to their betrayal?"

"We still treat both House Ravenwood and House Friere with value." Lord Renlar's eyes grew hard. "But there will be consequences for the choices they have made."

"And what about the empire?" Lady Bryren asked.

"They are people too. With loved ones, families, children."

"So we just let them sweep across our land?"

"No. They have brought the fight to us. And we will fight for our lives and for our land. But we can still fight with dignity and honor."

Lord Leo snorted. "I think you have a lot of ideals that sound good but won't stand up to the harshness of the battlefield."

Lord Renlar steepled his fingers together. "Perhaps. At the end of the day, we must each stand or fall by our own ideals. Choices will need to be made. And, like I said, lives will be lost. After all, this is war. But who will you be after the war? We don't want a repeat of our ancestors where they had to bury the truth of what happened four hundred years ago because of shame and regret."

Damien nodded in agreement as he tugged at his chin with a faraway look on his face.

Selene sat without moving, without speaking. It was taking everything she had just to sit there and listen. *Compose yourself. Don't let your emotions rule you.* She took a breath in and let it out slowly as the others continued to talk around her. She agreed with Lord Renlar. It mattered who a person was, even in the midst of making hard choices. She raised her head and stared out the window across the table. Perhaps her forebearers had acted with honor and dignity, even though in the end, they were betrayed. Was that possible?

It didn't make the treachery of the other houses any easier to swallow, but it gave her something to strive toward, compared to what her house was now: betrayers of the same magnitude as those who gave her family to the empire hundreds of years earlier.

They were all descendants of traitors. And yet . . .

She still wasn't sure who she could trust in this upcoming conflict.

Including herself.

4

"W"hy didn't you tell me?" Damien asked as he shut the door behind them, hurt lacing his voice.

Selene crossed her arms as she faced the windows inside the room. With each breath, the anger, hurt, and shock that had been storming deep inside of her came rising to the surface. The same question from a half hour earlier came rushing toward her lips. "How could I? After what I found out, I don't know if I can trust anyone."

"What do you mean?"

She rounded on him. "I was raised with the knowledge that my house had been abandoned, left at the mercy of the empire. If it hadn't been for Rabanna's abduction, we would have been wiped out. Only now I find out it wasn't an accident. It was planned by the very houses my family had trusted. The other Great Houses didn't just leave us—they gave us over to the empire. We were dispensable."

She raised her hand. "And not just that, but even now, when all of you thought we no longer had our gift, we were seen as inferior, as a token Grand House but hardly a power to be reckoned with. Is it any surprise that we've turned on you in the same way you turned on us?"

She could see the truth of her words on his face, and it struck her heart like an arrow. He *had* seen her as inferior at one point. Maybe even now? Hot tears threatened to run down her face as the dagger of betrayal dug deeper into her being. She dug her nails into her palms and blinked the tears away.

"Be prepared for anything. We will never be wiped out again." For the first time, she understood why her mother always spoke those words. "Maybe Mother was more right than she knew about not trusting anyone. That we can only count on ourselves."

"But how is that any different from what your mother is doing now?" Damien took a step forward. "She has turned against us and aligned with the empire."

He was right. Her house was doing exactly what had been done to them all those years ago. But at the moment, logic could not win over the hurt raging inside of her. She turned around and crossed her arms as if holding herself together, her cheeks hot. "When I was growing up, I wondered what my life would have been like if my house had not been razed by the empire all those years ago. Maybe my family would have been different. A loving, caring mother instead of one obsessed with power. A sister who would still be alive and also be a friend. Maybe I would have had a family like yours."

Her last words were like a javelin, which she aimed and threw right at Damien's heart. The moment she launched her words, she regretted it. It wasn't like Damien had the perfect family. And he'd lost them as well. She dropped her head. "I'm sorry. That wasn't fair."

"You ask if you can trust us—if you can trust me—so let me ask you the same question. Can I trust you?"

Selene turned around. "What do you mean?"

For the first time, Damien's eyes appeared cold, like blue flints of ice. "Ever since you came to Northwind Castle, there have been disturbances amongst my people. Nightmares, loss of consciousness, and one person was even sent to the infirmary. Not only that, you brought a dark, sinister being with you, putting my people in jeopardy."

Selene balled her hands into two tight fists. "That wasn't my fault. I had no idea at the time."

"But even when you did, you never said anything. What would have happened if things had continued? What if someone had died?"

Selene stared at Damien, caught off guard by his accusations. How long had these thoughts been haunting him? Did he think she did all of that on purpose? Heat rushed over her body, and she raised her head. "Fine. If we are asking questions, then let me ask you one: Why did you marry me?"

He narrowed his eyes and crossed his arms. "What do you mean?"

"Was it to save yourself?"

"I don't understand. . . ."

"Marriage rites would make it impossible for me to finish my mission, to kill you. Did you marry me to save yourself? Do you regret that choice now, when you could have been aligned with a different house? Like House Luceras?"

Damien stood deathly still, his face pale. The truth was written all over his body: Never had that thought entered his mind. The very answer she had secretly longed for. But the price . . . the price!

Selene turned around, unable to face him, barely able to breathe. The words were bursting from her before she could even think. Had she really been holding all of this in? What in all the lands were they even doing right now? There was a war coming and a treaty to be signed, and here they were fighting!

"Selene . . ." He spoke behind her in a choked voice, the sound piercing her heart. "I-I'm—"

The door burst open behind them. Selene twisted around just in time to catch the devastated look on Damien's face before he turned and headed for the doorway, where a messenger dressed in white held up two folded parchments. "Urgent messages for Lord and Lady Maris."

Damien reached for the notes. "Thank you,"

he said in a tense voice as he took the notes. The messenger turned to depart, and Taegis came in. Damien remained by the door as he opened the first message. His face tightened as his gaze moved across the page.

A chill went down her spine as she watched him.

He looked up, but she didn't need to hear his words. The message was clear in his eyes.

The war had begun.

"It's started, hasn't it?" Selene took a couple of steps forward, driving her emotions back behind an iron door. But that still wasn't enough to ease the tension that stretched between them.

Damien, too, seemed to have decided to put their heated words away for the moment. "The first message is from Lord Renlar. He just received word from Shanalona that House Friere was able to crack the wall open. The empire is now gathering north of Boldor, along the Friere and Vivek borders."

Selene curled her fingers. "So Lord Ivulf was able to break the wall."

"Yes." Damien looked up. "The second message is from your father."

"My father?"

"It is about the coalition. With Lady Ragna in Ironmond, Caiaphas has called upon the coalition to help him secure Rook Castle and the Magyr Mountains. If Commander Orion takes the mountains, he will have access to every part of the continent."

"Does my father know the empire has already breached our lands?"

"I'm not sure. I have a feeling Caiaphas has been planning this for a while. It makes strategic sense to secure Rook Castle for ourselves, and most likely he's been waiting for an opportunity before making his move."

Selene laughed softy. "I had always secretly wondered if there was more to my father. When he shared about the coalition, I knew. I don't think my mother ever realized the manner of man she married." Dart'an! Those words could be applied to her own situation right now.

Damien was carefully refolding the parchment when there was another knock at the door. Taegis answered this time. Another messenger entered the room.

"My lord, my lady." The man bowed. "An emergency meeting has been called for the grand lords and ladies. Immediately."

Damien caught Selene's eye. "It must be about the first message we received." He turned back toward the messenger. "We will be there directly."

"I will let the others know." The man bowed again and left.

Damien turned away and ran a hand through his hair. "It would seem there are things we need to talk about. In private. But we don't have any time at the moment." He looked back. "Can we speak about it tonight?"

An invisible hand clenched her heart, bringing back all the pain, hurt, and confusion from earlier, causing her breath to stall in her chest. But he was right. They needed to talk. She had said some hurtful things, and given the expression on his face, he knew he had as well. "Yes."

He offered his arm to her, but there was a wall between them. And she hated it. But she wasn't sure what to do. Not with her feelings. Not with the hurt swirling inside. But one thing she did know.

She didn't want to hurt Damien again.

5

Though only a few inches separated them, it might as well have been miles as Selene stood next to Damien in the meeting hall.

She loved him. So why did she say those things earlier? *What kind of person am I?* She clutched her arm to her stomach as Lord Leo brought a rolled parchment to the table and carefully spread it out in the presence of two priests dressed in white.

"These men are from the Temple of Splendor and will be witnesses to the signing of this treaty. The terms are the same as those we spoke of at Rook Castle a few months back. It is a pledge of our houses, our powers, and our forces to each other. I thought we would have one more day to talk, but . . ."

"The time for talking is over." Lady Bryren stepped toward the table. "And the time for action has come."

"Indeed," Lord Renlar said, his eyebrows drawn and his lips pressed together. "Together we stand. Or together we fall."

Lord Leo looked over to Damien and Selene. "Are you both prepared?"

"I am," Damien said without hesitating.

Of course he was ready. Damien was the one

who had moved for a treaty in the first place. As for herself . . .

Selene stared at the table, frozen. She was still processing Lord Renlar's words from yesterday. Could she trust those in this room? *How do I know? What do I do?* Did it even matter if she signed? She might be the head of House Ravenwood, but her mother was still the figurehead. And what power would she bring? Damien's accusations rang again in her ears. *What if I do more harm than good?*

She looked up and realized they were waiting for her. Dart'an! She nodded but didn't look anyone in the eye.

Lord Renlar spoke. "Then we sign together, a promise to uphold one another in this war."

Lord Leo stepped toward the table, took the quill in hand, and went first. Lady Bryren went next. Lord Renlar followed. The silence in the room was broken only by the scratch of the quill. Once Lord Renlar was finished, Damien stepped away from Selene and approached the table. After signing and placing the quill back in the inkwell, he turned toward her.

Silence filled the room again. It was her turn. Selene lifted her head and took short, even breaths as she approached the table.

At the table's edge, she reached for the quill and stared down at the parchment, at the beautifully detailed lettering that spelled out the treaty, at the embellishments along the tops and sides, indicating the importance of the document. Her hand hovered below Damien's signature, written in firm, bold letters.

Was this how her ancestors felt when they were signing the first treaty over four hundred years ago? Trepidation, fear, suspicion? Or did they trust their comrades so completely that there was never a doubt in their minds?

Another wave of betrayal washed over her as she remembered Lord Renlar's words. How could she put her name beside the names of those whose forebearers had lied to her own family? Would history repeat itself? Would Ravenwood be betrayed again?

Damien must have sensed the turmoil inside of her. He leaned in close. "Take as much time as you need," he said quietly, so as not to be heard by the others.

Her throat tightened. Despite her harsh words earlier, he still knew what she needed and showed it through his actions. Such kindness, even after her angry accusations.

No time to think about that now.

Selene sucked in a deep breath and nodded, the quill still in her hand.

Her word.

The names along the bottom of the parchment came back into focus.

Her word.

That was the only thing she could control. She couldn't say if the others would betray her house again, or if they would live up to the agreement set in this treaty. But she could. She would stand by her word. Her name would be her promise. She possessed the gift of House Ravenwood. And by her power, she would do all she could to protect not just her people but all people from the Dominia Empire.

That is what she would stand for.

Without another thought, Selene pressed the quill down on the parchment, and with a flurry of movement, her own name appeared below Damien's. *Lady Selene Ravenwood.* The letters were dark and bold with a flourish at the end. Strong, steady. Capturing exactly who she was and who—her lips turned slightly upward and her heart lightened for a moment—who the Light had made her.

She placed the quill down beside the inkwell and took a step back. The presiding scribe came over, checked the names at the bottom, then nodded at Lord Leo before carefully rolling up the parchment and placing it inside a decorative silver metal tube.

"It is done." Lord Leo looked around the room. "The treaty will be kept inside the Temple of Splendor."

"And now to the pressing matter at hand." Lord Renlar looked at those gathered. "The Dominia

Empire has come through the wall and is marching on our lands. We need to act now if we are to save the lives of as many people as possible."

Damien turned toward Lord Renlar. "Right now, it is your people who are in the greatest danger."

"Yes. I planned on leaving the moment the treaty was signed. My people are already being evacuated."

"To where, exactly?"

"North. We will defend Shanalona, but it is only to buy us time to get my people as far away from the empire as possible."

"And after that?"

Lord Renlar looked around the room. "Isn't that why we are here? I need your help."

Damien turned to Lord Leo. "Do you have a map? I have a few ideas."

"I'll have one of the servants retrieve one right away."

As Lord Leo conversed with one of the servants in the room, Selene watched the others talk, sharing thoughts, plans, and ideas. She glanced out the nearby window and held her palm up. What could she do? What *should* she do?

She had been trained to gather information and assassinate. She could work against the empire. She could find out secrets or kill those in power. Even now her fingers itched to hold her dual blades.

As fast as the thought came, she banished it and clenched her hand. *No. I will not go back to that. That is the way of my mother, of Rabanna. I must find another way, for the sake of my future. Darkness can never achieve goodness.*

When the servant returned with the map minutes later, Lord Leo took the vellum from him and unrolled it across the table. Damien, Lady Bryren, and Lord Renlar came to stand beside him. Selene looked among those gathered.

"Here." Damien pointed to where the Hyr River split into two tributaries before flowing into the sea. "We need to get your people past the river."

Lady Bryren looked over at Damien. "Are you going to try and raise the river? That's not your land."

"I don't know. What I do know is that long ago my ancestor helped House Friere raise the wall, combining their gifts of earth and water, which means I should be able to use my gift in places other than my own lands."

Lord Renlar rubbed his chin as he studied the map. "Even if you can raise the river, we still need to consider your power. I'm not sure if we can get my people far enough from the river before you need to raise it. My informants say the empire is moving quickly. We have very little time."

Lady Bryren placed a finger on the map. "I've already sent word to my reserves. A couple dozen wyvern riders can reach Shanalona in a little over a week, depending on weather and wind. Between your military and my own, we can at least buy your people time to reach the river. And I can fly both you and Lord Damien there in about the same amount of time. But that would be cutting it close." She looked up at Damien. "And we still don't know if you can raise the river outside your own lands."

Lord Leo cleared his throat. "Or what your water-wall might do to House Vivek's people."

Damien leaned forward. "It's the best choice we have right now. None of our troops are in position to reach the people of Shanalona before the empire does. My power might be the only thing that can save them."

Lord Leo shook his head. "Only if they are far enough away when you activate the barrier. And if they are not . . ."

The room became silent.

Selene remembered witnessing the terrifying force of the water barrier after her flight from Rook Castle. One reason Damien married her in the first place was to have his power recognize her in order to save her, to protect her.

She joined the others at the table. "What if by signing the treaty, Lord Damien's power now recognizes all of us as those he needs to protect?"

Damien looked at her, understanding filling his face—and a little bit of pride, Selene thought.

Lord Renlar nodded. "That makes sense. The treaty is binding, witnessed by priests, just as marriage rites are."

"Lady Selene's right," Damien agreed. "I believe it will work. In any case, we need to try."

"Yes," Lady Bryren said. "We should leave now. My consort and guards are already retrieving our wyverns. We can leave within the hour."

"Agreed," Lord Renlar said.

Damien glanced over at Selene, hesitations and helplessness flashing briefly in his eyes. There were still unresolved issues between them. Tonight, he had said. They would speak tonight. But if he left . . .

"One more thing," Damien said, turning back toward the others. "I have also received word from Caiaphas in Rook Castle. He is preparing to secure the Magyr Mountains in Lady Ragna's absence, but he will need backup."

"Caiaphas? Lady Ragna's consort?" Lady Bryren said. "That's an intrepid move on his part. I took him to be a more subservient kind of man."

"There is more to Caiaphas than many know. He's been planning this for years."

"With what forces?" Lord Renlar asked.

"A gathering of lesser nobles and citizens."

"From amongst the mountain people? Like a coup?" Lady Bryren asked.

"Not exactly . . ." Damien straightened up from

the table. "For years, Caiaphas and my father have worked to bring all of our peoples together, so when the time was right, both the Great Houses and the peoples of this land could work together. It was their belief that we were never going to win this with only our armies and our gifts—we would need everyone."

Lord Leo glared at Damien. "We took those rumors to mean insurrection against the Great Houses. We've been chasing those people for years. Only to find out now that House Maris has been behind it all."

"These people have always had one goal— to protect their people and their land. You must admit, there have been times our houses have only looked out for ourselves. That is why the coalition was formed."

"Still, that was overstepping the boundaries of your house and lands—"

"There's no time for accusations." Lord Renlar looked between Damien and Lord Leo. "Lord Damien, can you vouch for these people . . . this coalition?"

"I can. Caiaphas and his forces can be trusted to do what is good for our lands."

"And he's trying to secure Rook Castle?"

"Yes. But he reached out to the Great Houses to show his support and to ask for our help."

Lord Renlar nodded. "The Magyr Mountains are a strategic location. I had been wondering what we would do since Ravenwood holds the interior. But if we can secure the mountain region *and* raise the entire Hyr River, it will provide a chokehold on the empire's advancement. The only choice the empire will have is to go south."

"I agree," Damien said.

"Anyone else have a secret they need to share?" Lord Leo said, looking around. "Any secret groups or powers or ancient history? Or am I the only one in the dark?"

Selene could understand his anger. That same burn currently resided in her chest.

"Not at the moment," Damien said.

Lord Leo looked around the table. "Are all of you all right with this? That Ravenwood's consort and House Maris have been overseeing a secret coalition?"

Lady Bryren folded her arms. "If it were any other house, I would be concerned. But House Maris is the most noble of us all."

"And yet even House Maris was apparently a part of the conspiracy against House Ravenwood during the first razing!"

"What do you want us to do, Lord Leo?" Lord Renlar asked. "This treaty is a chance to trust each other once again. Will you trust Lord Damien?"

"But he's not going to Rook Castle."

Selene stepped forward. "No. But I am."

She saw Damien watching her from the corner

of her eye. "It is my home, my people. And I trust my father. As Lord Renlar pointed out, if the empire controls the Magyr Mountains, then Commander Orion will have access to every province. If we hold the mountains and raise the rest of the Hyr River, the empire will be forced to go south."

"To House Rafel's lands," Lord Leo pointed out.

"Yes. At this point, they are neutral, but their people are surrounded by hundreds of miles of forest. That itself will make it difficult for the empire to reach Surao. By then, I hope we will be able to convince House Rafel of our unity and determination to fight the empire. Lord Leo, will you join me in claiming Rook Castle and the Magyr Mountains for our alliance?"

He stared at her and his jaw twitched. "I will," he said finally. "My word is my vow. I do this for my people. House Luceras will help you secure the lands of House Ravenwood."

Selene bowed her head. "Thank you, Lord Leo."

Lady Bryren took a step back. "It is settled, then. Lord Renlar and Lord Damien will come with me, along with your personal guards. Lady Selene, Lord Leo, it will be up to you to secure Rook Castle and the mountain region. My riders should be here any minute, then we can take our leave."

"What about supplies?" Damien asked.

"We still have some from our trip. And we will hunt along the way. We must leave now if we want to reach Lord Renlar's people in time."

Damien nodded. "I understand. Please give me a moment with my wife." He looked over at Selene and held out his hand.

She gazed at him for a moment before taking it. As always, his skin was warmer than hers as he led her toward the windows, the same spot where Lord Renlar had shaken her world only yesterday.

The sky was still overcast, but no rain fell today. Damien stood between her and the others to give them some privacy. He gently gripped her other hand and held them both to his chest. "We don't have much time, so I wanted to say . . ." He let out his breath and bowed his head. "I'm sorry. I'm sorry for the words I spoke this morning. They were uncalled for. I have watched you over the months, and I've been inside your dreamscape. I know the battles you fight more than anyone else. You need someone to trust, so this is my promise to you."

He lifted his head. The light from the window made his eyes as blue as the deepest sea. A lock of dark hair hung down across his forehead, and she could see the small scar across his eyebrow. "I love you, no matter what. I will always love you. I will be the rock you can crash upon, and I will never move."

Selene didn't know what to say. All she could picture was the sea by Nor Esen, and no matter how hard the waves crashed upon those rocky cliffs, they never moved. That was his promise to her. He would always be there for her.

While her thoughts were on that image, Damien leaned forward. His breath was warm as he captured her lips and kissed her. A longing flooded her being, washing away the anger from that morning. All she wanted to do was wrap her arms around Damien and never let go. How could she hold him accountable for the choices of his ancestors? How could she not believe the words he spoke to her? He *loved* her. Either he was lying, or he was telling the truth. And she knew the answer deep down. No matter how their marriage began, she knew where they stood now.

"Lord Damien, we need to leave," Lady Bryren said behind them.

Damien drew his head back and pressed his forehead to hers. Selene clutched the front of his tunic. "The Light will be with you, Selene. You are never alone."

Then he withdrew. She felt strangely cold as she dropped her hands to her sides and watched him cross the room and join Lady Bryren and Lord Renlar. Lord Leo stared at her with an unreadable look.

They spoke for a moment, then headed out of the meeting hall. Selene turned and stared out the window, at the grey clouds and dull city below.

He was gone. Damien was gone. He was now heading out to war, and soon she would be too.

She placed a hand along the cold glass and bowed her head, her throat thick.

She never told him she was sorry. And that she loved him too. Instead, she had been caught up in the words he had spoken and his kiss goodbye. She knew without a doubt his heart toward her. But if he died somewhere out there during the war . . . if he never came back . . .

She curled her fingers.

He would never know how much she loved him in return.

6

"It appears we will be working together, Lady Selene."

Selene turned back from the window. Still next to the table, Lord Leo watched her with hooded lids and arms crossed.

She straightened up and held her chin high. "Yes, it does."

"If we are being honest, I don't like it." He looked away, his jaw tight. His light-colored hair brushed his broad shoulders, and there was a cut along his forearm. "I never liked House Ravenwood. And given what's been shared over the last few days, I like your house even less."

"I could say the same thing about House Luceras."

He looked back at her with his lips pressed together.

"I know your house is known as the House of Light. But I also know the secrets your family harbors. Even they were not above employing the skills of House Ravenwood, even though at the time you didn't know it was us." Selene stepped toward him. "It appears we have a choice. We can put the pasts of our families behind us and work together for the greater good of our people, or you can look down upon me and my house. Which will it be?"

Lord Leo dropped his arms and faced her. With a twist of his wrists, a broadsword of yellow light suddenly appeared in one hand and a light sphere the size of a man's fist in the other. He stared at her, the radiance from his weapons reflecting in his light blue eyes. "You don't scare me, Lady Selene. My family serves the Light."

"And you don't think I do?"

"A family who's done the things yours has cannot serve the Light."

Her heart pounded inside her ears. "You know very little about me. The things I have seen, the things I have fought. I know what the darkness—true darkness—looks like, and I have seen the Light. Do not presume to know who or what I follow. Instead, let my actions speak for themselves."

He stared at her for a moment before twisting one wrist. The light sphere disappeared, but his broadsword remained. "I will do whatever I must to protect my family and my people."

"So will I. But I will do it without resorting to the ways of my ancestors. I know my family's past. I will not repeat what they did."

He narrowed his eyes. "We shall see. This alliance between us is based on my trust of Lord Damien, and if Rook Castle and the Magyr Mountains fall to the Dominia Empire, then my own people are at risk. My house and my forces will join with your father's 'coalition' in securing Rook Castle. But know this"—he pointed his sword at her—"I will be watching you."

Selene raised her chin. "Then watch me, and see the kind of person I have become."

His sword disappeared. "For now, I will gather my troops and prepare for our journey to Rook Castle." He marched out of the meeting hall, leaving Selene alone with the silence and flickering candles.

After the door shut, everything inside of her collapsed. She stumbled toward one of the chairs and sank into it. The map lay on the table near her elbow. She ignored the vellum and placed her head in her hands. A rush of feelings swept over her, each one a wave threatening to pull her under.

Damien was gone. Animosity burned between her and Lord Leo. Grief over her sister continued to stab her in the heart. Her house had been betrayed.

How do I fight this? She curled into herself and held a fist to her heart. *I want to hate them. I want to hurt them. But I know it's not right. And I will only end up hurting myself. But I can't fight these feelings alone.*

Selene rocked back and forth in the chair. She didn't cry. The pain was much too deep for that. If only she could rip her heart out, or hide it again behind her familiar iron doors. But those doors had been blasted away, leaving a gaping hole that led straight to her heart. She couldn't hide anymore. All she could do was feel.

It . . . hurts.

"The Light will be with you, Selene. You are never alone." Damien's words came rushing back.

She lifted her head and stared across the table.

The Light will be with you.

The Light had been there when she faced the Dark Lady. And when her sister had died. And . . .

The Light was here now.

Selene slowly sat up, her heart stilling within her. The hurt was there, but it was as if a balm had been administered, soothing the pain.

"Lord Leo is wrong," she whispered. "So wrong. Anyone can serve the Light." She held her hand up in a fist and pressed it against her chest. "*I* serve the Light. No matter the darkness, no matter the hurt, no matter the betrayals—" Her voice hitched at the last word. She took in a deep breath and let it out slowly. "I can still choose the Light. And he gives me the strength to stand."

She closed her eyes and prayed. *I can do this through your power. I will forgive those who've hurt me. And I will ask forgiveness of those I have hurt. No matter what lies before me, let me be your light.*

After taking another deep breath, she stood

and headed for the door. Outside, she found Karl waiting for her in the empty hallway.

He bowed his head. "My lady."

"Karl, it is good to see you. I'm afraid we don't have a lot of time." She started down the corridor. "Lord Damien and Taegis have left for Shanalona."

"Taegis briefly informed me as he left with his lordship."

"Good." Selene let out a long breath. "You will be going with me. Back to Rook Castle."

"Rook Castle?"

"Yes. It is time for me to claim the Magyr Mountains for my people."

"I see. Then I will go with you and protect you, my lady."

"Thank you, Karl."

"Of course, my lady."

No, she wasn't alone. The Light was with her. And Damien, through those loyal to House Maris. Those who guarded her now.

She set her jaw and gazed ahead as Karl accompanied her back to her room. She didn't need those iron doors anymore. As a dreamkiller, she had trained to hide her heart. But to be a dreamwalker, she would need to let her heart be open. This would be her first step.

7

Hot air pressed against Lady Ragna's face as she waited outside the meeting tent for Lord Ivulf and Commander Orion to arrive. Canvas tents were spread out along the dry, arid land that stretched between House Friere and House Vivek. In the distance stood the city of Shanalona against a bright blue sky.

Soon there would be a razing. Just like four hundred years ago.

A sliver of guilt entered her heart, but only for a moment before she crushed it like she did every other emotion inside of her. Being a lady of Ravenwood meant having no emotions, no attachments. Feelings only got in the way of what needed to be done.

Lord Ivulf arrived first. He had discarded his fur cloak long ago, replacing it with a red silk tunic covered by a black leather jerkin and belt. His shoulder-length hair was held back with a steel circlet, highlighting the grey streaks running through his dark hair. His son, Raoul, was with him. The young man looked almost exactly like Ivulf did at that age, with those smoldering looks and black topknot secured by a gold band. For a moment, she wondered if Opheliana would take after Lord Ivulf as she matured. She already carried the mark of House Friere on her ankle. Would she also possess their looks?

Perhaps it was time to tell Ivulf of their daughter and bring her from Rook Castle. Until now, she had hidden away the young girl, but as time passed she could become useful. Having a daughter someday within House Friere and under her control would be valuable.

However, Ivulf might object to claiming a mute daughter. Lady Ragna tapped her chin. For now, she would simply approach Ivulf about moving Opheliana to Ironmond, then later she would reveal Opheliana's parentage.

A handful of guards accompanied the Friere men and joined her own contingent once Ivulf arrived at her side. Raoul took his place a couple of feet away, a dark look on his face, aimed at his father.

"Shanalona will soon be ours," Ivulf said with an air of confidence.

"And what about this Lord Renlar?" she asked. They had received word just days ago that a Lord Renlar, who was supposedly the son of Lord Rune, had taken control of House Vivek. How did she not know about him?

"He is currently not in Shanalona. Most likely he went to meet with the other Great Houses."

"That makes sense," she murmured. "His absence from Shanalona could work to our advantage." Then again, if he truly was Lord

Rune's son, he could still carry the gift of wisdom, making him a formidable enemy. And even worse, a second fulfillment of the Dark Lady's prophecy.

Commander Orion arrived at that moment, followed by his generals. Every time Lady Ragna saw Commander Orion, his height and broad shoulders, the way the sun highlighted the hard edges and scars on his face, she saw power. The power of the empire. The power of a man. The power that would soon be Ravenwood's.

Despite Lord Ivulf's own strong features, Lady Ragna found herself secretly disappointed. He was not as striking as Commander Orion.

"Follow me," Commander Orion said as he bypassed those gathered and entered the tent. Everyone followed without a word.

Commander Orion took his place at the head of the long table that took up most of the space. Lamps hung from support beams, lighting the area. Lady Ragna stopped to the left of him, while Lord Ivulf came to stand at Commander Orion's right side. Raoul stood behind his father. The rest of the generals filled in the areas around the table. The aroma of sweat and sand saturated the air.

Commander Orion looked around the room, as if weighing everyone there. Instead of cowering beneath his gaze, Lady Ragna stood proud and tall. She was here as his equal, and she would show it.

"Tomorrow we begin our assault on Shana-lona." His deep voice filled the tent. "Their walls are wide, and soldiers have been reported along the top, but compared to our army, our catapults, and Lord Friere's abilities, Shanalona will fall."

"What abilities might those be?" one of the generals asked.

"Our ally, House Friere, has the ability to manipulate and heat both earth and rock. He will use his power to heat the boulders we will be using in the catapults as well as create trenches or raise dirt mounds to stop or redirect their troops."

A few eyebrows were raised, accompanied by appreciative nods.

"That could cut down the time needed to take down the walls," the first general said.

"Along with setting fires within the city," replied another.

"And what about the woman?" another general asked. All eyes turned toward Lady Ragna.

"She has her own power, one that I will not disclose. Not yet," Commander Orion said. "But once we can utilize it, it will do more damage to the Great Houses than our entire army can do."

A trickle of sweat slid down the back of Lady Ragna's neck. The Dark Lady promised more power if they walked together each night. But nothing had come of it yet. The last thing she wanted to do was appear incompetent in front of Commander Orion. She would find a way to use the dreamwalking gift for the benefit of the empire. She just needed more time.

Commander Orion's eyes lingered on Lady Ragna. Could he see through her? "Now to discuss the next steps in our campaign. As we speak, there is a covert mission to take out the water lord of House Maris."

The first general spoke up. "The one who blocked us from the Northern Shores?"

"Yes. Once he has been taken care of, we will no longer have to worry about the barrier he erected around his land. It will fall, allowing us to continue our march north after we take Shanalona."

"Excellent," one of the men murmured.

Lady Ragna's fingers twitched, and another droplet of sweat trickled down her back. She hadn't heard from Amara in over a month. Not surprising, as there wasn't a way to communicate easily. Still, so much was riding on that girl. It would help to know Amara had accomplished her mission. If she failed, it would be a black mark against House Ravenwood, giving Ragna perhaps another reason to secure Opheliana into the good graces of House Friere.

Her eyes slid toward Commander Orion as he continued to lay out his plans. She also hadn't told him, or Lord Ivulf or anyone else, that Selene had succeeded her as head of House Ravenwood. That Selene's power was greater. That was a secret she would keep buried. If it came to light, it would be another black mark. She couldn't afford any hint of mistrust in this alliance.

An hour later, as the sun began to set, the meeting wrapped up. Lady Ragna left the tent ahead of the men, thankful for the cool breeze that blew softly against her heated face. The imperial base was finished, a small city made of thousands of tents set along the hills of sagebrush and sand.

The flaps of the tent moved, and Lord Ivulf joined her. "You are welcome to stay in my tent tonight," he said in a husky voice.

She waved him off as she watched the sun set over Shanalona in the distance, a fiery ball of red. "I'm busy this evening."

"With what?" A hint of suspicion entered his voice.

She wanted to tell him it was none of his business, but she didn't want to deal with his jealousy at the moment. She needed to keep him in a good mood for when she asked about relocating Opheliana. "I'm joining the Dark Lady tonight."

"I see. Then I'll let you go."

Even Ivulf was wary when it came to the Dark Lady. Seconds later, Raoul, his son, exited the meeting tent. The two wandered off together, their body language indicating a heated conversation. Once again, she wondered at the look Raoul had given his father right before the meeting.

Lady Ragna turned away and gripped her cloak tightly against her body. She would send a raven tomorrow to Captain Stanton to tighten security around Rook Castle and prepare Opheliana for her possible journey to Ironmond. She couldn't afford to lose Rook Castle to any surprise attack—whether from one of the Great Houses, the coalition she had been hunting for years, or even her own daughter, Selene.

As she walked between the tents, a moment of weakness came over her. Usually at this time of night, she would be in her chambers back at Rook Castle, either dipping her tired body into a hot bath filled with lavender-scented water or sitting before her mirror with Hagatha brushing her long hair.

No.

Her fingers tightened along the edge of her cloak. Power did not come to those who sought pleasure. She had a mission to accomplish. With the empire, the Dark Lady, and House Friere at her side, nothing would stop her from restoring House Ravenwood back to power.

Nothing at all.

8

After gathering a few supplies from their rooms, changing into their warmest clothing, and strapping their swords to their backs, Damien and Taegis met Lady Bryren on the roof of Palace Levellon. In the distance, over hills of green beneath an overcast sky, four wyverns appeared, gliding along the cool wind blowing over the city.

Damien folded his arms and curled his fingers inside the crook of his elbows. He hated leaving Selene this way. The words she had hurled at him that morning had left a mark deep inside. Did she really believe he married her to save himself? Hadn't she realized how much he'd come to love her over the last few months? Or was she reacting to all the hurt suddenly overwhelming her?

He sighed and ran a hand through his hair. He meant what he'd said to her. He would be her rock. No matter her words, he would be there for her. Through the storms. Through the waves. Through the war.

He would show her his love until his dying breath.

He looked up at the cloud cover. *Please, Light. Just let me return to her.*

Lady Bryren spoke. "Here comes Reidin and my two guards with their mounts. Lord Damien, you will ride with me. Your guardian will ride with Finn, one of my guards. When Lord Renlar and his own guard arrives, I will have him travel with my consort and other guard."

"Anything special we need to know?" Taegis asked.

Lady Bryren flashed them both a wicked grin. "Don't fall off."

Even a war didn't seem to put a damper on Lady Bryren's mood.

The wyverns arrived minutes later in a gust of wind laden with a heavy musky smell. They came down on their powerful hind legs first, then folded back their arms and wings. The copper-colored one leaned toward Lady Bryren with half-lidded yellow eyes. Reidin's wyvern was the color of magma, with powerful muscles and webbed wings. The Merek guards rode two smaller blue-grey wyverns that looked like they were from the same clutch. All four were the size of small houses and barely fit along the roof.

Damien took another breath and turned his head away. Ugh. That smell was going to take some getting used to.

Lady Bryren raised her hand and rubbed the copper wyvern along its narrow neck. "Shannu, I missed you."

The wyvern responded with a snort and a dip of its head.

Lady Bryren turned toward Damien. "Shannu will be your companion on this trip. Come here so she can get your scent."

Damien closed the distance between them, stopping near Lady Bryren and Shannu. Out of the corner of his eye, he spotted Taegis being introduced to one of the smaller wyverns.

"Hold out your hand so she can smell you. Keep your gaze on her. Show no hesitation. Wyverns despise cowards."

Damien turned back and did as Lady Bryren asked. He held his free hand up while looking the wyvern in the face. His hand never wavered, his temperature never rose. The only thing that indicated any fear was the sudden pounding of his heart. Could the wyvern hear that?

Shannu's eyes narrowed as she let out another snort, then sniffed his hand. She grunted and turned away.

"Well, apparently you're not the best smelling man, but she'll carry you."

Damien raised one eyebrow. He could say the same thing about the wyvern.

One of the guards approached Lady Bryren with a small padded leather saddle. The other guard had already started attaching a similar saddle to the large red wyvern. Both men were of medium build and looked exactly the same, right down to the spiky brown hair, thick eyebrows, and full beards. He suspected they were twins.

"You'll ride behind me on the second saddle," Lady Bryren told Damien as Finn looped the leather cinches around the waist of the wyvern. "My guards will carry your supplies in their saddlebags. Once Finn is done attaching your saddle, go ahead and give him your gear."

Damien glanced at her. "Is riding a wyvern like riding a horse?"

Lady Bryren threw her head back and laughed. "Even House Luceras's powerful war-horses cannot compare to the wyverns of the South. And I think you'll find flying is very different than riding." She eyed him. "You're wearing your warmest clothing, right? It can get a bit chilly up in the air."

"I am. I'm from the north, after all." He gave her a wink, and Lady Bryren laughed again. His lips twitched at her lighthearted response. Here they were, getting ready to go to war, and Lady Bryren could still find a reason to laugh. He sobered at the thought. They would need to find every reason to smile in the coming months.

Lord Renlar and his personal guard appeared just as Finn finished attaching the second saddle to one of the smaller wyverns.

Lady Bryren raised her hand as she headed in

his direction. "Lord Renlar. Good to see you. I hope to be in the air shortly. You will be riding with my consort, Reidin." She continued to speak to him while Finn and the other guard prepared the gear and the last two saddles.

Damien approached the edge of the roof and looked over the city, a shadow returning to his soul. His heart throbbed again with pain, and he bowed his head. He wished he hadn't said what he had that morning. Months ago, the morning of the Festival of Light, Selene had said he was a good man. But he wasn't. He was just a man. One who sometimes let doubts fill his mind and let anger get the best of him.

He knew it wasn't her fault that the Dark Lady was hunting her. Or that her vast power was overwhelming her and spilling across others. But he also knew Selene was strong. It had to take a strong woman to grow up in a family like hers, to choose to leave everything behind when given the chance, and to marry a man she didn't know for the greater good.

There was no other woman like her.

And he would never give her up.

Damien bowed his head as another cold breeze blew across the roof and his companions prepared for their trip. Then he began to pray.

"Lord Damien, we're ready to leave."

Damien lifted his head. All four wyverns were saddled. Finn, the one who had spoken to him, motioned toward Shannu. "I will help you onto Lady Bryren's wyvern."

Despite the trepidation filling his limbs and the somberness of where they were heading, he also felt a tiny burst of excitement. There wasn't a person alive who wasn't awed by the magnificence and power of the wyverns of the Southern Isles—and not one boy who hadn't dreamed of riding one.

Damien thought of his deceased brother, Quinn, with a sad smile as he approached Shannu. Quinn would have given his right arm to ride a wyvern. "I wish you were here to see this," he whispered.

Finn led him behind the massive webbed wings to the small saddle behind Lady Bryren's. They barely took up the space along Shannu's back. Once again Damien was awed by the creature before him.

The saddle Finn pointed to looked like any other, save for the long leather chaps that hung from the edge. Finn let out a sharp whistle, and a moment later, Shannu lowered her body.

"Once you're in the saddle, I'll attach the chaps to your legs. They'll help with the wind and help keep you on Shannu's back."

Damien nodded. He placed his boot into the stirrup, then swung himself onto her back. Despite her size, her girth was only slightly wider than a large horse. He settled into the saddle, then Finn began to wrap the thick leather ties from the chaps around his lower thigh and calf. Once he was done, he secured the ties and moved to Damien's other leg.

Damien could move his legs back and forth and to the side, but the chaps kept him bound to the saddle, which made sense. He looked up at the sky. The last thing he wanted to do was fall off. He gripped the saddle horn and waited.

As Finn finished tying the chaps to his other leg, Lady Bryren approached and hoisted herself into her own saddle. There were no chaps on hers. No doubt she had learned how to ride without the need of such safety harnesses; it gave her the freedom to disembark at a moment's notice.

Damien peered past Shannu's wing. Lord Renlar was already secured on the massive red wyvern, while Finn was helping Taegis onto his.

Lady Bryren glanced over her shoulder. "The wind is in our favor. We should make good headway today before we need to land."

Once Taegis's and Renlar's guards were in their saddles, the two Merek guards and Reidin raised their hands. Lady Bryren nodded, raised her own hand, then brought it down with a quick *whoosh*. She let out a shout in the old tongue, and Shannu heaved herself up onto the rampart.

Damien swayed in the saddle and clutched at the horn. Then, with great strength and a gust of wind, Shannu beat her wings and let go of the wall. Up she rose at an easy slant.

Damien felt like he had left his stomach back on the roof of Palace Levellon. He squeezed his legs tightly against the wyvern's body, thankful for the ties around his legs. With every pump of her wings, Shannu's body dipped, then rose. The air grew colder the higher they went. Lady Bryren's hair was a wild mess of copper braids and flowing strands. His own clothes whipped around his body as the air rushed across the wyvern's body.

Up they went, toward the overcast sky. Moments later, they entered what felt like a bank of fog. Cold, wet droplets scattered across his face and eyes. Damien blinked away the moisture and held on.

Then they broke through the clouds. Lady Bryren let out another shout, and Shannu leveled out twenty feet above the endless grey. Above them, the sun glistened with pure light. It was . . . amazing.

Damien inhaled deeply. It seemed harder to breathe, but he could still draw in a breath. While gripping the saddle horn, he chanced a look back. The red wyvern flew behind them, followed by the two blue-grey ones. The wyverns seemed to glide across the cloudy expanse, their wings spread, catching the wind, flowing along the unseen river of air.

Damien turned around and settled into his saddle with a sigh, savoring this new experience.

Hours later, the sun sank in the west behind them, and so did the wyverns. Patches of land were scattered between the clouds. Lady Bryren lightly tugged on the reins, guiding Shannu toward a large opening in the cloud cover. The moment they passed the clouds, the area grew dark, as night began to cover the land. They were approaching the Magyr Mountains. Far below, Damien could see twinkling lights from homes and small mountain villages set amongst towering pine trees.

Lady Bryren avoided the lights, steering instead toward what looked like a small meadow along a lone hill. Minutes later, Shannu touched down with a heavy thud. Damien let out his breath. As much as he enjoyed the open air, he felt even better back here on the ground. And the constant up-and-down movement had made his body ache.

Lady Bryren dismounted, then turned and began to untie the chaps across his legs.

"How are you doing, Lord Damien?" she asked as she unwound the first set of leather ties.

"Good, but sore."

Lady Bryren smiled in the dying light. "Not surprising. It took me weeks to grow accustomed to wyvern flight, and months to learn how to fight from the top of their backs." She went around to the other side and undid the other leather ties. "There you go."

Damien worked his legs free from the chaps, pulled his right leg over, and dismounted. The moment his feet hit the ground, his knees buckled beneath him.

"Whoa," said a deep masculine voice. "You must adjust to the land after flying all day."

Damien turned and found Reidin, Lady Bryren's consort, coming to his aid. Damien held a hand out for him to stop, then pushed up on his legs. A moment later, he felt right again and took a step. Reidin watched him with arms crossed and eyes narrowed, making him look menacing with his long black hair set in spikes around his face and the kohl lines beneath his eyes.

"You're right," Damien said as he took another step. "But I think I'm all right now."

Reidin raised one eyebrow, then turned and started untying the leather chaps stretched across Lord Renlar's legs. Lady Bryren came around Shannu and shook her head. "I should have warned you about that first step."

"I'm fine. Your consort's right; it's a lot like being at sea."

Lady Bryren looked in the direction of the red wyvern and rider. "Reidin is a man of little words, but he is always looking out for those around him." She smiled softly. "Including me."

Taegis came to stand beside Damien. He didn't seem to need any adjustment after the long flight. "What can I do to help, Lady Bryren?"

"Reidin and my two guards are unpacking what we need for tonight. Find some wood for a fire, before it becomes too dark."

"I'll help," Damien said.

The two men gathered dead branches and logs from the surrounding trees and brought them back toward the middle of the meadow, where the rest of the group was clearing an area, spreading blankets, and digging around in the knapsacks. Twilight had fallen, leaving the area in hazy darkness.

Damien put his load down while Taegis went about setting up a fire pit in the area Finn had cleared. Soon a fire began to burn, lighting the meadow with cheery light and warmth. The other guard started passing out rolls of dark bread and dried meat.

"Thank you, Erik," Lady Bryren said as she sat cross-legged in front of the fire, her leather split skirt spread around her. Reidin sat beside her, a towering shadow, and the two began to eat.

Erik brought Damien and Taegis food before sitting down beside Finn and handing the guard a roll. Lord Renlar stared into the fire, the orange light reflecting off of his dark skin and eyes, a piece of dried meat in his hand. He seemed to be deep in thought.

Reidin opened up a waterskin, took a drink, and passed it around. After everyone finished, blankets were claimed, and Taegis volunteered for the first watch.

Damien lay on top of the blanket with his hands behind his head and stared up at the night sky. The air was cool, but not cold. Spring was here and slowly thawing out the land. A sliver of a moon was making its way across the star-studded night. An owl hooted from the surrounding trees and far off, a timber wolf called out.

He sighed. Only this morning he had woken up beside Selene in Palace Levellon. And now . . .

Now he was at least a hundred miles away.

Never did he think he would miss the presence of another body near his. He rolled onto his side, his back to the fire, and held his hands next to his chest. Every part of him could feel the emptiness beside him. It would be weeks or even months before he saw her again.

He knew they each had a part to play in the war, but he had always imagined they would be standing together. Fighting together. He swallowed. So much could happen in the coming weeks. There were no guarantees in life. The passing of his family had taught him that.

He closed his eyes. *Please watch over her, Light. Watch over my wife.*

9

Every day started the same. Fasts were broken, blankets were rolled up, and the camp disassembled and packed away in the saddlebags once the wyverns arrived back from their nightly hunting. Then the small party flew all day, stopping once or twice for personal needs and a break. When dusk came, camp was reconstructed, and the wyverns sent out.

The scenery below gradually changed from the tree-topped Magyr Mountains to rolling foothills. Streams appeared like thin snakes weaving through the coarse green grass. Wisps of clouds hung high above the sky, farther up than where they were flying.

After the third day, plains of tall grass spread out beyond the foothills. Herds of pronghorn grazed amongst the golden fields. Small villages with thatched roofs, cultivated fields of barley, and shepherds with their sheep replaced the wild plains. Soon small towns appeared as they drew closer to civilization.

On the fifth day, great clouds of smoke appeared in the distance, dark and menacing. Damien leaned forward in his saddle, gazing past Lady Bryen's head. Yes, there was no mistaking it. Fires burned where the city of Shanalona stood.

Lady Bryren shook her head and steered Shannu to the right, where the air was clearer.

As noon drew near, the smoke grew thicker as Shanalona came into view. The city spread out over a wide area—ten miles at least—with whitewashed stone buildings, tiled roofs, and the occasional tree, all beneath a dark sky.

Damien gripped the saddle horn, his stomach churning. Were they too late? He glanced back but couldn't see Lord Renlar, only the red wyvern he rode. How could the empire have arrived so fast? They had to have marched almost every day. Then again, they had breached the wall close to a fortnight ago, perhaps longer, depending on the time it took for the message to arrive in Lux Casta.

Around the city stood a wall thirty feet high, but it only encompassed the inner part of the city. The rest was outgrowth over hundreds of years.

And to the east, past the wall . . .

Stood the might of the Dominia Empire.

A wave of heat washed over Damien as his heart leaped into his throat. Thousands of soldiers, tents, and massive wooden contraptions spread from the wall for miles under a darkened sky. More people than any city in all of the provinces. And every one of them was here to see to the destruction of Shanalona and the rest of the continent.

"This can't be," he whispered. Never had he imagined such an army. He had read about the first razing and knew the empire was coming. But it was a completely different experience to see the might of the empire with his own eyes. Not even if every military of the seven houses joined together could they stand against the empire.

He tried to swallow but found his throat dry.

No. He shook his head. *I can't think that way.* He lifted his hand away from the saddle horn and stared at his palm as the wind rushed past his body. *This is why we were given these gifts. To protect our people. All of our people.*

The red wyvern bearing Reidin flew past Shannu and led the way toward a towering palace near the center of the city. There were no people in the streets, no one looking outside the windows. It was as if the city were already dead.

Damien turned his gaze to the east. The wall still held, even though the outlying areas were on fire. If that was the case, then the empire hadn't broken into the city, not yet, and the people had already evacuated.

He let out his breath, and his body sagged. If nothing else, that was good news. But how far could thousands of people have traveled by now? Were they at the river?

He gripped the saddle horn again as the wyverns descended toward the highest and broadest roof of the palace. Within the courtyard and surrounding buildings, soldiers from Vivek's military scurried around.

Reidin dismounted and began to untie the chaps from Lord Renlar's legs. Lady Bryren did the same with Damien a minute later.

The air was warm and smelled of smoke and wyvern musk. Damien coughed and rubbed his eyes with the back of one hand before swinging his leg around and descending from Shannu's back.

As his feet hit the stone roof, a group of men appeared through a wooden hatch at the other end of the roof. All were dressed in leather and dark blue tabards with short swords at their sides.

"Lord Renlar," the first man said, leading the way.

Lord Renlar walked away from the red wyvern as Reidin took care of his mount. "Commander Akia."

"We've been waiting for your arrival. We received your message a couple of days ago, and I did as you commanded. The moment we learned the Dominia Empire had crossed the wall, I started evacuating our people north toward our strongholds there. However, there are many elderly and children, so the progress has been slow. Last I heard, they are still three days out from the river."

"As is to be expected. And the Dominia Empire?"

Commander Akia's face darkened. "Arrived two days ago. We've been putting up a fight along the walls. We have enough supplies to last at least a month. But these new weapons of the empire's are like nothing we've ever seen."

"Such as?"

Commander Akia looked toward the east. "They possess large wooden catapults that can launch what appear to be fiery boulders. They've been using them against the wall. There are cracks, but the wall is still holding. We've been able to repel the ladders and shot down two towers they erected. We're holding for now." He looked back at Lord Renlar. "The good news is I don't think they know about the flight of our people yet."

Lord Renlar nodded. "That is what I hoped for. The delay here should give our people enough time to cross the river." He motioned toward Damien, who then made his way to Lord Renlar's side. "Commander Akia, this is Grand Lord Damien of the Northern Shores. You know the power of House Maris."

Commander Akia bowed. "Grand Lord Damien, it is an honor."

"Thank you, Commander. I have come to aid your people. Once they have crossed the river, I will move the water barrier. As you know, once the water-wall is raised, nothing can cross it. Your people will be safe. I have also sent word for those along our borders to lend assistance with food, housing, and supplies."

"You are generous, my lord. Your aid will help greatly."

"My family has always believed in protecting all people." A pang stabbed him in the heart. That wasn't entirely true, not after what he had learned from Lord Renlar. There was a time when his own house sacrificed another to save themselves. Damien gritted his teeth. *Never again.*

"Commander!"

A young man reached the top of the stairs and waved a small folded message in the air. "A message from the front."

The men parted, allowing Commander Akia to reach the messenger. As he read the message, his face remained emotionless, but Damien had seen enough messages over the last year to know this one held dire news.

Commander Akia turned back just as Lady Bryren joined them. "It appears that at least two battalions and a cavalry regiment have broken away from the main imperial army and are heading north."

Lord Renlar let out his breath. "Right for our people."

"Yes, my lord."

"How long will it take them to reach the refugees?"

"Two days."

"The empire doesn't know about Lord Damien's presence here or our plan to raise the river. We need to buy our people enough time to cross the Hyr River. How many men can we spare to help our people?"

Commander Akia folded his arms, his eyebrows furrowed in thought. "I can send a regiment or two. If they ride hard and follow the hill line northeast of here, then cut across at the end of the valley, they can pass the empire's men and put themselves between our people and the empire. But it would be a suicide mission. Not many of them would survive."

Lord Renlar turned and looked over the ramparts toward the Dominia Empire. Smoke rose into the air in great billows where the outer city burned. Damien could almost imagine the thoughts tumbling through Lord Renlar's mind, weighing the cost of sending his men versus saving the rest of his people. It wasn't really a decision because there was no choice. The people of Shanalona came first. He knew he would be sending his men to certain death to give the people a chance to cross the river. A river they were counting on Damien to raise.

Damien ran a hand through his hair and down his neck. There was no guarantee he would be able to raise that part of the Hyr River, since it was not his own land. Did he dare hope Selene was right, that the treaty brought these people under his protection?

Lord Renlar turned around. "Send the regiments. Our people's welfare comes first. And our soldiers know that. They will be saving their own families by running interference."

Commander Akia pressed a fist to his chest and bowed. "Yes, my lord." Then he spun around and headed back to the hatch in the roof, along with his men.

Lady Bryren stepped forward. "My people should be here within a day. I will send Finn back to alert them to the situation and to bypass Shanalona and head to the border along the Hyr River."

Lord Renlar bowed his head. "Thank you, Lady Bryren. I thought we would have more time, but the empire appears to be as efficient as stories say. And now Shanalona burns."

"But the wall still holds."

The three of them looked out over the ramparts. "Yes," Lord Renlar said a moment later. "And we will hold it long enough to keep the empire's attention here. It's the people who need to survive. Cities can be rebuilt, and the libraries have already hidden away the most valuable tomes and books. But without people, it means nothing."

Damien stepped forward. "Agreed. I should leave shortly so that I can be ready at the river."

Lady Bryren nodded. "I will go with you. And my other guard can carry Taegis on his wyvern."

Lord Renlar raised his chin and folded his arms. "I will remain here with Commander Akia. When I can, I will send messenger doves to let you know what is happening."

"Reidin will stay here as well, and if the empire breaks through the wall, he will aid in your escape. As the leader and the final heir to House Vivek, we cannot afford to lose you. Your life and gift are important in this war. I'm sure Commander Akia would agree."

"I understand. This role is still new to me. My training as a scholar didn't prepare me for the realities I would face as a grand lord."

"None of us is ever ready," Damien said, remembering the hard choices he'd already had to make in the last two years. And more would come.

"Enough talk. It is time we left again." Lady Bryren looked at Damien. "Are you ready to go?"

Every muscle in his body screamed no. He was

tired and hot and sore. But now was not the time for rest. The people of Shanalona needed him. "I'm ready when you are."

"Good. I'll let my men know of our plans. We will leave shortly."

10

D amien held tightly to the saddle horn as the wind whipped past his face. The air was clearer here, away from the burning city. When it became too dark to ride, Lady Bryren and her guard Erik brought the wyverns down. No fire was made. A hasty meal of hard, round biscuits and meat was consumed, then blankets rolled out while the wyverns were let loose to hunt.

No one spoke. Sleep came in small snatches. By morning, Damien felt like he had been pummeled and left on the cold ground. Food and drink were shared, then they were back in the air.

A couple of hours later, he spotted the refugees of Shanalona making their way north. Thousands of people tramped across the long grassy plains, dressed in the bright colors of House Vivek.

Damien looked back. So far, there was no sign of the empire, and Lady Bryren had chosen a route to avoid being detected by those chasing the refugees.

As they drew near, people looked up and pointed. Everyone knew the stories about House Merek and their wyvern riders, but few had seen them. Lady Bryren brought Shannu down on the western edge of the people. Men dressed in blue tabards and leather armor broke away from the group and approached them.

"I am Captain Mursil. Are you here to help us?" the first man asked once he was close. He appeared young, no older than twenty seasons, along with the two guards on either side of him. Behind him, people slowed to catch a glimpse of the great beasts.

Lady Bryren dismounted, while Damien stayed in the saddle, his legs tethered within the leather chaps.

"We are. I am Grand Lady Bryren, and my companion is Grand Lord Damien. We are here to inform you that the Dominia Empire is coming and to assist in any way possible."

"The empire?" The captain's face paled in the sunlight. "The empire is coming after us?"

"Your commander has sent a contingent of soldiers to run interference and allow your people to get to the other side of the river. Once they are across, Lord Damien will use his power to raise the water."

"The empire . . ." the man murmured again to himself. His whole mind seemed centered on that thought as beads of sweat formed along his upper lip.

Lady Bryren reached over and clasped the captain's shoulder. "Look at me."

Captain Mursil raised his head.

"Now is the time for courage." She looked him straight in the eye. "These people need you."

Something unspoken passed between them. Moments later, Captain Mursil straightened up and pushed his shoulders back. His gaze was steady and his eyes clear. He pressed his fist to his chest. "I will see to it that the other captains are informed, my lady."

"Tell them time is of the essence. Get these people across the Hyr River as fast as you can."

"I will." He turned and headed back toward the crowds, his back straight, his steps determined. He stopped and spoke to the other guards, then all five spread out in different directions amongst the people.

The crowd continued to move northward, necks craned to catch a glimpse of the wyverns. Shannu watched the people with a bored expression before turning away and folding her wings in close to her body, blocking Damien's view.

Lady Bryren came around the wyvern's webbed wing, then fell against Shannu's side.

Damien stood in his saddle. "Lady Bryren!"

She held up a hand, her head still bowed. "I'm all right. Just give me a moment."

Damien reached down to start untying the leather chaps when Lady Bryren straightened up.

"Lord Damien, I'm fine. And we need to keep going."

"What did you do?" Damien asked, keeping his hand on the leather tie.

Lady Bryren let out a long, shaky breath. "I impressed upon Captain Mursil the need for valor. It is the last talent my family retains of our ancient gift, but it takes great effort. I'm sure you saw his fear. It was overwhelming him. If I hadn't acted, his fear would have spread. Instead, I infused him with courage. Now he will spread that to the others."

Damien let go of the leather strap and sat up. "Like a spark that starts a fire."

Lady Bryren smiled. "Yes. Both courage and fear can spread like a wildfire. I choose to spread courage. It will give flight to these people. And they will need it to cross the river."

"That's remarkable. I knew your house was known for your courage, but I didn't know you could give it to others."

"With each generation, our gift diminishes. But I still have the touch." Lady Bryren heaved herself up onto Shannu's back. "When used strategically, it can be powerful." She grabbed ahold of the reins. "Now it's time to head to the river."

As Shannu rose into the air, Damien thought back on how Selene calmed his nightmares on the anniversary of his parents' and Quinn's death. The gifts of House Merek and House Ravenwood were similar in some ways. If Lady Bryren could spread a seed of courage with a look and a touch, what could Selene do in the dreamscape to an entire world of sleepers?

They flew low over the people as they made their way to the river ahead. To the west stood the hills and forest that marked the tributaries of the Hyr River, the boundary between the lands of Vivek and House Maris, and where the water-wall currently flowed.

The refugees were close. If they pushed forward, they could possibly reach this branch of the Hyr River by evening or early the next day.

He turned around in his saddle. The other guard and wyvern followed close behind. He couldn't see Taegis beyond the wyvern's head but knew he was there. It was a comforting thought.

An hour later, they began their descent toward a river of blue. The sun steadily headed west toward the horizon. The people of Shanalona were no longer in view, just a wide open area of tall grass leading to the Hyr River tributary. Beyond the river were hills of trees budding in the springtime air, and Damien could sense the water-wall in the tributary that marked his own border.

Shannu skimmed across the river, then landed on the sandy bank. Lady Bryren dismounted and proceeded to untie the leather straps around Damien's legs.

Once he was free, Damien jumped down and

gave his legs a shake. Part of him felt like he could collapse in the grass and not move for an entire day, but there was no time for that. Instead, he turned toward the river and took a deep breath.

The last time he used his power was back on the *Ros Marinus*, when he took down the sea barrier in order to reach Lux Casta. The act itself had worn him out, but it was the overpowering thoughts that had filled his mind moments before that had sent him to his knees. As he let the wall down, all he could think about were all the men he had drowned in the past, both the imperial fleet and the Ravenwood soldiers.

Even now the memories swirled inside his mind, leaving him feeling nauseated. He took in another deep breath and pushed the thoughts to the side, then focused on the river ahead. Time to see if his power worked here outside his own lands.

Damien closed his eyes and centered on his heart, the place where his power resided. Then he placed his hands out. A tingling sensation started at his fingertips, then spread slowly up his arms. Yes, he could feel the water here.

One more test.

He bent his knees and turned his hands out palm up. He could almost feel the water on his skin, cool and soothing. He curled his fingers slightly as if gripping the water, then he brought his hands upward as if in worship.

The river rose. He could feel the sensation deep within his bones.

Damien opened his eyes. The river had risen a foot into the air. He could do it. He could manipulate the water outside of his own lands.

He let out a laugh and let the water drop with a resounding splash.

"I knew you could do it." Lady Bryren stepped up beside him.

"Yes." Damien stared at his hands. At least one of his doubts was assuaged. But . . .

He looked across the river, toward the unending plains of the province of Vivek. He could raise the water, but would his power protect any people not his own?

11

I hate waiting."
Taegis and Damien sat beside the river as the sun began to rise to the east. Lady Bryren and her guard had left during the night to assist the refugees. The air was cold and crisp. A few puffs of clouds hung in the sky, pink and orange in the light of the rising sun.

"I hate not knowing what is happening." Damien stared out at the river. "I hate the scenarios that keep playing out in my mind. What if the people don't arrive in time? What if my power doesn't recognize them as my people?" His throat constricted. *What if I have to make a choice between those who live and those who die?*

He lifted his hand and studied his palm. He didn't say the last thought out loud, but it was the strongest fear beating inside his chest.

Taegis leaned over and placed his hand on Damien's shoulder. Damien looked over at his guardian in surprise. Taegis wasn't one given to touch very often.

"It doesn't do any good dwelling on what might happen. Whatever the outcome, you can't change it right now. Worrying will only eat away at your strength. Instead, know what you need to do when the time comes, then let go. Save your energy for when the battle arrives."

Damien turned back as Taegis dropped his hand. He let out a long sigh, and his shoulders sagged. "You're right."

The wind continued to blow gently across the hills, and the trees creaked behind them. The sun rose, greeted by the songbirds.

Then he saw it. The first line of refugees.

Damien jumped to his feet. "They're here."

Just as he said that, he saw Shannu flying above the people and heading for his position. Damien spotted a long, sandy bank to the right, a place where the water was slow-moving and not too deep. The perfect place for the people to cross.

Shannu landed minutes later with a dull thud. Lady Bryren jumped from her back in a whirl of leather skirts and wild copper hair. "Lord Damien," she shouted as she ran toward him. "You need to be ready. The empire is closing in. I spotted the soldiers Lord Renlar sent, but it's going to be close."

"How close?"

She looked at the multitude making its way across the plains. "You'll have to raise the river immediately after the last person is across."

"But can't we give them time to get farther from the river? We don't know what my power will do."

Lady Bryren turned back. "You don't have a choice. We must save as many as we can."

Damien stared at her.

"Do you understand what I'm saying?"

"Yes." The word came out in one breath. He would raise the river and hope the treaty was enough to cover these people. If not . . .

He clenched his hand and turned his head. He hated war. He hated death. But a man in his position did not have the luxury of choosing pacifism. His duty was to use his power and position to save people. Make the hard choices. Choose life for some and death for others.

"Then I will leave the river to you. I need to get back and do whatever I can to stall the empire."

Damien glanced up. "One person against so many?"

Lady Bryren smirked. "Don't underestimate House Merek or our wyverns. Shannu will enjoy the battle."

With that, Lady Bryren spun around and headed back to her wyvern. Damien stared after her. Sometimes he wondered if House Merek possessed the gift of courage or just recklessness. But if her fire and bravado bought them time, then it was worth it.

Fear drove the people of Shanalona across the river. Taegis and the accompanying guards could barely control the refugees as they surged through the water. More than a few people lost their footing and fell into the river.

"Keep going, keep going!" a guard yelled, the water up to his thighs as he waved the people toward the other bank.

Another guard herded the people forward. "To the tree line. Make way for those still crossing the river."

Every few seconds, people turned to look back, eyes wide.

"How close is the empire?"

"Why did the grand lord evacuate us from the city? We would have been better off there."

"We're going to die—"

"Enough!"

Damien recognized the man yelling. Captain Mursil.

Captain Mursil stood on the other side of the river, but his voice carried to every person between himself and Damien. "Get your families across the river as quickly as possible!" he shouted. "Our military is fighting back and buying us time. If you value your life and fellow man, then move it!"

His words seemed to move the people along. Damien closed his eyes and took in a deep breath. If only the people knew what their new lord was willing to do to keep them safe. To be a leader meant to have one's decisions questioned. But from what he could see, Lord Renlar had made the right choice to evacuate the city, even before he knew Damien would be here to move the water barrier. Perhaps it was a glimmer of the gift of wisdom he carried.

Screams suddenly filled the air. Damien glanced up. Something large and black came hurtling through the sky. As it drew closer, he realized it was a boulder heading straight for the people.

Panic threaded its way through the refugees as they surged forward, pushing toward the river. The boulder landed within twenty feet of the people. More shouts erupted and chaos spread like wildfire. Captain Mursil tried to bring order, but as another boulder came flying, his voice disappeared amongst the noise.

More specks appeared in the sky. But they followed no trajectory, not like the boulders. Rather, they looked like they were flying. . . .

Wyverns. A clutch of them.

Finn had gotten the message to the other riders in time. Lady Bryren's people had made it.

Damien brushed a hand through his hair as he let out a sigh. They had a chance.

Minutes later, the battle between the empire, Shanalona's forces, and the wyvern riders commenced. The sound of thousands of swords clashing, battle shouts, and the roar of the wyverns echoed across the plains as the refugees crashed through the river. The empire pushed forward, intent on reaching the people.

Tension worked its way across his shoulders as Damien watched from the river shore. He could see the end of the crowd. They were almost to the river.

Another boulder hurtled into the air from the empire's strange contraptions, grazing one of the small red wyverns. The beast faltered, favoring that wing. His rider tugged on the reins, and the wyvern made its way to the river, the wind from its powerful wings brushing Damien's hair back as it flew overhead.

Seconds turned into minutes as the last of the refugees approached the water's edge. The empire drew closer, aided by their cavalry. The Vivek regiment hit their flank, but they barely slowed the empire's advance. Wyverns swooped down and moments later rose with enemy soldiers clutched in their talons, only to drop the men amongst the army in a terrifying bout of screams.

Damien shook his head as he watched the scene before him. Why was the empire so intent on going after the citizens? What benefit was there?

Then it hit him. They weren't interested in hostages. A live person could rise up and fight again. But if the population was wiped out, they could take what was left. And who was easiest to kill?

Ordinary citizens.

His nostrils flared, and a fire blazed up inside

his chest. Damien clenched his hands and took a step toward the river. His gaze traveled across the refugees forging through the water to the other side. His fingers tingled with his power, reaching toward the water ahead.

More boulders flew into the air, then crashed down on the plains, crushing soldiers and horses alike as the Vivek military cut across the battlefield to place themselves between the last of the people and the Dominia Empire. The air filled with shouts and thundering roars. Dust rose into the sky.

Mere miles now separated the advancing army and the river.

Damien positioned himself, ready to raise the water at the last moment. His power grew, sending another surge through his body, but he held back. "Come on," he whispered as the fighting forces drew near.

Just as the last of the refugees neared the riverbanks, a wall of earth shot into the air similar to the wall of water Damien created with his power. Dirt clods and grass flew high into the sky, along with a handful of people caught in the rupture. Seconds later, the dirt fell like rain across the area, and the bodies hit the earth with soft thumps.

Damien took a step back, his mind reeling as though he had been punched in the face. All he could do was stare ahead at the trench that separated the last of the refugees and soldiers from the river.

That power. The power to move the land and heat the earth. Only one family had that gift.

House Friere.

He knew House Friere had aligned with the empire, but to see Lord Ivulf's gift in action now . . . how could he? How could Lord Ivulf do such a thing?

"Ivulf!" he shouted as he sprinted to the edge of the river. The people behind him screamed and shouted, but he ignored the cacophony. He could possibly move the water from the river over to the crack and try to fill it, but that would siphon some of his power. And . . .

He looked across the river. Not knowing how deep the chasm went, he could even make things worse.

He swallowed hard as sweat stung his eyes and desperation filled his heart. There was nothing he could do.

His hands began to tremble, and he yelled again, letting out every ounce of anger and shock through his voice. The water rippled at the outburst of his emotions.

"Damien." Taegis's hand settled across his shoulder. "Don't waste your energy."

Taegis was right, but at the moment, he wanted to raise the water and let it explode across the imperial army. Even more, he wanted to find Lord Ivulf and—

He swallowed, then pressed his lips together.

No, he couldn't do that. He wouldn't become like House Friere.

With his whole body shaking, he was forced to watch the people of Shanalona struggle over the breach while the imperial army and Vivek's military drew closer.

Bodies littered the trampled grass beyond the chasm. Wyverns swooped down and caught more soldiers in their massive claws as their riders reached out with long spears. Thousands more still fought, but as the opposing forces drew closer, those dressed in blue were being swept into a sea of burnt orange and green.

Adrenaline poured across Damien's body as sweat became a second skin. *Light,* he cried in his mind. *How could this happen?*

A few people made it over the trench either by climbing or finding a fallen tree to span the chasm. But as he watched the imperial army draw closer, he knew there wasn't enough time.

One mile.

"They're not going to make it," Taegis said beside him. "It's time to raise the river."

Damien shook his head, his heart hammering inside his chest. "Don't say that, Taegis." His cheeks flushed as he watched two refugees rush into the river. "If I raise the wall now, then those still on the other side will be slaughtered." *Or even swept away.*

"But it will all be for naught if you don't raise the river in time and the empire crosses."

Damien stared at his outstretched hands. "What good is this power if I can't save everybody?"

Taegis stepped directly in front of Damien and looked him in the eye. "Even with this power, you will never be able to save everyone. You were never supposed to."

"Then why doesn't the Light?"

He could now see details on the uniforms of the empire's soldiers—the tassels, the rips, the bloody patches. He could hear grunts of pain and the screams of those dying. The two refugees made it across the river, but the empire was close behind and already stretching planks across the crack in the ground.

Taegis was right. If he didn't raise the wall now, then everyone would die.

Damien crouched down, every muscle in his body tight, and prepared to raise the wall. Sweat soaked his clothes and hair, and even the soft breeze wasn't enough to cool his body.

For a split second, his power faltered. It was the same feeling he had weeks ago before he brought the sea-wall down. Was his power fighting against the impossible choice he had to make about who lived and who died? Damien stared at his outstretched hands.

Taegis squeezed his shoulder. "You can do this. You *must* do this. Save those who can be saved."

Damien took a deep breath and raised his eyes. He ignored the sounds around him and focused on the river ahead until all he could sense was the presence of the water and his own power reaching out toward the source.

With a yell, he lifted his hands into the air.

With the same motion, the river shot upward in a tower of raging water and foam. It rose until it was thirty feet above the banks, then the water spread in both directions, consuming everything in its way.

His muscles bulged, and he let out a grunt as he held his hands up, letting his power pour out from him and into the water. His vision grew hazy, but he held on. He needed the wall to reach not just the nearby tributary in his own lands but all the way to the sea.

His eyesight blurred more, then darkened. His hands shook, and he could barely draw in a breath. Then he saw them: the forces of Vivek running for the river. But it was too late.

The wyvern riders dipped down and grabbed those they could before soaring over the water-wall, but it was only a handful. A few of the empire's men were caught up in the wall and sent screaming down the raging river, but most held back, choosing instead to pick off the remnants of House Vivek's forces.

Damien twisted his wrists, simultaneously locking the new water-wall in place and dropping the water barrier in his own tributary. His arms fell to his sides, and he took a step back. He stared ahead in horror at what he had done. It was just like that day at sea when his water-wall took out the small imperial fleet, only worse. He had condemned good men and women to death.

How can I keep doing this?

Something throbbed painfully inside of him. Damien looked down and gripped the front of his shirt. It was the same feeling from before. Like the ripping of his soul.

He took another step back, then fell to the ground. His cheek hit a rock, and Taegis yelled his name somewhere nearby. He closed his eyes and everything went black.

12

Selene stood on the steps that led up to Palace Levellon. The fountain trickled quietly nearby, splashing into the waiting stream below. A bright blue sky filled the expanse overhead, and a warm spring breeze blew across the landscape. At the bottom of the steps, the four Luceras siblings gathered: Leo, Tyrn, Elric, and Adalyn. They spoke quietly with each other, their expressions filled with love and affection.

Selene looked away. The familial sight was a private affair, and it reminded her intensely of what she had lost—not just Amara's death, but what they never had, and now never could. Even now her sister's ashes rested in a sealed urn, packed away with everything else for this journey: her final trip to Rook Castle.

Selene would not make the same mistake with Opheliana.

A moment later, Lord Tyrn stepped away from his brothers and sister and headed up the steps toward Selene. She had never spoken to the second brother and wondered why he was approaching her now.

"Lady Selene." He stopped on the step below hers and bowed his head. "May we speak for a moment?"

She stepped back in invitation, her brows furrowed. "What is on your mind, Lord Tyrn?"

He joined her at the top. Even though she was considered tall by female standards, Lord Tyrn was almost a head taller than she was, and thin, unlike his brothers, and with an intelligent look to his face. "I want to apologize for my brother," he said quietly, so as not to be overheard.

"Your brother? You mean Lord Leo?" she said, glancing down at the group.

"Yes. There is a lot weighing heavily on his mind: the death of our father, the sudden responsibility for our house and people, his worry for House Rafel—"

"House Rafel?"

"Yes. He is worried for Lady Ayaka."

Selene's frown deepened. Lady Ayaka—oh!

"I can see on your face you understand what I mean. It is something private between them, and they are still figuring out the logistics of a potential union. However, this war—and her father's unwillingness to join the alliance—has made it difficult."

"I had no idea," Selene murmured.

"I tell you this because my brother is a good man. He will do what is right. But it might take him some time to come around to you and your family."

"And what do you think, Lord Tyrn?" Selene looked him in the eye. "I'm sure you've heard everything by now, since you will be leading your people in your brother's stead."

"I think . . ." He paused. "I think we all have family secrets. I respect the fact that you have stepped forward about your own family's. Maybe someday the rest of us can follow."

Before Selene could ask what secrets House Luceras harbored, Lord Leo started up the stairs.

Lord Tyrn bowed again and stepped back. "Brother," he said, addressing Lord Leo.

"Tyrn." The two brothers clasped forearms. "Watch over everyone here while I am gone."

"I will."

"You've always had a better head for leadership, Tyrn. Don't let the council persuade you otherwise."

"I won't."

Lord Leo looked at Selene, and his face darkened. "Are you ready, Lady Selene?"

"I am. Thank you for the supplies and a horse."

"Then let us leave." He turned and headed back down the stairs toward where three horses were waiting at the edge of the fountain. They would meet with the rest of Luceras's forces outside the city.

Lord Tyrn let out a long sigh and shook his head in Lord Leo's direction. Maybe she wasn't the only one who needed patience with the newest grand lord. The thought bolstered her a little.

As Selene descended the stairs, Lady Adalyn

met her near the bottom. Every time Selene saw her, there was a tiny twinge in her heart. The bright sun highlighted the white-gold locks cascading down Lady Adalyn's shoulders, and the white gown accented her petite frame.

Lady Adalyn reached out her hand and grasped Selene's. Selene fought everything inside of her to pull back. Only Damien ever touched her, and she wasn't used to the unfamiliar gesture.

"Stay safe, Lady Selene."

Her look was one of innocence and purity, and it made Selene ashamed of her jealousy. "I will. And I will watch over your brother." She hadn't meant to say that, but the words slipped out.

Lady Adalyn's lips quirked. "Watch out for Elric. He can be a handful."

Selene had forgotten that Lord Elric would be coming as well. She remembered he was Quinn's friend from Damien's memories, and from what she had witnessed, he was a mischief-maker. "I will."

Selene pulled her fingers from Lady Adalyn and turned away. Only a small spark of envy burned in her heart. And even then, it was already vanishing. She wasn't Lady Adalyn. She was Lady Selene of House Ravenwood and House Maris. She was her own person and had her own path to follow.

Selene rode beside Lord Leo and Lord Elric an hour later. Behind them, the might of House

Luceras marched toward the Magyr Mountains. The farther they drew from the city, the heavier her heart became, as if a stone had replaced the living organ. Damien had left only days ago, but as time went on, it felt like he had taken her heart with him. Maybe he had. Maybe this thing that beat inside of her was only a shadow of what had once dwelt there.

She clenched her hand and held it to her chest. Her throat tightened as she remembered their last words, the accusations she had flung at her husband. *Why? Why did I do that?*

Fear. Hurt. Betrayal.

She had let these feelings get the best of her. And now she and Damien were both riding into battle with a chasm between them.

Selene lifted her head and gripped the reins tighter. *No. I will* live through this. *I will* secure my home. And I will see Damien again. And when I do, I will tell him the truth of my heart . . . that I love him.

That conviction grew, swallowing up her hurt as she accompanied the forces of House Luceras across hills of green toward the mountains ahead. She barely spoke to Lord Leo or Elric, choosing instead to keep her own company with the silent presence of Karl nearby. Every night she stared at the stars, placing her mind and her gift in the power of the Light before drifting off.

Her control over her dreamwalking was growing. She could sense the presence of thousands of sleepers around her, but she kept their minds at bay instead of pulling them into her dreamscape. Her power was no longer a wild, untamed gift.

But was her strength enough if the Dark Lady came back? And how could she use her gift to help in the war?

Each day brought evidence of spring: the budding of flowers, the stirring of insects, and the songs of birds. As they drew closer to the mountains, it appeared winter had finally lost its hold amongst the rocky cliffs, and bits of green shot through the hard ground.

Finally, after a week, they reached the foothills of the Magyr Mountains and King's Highway, which would lead them to the bridge that spanned the path to Rook Castle.

The soldiers set up camp as the sun set. Selene laid out her own blanket near the edge of camp, close to a fire. Out of the corner of her eye, she spotted Elric laying his own nearby. He looked up and waved at her.

Unsure of how to respond, she turned and placed her pack down before heading toward a grove of trees, her dual swords snug against her hips. Sometimes it was hard to believe that Lords Leo and Elric were brothers. They looked the same, with the light blond hair and blue eyes of the Luceras family, but that's where the similarity ended. Selene paused near a log as she remembered Damien's memories. How much alike had Quinn and Elric been? What would it have been like to have a brother-in-law like him?

She scrubbed a hand over her face, then finished her business. She would never know. The pain of her words stabbed her in the chest again. *"Maybe I would have had a family like yours."*

It had been a callous thing to say. Almost as bad as making Damien relive his nightmares. And the look on his face . . .

She shook her head and started back toward camp. *Can't dwell on that now. I need to focus on what's ahead.*

Almost a hundred fires burned as the Luceras army cooked and lay down for the night. Time was of the essence, so only the bare essentials were employed. Tents were a luxury for when they reached the mountains and not before.

As Selene approached her makeshift bed, she caught sight of Lord Leo speaking to one of the scouts at the edge of the camp. She leaned in closer, hoping to hear what news the scout brought.

"What should we do?"

Instead of answering, Lord Leo seemed to sense her and looked up. "Lady Selene, please come here."

Selene tightened her hold on her cloak and walked over. "Yes?"

"The scout here reports that a small company has been spotted near the base of the mountains, away from any village. And from what he can see, it's not a merchant's caravan or pilgrims. Is it possible this is your father's coalition?"

Selene frowned as her mind sifted through the possibilities. "It might be."

Lord Leo clicked his tongue with a scowl on his face. "I still don't agree with what your father and Lord Damien have put into motion, but they could be useful."

"Perhaps we should see what my father communicated to them?"

"Yes." Lord Leo raised his chin, the nearby fire reflecting in his eyes. "Your father appears to be more than any of us ever knew."

He had no idea. "I think I should be the one to approach them since I am Caiaphas's daughter."

Lord Leo turned back. "Agreed. First thing tomorrow morning, I will send one of my captains and a handful of soldiers with you."

Selene shook her head. "I don't think that is wise—"

"I will not send you alone. We don't know if this company is friend or foe." He looked directly at her. "And I'm not sure I trust you."

Her face flushed with anger. What would it take for Lord Leo to realize she was not like her family?

Time. It was going to take time.

Slowly she released her clenched fingers. "I understand. I will leave at first light. Your men better be ready."

"They will be."

Lord Leo turned and headed across the camp. Selene watched him while letting her breath out in one long sigh. *I can't lose it. It will only give him more fodder for his mistrust.* She closed her eyes. *I've changed. I follow the Light now. And by his power, I will do what is right.*

Selene was awake when the first rays of light touched upon the camp. She took a moment to wash her hands and face in the nearby stream, braid her hair, and adjust her swords around her waist before clasping her cloak around her neck. The scout from the night before was already waiting when she arrived, along with a handful of other men dressed in the colors of House Luceras. And of course, Karl, her constant shadow.

The scout bowed. "Lady Selene. Lord Leo sent us to accompany you and check out the group I spotted yesterday."

"Yes. Thank you for being prepared so early."

"It is our duty. This is Captain Lolan and his men."

Selene turned toward the young man at the scout's side and balked inside. Captain? The man appeared no older than she was, and not much taller either. He stared back with hazel eyes, his light brown hair brushing the edge of his armor.

"My lady," he said with a small bow.

"Captain Lolan."

"Shall we set off?"

Straight down to business. All right, she could do that. Selene turned her attention back to the scout. "How long will it take us to reach the company?"

"About midmorning."

"Then lead the way."

The scout was right. A few hours later, they spotted a company of about twenty people standing where the path to Rook Castle broke away from King's Highway. A wall of tall evergreen trees lined the slender path. The people gathered appeared like a traveling caravan, minus the bright colors and signs.

"Is that them?" Selene asked.

"Yes," the scout replied.

"I advise caution," Captain Lolan said.

"Yes," Selene agreed, "but we don't want to appear hostile. No weapons unless they are needed." Still, the subtle weight of her swords reassured her, just in case the people ahead were unfriendly.

Selene started for the group. The scout, Captain Lolan, and his men followed her lead. What kind of message had her father sent these people? He hadn't specified in his letter to Damien. Maybe he only had time to write a brief message. *Think, Selene. What would Father tell them?*

If it were her, she would tell them to be cautious and have a way to identify who was meeting them. The letter was sent to Damien, so her father must have assumed either she or Damien would meet them.

Does that mean I'm now part of this coalition?

She never gave Damien a straight answer months ago when he first invited her, but it would seem the answer had been made for her. If nothing else, the coalition was putting their lives on the line to help her secure Rook Castle.

Well played, Father. I'm now part of your coalition.

The more she came to know of Caiaphas the man, the more she realized how calculating her father had been—from his marriage to Lady Ragna, to her birth, to the current takeover of Rook Castle. Was it possible there was a drop of Vivek blood in him?

Three men broke away from the rest of the group and approached them. They were well dressed and carried themselves with a certain air. Out of the corner of her eye, she saw Karl's hand swing toward his sword. Captain Lolan stiffened beside her; apparently he recognized at least one of the men.

There were no visible weapons on them, but not for a minute did she think they came unarmed. The three men stopped ten feet away. Captain Lolan spoke first.

"What is a member of House Kaizer doing here?" he said, his eyes fixed on the man in the middle. He was taller than the other two, with flaxen hair and a sleek mustache.

"House business," the man replied. "Can't House Kaizer conduct matters apart from House Luceras?"

"Not if it jeopardizes our land," Captain Lolan said.

The nobleman's eyes grew hard. "Our land is not in jeopardy. At least not by my hand or by those gathered with me." His gaze roved across the rest of the group until his eyes met Selene's. There was a spark of interest and almost recognition.

Selene took this opportunity to step forward. "I am Lady Selene Maris, former lady of Ravenwood."

"You are Lord Damien's wife?"

"Yes. And partner in all of his affairs."

The nobleman seemed to like her answer. "And your father?"

"I am also privy to Caiaphas's knowledge."

"Then you are the one he sent?"

Not knowing who would come, her father must have given possible options. Now to take the lead her father and Damien had bestowed upon her. "Yes."

"Lady Selene, it is a pleasure to finally meet you. I am Lord Wynn of the lesser House of Kaizer. Is it safe to speak?"

"These men are with me for my safety. But they are on our side."

Lord Wynn studied Captain Lolan for a moment before responding. "Then as you know, we are here at your father's request. For years my family has worked with the coalition. It is my privilege to be here now and help in any way I can."

"Thank you, Lord Wynn."

"These two men with me are from the hill country. Behind me are those who were able to travel in a short amount of time. Those in the Magyr Mountains are preparing to help secure Rook Castle. We also have members coming up from the forest lands of Rafel, but it will still be another week before they arrive."

"I see." Damien had said the coalition stretched beyond the borders of the Great Houses, but to witness it now made it much more real. It was a true example of people from every province working together. If only the Great Houses could do the same.

"What are our orders?"

Selene looked up and stared across the expanse of conifer trees and mountaintops. Most of

Ravenwood's forces were probably loyal to her mother. However, if her mother thought Rook Castle was secure, then most likely the majority of the troops were stationed along the other strongholds around the mountains.

Selene tapped her chin as she glanced back to where House Luceras was making its way across the plains. If Lord Leo agreed, his forces could be a distraction, pulling out what few soldiers were located inside Rook Castle. While they fought, she would lead the coalition into the castle by means of the mine shaft east of here and secure the inside.

It could work, if she could convince Lord Leo.

She turned back to Lord Wynn. "We wait."

"We wait?"

"Until House Luceras arrives." Lord Wynn opened his mouth, but Selene continued. "We will use the forces of Luceras as a distraction to draw out those inside of Rook Castle. While they are engaged, I will lead you by another way into the castle, where we will meet up with my father."

"Another way?"

"I know of a hidden entrance into Rook Castle."

Lord Wynn slowly nodded. "I see. That could work."

Captain Lolan crossed his arms. "I also agree. It is better to wait for my lord to arrive."

Wynn rolled his eyes and looked away.

Selene sighed. Neither Damien nor her father had warned her that there would be another obstacle to overcome: the unity between the coalition and the Great Houses.

13

I'm not sure if I trust you to go alone." Lord Leo stood with his arms crossed and glared at Selene. Around them, the forces of Luceras set up tents and worked through drills. Near the edge of the forest stood the men and women of the coalition, waiting. The sun slowly made its way west, but warm rays still beat down on the people below.

Selene ignored the sweat collecting beneath her cloak as she stared back at Lord Leo. "So what do you plan to do? Follow me into the caverns?"

"Don't be mistaken. I will be the one leading the forces of House Luceras. But I would be a fool to let you go off into the caves by yourself. The Ravenwoods have proven to be very deceptive."

Her face flushed at his accusation. Selene balled her hands into fists and lifted her chin. "How can we work together if you continue to suspect me? What's it going to take for you to realize we are on the same side?"

Lord Leo remained silent. She couldn't tell if he was thinking about her words or just being stubborn.

Selene threw her hands up into the air. "Fine. Then send someone you trust."

He gave a small twitch before answering. Maybe her words were penetrating through his thoughts. "I'll send Elric. He may seem lighthearted, but he is more capable than you know. If he senses any duplicity, he'll take you out."

She ground her teeth together. As if Lord Elric could take her out. She wanted to remind him of what she was capable of in the dreamscape, but that would only add more fire between them.

Breathe. Just breathe. But her mind kept spinning. How could there be any unity between the houses when an attitude like Lord Leo's prevailed? Would she always be tainted by the dark history of her family? "If I secure Rook Castle, then will you consider that I am not in league with my mother and that I don't want to see the empire win?"

He folded his arms. "I will consider it."

"Fine. Have Lord Elric meet us within the hour."

She grabbed her pack—complete with Amara's urn—attached a waterskin, and cinched it shut. Then she curled her shoulders forward and bowed her head. *Damien, I miss you.* Her heart throbbed at the thought of him. She missed his cool, gentle composure. His soft voice. His comforting presence. *You'd know how to deal with Lord Leo. You'd know what to do. He wouldn't treat you like this.*

She wiped away the errant tear, then fortified

herself and straightened up. "I'm ready to go," she said as she turned around. Lord Leo was gone. She raised her head and searched across the men gathered, then spotted him thirty feet away, next to Lord Elric. The two spoke for a moment, before Lord Elric nodded. Both men turned and approached her.

"Lady Selene," Lord Elric said with his usual grin on his face. "It looks like we will be traveling together."

"So it does."

"I'll be bringing two guards along with me. I hope you don't mind."

"Of course." Lord Leo's words still rang in her ears, causing her body to flush again with anger.

"Let me retrieve my men, and I'll be ready to go."

Selene nodded and looked over the camp in an effort to bring her mind to the task at hand. Right now, they needed to infiltrate the castle and provide a stronghold. Now was not the time to deal with Lord Leo or any of the Luceras men. If nothing else, all her years of training had taught her how to focus.

Lord Leo cleared his throat. "I'm not sure when we will meet Ravenwood's forces, so I have no idea when we will arrive at Rook Castle. It may be up to you and your father's coalition to secure the castle. Do you think you can manage that?"

Selene hardened herself and turned back to

Lord Leo, biting down the desire to snap at him. "I understand." She took a deep breath and let it out slowly. "Fortunately, I know the secret passageways of Rook Castle. As long as you keep the military occupied, we should be able to take the castle."

"I am putting my people at risk, so I expect a victory. And no harm shall come to my brother. Do you understand?" His eyes were like a winter sky.

Her body tensed under his gaze, and she looked back fiercely at him. "I understand."

Lord Elric came to stand beside them minutes later with two Luceras guards, his pack in hand. His gaze darted between his brother and Selene, one eyebrow raised. "Shall we go?"

Selene took in another deep breath before speaking. "Yes. Between all of us, we have about thirty infiltrators. That should be enough."

"Excellent," Lord Elric said. "I've never broken into a castle before. This will be my first time."

Selene stared at him, taken aback by his cheerful, casual manner.

Lord Leo scowled. "Remember, Elric, this is serious business."

"I know." But his grin said otherwise.

Selene felt a foreign bubble of laughter suddenly rising up inside her chest. Perhaps it wouldn't be a bad thing to work with Lord Elric. They might even get along.

"What's your plan?" Lord Elric asked her.

She choked down the laugh and regained her composure. "It will take a day and a half through the old mines to reach the castle. During that time, I will go over the layout of Rook Castle and explain my thoughts as we travel, so as not to lose time."

"And Elric will decide if he likes your plan, and if it's in our best interest," Lord Leo added.

Selene's eyes flashed as she stared at him. *This isn't going to work,* a voice screamed in the back of her head.

"Calm down, brother. Remember, she is part of House Maris now. That is in her favor."

"I know." Resentment laced his voice.

Selene turned toward the hill where there was an opening to an abandoned mine. *No. I have to make it work. Father is counting on us. All of the houses are counting on us. We can't let Rook Castle fall to the empire.*

She breathed in through her nose. The faster she got away from Lord Leo, the better. Her mind and thoughts would be cooler, and she could concentrate on the plan at hand.

Lord Elric swung his pack onto his back. "Let's get going." He gave Lord Leo a haphazard salute. "Good-bye, brother."

Lord Leo sighed, but Selene swore she could see a smile tugging at his thin lips. "Good-bye,

Elric. I will see you at Rook Castle." He shot a warning look at Selene.

Selene ignored him. "The coalition is waiting for us at the edge of camp."

Lord Elric bowed. "Lead the way, my lady."

Selene wasn't sure how to respond, so she turned and headed for the group ahead, eager to start her journey.

As she approached those gathered who had come at her father's request, she was again impressed by the caliber of men and women her father had brought into this secret group. Retired captains, sons of lesser families, ex-militia, and a few merchants who knew a thing or two about subtle transactions and how to remain undercover.

Lord Wynn walked over to greet her. "Lady Selene. We are ready when you are." His eyes darted to Lord Elric and his two guards. "We're bringing more?"

"At Lord Leo's request."

Lord Elric shot Wynn a smirk. "Lord Wynn, what a surprise."

"Indeed," he replied, his face hardening.

Selene ground her teeth. If she had to put up with one more petty fight . . .

"All right, let's move out!" she shouted and started for the hills. Either they followed her, or they didn't. She was moving on. Her only focus was on securing Rook Castle and bringing Amara home.

· · ·

"How long have these mines been abandoned?" Lord Elric asked an hour into the mine shafts. Three people carried torches—one in the front, one in the middle, and one in the back. The light bounced off the uneven rock walls and wooden support structures. The air was cooler in here, and full of dust.

"Since before my great-grandmother's time. The silver was already scarce, but by the time my grandmother came into power, it was nonexistent."

"Interesting. I thought silver was a major source of Ravenwood's income. If the mines dried up, how has your family supported itself all of these years?"

"That is a question I cannot answer."

The other people talked quietly amongst themselves, their voices and the clap of their boots echoing along the mine shaft.

"By the way, please call me Elric. There are too many lords and ladies. I think it will be easier if you just refer to me by name."

Selene glanced over at the youngest Luceras. He was shorter and thinner than Lord Leo, and his light blond hair was kept short in a similar style to Damien's. "You know that's not proper."

He smiled, the torchlight bouncing off his youthful and handsome face. "I've never been one for propriety. Just ask my family."

She thought back to that memory she had seen in Damien's mind, of Elric and Quinn climbing the great oak tree when they were kids. Again, she wondered if Quinn had been the same as Elric: carefree and playful, with a hint of irreverence. What would it have been like to have a brother like him?

The mine shaft split into three different directions several hours into their travels. Selene stopped and stared at all three passages. It had been years since she last went this way, but one thing her mother always taught her was to see what the tunnels looked like from both directions so she wouldn't become disoriented.

"The one on the right leads to a cavern that meets up with another mine. That mine runs beneath Rook Castle."

"Amazing she can tell where to go," someone murmured nearby. "I'm completely lost."

"I hate this place. It's so dark and cramped."

There were more whispers as Lord Wynn came up to her side. "Perhaps this is a good time to rest."

Selene looked back at the group. Expressions were haggard and fatigued in the dim light and darkness. "I think you're right. Between this main hall and the three shafts, there should be enough room for people to split up and find places to rest."

"I'll let them know."

Another memory filled Selene's mind of Damien and his men as they escaped through the caverns to the Northern Shores. It was hard to believe that had been over six months ago. So much had changed. She raised her hand and looked at her palm. So much had happened.

"Hope you don't mind if I stay next to you," Elric said beside her. "I think my brother would want that."

"Of course," Selene said, mentally shaking her head and coming back to the present. It took her a moment to realize what Elric had said and what she agreed to.

"Where are we setting up camp?" he asked as he pulled out his blanket.

Those with torches were setting them in the rusty brackets attached to the walls as the others followed the passages in search of private areas. "How about right here?" Selene pointed to the passage on the right.

"Good idea."

The two men with Elric set down their packs while he laid out his cloak and blanket. As Selene watched the people scatter around the area, fatigue came crashing down on her. Lights like fireworks appeared across her vision, and she placed a hand against one of the support beams next to the mine shaft.

"Everything all right?" she heard Elric say as Karl took a step toward her.

"Yes, yes." She brushed a hand across her face as her sight returned. "Just . . . tired."

"Then lie down. I'm here, and so is Lord Wynn. And your guard. You're not alone. You can take a moment to rest."

Karl just watched her, but she could tell he was ready to catch her if she fell.

You're not alone.

Damien's last words.

Tears welled up in her eyes. Selene nodded and turned her back to everyone as she pulled out her own blanket and laid it on the ground. After downing a few gulps of water and a handful of grain, she laid her head on her pack, her face to the wall, her back to those behind her, and closed her eyes. It wasn't until this moment that she realized how much she was carrying on her shoulders: the coalition, securing Rook Castle, her own reputation . . . even her own sister.

How much longer could she last?

14

The darkness morphed into the dreamscape as Selene took flight. She flew high above the mountains, the cool air gliding beneath her wings. Below, snowcapped peaks and forests of green spread out as far as she could see. Everything was painted in the cool white light of the full moon, which softened the sharp edges of the mountains and brought a quiet calmness to the dark.

Along the valley she flew, letting the peace of the night fill her. A break in the trees appeared. She drew closer. It was a meadow filled with tiny white daisies. She swooped down to get a better look when she felt them: sparks of life, as numerous as the flowers dotting the hillsides.

She dove down toward the meadow, drawn by the feeling of vitality and life. As she lit on a branch of one of the towering trees that surrounded the meadow, transparent bodies appeared like spirits amongst the tall grass. Elric sat on a log, smiling and chatting with two men beside him. Others appeared at the edge of the forest. One of the women bent down to pick a wild daisy. Selene could sense her wonder as she held it in her hands.

Selene shuffled across the branch with her

claws, mystified by the scene. Did she bring them here? Her heart sped up. Was she losing control again of her dreaming? She stretched out with her senses. Yes. This was her dream. And someway, somehow, she had inadvertently invited her companions to share this place. But even as these thoughts flitted across her mind, one of the women laughed. Peace. She could feel it, like a soothing mist encompassing her within the dreamscape.

Was it a bad thing if she had brought her sleeping companions to this peaceful meadow? They had traveled all day, deep into the heart of the Magyr Mountains, heading toward battle. She could at least give them a quiet place to rest.

Selene closed her eyes and drew in a deep breath through her beak. She knew this place. She would come here often, using one of the caves, and lie in the sunshine while listening to the birds sing. For her, this was a place of peace, away from her mother's watchful eye and constant training. Here she could breathe easily and feel light.

Selene watched the people from her perch, listened to their amiable chatter and laughter and enjoyed the light of the moon.

Could she expand this place?

She glanced up at the star-studded sky.

Could she reach out beyond her companions to others in the physical world? Was it possible to reach her own people?

Selene left the branch in a flutter of black wings and took to the sky. High above she flew, past the trees and rocky cliffs until the landscape appeared like a blanket of green and grey beneath the moonlight. Then she closed her eyes again and stretched out her senses as she glided above the mountains.

She felt them. More sparks of life. Thousands of them, scattered across the mountains. Instead of pulling them into the meadow, Selene filled her being with that same sense of peace she had felt in the meadow below, then let it flow out of her.

There was a tugging inside her, like a memory trying to surface. She closed her eyes, her ears filled with the gentle sound of the wind, her nose filled with the sweetness of the night.

This is what the dreamer does.

It was more than a memory; it was a voice from the past, speaking to her here and now in this place.

The Nightwatcher protects those around her during the deepest parts of the night. The dreamer comforts the weary, inspires the broken, and brings peace to fearful minds.

This, my dreamwalker, is what you were made to do.

The Light.

Selene let her feathered body glide along the air, dipping down, then up again along the current. Damien prayed for his people almost every morning when he raised the water. She would do that too. She would pray for her own people here in the dreamscape. She would pray to the Light.

As she drifted along the wind currents, she lifted up her companions, then the people of the Magyr Mountains. Her thoughts shifted to Rook Castle, and she prayed for her father and little sister, and the servants and—

An image of her mother filled her mind. Her eyes flew open. Her body dipped down, and her wings faltered for a moment.

A throbbing ache filled her chest. Where was her mother now? With the Dominia Empire? At Lord Ivulf's side? How could she pray for her mother with such burning anger inside of her?

The sky, mountains, and meadow below faded into a dark grey, then into a fiery haze. Selene opened her eyes to the harsh, orange light of a lit torch overhead.

"Time to move," she heard Lord Wynn say.

Selene sat up and pushed her hair away from her face, the peace of the dreamscape disturbed by thoughts of her mother.

Everyone stood and began to stow away their belongings while someone passed out hard, round biscuits.

"I had this dream." A woman's voice echoed across the mine shaft. "We were in a meadow, and there were all these wildflowers."

"I did too," another woman said. "It was so peaceful."

"So did I," said a masculine voice. "It reminds me of a tale my mother used to tell about the Nightwatcher."

"Nightwatcher?"

Selene stopped, her pack half-cinched, and listened.

"It's an old, old tale still told in the forest country," the man explained.

"You're from the lands of House Rafel?"

"Just the very northern edge right next to the Magyr Mountains."

There was no more said about the Nightwatcher. Selene finished closing her pack and lifted it onto her shoulder. *Nightwatcher.* That's what the Light called her. Was it possible there were stories about the Ravenwoods in Surao? Stories that predated Rabanna?

She looked over her shoulder and found Lord Elric staring back with a thoughtful expression on his face. Did he know the dream was hers?

"You're not what I thought you would be." Elric spoke quietly to Selene as they led the company along another mine shaft, this one wider than the first.

"Oh?"

"I've known House Maris all of my life. And I've heard of House Ravenwood. Since your house has always kept to yourself, and the only time I met your mother was years ago, I thought all of you were like her. But you're not. For one thing, you smile—"

"I smile?" she said with a laugh.

"Yes. I never saw your mother smile when she visited. And she kind of scared me as a little boy," he said in a hushed tone.

Selene sobered. "I understand that. She scares me too."

"Really? Is that why you married Damien?"

"Hmm. Not quite." Though he was partly right. She did marry Damien in the beginning as one last hope for life.

"Do you love him?"

Selene shot him a look. Did every Great House ask such personal questions when they were together, or was it just Lady Bryren and Lord Elric?

Elric looked straight ahead. "My family had hoped my little sister would marry into House Maris."

"I . . . see."

"Do you know much about Damien's brother, Quinn?"

Her thoughts shot back to Damien's memories. "Very little. His death is still hard on Lord Damien."

"His death is still hard on all of us."

They walked on in silence for a while. Behind

them, others chatted quietly amongst themselves.

"What was Quinn like?" Selene asked.

The torchlight bounced off Elric's face and along the stony cavern. He wore a sad grin. "He was like a brother to me, even more so than my own brothers. He was always laughing and full of life. And we got into a lot of trouble together." He chuckled at that. "However, unlike me, he was still responsible. Maybe that was Damien's influence. Damien was always a quiet, steadfast counter to Quinn's outgoing, fiery personality. I never knew anyone so full of life. That's why his death—" His voice hitched.

Selene could almost hear him swallow before he continued, "That's why his death was so hard. How could someone so alive . . . die? And my sister—" Elric paused again.

"I'm sorry, I didn't realize how hard it would be for you to talk about him."

Elric choked out a laugh. "I like talking about Quinn. Light, I miss him so much. It's good to remember him. But it's hard for Adalyn. Only I knew how much she loved him."

Selene sucked in a breath. "Lady Adalyn loved Quinn?"

Elric turned and smiled at her. "If there was ever a perfect match, it was those two. When he died, I think he took my sister's heart with him. Leo had hoped she would marry Damien and unify our families, and she would have obeyed him, but I'm glad Damien married you instead. I'm not sure if my sister could ever love another man."

Selene stared ahead. She didn't know what to say. She could hardly breathe. All this time she had been jealous of the lady of light, only to discover the heartbreak of her past. Knowing how much she loved Damien now, to lose him would break her own heart. And then to have her brother pressuring her to marry the brother of the man she loved . . .

"I'm sorry." And she meant it.

Elric shrugged. "In a roundabout way, you saved my sister. I only hope that Damien also found love." He glanced at her from the corner of his eyes.

"You know that houses marry for more than love."

"Yes, I know. I'm all too familiar with marital treaties. Luckily, Leo's too busy with house affairs to be looking for a partner for me." He grinned at her, and for a moment, Selene thought of Amara. What would have happened with Amara if she were still alive? Would she have been at Rook Castle? Would she have joined them or stayed loyal to Mother? Would she have ended up marrying Lord Raoul? Or was it possible that she might have found a better man?

None of that would happen now. Selene swallowed the lump in her throat and readjusted her pack, the urn gently thumping her back with the movement. "I love him."

Elric looked her way. "What?"

"To answer your question, yes, I love Damien." Life was too short to hide her feelings.

He nodded and smiled. "I'm glad to hear that. I think Quinn would have liked you."

15

The atmosphere around Rook Castle was cold, even colder than usual, if that was possible with the absence of Lady Ragna.

Caiaphas leaned back and looked out the window of his study. A bright spring sun shone outside, and the Magyr Mountains were just starting to throw off winter's white wardrobe, allowing the deep green of the conifer trees to peek through.

It had been a fortnight since he sent a message to Lux Casta, and even longer since he secretly sent word to the coalition members nearby about his plan to take Rook Castle. And he hadn't heard from anyone since. Not that he was surprised. Security had tightened around Rook Castle, thanks to Captain Stanton.

He rubbed his chin in thought. Was it possible Lady Ragna had finally caught on to his plans? For years they had lived together: he the ever-submissive husband, she the brilliant and cunning grand lady. There had never been love between them. He married her for his own schemes, and she agreed to the arrangement at her mother's behest, never realizing he had orchestrated all of it.

Which brought him to where he was now:

poised and ready to assist the coalition and the remaining loyal houses in capturing Rook Castle.

But if Lady Ragna or Captain Stanton was suspicious of a coup . . .

Caiaphas stood and made his way around his desk, past the long line of bookcases and chairs where he usually read at night. Time to walk around the castle and find out what he could. At the door to his study, he spotted two guards nearby, and his eyes narrowed. Their usual post was at the corner of the converging corridors, not here in this hallway, and so close to his study.

He slowly closed the door behind him while keeping the two men within the periphery of his vision and headed the opposite direction. Seconds later, he heard the soft thump of their boots behind him. They could simply be heading in the same direction he was, but his sixth sense was already ringing bells inside his mind.

Instead of heading toward the main hall where he had originally been intending to go, he turned left at the next corridor. Sure enough, the guards were behind him, far enough away so as not to arouse suspicion, but close enough that he knew they were following him.

He didn't know all the secret passageways of Rook Castle, but he did know about a few of them. He ducked into one of the spare rooms before the guards came around the corner. The room was small and held an assortment of old furniture covered in white linen to protect from dust and sunlight. He bypassed the ghostly furniture and headed to the far back of the room, where there was a hidden lever just below a set of shelves. He could hear the muffled voices of the guards on the other side of the door, no doubt trying to figure out where he went.

A small smile slipped across his lips as he pressed down on the lever and a narrow door opened to the right of the shelves. He quickly entered and shut the door behind him. He had discovered this particular secret passage when Amara disappeared into this room and failed to close the door behind her.

Amara.

He let out a long breath as he made his way through the dusty darkness, his hand sliding along the uneven stone wall. Where was she now? The last he had seen of her was over a month ago, and he knew she hadn't gone with her mother. So where did she go? His heart warbled at the thought of her on a mission. He was never very close to Amara, not like Selene. But she was still his daughter, his flesh and blood, and there were times, like now, when he wished he could have gotten to know her better.

Instead, it seemed she became more like her mother every day.

The passageway split. He took the path on the left that led to the servants' common area. After a minute of walking in the dark, he reached another narrow door. He pressed the side of his face to the wooden surface and listened. Silence.

After waiting a few seconds more, he pushed the door open and entered the room. A long wooden table took up most of the common room, with a staircase to the left that led up to the servants' quarters. The fireplace on the other side was empty and cold, just like the room.

Caiaphas slipped across the stone floor to the other door and let himself out. The guards had now confirmed his suspicions that something was up and he was being watched. He needed to find out why.

He made his way along another corridor toward the barracks. First place he would check was with those under Captain Stanton. Most were loyal to the man, but one was secretly with the coalition.

Gavin was not in the barracks. In fact, the barracks were empty. Caiaphas paused with a frown on his face as he looked around the dark, grey rooms. There were neither voices nor the sounds of training. He could believe that most of the soldiers would be gone, but not all of them. He narrowed his eyes. Where were all the men?

He stepped out of the barracks and continued his hunt for Gavin, taking care to keep out of the sight of the other guards and servants. He headed toward the library on the next level. At the top of the stairs and just around the corner, he spotted the golden-blond hair of the mountain boy near the double doors.

After making sure no one else was around, Caiaphas made his way down the hall as if he had a purpose and had no time to speak to anyone. His facial expression was focused, and his eyes stared straight ahead. Just when he reached the doors, he took a sharp right and entered the library.

"Follow me," he said in a low voice.

Gavin followed without saying a word.

The library was cool and dimly lit. It was a quarter of the size of the library in the palace in Shanalona, and Caiaphas often missed the halls of knowledge from his former home. He paused by the second bookcase and appeared as though he was searching for a title amongst the leather-bound tomes that lined the third shelf.

"It appears that I am now being followed by the guards. Do you know why?"

"Captain Stanton wants you watched."

"Why?"

"He didn't tell us."

Caiaphas pulled out a book with a dark cover and began to undo the thin leather ties. "Do you think he suspects our plan?"

"I think he knows something is going on, and not just in Rook Castle."

Caiaphas slowly nodded while his mind began

to spin, stretching across all the possibilities. "Explain."

"I overheard one of the soldiers saying that the forces of House Luceras were spotted on the King's Highway with banners flying."

"When was that?"

"Yesterday. Most everyone left yesterday afternoon. This morning is when Captain Stanton assigned a handful of guards to keep an eye on you."

Caiaphas slowly nodded. That made sense. But was it for his protection, or due to suspicion?

"I also overheard that Lady Opheliana was to be sent away."

His head shot up. "Why? Where?"

Gavin shook his head. "I don't know."

"Do you think she is in danger?"

Gavin frowned at Caiaphas. "Why would she be in danger?"

Caiaphas snapped the book shut and placed it back in the empty spot on the shelf. "We may have run out of time," he murmured and spun for the door.

"Sir?"

"I believe that Captain Stanton's orders are from Lady Ragna herself. She is securing Rook Castle. I can't let her take Lady Opheliana." He turned toward Gavin. "I'm going to retrieve her ladyship. I need you to find out what Captain Stanton is doing right now and meet me in my own rooms."

"But, sir, I've been assigned to guard this area."

Caiaphas shook his head. "I need you more. I don't know how long before help comes, either from the leader of our coalition or from the coalition itself. What I do know is Lady Ragna is on the move. Now go."

Gavin slapped his boots together and pressed a fist to his chest. "Yes, sir."

Caiaphas stole down the hallway toward the nursery. The future. He needed to think about the future. Which meant he needed to keep Opheliana here and not let her leave the castle. Once the coalition secured Rook Castle, she would be safe on their side and not with the empire. But until then, he would guard the little girl personally.

Even if she wasn't his own daughter.

Caiaphas stepped into the nursery and paused. The room was warm and smelled like lavender. The walls were paneled with dark wood, and a small table stood in the corner, topped with three blocks and a doll with a painted face. Beyond, next to a window filled with light, stood a little girl with long, dark auburn hair that hung down to the blue sash around her waist. She seemed to be intently watching something outside, her entire being enraptured by whatever it was.

He shut the door softly behind him and stood still. Neither she nor her nursemaid realized he had entered the nursery, given the humming that continued uninterrupted in the other room. He watched Opheliana, a mixture of sorrow, hurt, and anger twisting inside his middle.

She was the physical manifestation of the indiscretion of his wife. Proof of unfaithfulness. He had known about it the moment the girl had been born, and yet never let on of his knowledge, playing along with the notion that the girl was his.

But the accompanying hurt lasted only a moment before he looked away and shook his head. This young girl had no say in how she came into the world. She was a lot like him: unwanted and hidden away by the Ravenwood family. But what people of power usually never realize is that truly powerful people are the ones who grow in the shadows, unnoticed, shaped by their surroundings.

Opheliana would be her own person. He would make sure she grew up to fulfill her own destiny—not of Lady Ragna's choosing, but of her own. She would be the perfect new leader for House Friere, should there be need of one someday. After all, war brought about many changes.

He crossed the first room and entered the second. Opheliana seemed to sense his presence because she turned from her spot at the window and looked up at him with a curious expression.

The humming nearby stopped. "Sir!" the

nursemaid cried and stood, her needlework falling to the floor. Her brown hair was gathered at the nape of her neck, just below the white cap she wore over her head. An oversized apron covered her ample body. "What are you doing here?"

Caiaphas turned his attention to the nursemaid—her name was Maura, right? "I've received word that Lady Opheliana might be in danger."

"Danger? From whom?"

"The empire." He wasn't sure where Maura's allegiance lay, and he didn't want to risk that she was loyal to Ragna.

"The empire is here?"

"It will be soon." But not if he could help it. "We need to move her ladyship to my rooms. I will personally guard her until help comes."

The first inkling of doubt entered the plump nursemaid's eyes. "But I am in charge of Lady Opheliana's welfare."

"Then you must come with me as well."

That seemed to appease the woman. "What do we need?"

"Just you and the little one."

Caiaphas approached Opheliana. She looked like a blend of Selene and Amara, but with the telltale amber eyes of House Friere. He mentally shook his head as another flash of hurt washed over his heart. No. He would not make this child bear the sins of her mother. He would watch over her as if she were his own.

For her own sake and for House Friere's.

He went down on one knee and stared into Opheliana's eyes. "Would you like to visit my room? I have lots of pictures and windows."

She cocked her head to the side and studied him.

He stared back in amazement at her thoughtful look. She seemed to possess quite an intelligence, despite her lack of words.

"And we might have a guest soon." He wondered who might be coming with the coalition. Lord Damien? One of the lesser lords? Perhaps . . . Selene? Was she the one leading the coalition here? It made sense. Selene would know the best ways to infiltrate the castle. At any rate, her name might help convince the girl. "I'm hoping to see Selene. Do you want to see her?"

Opheliana's eyes widened with delight, and she nodded vigorously. Caiaphas smiled back. "Yes, I've missed her too. Come here, little one. Let's go."

Opheliana held out her arms, ready to be lifted. Caiaphas took her and stood up. He looked back at Maura. "Ready?"

"Yes. Will we really see Lady Selene?"

Caiaphas turned around and headed for the outer door. "I hope so."

Maura caught up to him, and the three of them

headed out into the hallway. He would need to be careful making his way back to his rooms. There was no telling what Captain Stanton might do if he found out Lady Opheliana was in his possession.

Opheliana looked ahead with a soft smile, her arms wrapped around his neck. Caiaphas felt a pang in his heart as he held the little girl. He should have made more of an effort to see her. But the pain of knowing her parentage had kept him away, stealing what he now knew: Opheliana was a special girl.

He would do better. He knew better. She might not be his, but he could raise her and be her guide. As they rounded the last corridor and approached the door to his own rooms, he turned his head and whispered in her ear. "You will do amazing things, my child. But first, I must make sure you live."

16

Rook Castle. Just as Selene remembered it. The same grey stone walls. The same cool mountain air. The same mountain views. It was late afternoon and the sun was already making its way toward the nearest mountain peak.

She stood for a moment in the small cavern opening, the one below the guest room, the same room where six months before she had almost taken Damien's life.

How much had changed since that fateful night.

"Where are we?" Elric asked.

"Below one of the guest rooms in Rook Castle."

Elric looked up. "I see a balcony. Are we going to climb up there?"

"Yes."

He grinned at her. "I like your style."

Lord Wynn snorted nearby.

Selene checked her blades. "I'll go first and scout out the room." Karl took a step toward her. "And Karl will go with me."

Karl gave her an appreciative nod. He had been her silent shadow during this entire trip, and she was thankful for his quiet presence.

Selene went first, stepping to the edge of the cavern, twisting around, and scurrying up the side. In some ways, it felt surreal to be home. The woman she had been when she had left this room was quite different from the one entering. The Light she had seen inside of Damien was now a part of her.

She brought her legs over the stone railing and landed by the double doors. After a brief glimpse through the glass, she opened the one on the left. Karl followed her in.

The room appeared as it always had: the four-poster bed, bearskin rug, doors leading to other bedrooms, and the main door. Her eyes strayed toward the bed, to the corner where she had first knelt and entered Damien's dreams.

"Does it feel strange to be back?" Karl asked quietly.

She paused before answering. Was he remembering that time as well? "Yes. I'm no longer the same woman I was before."

"I agree."

Before she could reply, Elric joined them.

Selene, Karl, and Elric checked the room. "It doesn't look like anyone has been in here for a while," Selene said. "Tell Wynn to send up a handful of others. Karl and I are going to check the hallway."

Elric nodded. "Yes, my lady."

Selene carefully placed her pack in the corner where her belongings and her sister's urn would be safe before pulling out her swords. She turned back around. "Karl, I'll have you get the door. I want to be prepared just in case."

"Are you sure you're ready?"

Selene frowned. "What do you mean?"

"This is your former home, with the men and women you grew up with: guards, servants, friends. What will you do if they discover us?"

Selene let out her breath and held up one sword, her eyes trailing the sharp edge to the point. "I don't want to take anyone's life. But we need to secure Rook Castle. If possible, I will attempt to discern who is loyal to my mother, but . . ." She looked up. "I will do what I need to for this mission." She could feel the gravity— and strength—in her words. If there was any good that came out of her childhood and training, it was her focus on the mission at hand. But she would be careful.

"Not many men—or women—would be ready for such choices."

"It's what I was trained to do. Ready?"

"Yes, my lady." Karl passed her and slowly opened the door, careful of any sound it made as it swung inward. He peeked into the hallway, then motioned silently with his hand.

Selene stepped out into the corridor. Another wave of familiarity washed over her. Memories rushed across her mind: slipping through passageways, learning how to walk silently across the stone floor, training in the caverns below, listening to her mother's lectures, and learning the secrets of House Ravenwood.

A cold sweat sprang up across her forehead as the edges of her vision went dark.

"My lady, are you all right?" Karl whispered nearby.

"Yes." She brushed the side of her face with her arm, and her vision returned. Maybe her words to Karl had been a bit more confident than she was experiencing now. "We need to find my father."

As they advanced down the hall, other priorities tugged at her. Should she first find Opheliana? Should she make sure Renata was still alive, or had her mother done away with the invalid girl?

Selene shook her head. No. She needed to find her father first. He would know what was going on and what to do next. She gripped her swords and turned right. He would either be in his study or his rooms.

Together, Selene and Karl silently made their way through the silent, cold corridors. No humming from any nearby servants, no shuffling of feet. The castle was empty of life. Selene frowned. Where were the servants? The guards?

Just as they approached the living quarters and Selene opened her mouth to whisper her concerns to Karl, there was a shout and the pounding of boots.

Selene and Karl both ducked into a small alcove beneath a set of long windows. They pressed their bodies against the wall, and Selene readied her swords.

"Why are we arresting Lord Caiaphas?" a guard asked as they passed, never glancing toward the shadows.

"Captain Stanton's orders. And we are to secure Lady Opheliana."

"Secure her? From what? Her father?"

"All I know is what I've been told to do."

The boot steps faded as the four men disappeared.

Selene stared ahead at the wall, her heart pounding. They were arresting her father? Did they know about the coalition? And why was Ophie with him?

Ophie.

Her heart clenched at the thought of her sweet little sister.

"Don't let Opheliana die. Or be taken by House Friere. She's all I've ever cared about."

Selene took a shaky step forward as Amara's last words echoed inside her head. *I will save her, Amara. I will fulfill your last wishes.*

Grief pierced her gut as Selene started down the hall. She thought she had finished mourning Amara, but being here again where they had lived and fought and doted on Ophie brought all the hurt back.

She gripped her swords and picked up her steps. Ahead, she watched the men disappear around the corner, right near Father's rooms. She hurried to the corner and peeked around to find them pounding on the door.

"Open up. Captain Stanton's orders."

She surveyed the men with one quick glance. Only two had their weapons drawn, and one appeared uncomfortable with the situation, given how his hand was twitching at his side, and he kept wiping his face with the other.

The door slowly opened.

"Can I help you?" asked a clear male voice.

Selene swallowed, her entire being focused on the guards and door ahead. Father.

"You are hereby arrested on Captain Stanton's orders. Please come quietly, sir."

"Why?"

The first guard stuttered for a moment. "On the account of stealing away Lady Opheliana."

"I didn't steal her away. She and her nursemaid are visiting me. Is it wrong for a father to visit with his daughter?"

Selene's heart plummeted. Amara had revealed to her the truth behind Opheliana's parentage. Did her father know as well?

The first guard rubbed the back of his neck, and the two with swords drawn looked down and shuffled their feet. The last guard appeared even more agitated.

"I'm sorry, sir." The first guard lifted his head. "But Captain Stanton's orders—"

"Perhaps Captain Stanton is mistaken. Why don't you go and ask the good captain to come here himself? Then we can find out what is going on."

"Maybe he's right," the agitated guard muttered. The other two nodded in agreement, their swords now hanging at their sides.

Selene pressed her lips together, waiting to see what the first guard decided, her fingers wrapped tightly around the hilts of her own swords. She would be ready if the guard insisted on arresting her father.

The first guard stepped back. "Perhaps I was misinformed. I will speak to Captain Stanton."

"Good idea." She could almost hear the smile in her father's words, and she stood in amazement at the wisdom he had used with the guards. Once again she wondered if he was distantly related to House Vivek.

The four guards turned and headed down the corridor opposite of where Selene and Karl stood. The door to her father's rooms shut. Selene waited until the footsteps had faded, then stole across the hallway. Her entire body buzzed with adrenaline. She hadn't seen her father since the night of the gala. The thought of seeing him now—and Ophie—brought a wave of nausea across her middle.

I can do this.

She approached the door, slid her swords back

into their scabbards, and knocked. There was a shuffle across the floor, then the door opened.

Caiaphas stood in the doorway, frozen. The only hint of an emotion was the wideness of his eyes. Finally, his lips moved. "Selene," he whispered.

She only nodded.

He stepped back and motioned her inside. "Come in. Hurry."

She entered, Karl close behind. Her father shut the door and turned. Selene wasn't sure if she was going to vomit or cry. She held a hand across her middle, and for a second, she had her emotions under control.

Until Ophie peeked around the corner.

Then the tears came in a rushing torrent.

Selene fell to her knees as her sister came running up to her. "Ophie," she choked out, smothering her face in her auburn hair. "I missed you so much!"

Little arms wrapped themselves around her neck, which made her cry even more. Every part of her that she had been holding back broke loose. She wasn't sure how long she knelt there, holding Ophie. Eventually, she felt a warm hand on her shoulder, which brought her back to reality.

Selene wiped her eyes and glanced up. Her father stared down at her with a tender look on his face. "Selene," he said again.

Selene kissed the top of Ophie's head and stood. She stared at her father. "I missed you too, Father."

His eyes sparkled. Selene had never seen him cry. "And I missed you."

He held out his arms, and Selene entered his embrace. He smelled like the books he was always reading: a warm, woodsy, vanilla smell. The hug only lasted a moment before Caiaphas stepped back, this time with a more studious look. "Are you here alone?"

"No, we received your message at Lux Casta." Selene took a moment to wipe her face before continuing. "Lord Luceras is leading his forces through the mountain pass as a distraction so I could lead the coalition secretly into Rook Castle."

"The coalition? Are you a part of it now?"

Selene hesitated. "Yes. I'm here in place of Damien."

"It seems there is much for us to talk about, but it will have to be done at a later time. It appears your mother is attempting to secure Rook Castle through Captain Stanton."

"Is that why those guards were here to arrest you?"

"I believe so." His lips turned up in a wry smile. "Captain Stanton is going to find out how hard it is to remove an old man from his rooms."

"And Opheliana?" Selene's affectionate gaze

fell on her sister, who was still clinging to her legs.

"Your mother wants her removed."

Selene's head shot up. "To where?"

"I suspect Ironmond." His face faltered.

"You know?"

He let out a long breath. "Yes. But it doesn't matter."

Her heart swelled again for her father. "Amara told me."

"Amara?"

"My lady," Karl said, stepping forward. "We should do what we came here to do."

"You're right. Father, the coalition is here and ready to take Rook Castle."

Her father was all business now. "How many?"

"About thirty."

He slowly nodded. "Using the forces of House Luceras to draw the military out was a good plan. It won't be easy, but I think with the coalition's help, we can secure Rook Castle."

Selene laid a hand on her sister's head as she faced her father. "What should we do with Opheliana? I don't want her caught up in the fight."

Caiaphas nodded. "I agree. And I don't want to see Captain Stanton get ahold of her. But I will need your help taking Rook Castle. We are the only ones who know the castle."

"But sneaking back to where the coalition is

waiting is risky enough without bringing Ophie and Maura." Selene glanced at Karl. He seemed to guess what she was about to ask by the darkening of his features. "Please, Karl, stay here with my little sister and protect her."

"My duty is to you, my lady. If anything were to happen to you, Lord Damien—"

"Would understand. If he were in my place, and this was Quinn"—she patted Ophie's head again—"he would understand why you left my side. To protect my family."

He pursed his lips together. "I don't like it." His shoulders sagged. "But I understand. I will stay here and watch your sister." His voice was quiet but serious as he said, "Please be careful."

"I will. Lock the door behind us."

"Yes, my lady."

Selene looked at her father. "Ready?"

He stepped over to the desk that stood near his bed, pulled out the drawer, and withdrew a small silver blade. "It's not much, but I'll use it if I have to. Now, let's go."

17

Selene crept into the hallway, expanding her senses for any sound or movement. Again, she wondered where the servants were. Did Father know? Were they simply in another part of the castle? She hoped so; she didn't want to involve anyone unnecessarily in the upcoming conflict.

Just when she thought they would reach the guest rooms without being noticed, a maid came walking around the corner with a stack of folded linens in her arms. At the sight of Selene, her eyes went wide, and the linens fell to the floor. Before she had a chance to say anything, Selene was already reaching forward to cover the young woman's mouth.

"Hmph!"

Keeping her mouth covered, Selene swung the girl around, wrapped her other arm around her body, and pulled her close. "We are here to help you," she whispered in the maid's ear. "Do you know who I am?"

The head bobbed.

"Do you know the man in front of you?"

Again, the head bobbed.

Wait. Selene frowned. She knew this girl. Mira. She was always bringing Father's tea to his study. "I don't know what's been said about me, but please give me a moment to explain. I am here to help you and all of those who live here in Rook Castle. Will you let me?"

The maid hesitated.

Caiaphas gave her a soft smile. "You can trust us, Mira," he said quietly.

Mira nodded.

Selene let out her breath. "All right. We are heading to the guest room with the bearskin rug. Do you know which one that is?"

She nodded again.

"Good. I'm going to let go of you. Don't say anything. Just come along with us." Selene slowly brought her hand away from Mira's lips. The maid's face was pale as she turned around to pick up the linens. "Follow me. My father will bring up the rear."

Just as they rounded the corner, a group of men appeared at the end of the hallway, led by Captain Stanton.

Selene halted, her heart jumping into her throat. Of all the people to meet at this moment . . .

Captain Stanton spotted her at the same time. He appeared as he had a year ago: with long, stringy black hair that brushed the top of his tunic. Black leather jerkin, dark pants, and boots. His usual lidded eyes widened in surprise, and his lips parted. The shocked look only lasted a moment before his face morphed into a smug grin. "Well, well. Lady Selene, what a surprise."

"Captain Stanton," Selene said coldly, placing herself between the maid and her father. Adrenaline swept across her body, leaving her in a chilled sweat.

The guards whispered around him as he stepped toward her, his hand edging to the sword at his side. "What is the traitor to House Ravenwood doing here in Rook Castle? You've been banished from the Magyr Mountains."

"I'm here to keep the mountain nation from falling to the empire. Something you're failing to do."

"The empire?" Captain Stanton laughed, and there were snickers from the other guards. "Why do we need to fear the empire?"

Selene licked her lips. They were close to the guest room where the coalition was assembling. There was a chance the others could come to her aid. But they might not hear the commotion outside, which meant it was up to her to keep her father and Mira safe.

Selene reached for her blades. Captain Stanton followed her movement with a tightening of his lips. "Do you mean to fight us? Those of us loyal to House Ravenwood? Apparently once a traitor, always a traitor." In a flash, he had his sword in hand and closed the distance between them.

Selene raised her weapons just in time to meet the edge of his blade. She deflected his blow and bounced back.

"Run!" she yelled to her father and Mira without taking her eyes off Captain Stanton. The other guards were drawing their swords behind him.

Selene used her left blade to deflect, then jabbed with her right, the tip of her sword meeting his leather jerkin.

"Ah, so you can fight, little raven," Captain Stanton said, stepping back with a grin.

Little raven?

Memories of the Dark Lady came rushing back. Selene trembled as all the blood rushed from her extremities.

He laughed. "What, are you scared now?" He slashed at her again.

Selene knocked his blow away with her left blade and jumped back.

"Is that all you're going to do? Retreat? Come at me!"

As another guard moved forward, Captain Stanton glanced over his shoulder. "Stay back! She's mine."

Selene drew in deep breaths as the men retreated. The air was like razor blades in her chest. She couldn't see Mira or her father. Hopefully that meant they had listened to her.

Captain Stanton took a step forward, then sent multiple slashes her way. Selene deflected every one of them except for the last. The tip of his sword reached past her own blades and swept across her right cheek, sending a stinging sensation across her skin.

Her eyes watered, and she took another step back.

"What, never been cut before?" Captain Stanton grinned, his black hair hanging across his face. "I can do more than that."

Selene resisted the urge to reach up and touch the area, keeping her swords out and ready instead.

"You know, I always wanted to fight you." He raised his sword and pointed it at her. "I knew there was more to you than a beautiful face."

Her jaw clenched as rage blossomed inside her chest.

"By the way, whatever happened to Lady Amara?"

Selene froze.

"She never returned from her mission to Lux Casta. I assume she failed, as I knew she would—"

With a roar, Selene charged. Her blades were a whirlwind, slashing, first her right, then her left, then her right again. All Captain Stanton could do was raise his own sword and deflect.

She caught a glint of fear in his dark eyes as he raised his blade again and caught her own sword. She shoved it away with her left, pinning it to the wall, and brought her right blade to his chest.

They stared at each other, panting.

"So," he said as she watched his Adam's apple bob, "are you going to kill me?"

Selene held her breath. Kill him? Her eyes trailed to the point of her blade where it waited just above his heart. Just one thrust and he would be dead. But could she do it?

I have to. I have to save Ophie.

She steadied the grip on her blade as his mouth slowly split into a smile, and the guards drew close around them. "I knew it. You can't do it—"

Something flew past her face and hit the soft area above his collarbone.

Captain Stanton's eyes went wide. A moment later, a trickle of blood escaped his lips. He let out a groan and started sliding down the wall beneath her blade.

Shocked, Selene stepped back. A red stain began to spread across his skin. The guards stared at their captain as he collapsed to the floor, a small silver knife trembling just below his neck.

"Maybe she can't," her father said calmly from behind her. "But I can."

Her father had killed Captain Stanton.

The door down the hall burst open beyond the guards, and Lord Elric emerged with a polearm of white light in hand, followed by Lord Wynn and members of the coalition.

A couple of the guards drew their swords and faced the newcomers. One, however, turned for Selene. "You traitor!"

Adrenaline guided her movement. Swing, slash, and her left blade found his forearm . . . and it kept on going, severing his hand from his body. His sword and limb dropped to the floor as the man pulled his bloody stump to his body and cried out.

Selene stared at the guard, her mind numb and detached from her body.

"Are you all right?"

She heard the words but couldn't seem to figure out who was talking to her or where to look. All she could do was stare at the wounded man and at Captain Stanton, who lay on the ground behind him.

"Lady Selene?" A hand touched her arm.

Selene leaped back, bringing her blades up in front of her.

Elric's face went in and out of focus.

"My lady?"

Selene blinked and drew in some gasping breaths. "I'm all right." She went to lift her hand and wipe her face, then spotted the blood on her left blade.

No, she wasn't. Nausea filled her throat. She was going to vomit. Clenching her jaw, she took two deep breaths through her nose, gripped her swords, and looked up. This wasn't the time to lose control. Using every ounce of strength she possessed, she pulled herself together.

At the same moment, her old resolve came

flooding back, giving her the will to stand. "We still need to secure the castle. Lord Wynn, take a group and head to the barracks. My father will lead you. Lord Elric, come with me. We will check the corridors and make our way to the ramparts. I need one group to stay here, tie up the guards, and secure this area. And get this man a healer."

"Yes, my lady," a chorus of voices shouted. Lord Wynn gave her a look of wonder before collecting a few of the members. Her father passed her, but not before sending a respectful nod in her direction. Elric instructed three of the men to tie up the guards, then joined Selene.

"This way," she said and started along the corridor. Emotions threatened to surface, but she held them down with an iron grip. The feeling was familiar, almost as if stepping back into Rook Castle had brought back her cold veneer. There was a job to do, a mission to accomplish. There was no time for shock or grief.

There was concern on Elric's face as he looked at her, the first time she'd seen him serious. It only made her crawl deeper inside of herself. Once they had Rook Castle secured, she would allow herself the luxury of feeling again.

The few servants they met acquiesced immediately, either because of their militant presence or because of Elric's charming smile and smooth words. Selene believed it was the latter.

Once they reached the ramparts, the group spilt into two and each made their way along the rooftop of Rook Castle, rounding up the few guards present. When Selene met Elric on the other side, he approached her with a wary smile. "We barely met any opposition. How about you?"

"No. The few guards we ran across came willingly. I think those who were loyal to Captain Stanton were with him when . . ." She shook her head and looked away. His words echoed inside her head.

"I knew it. You can't do it."

How wrong he had been. If it hadn't been for her father's dagger seconds before . . .

"Why don't we head back and meet up with the others?"

Selene brought her mind back. "Yes. We should do that. . . ." Her words faded as her eyes fell upon the small cluster of homes within the castle courtyard. She could see the small wooden door that led into Petur's home. The memories of Petur, Hagatha, and all the guards and servants who she had visited in their sleep came rushing back. And above all, one particular memory stood out.

Renata.

Was she still alive? Or had her mother—

Selene clutched the stone rampart in front of

her, taking in deep breaths. Cold beads of sweat collected along her forehead.

"Are you sure you're all right?" Elric asked beside her. "Sometimes seeing death for the first time can be a real shock."

Selene let out a shaky laugh. "Just being back here is a shock." She pressed her lips shut. That was more than she had meant to let on.

He gazed at her, then shook his head. "My brother completely underestimated you. You were amazing. The way you moved your swords and your body . . . I'm not even sure if Leo could keep up with you."

Selene wasn't sure how to answer. She could still see the man's hand on the ground next to his sword, the pool of blood—

She faltered for one step, then took back her shaky body. The stares from the others began to press in on her. She straightened up and turned back around. "We should meet back up with Lord Wynn, and possibly do another check around the castle and courtyard. Then we can position our own people and shut the gates."

"I agree. What forces remain will be pinned between my brother and the castle. Hopefully they will surrender with very little fight."

"I hope so as well."

Elric spoke with the other members of the coalition, then they started making their way back, leaving a handful to stay along the walls.

Selene walked beside him, her stomach clenched tight. When the castle was secured, she would do two things.

First, she would make sure Opheliana was safe.

Then she would finally find out what had become of Renata.

18

"There is nothing weak about not wanting to take a life." Caiaphas stood across from Selene near the front gates of Rook Castle that evening. The coalition and a handful of guards were gathered in the middle of the courtyard. Rook Castle was theirs, and now they waited for House Luceras to arrive. Night had fallen across the area. Stars appeared in the sky above, and a timber wolf howled in the distance.

"I know," Selene said quietly.

"If I hadn't been there, you would have done what you needed to, to protect your sister and yourself, along with everyone else."

She knew that only too well. Her blade had been poised and ready to pierce Captain Stanton. No matter her training, the fact that she had been ready to take a man's life shook her. The way she had been cold and calculating, ready to do whatever she had to, to keep her sister and others safe.

"I didn't want you to carry that weight, not yet."

Selene looked up.

"Someday you probably will. But I had an opportunity, and I took it. It was my way of taking one burden away from you."

She eyed him warily. "Have you killed before?"

He hesitated. "Yes." The cords along his neck bunched together. "If you want to protect those you love, sometimes your hands get bloody."

Bloody. Ha. Her hands were already bloody. She might not have killed Captain Stanton, but she certainly had maimed the guard. She held her arms out. "Then what is all of this for? Why did I run away when in the end I'll become a killer anyway?" Out of the corner of her eye, she spotted Lord Elric watching their exchange. She dropped her arms and turned away from his perusal.

"A killer? No. The difference between you and your mother is that your compassion is what guides you. Ambition and hatred are what drive her. You will only take a life when you need to and only at extreme costs. Your mother doesn't care who she takes out, not if they are in the way of her goal."

Selene stared at her hands. "But isn't murder, murder?"

Her father shrugged. "Perhaps. But as a leader, you are called to make those hard choices: who lives and who dies. If you had let Captain Stanton live, then in a sense, you were letting others die. But if Captain Stanton died, then you chose to let others live. In those instances, someone has to die. And you had the power to choose who did."

Selene crushed her hand into a fist. "I hate this."

"I did too, when I was young. And I still do. But I've made peace with myself. I will protect those I love. Let love, not hatred, be your guide."

"And the Light?"

Her father laughed softly. "I follow some of the tenets of the Light. So yes, also let the Light guide you as well."

What did that mean? Was her father a follower of the Light? Or only the idea of the Light?

"Could I ask you one question while we wait?" her father continued before Selene could puzzle out what he meant about the Light.

"Certainly."

"Captain Stanton mentioned something about Amara going on a mission. Do you know anything about that?"

Selene went rigid. Even now, Amara's ashes were tucked safely within her pack, waiting to be released across the Magyr Mountains.

Her father's face fell. "I can see by your face that you know something, and it's not pleasant."

Selene turned away and held her arms against her midsection.

Horns sounded around the castle.

Caiaphas ignored them as he approached Selene and placed a hand on her shoulder. "You can tell me when you're ready. Amara was my daughter too. I wish . . ." He sighed. "Maybe I could have done more for her."

193

"House Luceras has arrived," the gatekeeper shouted.

Selene turned around and placed her hand on her father's. Tears prickled her eyes. "Amara was free in the end. Free of our mother, free of our destiny. She died in peace and in the Light."

There was a slight tremble to her father's lips, then he straightened. "Thank you, Selene."

"I brought her ashes back with me. I hope that when the time is right, we can release her across the mountains."

"That . . . that would be nice." This time a tear accompanied his words. Selene turned away. If they kept talking about Amara, she was going to cry too, and this was not the right time for tears.

Lord Elric reached the gatehouse and spoke to the gatekeeper. "Are you sure?" she heard him say.

"Yes," the gatekeeper said. "They come wearing the tabard of the House of Light, and their banner waves ahead of them."

Selene glanced at her father. "What do you think? It wouldn't be hard to take the tabards off dead soldiers and hoist up the Luceras banner."

"True. Let us see who rides toward Rook Castle."

"I agree."

Selene and her father joined Elric at the top of the gatehouse and shared their suspicion.

Elric nodded. "Yes, that could be true. But,

meaning no disrespect, the chances of Raven-wood forces taking out House Luceras are slim. Your house is not known for its military prowess."

"I agree," Selene said. "And given how many guards came to our side once we took Rook Castle, I'm hoping more surrendered."

Elric headed back toward the staircase. "I'll tell the men and women here to be prepared. Go ahead and tell the gatekeeper to open the gates once I give the signal."

Selene nodded and turned her attention back toward the bridge. Hundreds of torches burned in the darkness, from the front of the troops all the way toward the trees on the other side of the bridge and along the road.

As she watched, the soldiers stepped aside to allow a figure to approach the gates. His uniform was covered in blood and mud, but there was an air to the man, and a certain splendor to his uniform that set him apart. Even before he took his helmet off, Selene was certain who he was.

Lord Leo.

At the same time, Elric lifted his hand in signal that he and the others were ready.

"It appears Lord Leo was successful," her father said as he gripped the ramparts. "But I wonder how many Ravenwood soldiers died for his victory."

Selene agreed. And how many more lives

would be lost because of the choice her mother and House Friere had made? *Why, Mother, why?*

As the gates slowly swung open, Selene made her way down from the wall and came to stand beside Elric. "I saw your brother."

He let out a small laugh. "You did?"

"Yes."

"That's a relief. I was certain it was Leo, but . . ." He shrugged.

She knew what he meant. The appearance of Ravenwood would have meant not only the fall of the Luceras military; it would have meant the fall of his brother as well.

The gates opened. Selene, Elric, and her father met the first line of soldiers as they entered. Lord Leo's light blond hair gleamed in the torchlight as he passed beneath the archway and into the courtyard of Rook Castle.

There was a hearty greeting between the Luceras brothers near the gates before Lord Leo turned to Selene. He sobered, but there was a look of grudging respect on his face. "Greetings, Lady Selene. It would seem that your coalition did their part."

"Same to you, Lord Leo. Thank you for helping us secure the Magyr Mountains."

"I have injured men and prisoners, and I require food and places to sleep for my army."

Selene nodded and gave directions to the infirmary, dungeons, and barracks, then stepped back and watched as wave after wave of Luceras soldiers marched across the stone bridge into Rook Castle. Their white tabards were stained, and quite a few men sported bruises and cuts. Those badly injured were supported by others or carried on makeshift stretchers.

When the prisoners came by, Selene took a step back and held a hand to her chest while keeping her back straight. There was pain in seeing the tabard of purple and black march in front of her, and for a moment, she felt like she had betrayed her people. Two Ravenwood soldiers glared at her as they marched by, hands bound behind them. Then one stopped and spit at her. "Filthy traitor!"

His words hurt more than the spittle dribbling down her cheek. Lord Elric spun around, pulling his light-infused polearm from thin air, and stepped toward the man. He shoved the weapon beneath the man's chin. "Never spit at a lady!"

"What lady?" the man said with a smirk.

Elric pressed his polearm forward until it sizzled at contact with the man's skin.

The man cursed and stepped away, the light from the polearm reflecting in his eyes.

"Lord Elric, stop." Selene placed a hand on his arm.

Elric turned around as the man stumbled forward and caught up to his compatriots. "He had no right to call you that." He pulled out a handkerchief and wiped her cheek, his polearm still next to his side. "They are the traitors, siding with the empire."

"My mother is very good at twisting words. He has been deceived."

"Maybe, maybe not. Still, that's no way to treat a lady."

Selene didn't have a comment. Part of her still felt like a traitor to her people, but in a different way. The mountain people didn't know the whole story, of how her family had been deceiving them for hundreds of years, claiming to use their gift to help them when in fact, from what she had seen, they still lived in poverty.

She dropped her hand and searched the sky until she could see the topmost battlement of Rook Castle and the stars twinkling above. Yes, she was a traitor. A traitor to the old ways of Ravenwood. But those ways stopped now. She would forge a new path. A path where she would bring peace to her people.

19

"Selene!" Damien sat up in bed, gasping for air.
"She's not here, your lordship."

Damien sat back against the pillows and slowly took a breath. He couldn't remember the dream. Only an immense feeling of longing and loneliness, and Selene's face swathed in shadows. Then he frowned and looked to his right. "Healer Sildaern?"

A dark-haired man sat in a chair by his bedside. A fire burned in the middle of the floor, the orange light flickering off the sides of the canvas tent. On the other side of the tent were a small table and chair. The rest of the area was cloaked in darkness.

At the mention of his name, Sildaern bowed his head, his long black hair falling over one shoulder. "Yes, my lord. I arrived this afternoon with the troops from Brightforest Citadel."

"Admiral Gerault is here?"

"Yes. I joined up with the admiral after he set up a patrol along the sea. We reached the border between the Northern Shores and House Vivek two days ago and then met up with the refugees from Shanalona. Admiral Gerault has set up another patrol along the water-wall you created in the Hyr River as well and provided whatever supplies and tents he could muster for the refugees."

Damien let out a long breath. "Thank the Light." He placed a hand against his head. "How long was I out?"

"According to Taegis, you fell unconscious after raising the water-wall yesterday."

"A whole day and a half?"

"Apparently so."

"Why?"

"Well . . ." Sildaern steepled his long, tapered fingers together. "A gift like yours is a powerful one that takes a heavy toll on your physical body. Between the sea boundary and now moving the water barrier in the Hyr River, you've pushed your body to its maximum capacity."

Damien narrowed his eyes as he stared at the fire. Was that it? No, he felt there was something more. He felt as if there were something blocking his power inside of him. A wall of his own making . . .

The tent flap flew up and Taegis walked in, bringing with him the night wind and the smell of smoke.

"Healer Sildaern—Lord Damien, you're awake."

"I am. And ready to leave this bed." He pushed back the wool blanket and swung his legs around. "How are the refugees doing? And Lady Bryren and her soldiers? Any word from Shanalona and Lord Renlar?" He refused to dwell on the people and soldiers lost. If he did, he might not be able to bring his mind to the present. Instead, he reached for his leather jerkin at the foot of his bed and shoved his arms through it.

"Admiral Gerault is working with House Vivek's men to see that the refugees are taken care of. Lady Bryren and her people are currently hunting. As far as Lord Renlar, we have received no word from him."

"When can we expect Lady Bryren back?" Damien sat down again and began to pull on his boots.

"She should be back anytime now."

"Good. I want to discuss our next strategy."

Healer Sildaern rose from his chair with graceful ease, his head bowed. "My lord, until then I advise you to rest in here. I will have food brought to you."

Damien wanted to protest, but he knew Sildaern was right. And the man could be quite stubborn. "I will wait, then."

"Very good." He swept back his green robes and left the tent.

Damien rubbed his face with one hand, then looked up. Taegis crossed the room and took a seat in the chair Healer Sildaern had vacated moments ago. They sat quietly for a minute before Taegis spoke.

"How are you really feeling?"

Damien let out his breath and stared ahead. "You said my father passed out before when he used our gift."

"Yes. Once or twice. He said it was from the intensity."

"Was that the only reason?"

Taegis narrowed his eyes. "What are you saying?"

Damien leaned forward and placed his elbows on his knees. "I think there's something more going on."

"More than just exhaustion?"

Damien ran a hand through his hair and along his neck. "It's—it's like there's a barrier inside of me, a mental block. And it's growing stronger."

"A barrier?"

"It's not a weakening of my power . . . more like something is stopping the power inside of me. Like a dam along a river. I can feel it, in here." He pressed a finger to his chest. "And here." He pointed to his temple and let out a shaky sigh.

"How long has this been going on?"

"I've known of it since I lowered the sea-wall weeks back. But I think it first began when I took out that small imperial fleet last year."

"The first time your power took another's life."

Damien hesitated. "Yes."

Taegis sat back. "Life has always been sacred to you. People aren't just masses—each one has a face, even the enemy. So when you take a life, it becomes a weight you carry. A weight you won't let go of."

"I know."

"But you have to."

Damien looked up. "What?"

"Your heart may well be hindering your gift. You need to let go, or you will never heal. And that could be devastating for everyone."

Before Damien could say more, the tent flap lifted up and a soldier wearing the colors of House Maris walked in with a tray in hand, followed by Healer Sildaern.

"My lord," the man said as he brought the tray over. On top lay a wooden bowl with some steaming soup inside.

Damien took the tray. "Thank you."

The man bowed and left. Sildaern came to stand beside Damien, his hands folded and tucked within his green robes. "Is there anything else I can do for you, my lord?"

Damien lifted the spoon and stirred the soup. "No, not at the moment." His heart felt heavy inside, as if he had swallowed a boulder, and it was now lodged inside his chest. How could he do as Taegis suggested? Letting go felt like it cheapened the lives lost by his hand.

Healer Sildaern seemed to sense Damien's tension. "Then I will join the healers who came with the refugees and leave you to eat."

Taegis stood as well. "I need to speak to

Admiral Gerault. If I see Lady Bryren, I will let her know you wish to meet with her."

"Thank you, Taegis."

The two men left the tent, leaving behind a wake of silence. Damien dragged his spoon through the liquid once more before he placed the tray at the end of the bed and leaned forward, holding his head in his hands.

He closed his eyes and pictured Selene, her long black hair hanging to her waist, her dark eyes looking into his. Was she at Rook Castle now? Had they been successful? Was she safe?

More than anything, he wished she were here right now, with him.

He sighed and rubbed his temples before picking up his bowl and proceeding to eat.

"There you are." Lady Bryren stormed into the tent, flaps flying behind her. "Your guardian said you were awake. I just received word from Lord Renlar and wanted to pass it on to you."

Damien swallowed the last of his soup and placed his bowl down. "I thought you were out hunting."

"We were. But we're back now. Come, there is much to discuss." Lady Bryren spun around, the braids and beads in her copper hair flying around her face, and she left the tent as abruptly as she had entered.

Damien stared at the fluttering tent flaps, then laughed. Count on Lady Bryren to lift his spirits, even if she didn't know about the darkness he was fighting within himself.

That last thought sobered him as he stood. Taegis's words haunted him: *"Your heart may well be hindering your gift."*

He placed a hand on his chest. If that was true, how did he choose between his heart and his gift? How did he remain true to himself when his gift could be so destructive?

Lady Bryren ducked her head inside. "Are you coming? I swear you're as slow as an old wyvern."

Damien dropped his hand and stood up. "Yes, yes. I'm coming."

"Then hurry yourself!"

"Aye, my lady."

Lady Bryren snickered as she turned and disappeared. Damien followed, a frown on his face. How did the other lords and ladies balance their gifts, their people, and their duties?

His initial thoughts dissipated as Lady Bryren led the way across the camp. He glanced around as he followed her, amazed at how a makeshift base had come together in such a short amount of time. Hundreds of tents were lined up in rows along the valley, several miles beyond the Hyr River. The air was warmer now, despite the dull grey sky above, and the grass a little greener than it had been a week ago. Spring was here, as if to say nature cared little about the affairs of humankind.

Near the center of the camp stood a cluster of oversized tents with the flags of House Maris and House Vivek flying together in the wind.

Lady Bryren ducked into the closest tent. Damien followed.

Inside a map was spread on top of a long table positioned between the tent poles. Lanterns hung from the ceiling. A handful of chairs were scattered around the perimeter. Reidin, Bryren's consort, stood near the back, along with Admiral Gerault, Taegis, and several captains dressed in the dark blue of House Vivek. Lady Bryren bypassed the chairs and table and took her place by Reidin.

Admiral Gerault bowed. "Lord Damien."

Damien nodded in his direction. "Admiral."

"I was just telling the Admiral you were awake and was going to retrieve you," Taegis said, "but apparently Lady Bryren beat me to it."

"Yes, she did. Almost dragged me from my tent." A smile played along his lips. Lady Bryren appeared not to have heard him as she whispered something to Reidin. He nodded to her, then turned and made his way out of the tent.

"Gentlemen," she said, turning her attention to the men present as they made their way around the table, "I have received word from Lord Renlar." She reached into the folds of her leather split skirt and pulled out a small piece of parchment. "It came by dove this morning. Lord

Renlar and his forces are holding out against the empire, but he's not sure how much longer the city wall will stand." She looked up. "He's asking for help with a tactical withdrawal."

"He's deserting Shanalona?" one of the Vivek captains sputtered. "How could he give up our city?"

"There must be a strategic reason." Admiral Gerault folded his muscular arms across his chest. His chestnut hair was pulled back in a similar fashion to Taegis's as he gazed down at the map on the table. "I don't believe the leader of the House of Wisdom would leave if it wasn't for a greater purpose."

"There is," Lady Bryren answered. "He writes that the empire has a series of catapult-type weapons that are wearing down the walls. There are already a few cracks. He believes they can hold for a while longer, but eventually the city will fall. And if he is to lose Shanalona, then he wants to make sure he saves as many of his men as he can."

That made sense, but the thought of losing Shanalona . . . Damien leaned forward and pressed his fingers against the wooden table. Shanalona wasn't razed during the first war with the empire, but many of its buildings and libraries had been burned to the ground and much of its history lost. Were they cursed to relive the past? Could he make the same decision if he were in Lord Renlar's place? Could he give up Nor Esen?

More murmurs rose from those who were part of House Vivek's forces.

"Do we know what the other houses are doing?"

"Yes. House Luceras is currently securing Rook Castle."

The others hushed at his words. Admiral Gerault nodded. "Good. If we hold the north and the mountains, we can control where the empire goes next. Do we know how they are faring?"

Lady Bryren spoke up. "Not yet. Hopefully we will receive word from Lord Leo or Lady Selene."

Admiral Gerault looked down at the map. "If Lord Renlar withdraws, the best place to send him is westward toward the Magyr Mountains. The empire has its army stretched from Shanalona to the Hyr River. I doubt the empire will suspect Lord Renlar will head west, especially if they believe they hold Rook Castle. If he and his men can escape during the night and head across the plains, we could send Lady Bryren and her wyvern riders as a vanguard and have Lord Leo and his forces meet Lord Renlar."

Lady Bryren pointed at the map between Shanalona and the mountains. "That's assuming Lord Leo has taken Rook Castle."

"He will, if he hasn't already," Damien said.

"My wife is with him, and she knows every inch of that castle and the surrounding mines. Ravenwood's military is not strong, especially not compared to House Luceras's. I'm confident we will take Rook Castle."

"Well, in any case," Lady Bryren replied, "House Merek will protect Lord Renlar and his men. I doubt the empire will have time to move those catapults they were using against my riders and follow us south."

One of the captains from House Vivek stepped up. "While Lord Renlar is heading west, we can take a contingent of soldiers from both our house and House Maris and move along the banks of the Hyr to the Magyr Mountains and meet up with House Luceras and Lord Renlar at the northern foothills."

Damien slowly nodded, his gaze moving along the map. "Good idea. I will then lower the river for a moment so we can cross and rally with House Vivek. Then the empire will have to make a choice: meet with our forces or head south toward the forests of House Rafel."

"Does House Rafel stand with the empire?" the Vivek captain asked hesitantly.

"No, they are neutral at the moment." Damien narrowed his eyes as he stared at the map.

"But what if the empire forces the issue? Would Lord Haruk side with them to save his own people?"

"I don't know," Damien answered, finally looking up. But the captain had just voiced his own apprehension.

"Then we need to be prepared," Admiral Gerault said. "And with our forces joining those of House Luceras on the east side of the Magyr Mountains, we will be ready."

20

For three days Damien marched with his men and House Vivek across the land along the Hyr River toward the edge of the Magyr Mountains while Lady Bryren led her wyvern riders to assist Lord Renlar. The water-wall not only provided cover from the enemy, but any imperial soldier who came near it was also washed away in the torrential waves.

As they reached the border between his own lands and that of House Ravenwood, Damien came to stand in front of the river. It was warm and muggy and nearing evening. The troops gathered behind him as he prepared to lower the barrier so they could cross. For a fleeting moment, he wondered if his father ever thought there would be a war. Or that the gift of House Maris would be used to save so many of the people of these lands.

Damien let out a deep breath, sank down into position, placed his hands up, then stretched out with his gift. A moment later, the weight of the river settled across his arms and shoulders. He let out a grunt and slowly let the water down. There were gasps and exclamations of awe from the men behind him.

His arms and body began to shake from the

exertion. Sweat dripped down the sides of his face. Somewhere deep inside, a blockage to his power was making it even harder to bring down the river. Fear niggled at the back of his mind. Would there come a point when he would no longer be able to access his power?

The moment the river settled into its bed, Damien fell to one knee, his vision moving in and out of focus. A hand gripped his shoulder, but Taegis didn't say a word, just gave him a reassuring touch.

Damien remained where he was, watching as the men around him began to trudge across the river. Stares were sent his way, but he ignored them. He bowed his head and breathed in and out. Soon, when everyone was across, he would need to raise the water again, and he wanted to make sure he had all his strength in order to do it.

The sun slowly started to sink, and the wind blew through the nearby trees. Damien finally stood and watched as Admiral Gerault and his men steered the combined forces of House Maris and House Vivek across the river. An hour later, the last handful of soldiers and supplies crossed.

Damien gripped the front of his tunic. His chest ached, but whether because of his power or something more he couldn't tell. *Just one more time,* he thought. *I just need to raise it one more time. I can do this.*

"Ready?" Taegis asked.

"Yes," Damien replied.

The two men stepped into the river. The icy waters brought a gasp to his lips, but Damien kept it behind his teeth. They forged ahead until the water was up to his waist. Past the banks on the other side, the army was already getting fires going and preparing for the evening.

Damien swung his body back and forth, pressing against the strong current, taking care to watch his step. The current grew weaker as he reached the other side and finally stepped out of the river. His wet clothes clung to his legs and body.

"Do you need more time?" Taegis asked, coming to stand beside him.

"No, I can do it now." *I think.* That shard of fear again splintered his already aching chest. "But it might take a lot out of me."

"I'll be ready."

It was even harder this time as Damien started to lift the river. Yes, there was definitely an impediment to his gift. Only a trickle of his power was making it through the dam. Panic began to take hold of his body, causing his heart to race. Would he have enough power to lock the river in place?

Cold sweat combined with his wet clothes caused his body to shiver violently as he hoisted the river up with all of his might. Already darkness was overtaking his vision. *I need . . . to finish.*

Just when he thought he would lose consciousness, Damien twisted his wrists. There.

Then he fell down, down, down into darkness.

After what seemed like an eternity, Damien slowly opened his eyes and sat up. He pressed a hand to his head as he caught sight of Taegis sitting near a fire, the night sky deep and dark overhead. The air was quiet and warm, save for the soft murmur of voices and the occasional chirrup of an insect. Hundreds of other campfires were burning low with men sleeping all around them. "It happened again, didn't it?"

"Yes," Taegis said quietly. "But thankfully you were not out for long."

Damien let out a sigh. "How did the soldiers react?"

"Hardly anyone noticed when you slumped over, but those who did were alarmed. I explained to them how much it takes out of you to do what you do."

"I see." It was partly true, but not fully. He was strong enough to handle his gift. This . . . this was something more.

Damien looked up, banishing those thoughts. "What's next?"

"We head out tomorrow. It will still take a lot of hard marching to reach the foot of the Magyr Mountains. By the time we arrive, Lord Renlar should be there, along with Lady Bryren's wyverns."

"If they were successful."

Taegis let out a small laugh, which made Damien lift his head. "You know House Merek. Unless the empire has found a way to combat Lady Bryren's reckless courage, they will be successful."

Damien laughed. "True. However, I'm sure Commander Orion has come up with something. Some kind of weapon besides catapults."

"Perhaps. But it's likely that he was unaware that the wyvern riders were coming to assist Lord Renlar," Taegis pointed out.

The two men sobered as someone nearby began to snore. Damien lay back down. Best to get what sleep he could before morning came and they began their long trek toward the mountains.

As he tried to find a comfortable position on the hard ground, his thoughts turned to his wife. Where was Selene now? And did she miss him as much as he missed her?

The mountains came into view by the fourth day, tall and proud in the distance, with white caps of snow and green hills along the edge. Damien stared at them. Deep within those tall peaks stood Rook Castle and, hopefully, Selene. The thought of seeing her again created an agonizing desire inside of him. Never did he think he would miss someone that badly. It was as if she were a part of him now, and he had been living with only half of his heart.

It had been weeks since they parted, and Damien couldn't help but recall the hard words that were spoken between them. He remembered again her accusation that he had only married her to save himself. Not only was that not true, it was the complete opposite. If she truly believed that, then he would be sure to show her otherwise until every thought of his intentions toward her were washed away and only his love for her remained.

As they approached the foothills, smoke could be seen in the distance. Was it from Lord Renlar and Lady Bryren, or the Dominia Empire?

Word spread across the troops to be ready as they made their way toward the hills. There was no sign of the empire, or of any other people. No sound either, other than that of their own soldiers and the wind as it blew through the tall grass.

Then, as the sun began its descent toward the mountains, a sprawling camp was spotted in the distance. It was too disorganized to be the empire, and the banners of burnt orange and green were not visible. A wyvern appeared moments later, circling the camp before landing on the near side.

A half hour later, they reached the camp. Lady Bryren was the first to greet them, her leather split skirt whipping around her boots as she approached. Lord Renlar was close behind.

"We were victorious," she said with a wide grin. "The empire retreated like a whipped dog with its tail between its legs."

Lord Renlar appeared more sober and tired. "True, but we have many injured. And we lost some good soldiers."

"Do you have any healers?" Damien asked.

"Hardly any. They are doing what they can for my men."

"Healer Sildaern from House Rafel is with me, along with a handful of healers under him."

"House Rafel?" Lord Renlar said, his eyebrows shooting up in surprise. "Did Lord Haruk join us?"

"Unfortunately, no. Healer Sildaern has been serving in my house for the last couple of years."

"Oh." His face fell, and Damien knew exactly how he felt. There were healers, but none with the gift of healing that House Rafel possessed. Which meant more lives would be lost. "At least we are safe for the time being, thanks to Lady Bryren and her riders."

Damien turned and gave directions for Healer Sildaern and the other healers to aid the injured, and also for food and supplies to be brought into the camp.

"You had to leave Shanalona more quickly than you thought," Damien observed.

"Yes," Lord Renlar said. "We were not expecting the empire to take the walls as fast as they did. Their catapults are more powerful than our own, and many of the boulders were set ablaze by what appeared to be the power of House Friere, or some similar accelerant. I thought we were ready, but . . ." He shook his head and Damien could see the distress across the young lord's face. "They are not the same empire that came four hundred years ago. It's going to be a hard battle to win."

At least Lord Renlar didn't say they were doomed to fail, Damien thought, as he noticed a few men listening in on their conversation.

Lady Bryren clapped Lord Renlar hard across the back, causing the man to stumble forward. "No fear. If we work together, then the empire is no match against us." Her courage was such that Damien could feel it seeping into his own weary body, and he watched Lord Renlar's eyes brighten a little and his lips turn slightly upward.

But only five of the seven houses were working together against the empire. Deep down, he was sure it would take all seven to push them back, just as it had centuries ago. Perhaps House Rafel would come to their side. But House Friere?

Damien couldn't see that happening.

21

Commander Orion stared hard at Lady Ragna. "Your daughter failed."

Lady Ragna bristled. "What do you mean?" she asked, a layer of ice entering her voice.

The rest of the people inside the meeting tent went deathly silent as all eyes turned toward the commander and Lady Ragna.

"My men just returned from chasing the refugees north. The river barrier was raised and took at least a hundred men with it."

"The river . . . was raised?" Amara had failed in her mission? Ragna blinked, the only evidence of the shock she was feeling inside. Amara wasn't that gifted, but she was sure her daughter's tenacity would see her through to the end. Where was Amara now? A prisoner? Dead?

"The water-wall is in place, which means many of the people of House Vivek still live. People who can still fight. And Lord Damien is still alive as well, one of the greatest threats to the empire, not only because of his gift but because of his leadership. If it wasn't for Lord Ivulf's quick action in breaking the ground with his power, more would have crossed the Hyr River."

Lord Ivulf bowed toward Commander Orion,

which only made Ragna's blood boil. She pressed her lips together and didn't respond.

Commander Orion continued, ignoring her silence. "I sent two companies after Lord Renlar and his men, but I haven't heard back yet. However, a messenger arrived, stating he had seen wyverns in the distance. I'm assuming this means that Lord Renlar has also escaped."

There were grumblings under the breath of those present, and Ragna caught Raoul smirking, as if he enjoyed her misfortune.

"So now we need to discuss the next steps in our campaign." Commander Orion looked around the table, his eyes lingering on Lady Ragna, then Lord Ivulf. She could see the displeasure clearly on his face, but she refused to apologize. There were mistakes made. She would try harder.

"The north is no longer open to us. And it would seem that most of the Great Houses are working together."

One of the generals grumbled at the end of the table. "We wouldn't have this problem if Lord Damien had been dealt with."

"True," Commander Orion said, sending another look at Lady Ragna. "But focusing on the past will not help us move forward. The water-wall is raised, and it cannot be taken down, correct?"

"Yes," said Lord Ivulf, speaking up for the first

time. "Unless Lord Damien dies. Then all of his barriers fall with him."

"And most likely he is on the other side of the wall?"

"I would think so."

"Then we need other options."

"Do we know where Lord Renlar retreated to?" Ragna asked.

"Not yet. I have scouts searching. But he probably has the wyvern riders with him by now. That means House Merek, House Vivek, and House Maris are working together."

"What about our messages to House Rafel?" one of the generals asked. "Have they chosen to align with us?"

Commander Orion's face darkened, causing his scar to stand out. "Lord Haruk insists on remaining neutral."

The men around the table began to smile as they glanced at each other. "Lord Haruk must not realize the empire recognizes no neutral parties," one of them said.

Commander Orion's lips turned upward. "No, he does not. You are either for or against us. . . . Am I right, Lady Ragna and Lord Ivulf?"

Ragna narrowed her eyes. Was Commander Orion threatening them?

"We are with you," Lord Ivulf said. Raoul stared at his father with a dark look on his face. Lady Ragna felt a hint of that emotion herself.

"Lady Ragna?"

She turned to Commander Orion. "House Ravenwood stands with the empire as well."

"And what would you say if we chose to move against House Rafel?"

"In what way?" Lady Ragna asked.

Commander Orion looked over his men, then back at her. "The empire is not interested in people, only in resources. The fall of a house, a city, or even a nation does not concern us. If House Rafel does not want to join us, then we will wipe them out. We can't afford House Rafel choosing to join the other houses. The more houses that join together, the more powerful they will become. Isn't that what you said, Lady Ragna?"

She nodded. "Yes, it is true. The healers of House Rafel are equal to none. If House Rafel were to join the others, it would be that much harder for your forces. It is better to pick off an individual house, as we attempted to do with House Vivek, instead of facing the combined forces of the Great Houses."

"What's your plan, then, Commander?" Lord Ivulf said from the other side of the table. "There are hundreds of miles of forest before you would even reach the city of Surao."

"Yes. Hundreds of flammable woods."

"Flammable woods?" Lady Ragna's mind raced. "Wait, are you suggesting we light the vast forest of House Rafel on fire? Didn't you say you needed resources?"

"We do. But why send an army to take over a nation when nature can fight for us? Not only would it take care of House Rafel, it would clear the way so we can move on House Merek and Burkhard in the south and House Luceras and Lux Casta to the north."

His plan made sense. Terrifying, yet practical sense. The area south of the Magyr Mountains tended to be dry, even with a lot of snowfall. Set a couple of fires and the forest would catch flame, doing quickly what would take the entire imperial army too much time and resources.

Take out House Rafel.

The thought of all the destruction to life and land made Lady Ragna feel physically ill. Even in her wildest dreams she never thought the empire was capable of such devastation. But she held her feelings tightly inside. "It could work," she said slowly. "But fires can be extinguished with water, no? You'll have to watch for Lord Damien. If he can somehow make his way down south, he could possibly put out the fires with his water gift."

"Then we will assign a handful of companies to patrol any rivers running through the forest." Commander Orion turned his attention to Lord Ivulf. "House Friere has a stronghold near the Drihst River, correct?"

"Yes, we do."

"Then we will send your men from there."

Lord Ivulf balked. "My men?"

Commander Orion raised one eyebrow. "Is that a problem?"

Lady Ragna saw a spark in Ivulf's eyes, but it disappeared as fast as it came. "No, we are happy to assist."

Raoul curled his lip. It was clear he did not approve of his father's ready acquiescence to Commander Orion's request. Even she had noticed how the soldiers from Friere were the first ones sent into battle.

"We will start the fire in the northwest corner of the forest and allow it to spread," Commander Orion continued. "Not only will it block any help from House Vivek and Lord Renlar, if they are indeed taking shelter along the foothills of the Magyr Mountains, but there are also very few small rivers near there, according to the map Lord Ivulf provided. We will send House Friere's men to the south, along with a handful of my own, and they will keep me informed of their progress. As Surao and the surrounding forest are burning, we will first march south for supplies, then toward the western side of the continent. If Lord Maris does show up to stop the fires, then we will be more than ready."

Lady Ragna nodded, although she was again struck by how Commander Orion was using Lord

Ivulf's men as expendable pawns. "I'll send a raven to Rook Castle to have Captain Stanton send my forces east over the mountains to capture Lord Renlar."

Commander Orion folded his arms across his chest. "Yes, that would be good. It would at least make up for your daughter's failure. And it will leave us one less house to deal with."

Lady Ragna's back stiffened at his words, but she kept her face emotionless.

After another half hour of talk, those inside the tent were excused. Lady Ragna stepped back out into the heat. She waited for Ivulf, but he only nodded to her as he exited with his son, heated whispers being exchanged between them. Slowly, the other generals left the tent. The sun began to set, and a cool breeze sprang up, blowing across her flushed face.

She hadn't heard back yet from Captain Stanton about Opheliana or her transfer to Ironmond. Once her daughter was safely away from Rook Castle, she would consider sharing her news with Lord Ivulf.

"Lady Ragna, I would like to have a private word with you."

Commander Orion stood in the entrance and turned back inside without waiting for her to comply. Dart'an, was he going to reprimand her again for Amara's failure?

Once inside, he studied her with a raised

eyebrow. "Have you been able to expand your dreamwalking?" he finally asked.

Her dreamwalking? Her heart slowly relaxed its beat, and a smile spread across her face. She hadn't been prepared to say anything just yet, but now seemed like a good time. "I've had a breakthrough with my gift."

He nodded curtly. "It's about time."

She ignored his subtle barb. His tone would change once she shared what she had been able to accomplish. "As you know, my family can enter a person's dream with just a touch and manipulate his or her greatest fear until their heart gives out. I've been working with the Dark Lady, and with her power, I can now enter a dream without touching the person."

"Just one person?"

She scowled. "Yes, so far. But it is the first time my family has ever been able to do such a thing."

"Your other daughter can't?"

Lady Ragna paused. Could Selene? Surely not. It had never been done before. And she herself could only do it with the Dark Lady's help. But then again, Selene's power had become strong enough for her to be recognized as the true head of House Ravenwood—

"Lady Ragna? Can she do it?"

She looked up. "No." But now a seed of doubt was planted in her mind.

"And you can only do it with the Dark Lady's help? To just one person?"

"Yes." Her jaw tightened. He made her sound weak.

He paused thoughtfully. "This could be helpful, especially if you can enter a mind like Lord Damien's. Can you do that?"

"Not from here. Even without having to touch a person, I have not yet figured out how to overcome the distance." It was true that she had been able to enter one of the prisoner's dreams without touching him, but she had been on the other side of the tent. And even then, it had come only with great force.

"If you can enter a dream without touching a person, what about multiple people? Is it possible to enter more than one dream?"

Lady Ragna's mind spun. She'd never tried to enter more than one dream at the same time. "It might be . . . possible," she answered slowly. "But I fail to see the need."

Commander Orion ran a finger along his scar. "If you can enter into one person's dream and kill them, what's to say you can't kill an entire army in their sleep?"

Lady Ragna stared back at him, horrified. Kill an entire army?

"Or instead of killing people in their dreams, could you trap them there?"

"Trap them?"

"Yes, so they can't wake up."

Her eyes went wide. "Like a death sleep," she murmured, her mind turning the thought over. Her thoughts flashed to Renata, the servant girl whose mind Selene had shattered. Could Lady Ragna do that to an entire army?

"Killing the sleepers would be optimal," Commander Orion said, still rubbing his scar. "But if you could trap the alliance soldiers, it would still benefit our campaign." He dropped his hand. "See what can be done. If distance is the problem, I will arrange for you to be secretly escorted closer to the enemy camp. Perhaps I'll send you west to where we think Lord Renlar is. I want to know if you can do it."

He turned abruptly and walked toward the door. "I expect to see results, Lady Ragna," Commander Orion said, his voice hard. "No more failures. Do you understand?"

His tone of voice made her bristle. "Yes, Commander," she said, wanting to bare her teeth. She understood perfectly. She understood how Commander Orion seemed to have forgotten it was her connections and gift over the last five years that had paved the way for him to enter these lands. His mind, although doubtlessly powerful, was still susceptible to her abilities.

But the flare of anger quickly burned out as misgivings crept into her mind like shadowy fingers, probing the deepest parts of her soul. She was selling out the other houses, one by one, and walking a fine line with Commander Orion and the empire.

If she wasn't careful, she might find herself with nowhere to turn.

22

Selene walked down the corridor toward the infirmary. Now that Opheliana was safe and the coalition and alliance forces had fully secured Rook Castle and the surrounding area, it was time to fulfill the second promise she had made to herself: to find out if Renata still lived.

Her stomach tightened with each step, and fear pulled at her, trying to turn her back. The hallway was cold and dimly lit, and the moans of injured soldiers raked across her ears, adding weight to her heart. She passed by rooms filled with the wounded, both Luceras and Ravenwood. The subtle stench of blood and decay permeated the air.

Selene ignored the smells and continued on. The last time she had seen Renata, the girl had been staring up at the ceiling with an unfocused gaze, her face pale, her body tucked beneath a woolen blanket. Like a living corpse.

Bile filled her throat. She placed her hand against her middle. *I can do this. I* need *to do this. I will do whatever I can to help Renata. I owe it to her.*

If she is still alive.

Selene reached the door to the infirmary and walked in. Beds and mats were laid out wherever there was space, with only narrow gaps between the bedding to allow the healers to access the patients.

She spotted the head healer at the end of the room, dressed in simple pale robes and silver hair bound up in a swath of matching cloth. She stood beside a long table, crushing something inside the stone mortar with her pestle.

As Selene made her way toward the healer, a man lying on a mat lifted his hand toward her.

"Please," he whispered in a raspy voice.

Selene paused. She recognized him as one of the members of the coalition, a young man with just the beginnings of a beard. His arm was bandaged, and his cheeks looked flushed. Before she could stop herself, Selene knelt down. "Yes?" she said as she grasped his fingers between her own.

"So . . . tired."

"Then sleep. I will help you."

He closed his eyes. Then Selene shut her own. Within seconds, she sank into his dreamscape. It was dark and cold, like a winter morning under a mournful sky. Instead of immediately changing into her raven form, Selene walked along snow-covered ground. With each step, she imagined grass, like the rolling hills of Serine, and a warm sun overhead. The clouds parted, allowing light to break across the dreamscape. Grass shot through the snow until the ground glimmered with new growth. Selene hummed softly as she walked, changing his dreamscape until she felt a peace settle across the soldier's physical body.

"There you go, my friend," she whispered before changing form and taking flight.

Moments later, she broke through the dreamscape and found herself back in the infirmary. The man's hand fell from hers, his chest rising and falling in even breaths.

Selene stared down in wonder. She glanced from her hand to his. She did this. She brought him peace. With her gift. The same gift that a year ago she was using to evoke nightmares. She glanced at those around her. Could she do that to all of them?

Selene stood and crossed the room to the head healer.

The healer looked up at her approach. Her mouth turned downward, accentuating the wrinkles across her aged face. "My lady, I was not expecting you."

Selene wondered what else the older woman was thinking, but pushed on. "I'm here to check on someone."

"A soldier?"

"No." Her heart began to pound in her chest. What if her mother had ordered Renata to be put to death? "Her name was—is—Renata."

The old woman coughed before answering. "Renata? You mean that servant girl with the addled mind? I've taken care of her for almost a year."

Selene's relief at hearing Renata was alive was tempered by the subtle accusation in the healer's eyes. Did she know? No, she couldn't. Mother would have never revealed what happened.

"Can I see her?"

The healer folded her arms. "Why?"

"Because she was my servant. And . . . a friend." The truth of her last word hit her like an arrow to the chest. Yes. Renata had been her friend. And right before she came into her gifting, Selene had promised herself that she would draw that shy girl out. Now, after causing so much damage, she had to see if her gift was capable of mending Renata's mind.

The healer's face softened slightly. "Come, follow me."

Selene followed the head healer around the beds and mats, stopping as the woman adjusted a pillow or spoke a word to one of the soldiers. When they reached the outer door, the healer turned right and headed down to the end of the wing. At the second-to-last door, she stopped and turned.

"Renata has been like this for months. I've done everything I can for her, but nothing has changed. She never wakes up. And I must warn you, she does not look like she did when you last saw her."

"What do you mean?"

"You'll see for yourself."

The healer opened the door. The room was small and cold, with a single square window on the other side. A bed was on the right, a single figure on top, buried under a mound of blankets.

"Your mother hinted at first that I shouldn't let the girl live, but as a healer, it is my duty to save life, not take it." She nodded at Selene and silently made her way back down the corridor.

"Thank you." The words came out in a choked whisper. Selene's hands shook as she stepped into the room. She knew it would be difficult to face her greatest mistake, but never did she realize how much until this moment.

Renata lay in the bed, her cheekbones hollow and her face pale. Her hair surrounded her like brittle stalks of wheat scorched by the sun.

Selene stood near the bed, her legs frozen. All she could do was stare at her former servant girl. The nightmare came back as vivid as that night: Renata's horrifying memories, Selene's reaction, and the dreamscape shattering around her.

"Renata," she whispered. She stumbled toward the bed. At the edge, she fell to her knees and grasped the blankets. "I'm—I'm—" She buried her head in the quilts and sobbed.

I'm so sorry!

Her whole body shook as her heart broke for the girl with the shattered mind.

Light, what do I do? What can I do?

She lifted her head and stretched out her fingers toward Renata's face. Gently she touched the girl's cheek and closed her eyes. She was more terrified to reenter Renata's dreamscape than of anything she had ever done before. Her heart beat so hard it hurt inside her chest.

But I must. I must undo what I did. If I can.

With that thought, Selene dove into Renata's mind.

23

Darkness. All around Selene was darkness and cold. She clutched her arms across her chest and took a step forward. Was this how Renata had been living all this time? In this shadowy place?

She took a few more steps, her entire body succumbing to the chill around her. And the silence . . .

This place was one of nothingness.

Part of her wanted to change into her raven form and fly toward the boundary of the dreamscape above. Panic clawed at her throat, and she lifted her arms, ready to do just that.

No. She stared at the boundary, a thin, grey line barely visible within the darkness. *No. I came here for a reason.*

She dropped her arms and started moving forward again. The dreamscape pressed down on her like a smothering smoke, dulling her mind and pervading her with a sense of hopelessness.

No wonder Renata appeared as she did in the physical world. There was nothing here, nothing but darkness and bitterness.

Then she heard it. Metal grinding on metal.

Selene made her way through the hazy shadows and gloom toward the noise. A minute later, she spotted a dark sphere rotating just at the edge of her vision, with chains encircling the orb. Around and around the chains went, revolving with the sphere.

She knew that orb. It was Renata's soul.

Selene approached, wary and heartsick. A year ago, as a dreamkiller in training, she would have already locked her emotions away. But as a dreamwalker, that was not an option. She couldn't do that, not if she was going to help Renata.

Once she was a foot away, she stopped and squeezed her arms tight. Around and around the thin chains went, imprisoning the orb. She stared at the sphere, the living essence of Renata's being.

Light, please show me what to do. The words came from the deepest part of her, rising upward and vanishing into the dreamscape. She closed her eyes. *Please.*

A wind stirred across the dreamscape, and with its gentle caress came the words *show her what I've shown you.*

Selene opened her eyes. She lifted one hand and stared at her palm, barely visible in the dim shadows. *Show her . . . what I've seen? Nightmares . . . and death . . . and hurt . . .*

And the Light.

Her breath hitched. Yes. The Light. Just like she showed Amara.

Selene knelt down. "Renata," she whispered

toward the orb. "I don't know if I can mend your mind and free you from this place." She swallowed. "But there is one thing I know I can do."

She reached out—fingers spread—and placed her palm on the revolving orb. The sphere slowed until it came to a stop and all became silent. Then a small light appeared, shining out from beneath her palm. "Renata, let me show you what I've discovered over this last year."

Selene closed her eyes and opened her heart. There were no words for what came forth, only images and feelings. The darkness she had felt when she first discovered what her family did with their gift. The despair of a bleak future. Then the first time she saw the Light.

"This," she whispered and pressed her hand, "this is when I realized there was hope."

The orb pulsed beneath her, then shifted. Selene opened her eyes. The orb began to morph until Renata lay beneath her hand, gaunt and sickly, with dark circles under her eyes and blue-tinged lips. Slowly her gaze turned to Selene.

"Renata," Selene said through a tight throat. Before she could think, she bent down and gathered the frail girl into her arms and held her tightly. Renata was cold to the touch and shivered within her embrace. "I'm so sorry, Renata!"

"You . . . came." Renata's voice trembled—not with fear, but with relief.

Selene's lips quivered. Had Renata been waiting for her? For anyone? It made her heart hurt even more to think her servant girl had been waiting all this time in this dark place. "Yes, I came," she said with blurry eyes. "But I don't know if I can rescue you."

Renata slowly closed her eyes. "I-it is enough that you came."

That familiar stutter sent another pang of grief into Selene. She bowed her head and wept as she held Renata in her arms.

"Sh-show me more," Renata whispered.

"Show you more?"

"M-more of the Light. It is w-warm."

Selene swallowed hard and nodded. She cupped Renata's thin face and opened her heart, mind, and memories to the girl. Everything she had felt, everything she had experienced over the last year: her fears, her struggles, and when she made the quiet choice to follow the Light for the rest of her life.

As if in response, a light began to enter Renata's dreamscape like the first rays of dawn: subtle and warm, burning away the shadows and nothingness.

"I a-always wondered if the Light was real."

Selene raised her head. "You knew of the Light?"

"Y-yes." The word came out as a whisper. "My g-grandparents followed th-the Light."

Renata's breathing slowed, and she relaxed in Selene's embrace. "Th-thank you, my l-lady."

Light came over the dreamscape like a sunrise, sending rays of yellow, pink, and orange across the area. At the same time, Renata's head sagged against Selene's chest. It took her a moment to realize Renata was no longer breathing.

"Renata?" Selene whispered. "Renata?" Her breath stuck in her throat as she stared down at her peaceful visage.

Renata was gone.

Selene tightened her hold around Renata and began to rock back and forth as one tear, then another one fell. It was just like when Amara died. For a split second, she wasn't sure if opening her heart was worth all the pain and heartache she was experiencing now. It was as if her very heart had been ripped from her chest and squeezed in a tight grip. She could barely breathe through the pain.

"Renata, Renata," she whispered over and over again.

The dreamscape continued to fill with warm light even as the air grew cold around her. Then, like a wisp, Renata faded away.

Selene leaned forward and covered her face with her hands. Is this what it meant to be a dreamwalker? Her hand curled into a fist next to her chest. "Light," she breathed. "This hurts."

After a moment, Selene staggered to her feet.

She closed her eyes and spread her senses across the dreamscape. Renata was gone, but there was another presence here. Warm and brilliant.

The pain is gone. She is at rest now.

Selene stared down at the spot where Renata's soul had been minutes ago. The black orb encased in chains had disappeared. She was free. And at peace.

Selene marveled at the miracle. "And I helped usher that in. But still . . ." A burning ache filled her throat. The dreamscape was becoming faint all around her. It was time to go. She spread her arms out and transformed into a raven. She flew toward the thin line between the dreamscape and reality. Just as she passed the barrier, Renata's dreamscape faded completely.

Renata lay on the bed where Selene had first found her. There was a soft smile on her face, and her eyes seemed to be focused on something far off, even with the spark of life gone. Selene gently closed the girl's eyes, her own body heavy. What did Renata see at the end? The Light?

She swallowed hard, and her hand began to shake. If only she had been able to repair Renata's mind—

"No," she whispered. "That is not my gift. I am not a mind mender. I am only a dreamwalker."

Selene pushed up off the ground and headed out. She would need to let the head healer know that Renata had passed away and to make arrangements for the body to be burned.

With heavy footsteps, she exited the small room. There would be more joining Renata. Already two men had died, both Ravenwood soldiers. And more were close to death. The pyres would soon be lit. As the only member of House Ravenwood present, she would oversee the burning, then help spread the ashes, as was the custom of the mountain people. She would make sure Amara's ashes joined the others, and together they would fly above the Magyr Mountains.

This was the path of the dreamwalker, and this was her responsibility as head of House Ravenwood. And hard as it was, she would walk it.

24

As Lord Leo and his forces secured the strongholds around the Magyr Mountains, more and more soldiers were brought back to Rook Castle, either for healing or to prepare their bodies to be taken back to Lux Casta. Selene spent her waking hours overseeing the pyres of her own people and providing for those grieving.

When night came, she went to the highest tower, knelt beneath the night sky, and walked the dreamscape, soothing minds, driving away nightmares, bringing light and hope to the souls inside the castle and mountain villages. Still, each day brought death as soldiers passed away. She hated those dreams the most, watching people fade from the dreamscape.

At last the first of the ashes were released across the mountains from the balcony on the north side of Rook Castle. Selene spoke a prayer over the remains, then watched as families let go of their loved ones. When the time came for Amara, Caiaphas joined her at the railing, and together they let her ashes fly into the wind. Selene had already spent her tears, and now she just stood with a heaviness in her chest while her father wiped his eyes.

It was done. Amara was gone. But someday she would see her sister again.

The sun slowly rose above the mountains a couple of days later, its rays spreading light across the trees and cliffs. Selene gripped the stone railing around the topmost tower and pulled herself up, drained. Last night had been different. A shadow had appeared during her dreamwalk, barely visible, but she knew that familiar feeling.

The Dark Lady.

However, instead of engaging her, the Dark Lady seemed to merely be watching her while staying within the shadows of the dream world.

Selene closed her eyes and bowed her head. She knew eventually the Dark Lady would be back. For hundreds of years the dark one had held sway over her family. But now she was a threat to the Dark Lady's power. And sooner or later, the Dark Lady would come for her.

She also hadn't seen the dark priest since her arrival. Her father hadn't seen him either, not since Lady Ragna left. Perhaps he left as well. But she wasn't so sure—

"Selene?"

She glanced back and found her father emerging from the stairs that led up to the tower. "Karl said you were up here."

She turned back toward the mountains, the wind pulling at her cloak and rustling through the trees, a sound much like the sea waves.

He stopped beside her, and they both stood silently at the top of Rook Castle.

"Thank you for what you're doing," he said, breaking the quiet. "I knew the dreamwalking gift was capable of many things, but I never thought of it as a balm. I believe many of our soldiers live because you give them hope during the night."

"It's the least I can do." She thought again of the shadow within the dreamscape and curled her fingers along the stone railing. She had to remain strong. Vigilant. Ready for the Dark Lady, or else those within her care would suffer.

"Lord Leo should be back tonight. Once we hear from him—and if his campaign was successful—we will send a letter to the others."

Selene turned her attention back to her father. "And then we will hold the entire Magyr Mountains." She paused. "Does it seem like it's been too easy?"

"Too easy?"

"Yes, that we're winning. The empire hasn't seemed especially threatening so far."

Her father shook his head. "We've been fortunate that we were able to take Rook Castle. But I don't think Lord Renlar or the people of Shanalona would feel as though it's been easy. The last carrier bird brought a message that they lost a fourth of the refugees at the Hyr River, not to mention most of the men sent to help the people. And the city of Shanalona fell."

Selene let out her breath. "You're right." She had been focusing only on her own lands. The thought of House Vivek's losses brought a tightness to her throat.

"But you're right too, in a way. Two things have happened that I don't think the empire was counting on. First, a new and capable leader rose up to lead House Vivek. Yes, Shanalona fell, but many of the people lived. Second, the coalition. Between the coalition and Lord Leo's forces, we've been able to secure Rook Castle and the center of the continent. The empire might not know that yet. And on top of that, they still haven't been able to stop Lord Damien. His water-walls are most likely the biggest thorn in their side."

Damien.

An image of him filled Selene's mind: his dark hair and piercing blue eyes, that smile that lit up his entire face, the way he smelled, and the warmth of his body. She missed him so much it was almost a physical ache. She hadn't ventured past the mountain borders during her dreamwalks to search for him. Maybe she should, but shame held her back every time she thought about it. She could forgive him, but she couldn't forgive herself, not until she saw him in the real world and could speak to him face-to-face again.

Silence stretched between them, broken by the warble of a bird nearby.

"What do you think Commander Orion will do next?" Selene finally asked.

"I've been wondering that myself. He doesn't seem interested in taking prisoners, which means he will have no qualms using absolute force to take these lands, no matter the loss of life. That makes him a dangerous man."

Selene turned toward her father. "So what do we do?"

"Be ready. Send forces when the alliance needs them. And contact House Rafel. Commander Orion will not let Lord Haruk remain neutral, no matter what he thinks." Caiaphas leaned across the railing. "Stubborn man," he added under his breath.

"And if Lord Haruk continues to refuse and the empire comes for his lands?"

Her father dipped his head. "I'm not sure."

"We wouldn't help them?"

"It's more complicated than that. There's not much we can do if Lord Haruk refuses our help."

"Would he really do that?"

"Like I said, he's stubborn. And there seems to be something holding him back. Whatever it is, it could spell the demise of his land and people."

"What do we do if the empire heads south?"

"I think we try to head them off first with our own forces. But in the end, we might have to let the empire have House Rafel."

"*What?*" Selene spun her head around. "How could you say such a thing?"

"We only have so many soldiers. If we can't stop the empire without massive loss, then we might have to retreat and find another way."

It made sense. And yet how many people would die because of Lord Haruk's decision?

Caiaphas stepped back from the rampart. "Let us hope it doesn't come to that. And in the meantime, you should rest. I've seen how much you've been caring for others. Be sure to care for yourself, or you won't be any good to anyone. We can talk more tonight."

Her father was right. Perhaps she was stretching herself too thin between helping those in the infirmary, overseeing the work at Rook Castle, and dreamwalking every night. With the Dark Lady back, it was only a matter of time before there was a confrontation. And when that happened, she would need all her strength to fight the dark one and keep everyone safe.

25

Raoul Friere stood in the shadows of an alcove, watching the Dominia Empire loot the city of Shanalona as the sun set to the west. Fires burned in the streets, lighting the way for the soldiers to pillage homes and shops, bring back spoils, and eat and drink their fill.

He'd visited Shanalona a handful of times while growing up. The trade route between House Friere and House Vivek was always busy, filling both cities with the bounty of the other. Shanalona was a city of colors and life, of silk and wine, of laughter and debate. In contrast, Ironmond was a fortress with little color and little life, full of ancient military history, a token to its survival in the barren wastelands of the south.

Watching those familiar streets burn left an uneasy feeling in his gut. Was it guilt? Or maybe this was simply not the way he would have taken over Shanalona.

He left his spot by the wall and made his way south, keeping his hood up and following along the edge of the buildings so as not to be observed.

The soldiers in the streets became more boisterous as wine and ale flowed freely. Raucous laughter echoed across the plazas, and the smell of roasting meat filled the air. The revelry would provide the distraction he needed to meet covertly with the officers of House Friere. No one would notice a handful of men missing when there was food and drink to be had.

The plunder of Shanalona would supply the Dominia Empire for a while, but then where would the empire get food enough to feed tens of thousands of soldiers? Especially now that the north was closed to them? The captains of House Friere were already quietly asking those questions, wondering if their own cities and villages would be next. Father didn't hear the grumblings. He was only focused on winning Commander Orion's favor.

Raoul slipped around a corner and continued along a narrow, deserted street. Not that he cared about the villages. The villages existed to provide for House Friere. No, what he cared about was what the empire was taking from his future. If what he had seen here in Shanalona happened within his own lands, there would hardly be anything left once he became grand lord. The land and resources would be as barren as the wastelands around them.

The last few days had given him everything he needed to move forward with his plan. During the Shanalona campaign, it was Friere soldiers who were put on the front lines, ahead of the empire, and many had died. Those who remained were not happy about it. Even tonight there was subtle talk amongst the soldiers of Friere, quiet rumblings that hushed every time a Dominia soldier walked by. But it was there, beneath the surface, like molten rock, words of an uprising.

And he was with them. He wasn't the only one who doubted Commander Orion and his people would share power with those whom they deemed lesser when the war was done.

The farther south in the city he went, the quieter it became. He turned a corner, his body tight. This was not the future he wanted, one where he was lord in title only, with no land, no people, nothing of note. He wanted more. He wanted what should rightfully be his. And the doubts and dismay of the captains and soldiers could work in his favor to gain back his land.

However, they would have to be careful. Making plans inside the enemy territory was akin to tiptoeing across a den of slumbering vipers. One misstep and death would come swiftly and violently. But if there was one thing that burned inside the soul of House Friere, it was a reckless courage that could rival even that of House Merek.

He made his way silently between the buildings until he spotted the shabby old tavern one of the captains had suggested for the secret rendezvous. As the captain had predicted, no one was around. There was nothing worth looting on this side of town. This section of the city was less ostentatious, the home of the common folk.

Raoul smiled. Perfect.

He checked his surroundings once more before approaching the dilapidated building and going inside. The interior was dim, save for a light that glowed from the room past the bar. He made his way around the tables, past the counter, and into the back room. A single lamp hung from the rafters, casting more shadows than light. Six other men sat around a long table, ranging in age from respected elder to a man not much older than Raoul himself.

"Lord Raoul," the men said as they stood and bowed.

"Gentlemen," Raoul said in return.

The captain who had arranged this place spoke first. "I've checked the perimeter twice and have a handful of our men on watch just in case looters come this way. We should be able to speak freely."

"And you trust these men?" Raoul asked, addressing the captain.

"Yes. They are loyal to House Friere and wish to end our alliance with the empire."

"Thank you . . ."

"Marco, from House Tesoro."

He knew the rest of the men gathered: two were generals and the other three were from other lesser houses like Marco's. All six were leaders in their own right and between the seven of them, they had the power to change House Friere's destiny.

"Gentlemen, I'd like a report from each on any intel, troop movements, orders, or rumors," Lord Raoul said, settling into a chair at the head of the table.

"Dissension grows by the day. Our people are becoming angry and bitter," Lord Carone said. "I'm doing what I can to keep their words quiet."

"I think Lord Ivulf forgot about the skirmishes along the border long before the empire crossed the wall," General Manella said. "I pushed for Lord Ivulf to go to the Assembly last harvest so that our grievances could be addressed. Instead, here we are, fighting alongside the very men who harassed our people."

The other lords nodded.

"Lord Ivulf can say all he wants about the spoils of war, but none of it will be ours. It will all go to the empire in the end, mark my words." Lord Carone wagged a finger. "We need to pull out. The sooner, the better."

"I agree," Raoul said, "but we need to do it carefully. If the empire suspects a rebellion, everything will come crashing down around us."

A few of the men bobbed their heads in agreement.

General Manella leaned forward. "We can't do

this by ourselves. Have we considered finding a way to contact the other Great Houses?"

A hush fell over the men. "Yes," Lord Carone finally said. "Although I don't know if any of them will believe us. So it would have to be you, Lord Raoul, a member of House Friere, who approaches the alliance."

"We are in agreement?" A thoughtful expression spread across Raoul's face as the other men nodded. These men were of the highest stature in the lands of House Friere, and here they were, deferring to him. "In that case, I will begin searching for a way to contact the Great Houses."

"What about the daughters of House Ravenwood?" Captain Marco asked. "Perhaps they feel as you do about their house's connection to the empire."

His face darkened. "Lady Amara is either dead or imprisoned."

Captain Marco's eyes grew wide. "Lady Amara?"

"Yes." He couldn't go into detail with these men about her mission and its failure. Even now the thought angered him. Neither had really liked the other, but they did understand each other. They were goal-driven and ambitious. He had admired her fierce desire to go beyond herself and her status. If she had been first daughter, he might have even been tempted to form an alliance.

Instead, she had given her freedom and perhaps her life for the Dominia Empire.

That was not going to happen to him.

"What about Lady Selene?" asked General Manella. "Her connections with House Maris could help us gain an audience with the alliance."

Raoul let out a bitter laugh. Selene had once been a desire of his, and he had fallen for her sultry looks. Even now, there was a part of him that still coveted her and her power. "Perhaps. But her whereabouts are unknown. It would be better for me to wait for a contact opportunity with her and take whatever one comes."

Lord Carone crossed his arms. "Yes. We must tread carefully. This is a dangerous game we're playing."

"But well worth it," General Manella said. "I have no desire to be a slave to the Dominia Empire. Who knows, one of us might be in the next unit sent to the front lines. If this war keeps on going as it has been, there will be no soldiers of Friere left."

The other men murmured in agreement.

Lord Raoul looked around the room. "Then while I seek out a diplomatic contact, the rest of you quietly continue to gather our forces. Be careful, though. One word and we're all dead."

They all nodded.

"Until then . . ."

"May the sun rise on House Friere," they all said in unison.

Raoul held his hand in a fist, a fierce smile on his face. The sun would always rise on House Friere.

26

*D*eath sleep.

The words spread across the camp faster than the wind, bringing fear in their wake. Healers moved from tent to tent, trying every remedy they could to awaken those who had fallen into the death sleep, but nothing seemed to be able to rouse them.

Damien stood beside his own tent as the cold morning mist slowly dissipated along the foothills of the Magyr Mountains, that same dread clutching his own heart. It reminded him of the plague that swept across the Northern Shores almost three years earlier: the fear, the panic, the hopelessness. The only difference was the soldiers were still alive. Those who succumbed to the plague never came back.

Healer Sildaern exited one of the tents nearby, his face tight. His hair, usually kept tied to the crown of his head, had come loose and spilled across his shoulders in a sheet of black.

"Healer Sildaern," Damien called out.

The healer looked up as he approached. The dark circles under his eyes matched his unkempt hair. "Lord Damien," he said wearily.

"Do you have any idea what is causing this?"

Healer Sildaern shook his head. "I've never

seen anything like it, nor read of such a thing either. Everything I try doesn't work. The soldiers keep on sleeping." He ran his fingers through his long hair, disheveling the black strands even more.

"How many are affected?"

He gestured across the sprawling camp. "Twenty so far, counting the one in the tent behind me. I'm ordering those affected to be quarantined. If this continues, we will need to find a way to keep the men nourished. I just hope it doesn't spread, whatever it is."

"So . . ." Damien swallowed. "This isn't another outbreak of the plague?"

Healer Sildaern's expression softened. "No, my lord. The men sleep, but they are not sick. At least for now."

The words comforted Damien only a little. "Let me know if you find out more."

"I will."

Damien watched Healer Sildaern disappear around a row of tents. If it wasn't the plague . . . He ran a hand through his hair. *Death sleep.*

He glanced up at the Magyr Mountains in the distance, still snowcapped and beautiful beneath a cloud-studded sky, thinking of House Ravenwood's lands behind them. Selene had said her family could only enter a person's dreams through touch. But the last few months had proven the gifts they carried were evolving.

Had Lady Ragna and the empire found a way to weaponize the gift of dreaming?

He needed to speak to Lord Renlar and Lady Bryren immediately.

After sending word to Lord Renlar, Damien found Lady Bryren at the far edge of the camp by her wyvern, Shannu, rubbing the great beast's neck. The morning light glinted off Shannu's copper scales, and her reptilian eyes glimmered yellow as she lifted her head and stared at Damien. At her movement, Lady Bryren also turned around.

"Lord Damien, what brings you out this morning?"

"Have you heard?" Shannu's strong musky scent filled his nostrils, and he fought the urge to cough.

She frowned. "Heard what?"

"About the death sleep spreading across the camp."

Her hand dropped from Shannu's back. "What are you talking about? I've just arrived back from a hunting expedition."

As he gave her a quick explanation, her frown deepened, and she let out a low whistle.

"I assume you've just informed Lady Bryren of the situation?" Lord Renlar asked as he approached.

"Yes. Though Healer Sildaern and the others are searching for the cause, I don't believe they will find anything."

"I thought the same thing the moment I heard."

Lady Bryren looked back and forth between the two men. "What do you mean?"

Damien sighed. "A dreamwalker can only enter into a person's dreamscape through physical touch—or so we thought. Selene is now capable of entering the dreamscape even over distance. Either Lady Ragna is near, or she has somehow found a way to stretch her gift beyond her limitations. Possibly by the power of her patron, the Dark Lady."

Lady Bryren narrowed her eyes. "Lady Ragna," she seethed. "I've heard of this Dark Lady but didn't realize that House Ravenwood was involved with her."

Lord Renlar looked at both of them. "If this is a corruption of House Ravenwood's gift, we need to contact Lady Selene as soon as possible. She may be the only one who can stop it."

"But do we know where she is?" Lady Bryren asked.

"A message arrived yesterday that she and Lord Leo have secured not only Rook Castle, but also the Magyr Mountains."

"Then we should send a message."

Damien shook his head. "A letter will not suffice. I need to go to her and explain in person."

"I agree," Lord Renlar said. "If it is Lady Ragna who is causing this, then we need to get you away from here and to Lady Selene. She is the only one who can keep you safe. The last thing we need is for you to fall under this death sleep—or worse, for Lady Ragna to kill you. If you die, the barrier to the north falls."

Lord Renlar was right.

Lady Bryren placed a hand on Shannu's neck. "I need to stay here with my riders for the time being, but Reidin can take you, and Finn can carry your guardian. It's a little over a day's flight from here to Rook Castle."

"And while you're gone, we will start marching toward the Drihst River," Lord Renlar said. "The empire will eventually be heading that direction since the north is now closed. It is time we did the same."

"I'll let Admiral Gerault know so he can assist you. And I will convey that news to Lord Leo, if he is at Rook Castle, so he can mobilize his own troops."

"The rest of my forces should be making their way along the southern continent," Lady Bryren added. "I'll plan on flying out to meet them and guide them to the Drihst River."

"I will also send out scouts," Lord Renlar said. "I'm not sure how close Lady Ragna needs to be in order to use her gift on our men, but if she is near, I will try to flush her out, or at least send her running."

"Then we meet at the Drihst River?" Damien looked at Lord Renlar, then at Lady Bryren.

"Yes," Lord Renlar said. "It will take at least a couple of weeks to reach there by foot."

Lady Bryren nodded. "Same with my people, likely longer. Because of Lord Haruk's stance, we have been forced to travel along the southern coast."

"Then we shall see each other again at the Drihst River in about one month."

"Yes," the other two repeated.

"May the Light be with you both," Damien said with a bow before turning and heading back into camp. One month. In one month, five of the seven Great Houses would converge on the Drihst River in preparation to meet the empire. But would the power of five houses be enough to stop Commander Orion?

Moonlight spread across the mountains and jagged valleys below as the two wyverns began their descent toward Rook Castle over a day later. A timber wolf howled and moments later was answered by its pack.

Damien held on to the horn, fatigue eating away at his muscles. No matter how many times he rode these great beasts, they were nothing like riding a horse. Even now, the heavy musk rising from the red-toned scales filled his nostrils, and the constant up-and-down motion from the wings made him long for firm ground.

The towers of Rook Castle came into view,

dark purple banners rippling in the night air against the pale moonlight. Reidin pointed down below toward the highest tower.

Damien followed the direction and spotted a small figure kneeling at the top of the tower. Who would be up there at such an hour? A watchman? Perhaps. But why was he kneeling? And wearing white—

Wait. That was no watchman. No man for that matter either. His breath hitched in his throat. There was no mistaking that long dark hair and those feminine features.

His heart stopped inside of him.

Selene.

Damien leaned forward, enraptured by the sight of his wife. Kneeling there beside the stone ramparts, dressed in a pale gown, she appeared like a seraph from the ancient stories, the ones who made supplications toward the Light. His breath caught as he considered that maybe she was doing the same.

"Can you land on the ramparts of that tower?" Damien yelled over the wind.

Reidin nodded and motioned his intentions to Finn before tugging the reins slightly to the right. The wyvern adjusted his descent, circling toward the tower below. The wyvern that bore Finn and Taegis continued toward the courtyard.

Selene made no movement as they approached.

She had to hear them; the sound from the wings alone was almost deafening. But she never moved.

Just as they reached the tower, the wyvern pulled up and extended his powerful hind legs toward the rampart. Damien held on to the saddle horn and tightened his grip with his legs. The wyvern clutched the low wall with his talons and settled down like a bird coming to rest on a branch. He tucked back his leathery wings and waited for Reidin's next command.

A cloud began to pass across the moon, sending a dark shadow across the tower. Damien undid his chaps, pulled his leg over the back of the wyvern, and climbed down, careful not to kick the wings nearby.

The wyvern gave out a snort as Reidin dismounted and spoke softly to the creature. Damien bypassed both as he walked toward Selene. She still knelt where he had first seen her, her head bowed.

Damien lifted his hand toward her. "Selene?" he whispered. He took a step closer. "Selene?" he said a bit louder.

The hatch door to the right opened, and a guard scrambled through the gap. He hurried to his feet and pulled out his sword. "Hold it right—Lord Damien?"

Damien's brow furrowed as the guard came into focus. "Karl?"

Karl lowered his blade and bowed. "My lord, we were not expecting you."

"An urgent situation has arisen with the alliance, which required that I come personally to Rook Castle." He looked back over at Selene. "What is going on here?"

Karl sheathed his blade and stepped forward. "Lady Selene has been coming here every night since Rook Castle was secured."

"Why?"

"She comes here to use her gift."

Damien turned back toward Selene as the moonlight reappeared. On closer inspection, he found her eyes closed. "She's dreamwalking? Right now?"

"Yes. Ever since we arrived, she has been dreamwalking every night. At first, it was to comfort those hurt during the battle. Now she comes up here to watch over all of us."

Damien stared at his wife again, warmth spreading across his heart. He slowly walked toward her, the warmth changing into a beautiful ache inside his chest. *Selene, you're finally discovering who you are.*

He reached his hand out, then stopped. She appeared to have become even more beautiful during his absence, and all he wanted to do was draw her to himself. But if she was dreamwalking, then his news, and his embrace, could wait.

His news. He let out a long sigh and ran a hand

through his hair and along his neck. Why must there always be shadows across their lives?

Damien. Her heart whispered his name the moment she sensed him land along the rampart. It took everything inside of her not to burst from the dreamscape the moment she saw him dismount from the back of the wyvern. But she had a job to do, and she would finish it.

She submerged herself back into the latest dream, back into her raven form, and circled above the mountain meadow where a man sat alone in the grass, his face toward the sun. The sky was robin egg blue, with a handful of white puffy clouds. Wild daisies bent their heads as a cool mountain breeze swept across the area. Tall pine trees surrounded the meadow like guardians of nature.

It was a hidden meadow she had found deep within the Magyr Mountains, and now it served as a place where she could pull those who were fading away and give them one last glimpse of life.

The man below was dying. She didn't know his name or where he came from, other than he was part of the coalition and had assisted her father in freeing the Magyr Mountains. Even now she could feel his soul slipping away from his body, and the thought of more life lost broke her own heart.

But she held herself in check. It was not in her power to stop death; she could only soothe those moving on and remind them of the Light, the one who gave them life in the first place.

Selene settled on a branch of a nearby pine tree and closed her eyes. She drew upon her memory of the first time she heard the monks from Baris Abbey chanting, their voices blending in with the wind and the waves. The Chant of Light was sung to remind the people of Nor Esen that even though winter brought darkness and snow, life would come again.

The Light would come again.

She took hold of that memory and then let the music flow from within her into the dream.

The man raised his head, his eyes unfocused as he listened to the chant filling the meadow.

She didn't know if he was a follower of the Light, or just a man trying to make it through life. She only hoped she could remind him of something more, something outside himself, of the one who loved him more than anything else. It was his choice to acknowledge the Light at the end or not. She was simply here to show him the Light one last time.

His soul was almost spent, like a mist evaporating on a warm summer day. As the chants faded into the air, he smiled up at the sky.

Then he was gone.

Selene stared at the empty spot where he had

been sitting moments ago. Then she spread her wings and flew down where the grass was slightly bent and one daisy lay broken on the ground. She landed, changing into her human form.

She fell to her knees and curled her body forward. He wasn't the first one she watched pass away, and he wouldn't be the last. In some ways, bringing peace and reminding people of the Light was harder than searching out secrets and nightmares. In the latter, she had learned to hide away her heart and never feel. But this new way of dreamwalking required her very heart to connect her to the dreamers. There was no hiding, no locking her feelings behind iron doors. The only way she could inspire and comfort others was by using her heart as a doorway into their dreams.

She pressed her forehead to the grass as she spread her hands out, palms up. It was how she ended every dreamwalk. She still didn't have words yet to go with her supplication, but as she had learned from Damien, her gift came from the Light, and so she offered it back to him each night.

A moment later, she stood. Heaviness from her latest walk mingled with longing to see Damien again. She held out her arms, transformed into a raven, and flew up toward the dream barrier.

Seconds later, she sank into her body. She

tucked her hair back and glanced behind her. Damien was standing there, watching her, his face illuminated by the moon's pale light.

Damien.

It had been over a month since she had last seen him fly away with Lady Bryren toward Shanalona. So much had happened in that time.

She rose to her feet just as he closed the space between them. He pulled her in tight, his hands spread along her back, and he whispered in her hair, "I missed you."

She gripped him just as tightly. The last few weeks of using her gift to help those hurt and dying had taken a lot out of her. If not for the Light's strength each time she used her power . . .

"Why are you crying?"

Selene looked up and blinked. Damien placed a hand on her cheek and his thumb paused. "And you have a small scar here."

She reached up and touched the area. The cut Captain Stanton had given her during their fight.

"It appears we both have stories to tell."

"Yes," she whispered. She pressed her face to his chest. "But right now all I can think about is how much I missed you." Lands, how she had missed him. All of him. His strength, his kisses, his voice, and his scent. Her nose wrinkled. There was a hint of wyvern on him. But no matter. He was warm, and he was here.

"I've finally discovered who I am," she said

quietly a minute later. "And what it means to be a dreamwalker. I've been helping others in the dreamscape—feeling their pain, watching as their souls fade away."

"I know." His voice rumbled through his chest. "Karl said that's why you're up here. And that you've been here every night since you arrived."

"It's . . . hard." Her voice cracked. "Harder than anything I've ever done."

"The gifts we have been given take great strength of heart and mind and spirit."

Selene squeezed her eyes shut. Her husband knew that only too well.

After a moment, she raised her head. "Damien?"

"Yes?"

She pulled back but kept her hands on his chest. "I am sorry for what I said that morning. Because of that, I never had the chance to say what I really wanted to." She gazed into his blue eyes. How long had she been waiting to say these words? Why had it taken her so long? "Damien, I love you."

He stilled. She could almost see her words seep into his being and spread, leaving a look of wonder on his face. He placed his hand on her cheek again as his gaze roved across her face, studying her while his thumb played with the corner of her lip. Her heart thumped wildly in her chest. She reached up and brushed a dark lock from his forehead, noting the slender cut just below his eye. So he, too, had a scar.

"Selene." Before she could respond, he tipped her chin and kissed her.

They barely noticed the wyvern lifting up from the ramparts or Karl climbing back down through the hatch. All she knew was that Damien was here with her, and his presence filled her body and mind.

Thank you, Light, for bringing him back to me.

After a minute, he drew away, but he never let her go. Selene placed her head on his shoulder, her face tucked close to his neck, one hand on his chest, the other around his waist. Somewhere far below a cricket chirped.

"Will you continue dreamwalking tonight?" he asked.

"No." She swallowed as she remembered the man's soul fading away. "Tonight was enough. Are you tired?"

"Yes. Until I saw you. It was worth riding all night." His fingers tenderly moved through her hair.

"But why are you here? We received no word of your coming." She felt him stiffen, and a shadow fell across her heart. "Damien?"

"I bring news from the alliance camp. We seem to be under attack."

"Under attack? Are you here to ask for

reinforcements?" But they could have sent a messenger bird for that. Instead, Damien had come here personally.

He turned his face away, the moonlight highlighting the sharp features of his face. "People are falling asleep and not waking up. It's like a death sleep."

"A . . . death sleep," she whispered.

"Yes." He turned back toward her. "And we think it might be the doing of your mother or the Dark Lady. Or both."

Selene stepped back and placed her arms across her stomach. "Did you see her? Did my mother somehow infiltrate your camp?"

"No, not that we're aware of."

"Then how—"

"We think she is doing it without touching them."

Selene spun around and stared out across the mountains. *This . . . this can't be.* Waves of emotions hit her like the crashing of the sea. The euphoria of seeing Damien and of finally speaking those words that had been building up inside her faded as he gave voice to one of her worst fears: Her mother's power had grown.

"Are you sure?" she asked as she reached forward and gripped the ramparts.

"We're not completely certain, but Healer Sildaern said this is no disease, and . . ." She heard him sigh behind her. "It's just like when the

Dark Lady was visiting you back at Northwind Castle."

She could barely swallow past the lump in her throat. "H-how many?"

"Twenty men so far."

It couldn't be. No Ravenwood woman had ever been able to use her gift without touch until her. And so many? When the Dark Lady was stalking her in Nor Esen, only a handful had been affected. Then again, she hadn't been targeting the dreams of others. But her mother would be.

Was that why the Dark Lady had recently been appearing in her dreams? Was she following her, watching her, so she wouldn't sense what her mother was doing?

Selene clenched her hand. "Those affected are in the alliance camp?"

"Yes," Damien said behind her.

She hadn't stretched her power beyond the mountains, but she would try tonight. She turned around. "I'm going to try to awaken them. But it's going to take a lot out of me."

Damien walked toward her and stretched out his hand.

She stared at his fingers, then looked up.

"I will be right there beside you while you sleep."

"Thank you," she whispered as she took his hand. It gave her strength to know he would be there, holding her while she dreamwalked.

He gave her a soft smile. "Let us head into the castle."

"Yes. I've been staying in my old room, but there is space for both of us." *Both of us.* The thought made her stomach tighten and her heart speed up. She never realized how much she would miss sharing a bed with another until Damien was gone.

He leaned over and kissed her cheek. "Lead the way."

27

The moment Selene entered the dreamscape, she took flight in her raven form above Rook Castle and started toward the eastern side of the mountains. This castle, this land, it was not real, but this was how her mind formed her dreamscape, and it would make it easier to search for the alliance camp in the dream world.

She flew high above the trees with the moon lighting her way, the wind rushing past her feathered body as she made her way east. The mountain peaks slipped by beneath her, each one growing smaller until she reached the foothills that surrounded the Magyr Mountains. Then she sensed them: thousands of sleepers nestled together.

She banked to the right and continued toward the sleepers. The feeling of darkness grew as she reached the alliance. Instead of tents spread out, the people appeared as translucent silhouettes gathered along the grassy plains, separate dreams playing within each mind.

Selene touched down at the edge of the gathering and transformed into her human body. The closest soldier sat amongst the grass, his knees drawn up to his chest. Another one lay on his side. Others were rambling along or lying on their backs. Each sleeper was a mind waiting for her to touch and enter.

Selene walked by the translucent bodies, careful not to brush against them, following the feeling tugging her along, following the darkness.

There.

She looked up. Just outside the camp, the shadows grew stronger. She stretched out her senses, searching for any hints of the Dark Lady. Nothing. That didn't mean she wasn't here, though. Or her mother.

Selene transformed again and swooped toward the men lying on the ground where the shadows were strongest. Unlike the other dreamers, they lay on their backs, their wide pitch-black eyes gazing up at the night sky but not really seeing it. It was as if the darkness had seeped into their souls.

Damien was right. It looked exactly like a death sleep.

"Who did this to you?" Selene whispered, vacillating between anger and apprehension. Could she enter their minds and wake them up? What would she find inside?

She knelt down by the closest body, the man's skin pale beneath the moonlight, and reached out her hand. She hesitated, then placed her hand over his heart.

Darkness enveloped her senses. Her own heart thudded in her chest, but she held her fear in check. This was her sphere of power. And she had learned so much over the last few months about the Light, about life, and about her gift.

She could do this. She would bring light into this darkness. She spread out her fingers and concentrated on her palm.

I follow the Light, and his light dwells inside of me.

A small orb appeared, like a ball of white flames. She smiled. Just like Damien's soul.

The light spread across the area, devouring the shadows.

She held her hand higher. *Awaken, sleeper.*

His consciousness began to stir.

The shadows cannot hold you.

Memories began to flash across the horizon of the dreamscape as his mind took hold again.

Come into the light.

He moved as the last shadow faded from the dreamscape. His mind was free again.

With a caw, she transformed into a raven and left his mind, passing the barrier and then into the next dream, awakening each sleeper trapped in the shadows. There was no hint of the Dark Lady or her mother. Perhaps they only ensnared the soldiers, then left. Maybe that was all they could do. The thought encouraged her a little. But it meant she would need to stretch herself even more each night and search for anyone caught in this death sleep.

Exhaustion hit her like a wall as she finished awakening the last soldier. She could barely change into her raven form, and each pump of her wings took all the strength she could muster as she flew toward the dreamscape barrier.

Just as she reached the top, a great wind hit her, tossing her to the left, spinning her through the air. Selene fought against the wind and righted herself. Smoke began to pour into her dreamscape: thick, black, and noxious. The wind spread the smoke until her whole dreamscape was filled, and she could hardly see. Then the screams began.

Before she could react, the dreamscape began to spin around her like a child's top. She was tossed from one dreamscape to the next, with visions of fire and fear. A forest fire, with entire hills blazing. Each dream captured the same image, moving so fast through her mind that she felt like she was going to retch.

I need to get out of here.

Selene fought against the wind and smoke, pressing her already exhausted body to the limits. With one last surge of energy, she lifted her head, spread her wings, and shot upward through the darkness. Her eyes watering and her lungs burning from the toxic fumes, she pushed until she reached the dreamscape barrier.

With one last thrust of her wings, she burst out of the dream world.

. . .

Selene woke with a start and sat up in bed. Her body dripped with sweat as she gasped for air. Human screams still echoed inside her mind. She could even smell the billowing smoke and feel the thick darkness closing in on her. She lifted her hand and pressed her fingers to her forehead. What had just happened?

"Selene?" Damien lay on the bed, blinking back the vestiges of sleep. "Are you all right?"

She pressed a hand to her face. "I don't think so."

At the concerned sound of her voice, he sat up. "What do you mean?"

"The dreamscape . . . something happened." She began to shake. "I found the men caught in the death sleep and freed them, then . . ."

He moved until he was next to her and pulled her to his side. Just being next to him helped her gain control. "Something's happening in the real world."

"Let's start from the beginning. Tell me what you saw."

Selene swallowed. "Fire and smoke. And dreams. Not just from one mind, but many. It was like I couldn't control my power. I kept moving from one dream to another, all of them terrified of this fire."

"Did you recognize anything?"

"No. It looked like a forest fire. Except the

trees . . . they were different from the ones here in the Magyr Mountains or the Northern Shores. I would almost say they were like—" Her eyes widened, and she turned toward Damien. "I think it was the great forest around Surao."

Damien furrowed his brow. "The lands of House Rafel?"

"Yes. I think . . ." She sucked in a quick breath at her next thought. "I think I was seeing the dreams of those who live in the forest."

"Wait, your power reached the people of House Rafel? From here?"

She placed her hands down on the bed to brace herself. Just this evening she wasn't sure if she would be able to reach the alliance camp, and now she may have been able to access the minds and dreams of those who lived even farther away.

"Is that possible?" Damien asked again beside her, his voice incredulous.

"I . . . I think it is." The image the Light showed her that night in the garden of Lux Casta came back, of her flying above the highest part of Rook Castle and the rest of the lands spreading out around her. *"I am everywhere."* That's what the Light said. But did he also show her those images to reveal to her just how far her dreamwalking gift could reach? Could her gift really pass all borders and reach all people? The very thought of such power shook her to her core.

"We need to find out if something has happened down south with House Rafel," she said.

"I agree." Swinging his legs over the side of the bed, he grabbed his clothes from the floor and started pulling on his pants. Selene moved to her own side of the bed and stood. Outside the window, it was already promising to be a beautiful day. Her hands trembled as she reached her changing screens and grabbed a simple dark blue gown and began to tug it over her head. Shock tingled along her limbs. A moment later, a wave of dizziness hit her, and she sagged against the wall.

Strong hands gripped her arms and held her up. "Selene, are you all right?"

"Yes." She shook her head, and her mind cleared again. Damien gazed at her with a worried look. "I'm just shaky from what I saw." *And exhausted from pouring out my power in the dreamscape.*

"I understand." He pulled her close and held her. The warmth from his body brought stability back to her.

She took in a deep breath. "I'm feeling a bit better."

"Are you sure?"

"Yes. Go to my father and tell him what I've told you. He'll be able to send a raven."

"I'll have Karl and one of the maidservants come here to be with you."

Selene nodded. As much as she wanted to go with Damien, the fiery dreams still swirled in the back of her mind. Damien stepped out of the bedroom a moment later, shutting the door softly behind him.

Selene crossed the room and sat back down on the bed. The covers were in disarray from sleep. She bowed her head and gripped her fingers in front of her. If this was real—if within the dreamscape she had seen what was happening to the people of House Rafel—then the Light also knew. Perhaps that's why she had seen it. He'd shown her.

She closed her eyes and began to pray. *Please, Light, help us.*

"It's even worse than we thought." Caiaphas leaned back in his chair in his study. Lord Leo and Lord Elric had been summoned, and now they stood around the desk alongside Damien. Selene stood by the window, her body half-turned, her fingers along the windowsill. "A message arrived from Lady Ragna to Captain Stanton. Apparently word has not reached her yet that we have Rook Castle. That is in our favor. And her message gives us insight into what the empire is doing next. Or"—he glanced at Selene—"has already started."

"What did the message say?" Damien asked.

Caiaphas lifted the note. "In essence, she has

issued an order for Captain Stanton to send most of Ravenwood's forces east to capture Lord Renlar. And she sends a warning that the empire is set on destroying the forest around House Rafel in order to reach the western side of the continent."

"A forest fire," Selene murmured, the nightmares coming back. She saw Damien cast her a worried look through the reflection of the window.

Lord Leo tapped his chin. "Well, we have one advantage. Ravenwood's forces will not be capturing Lord Renlar or his men."

Lord Elric was watching Selene with a curious expression. "Lady Selene, if what you saw is real, then the empire has already set the fire around Surao."

Lord Leo's eyes narrowed. She still wasn't sure what he thought of her gift or if he even trusted her.

Selene ignored him as she turned toward the others. "So what do we do?"

Her father stood. "We need more information. Where is the fire, where is it heading, and how bad is it? And second, we need to find out how this death sleep is occurring. Do you have any thoughts, Selene?"

She shook her head. "I don't know if it is the work of the Dark Lady, Mother, or both. I didn't see or sense either of them last night."

Caiaphas grimaced. "I'm afraid that is one area where we cannot help you."

"I know."

"But we can do something about the fire."

Lord Leo took a step forward. "That could be tricky. I'm not sure if Lord Haruk will let us enter his lands to help him and his people."

Caiaphas nodded. "Without Lord Haruk's permission, we would be trespassing on his lands as much as the empire has."

Damien looked at those gathered around the desk. "It doesn't matter. We can't let those who live in the forest die because of treaty agreements. In fact, the empire might be counting on that. They tried to destroy House Vivek first by killing Lord Rune and Lady Runa, then by going after Lord Renlar and Shanalona. Now they are going after House Rafel. If the empire can isolate each of our houses, then Commander Orion can pick us off one by one. We can't let him do that. I will go. If Lord Haruk becomes angry at our intervention, then I will take the blame."

"What are you saying, Lord Damien?" Lord Leo asked.

"I'm going to go to the forest. If I was able to raise the Hyr River outside my land, maybe I can use my gift over other rivers to put out the fires."

"How would you do that?" Caiaphas asked.

Selene was wondering the same thing. If there was more to her gift, then perhaps there was more to Damien's as well. And what about the other houses? Wasn't it this kind of creative thinking that had brought the powers of House Maris and House Friere together to build the wall between their lands and the Dominia Empire?

"Instead of raising a water-wall," Lord Elric mused, "you would . . . bring the river up, then spread it over the fire?"

"Yes, that's exactly what I'm thinking."

"How would you get there?" Lord Leo asked, crossing his arms.

Damien pressed his fingers along the desk. "I'll ask Reidin to take me via wyvern." He looked at Caiaphas. "Do you have a map of House Rafel's lands?"

"Yes," Selene said, answering for her father. "At least, we might. My mother had elaborate maps of all the lands, if she didn't take them with her."

Caiaphas frowned. "Do you know where she would keep them?"

"Most likely her rooms. Or our training area below the castle."

"Training area?" Elric asked.

Damien raised his eyebrows. "You have a secret training area below Rook Castle?"

That's right, she had never mentioned that to him before. He had only seen her train in a deserted corner of the bailey. Lord Leo opened his mouth to say something, but Selene cut him off. "I'll go now. I'll check Mother's rooms first," she said, noting the hint of discomfort on her father's face at the mention of her mother's rooms.

"I'll speak to Reidin," Damien said. "I'm sure Lady Bryren will understand our need for her consort's help."

Lord Leo nodded. "My brother and I will inform our generals to prepare our men. We will be ready to either reinforce Lord Renlar's forces or head south to Surao. Or both."

Caiaphas glanced at Lord Leo. "I will speak to the coalition and provide you with any supplies and soldiers you may need."

"Thank you, Caiaphas."

Damien straightened up. "Let's meet back here this afternoon so we can plan our next steps."

"Agreed," Lord Leo said.

Everyone split up, each one heading toward his or her errand. Selene turned down the hall where her mother's bedchambers were. A chill went down her spine as she remembered the last time she had visited her mother's rooms. It was there her mother had announced their alliance with the Dominia Empire and given her the assignment to kill Damien.

At the door, she stopped. She wanted nothing more than to run as far as she could away from here. As if in response, her body was already sweating and her heart racing, ready to take flight. Instead, she took a deep breath and gripped the handle, then pressed down on the lever. The door opened without a sound.

The inside of her mother's chambers looked the same as always. Two ornate chairs sat in front of an empty fireplace. Sunlight streamed in through a nearby window. The door to her mother's bedroom was open, revealing the lavish four-poster bed with a dark red coverlet. The door beside her bedroom was shut, the one that led into her mother's private study.

Selene's eyes stole across the room again, settling for a moment on the portrait of Rabanna Ravenwood that hung above the fireplace. There was an air of coldness to her, even in the painting. And her eyes . . .

Selene turned away and shuddered. Hatred as black as death filled Rabanna's gaze. How could her mother not carry the same hatred when she was constantly viewing this portrait?

A shadow moved out of the corner of her eye. Selene spun around and stared at the corner where an ornate wardrobe stood. Nothing. The silence began to seep into her, a cold and deathly quiet.

Remember why you're here.

She straightened up, her resolve returning. Find the collection of maps and take them back to the others and—

Another shadow moved, this time near the

fireplace, followed by a scraping noise within the walls.

A shadow, just like the one in the dreamscape.

The door to the study creaked open.

Selene reached for her blades, only to realize she hadn't strapped on her swords this morning.

Before she could hide, the dark priest stepped out of her mother's study. He lifted his chin, his dark cowl pulled back, revealing his wooly white hair. His watery blue eyes came to rest on her.

For a moment, they simply stared at each other. *He never left.*

Where had he been hiding? In the caverns below? In some cave in the Magyr Mountains? Why hadn't they found him before now?

"Lady Selene," he said at last, his voice raspy.

"Priest," she replied, her voice in control, but her body rushing with adrenaline. "Where have you been?" She snapped her lips shut, years of respect for the dark priest stopping her from saying more.

"There was still work for me to do here." He stepped out of the study and closed the door behind him.

"What work?" Selene asked, her throat tight.

"There is one last message for Ravenwood."

More riddles and prophecies? Like the one about the threat from the north? Selene watched as he crossed toward the door. She needed to go after him; he was a danger to the alliance. But her legs refused to move.

He stopped and turned. "You have nothing to fear from me. I have no issue with you. I serve the Dark Lady, and it is not in her plan for harm to come to you." He pulled up the cowl of his cloak and continued across the room.

"What do you mean?" she called out.

He stopped again. "I see a raven living again in Rook Castle."

"Who?"

"I do not know." He reached the outer door. "That is my last message. There will be no reason to search for me; I will be gone before night falls. Farewell, Lady Selene."

She still couldn't move. Instead, she stood frozen as the dark priest shut the door behind him, leaving her again with the silence.

"I see a raven living again in Rook Castle."

What did he mean? Amara—Selene swallowed hard—wasn't coming back. And Opheliana wasn't a Ravenwood. Did he mean her?

If she had not met Damien and had chosen instead to remain at Rook Castle, this would have been her future as grand lady of Ravenwood. These would have eventually been her quarters, once in a while shared with some consort her mother had chosen for her.

Instead, by the power of the Light, she had broken free.

That thought poured strength and fire back into her body, releasing her body to move. She ran for the door and wrenched it open. Peering down the corridor, she looked for the dark priest. But like a ghost, he had vanished. She stood in the doorway a moment more, torn between pursuing him or letting him go. Finally, she took a step back into her mother's chambers. The dark priest never lied. He would be gone, just like he said. He had delivered his last message, and there was no reason for him to stay. Right now, there were more pressing issues, and people's lives were at stake. She needed to let him go.

Selene turned back inside and headed across the room. She ignored the portrait of Rabanna, ignored the shadows in the corner, and went into her mother's study to search for the maps.

The Dark Lady had no control over her future. But then who was the raven the dark priest spoke of?

She paused in the doorway to the study and glanced down, placing a hand on her middle. Was it possible that someday she would carry the future of Ravenwood? That not all was lost? An image of a little boy with dark hair and dark eyes filled her mind. A new raven, one who would grow up knowing about the Light and why they were given the gift of dreamwalking. A leader for the people of the Magyr Mountains. A new beginning.

She dropped her hand and stared at the wood grain across the surface of the door, a fierce desire taking hold of her. This image—this future—this was worth fighting for.

28

By that afternoon, a thin haze of smoke had slowly spread across the mountain range and around the castle. A dove arrived with the latest imperial movement: The Dominia Empire was making its way south along the lands of House Friere.

Damien placed the message on Caiaphas's desk next to the maps Selene had found. "It would seem Commander Orion is preparing to set up his base near Ironmond before marching across the southern continent after the fire has done its work."

"I hate to say this, but his plan is brilliant," Lord Leo said.

"What?" Elric stared at his brother.

"Leading an army through a forest would not be an easy feat. Let the fire take out not only your enemy, but also the obstacle that prevents you from crossing. Now the path will be clear."

Caiaphas nodded. "He's right. All the more reason to stop the fire. And hopefully by doing so, we gain the favor of House Rafel."

Lord Leo placed a finger on the map, next to the forest. "If House Rafel joins us, and the rest of House Merek's forces are able to meet up with us—and we are able to stop the fires—then we will have a line of defense all along here." His finger slid from the Hyr River, along the eastern side of the Magyr Mountains, and down along the Drihst River.

"And with Damien already near the forest, he can raise the Drihst River," Elric said.

"Maybe." Damien stared at the map, his stomach knotting up inside of him. He hadn't told anyone except Taegis about his blocked power. Selene caught the odd tone in his voice and sent a curious look his direction. Not even she knew. Why? Because of shame? Fear?

"We may not want to raise the river." Lord Leo looked around the desk. "We can't run from the empire forever. If we fight along the Drihst, perhaps we can push the empire back, even back to the wall."

"But with House Friere on the side of the empire, there is no raising the wall again," Elric pointed out.

"Then we fight." Lord Leo clenched his jaw. "We fight until the empire is no more."

There was a knock at the door. Everyone turned as it opened, and Taegis peeked in. "Lord Damien, Reidin is ready to go."

"Thank you, Taegis. I will meet you on the rooftop."

He bowed his head. "Yes, my lord."

"Be careful, Lord Damien," Caiaphas said as he came to stand next to him. "The empire might suspect you will try to intervene with the fire and will be looking for ways to take you out. After all, you are one of the greatest threats with your ability to raise waters."

Damien nodded. "I will be careful." He looked at those gathered. "This is it." He began to roll up the map of Surao to take with him. "I'm not sure where we are going to land yet. We'll have to take a circuitous route around the fire and smoke."

Selene looked out the nearby window. "If there is already this much smoke here in the mountains, I can't imagine how bad the fire is down south."

"I know." Nausea filled his throat as he finished rolling the vellum. How could Commander Orion do such a thing? All the people . . . all the destruction. Then again, this was the same empire famous for annihilating the other side of their borders. Rumor was, there was nothing left but barren wasteland and ruins on the other side of the continent. Would that happen here as well?

He found Selene staring at him when he lifted his head, her eyebrows drawn together.

"May the Light be with you on your journey," Lord Leo said.

"And may he be with you as well, Lord Leo."

Elric clapped a hand on his shoulder. "Be safe, Damien."

"I will, as much as I can be."

When the Luceras brothers left, Damien turned

to Caiaphas. "Please watch over my wife while I am gone. And keep an eye out for the dark priest, in case he has decided not to leave after all. I don't like the idea of him roaming Rook Castle."

"I will. But it must be done diplomatically. There are many followers of the Dark Lady still here." Caiaphas moved away from his desk. "I will give you both a moment alone."

"Thank you, Caiaphas."

The moment the door shut behind him, Selene slumped forward as if she were a puppet cut from a string. She gripped the front of her gown, her other hand on the desk to brace herself. "I don't want you to go, but I know you need to." She looked at him with glistening eyes. "You can save those people. You are one of the strongest, kindest, most extraordinary men I know—"

He never gave her a chance to finish her thought. Instead, he moved in and kissed her, memorizing her smell, her lips, her hair. By the time he was done, her braid had come loose, and they both were breathing hard. "That's to remember me," he said with a smile.

She grinned back. "I like this better than how we last parted." Then her face sobered. "The Light be with you, Damien."

"He is, and he is with you as well. Be strong."

"I will. And I will be watching over your dreams from here."

He kissed her again, this time tenderly, then left

the room. Minutes later, he met Taegis, Reidin, and Finn on the roof of the topmost tower, the same place he had seen Selene dreamwalking the night before. Barely any sky was visible with the smoky cover, and he fought back a cough.

Lady Bryren's consort and his guard were dressed in leather, with the customary kohl around their eyes and hair in wild spikes around their faces. Damien was thankful for Reidin's assistance, especially because by helping him, more time would pass before Reidin would be back with Lady Bryren. However, Damien was definitely tired of riding the great beasts. The people of House Merek were special people indeed to have such a bond with the wild wyverns—and to be able to stand the scales and the smell.

Reidin passed around long wet strips of cloth. "To breathe through," he explained, handing one to Damien. "You don't want to inhale too much smoke."

Damien nodded and tied the cloth around his face. It helped a little. Then he approached the large red wyvern Reidin rode. By now, he needed no assistance tying the leather chaps to his legs.

Reidin settled into the saddle in front of him. "Ready?" he yelled through the wet rag, glancing at Damien over his shoulder.

"Yes," Damien replied, his voice muffled as he made sure the last strap was secure.

Reidin signaled to Finn, who signaled back. Then with a sharp whistle, Reidin's wyvern lifted up on his powerful haunches, spread out his wings, and took to the sky.

When they reached the edge of the forest days later, the devastation was more than Damien had anticipated. Black husks of trees smoldered below as the raging inferno continued to devour the great forest. A wind blew westward, sending the smoke away but also driving the fires toward Surao.

When dusk came, the party landed on an untouched patch of land Reidin had spotted from the air. Finn was careful to clear away all the debris before building a small fire. Food and water were shared, then Damien brought out the map Selene had retrieved from her mother's study. A dozen small rivers and creeks ran through the forest from the eastern edge of the Magyr Mountains. They wouldn't provide much water, but it was a start.

"The fire seems to have started from the northeastern corner, given the burn pattern," Reidin said as he placed another log on the fire.

Damien consulted the map. "What if we start here?" he asked, turning the map around toward Taegis and Reidin, his finger on a small tributary.

Reidin slowly nodded. "If the fire has spread,

there is another small river nearby and a creek, if we need to go that far."

"Then that's where we'll head." Damien carefully rolled the vellum and placed it securely back in his pack, then pulled out a blanket. The others did the same.

Damien folded his arms behind his head as he lay on the ground and gazed up. There were no stars. Even though the smoke had thinned due to the wind, clouds covered the sky. Reidin and Finn talked in low voices nearby, and Taegis settled down next to him.

Damien wasn't ready to sleep yet. His body was fatigued, but his mind was not. All he could think about was what he had seen over the last day. So much destruction. So much death.

"You're thinking about the fires, aren't you?" Taegis asked quietly.

Damien let out a long breath. "Yes."

"There's nothing you can do about it right now. Worrying will only make you feel worse."

"I know." He placed a hand over his heart. But that didn't stop his mind from racing from one thought to the next. What if his power failed him? What if he could only raise the water and not spread it? What if it wasn't enough to save Surao?

"Let me tell you a story," Taegis said, interrupting his thoughts, "since you're clearly still worrying."

Damien let out a weak laugh. How well his guardian knew him.

"There was a time when your father was still learning to control his gift over the waters. It was shortly after the match had been made between your parents. So in order to get to know your mother more—and hopefully impress her—he decided to take her out to one of the small tributaries that ran into the sea near Nor Esen to show her his ability. Of course, as his personal guard, I accompanied them. It was winter, and even though it had been warm recently, there was still a thin sheet of ice across the water.

"When he went to raise the creek, the water bubbled under the ice, then shot up, sending shards of ice and freezing water into the air. And his control was not that good, so not only did the water shoot upward, it went outward as well, drenching all of us.

"Your mother stood there, her arms crossed, shivering, with a stern look on her face. 'I'm not impressed,' she told him flatly. Your father's face turned bright red, even his ears. I'd never seen him so embarrassed before. I couldn't help myself, and I started to laugh."

Damien turned toward Taegis. "You laughed at my parents?"

"Yes. There we were, cold, wet, shivering and uncomfortable, and I burst out laughing. Your father shot me a look that would have killed me on the spot if it could have. A moment later, your mother started to laugh too, her voice like a bell echoing through the trees."

Taegis let out a happy sigh and folded his hands over his chest. "I think that's when your mother first started liking your father. Not because of his name or what he could do, but because he was human, just like the rest of us. Just a man with a heavy burden to carry."

"And how did my father respond?"

"He laughed too. Then we went back to the castle for warm clothes and tea."

"I've never heard this story before."

"It might have been one they kept to themselves. Or—" Taegis chuckled—"maybe your father didn't want you using your power to impress a girl."

"Yeah, well, I didn't have much opportunity to do that." Or had he? When he raised the first part of the river, all he could think about was saving Selene and his men, not about impressing her. But he did remember the look on her face afterward, one of awe and fear. And her words of gratitude.

His and Selene's love story was very different. But for a moment, it was nice to imagine a time when things were innocent and simple and to remember his parents.

Damien sighed and brought his arms back beneath his head. "Thank you, Taegis."

The knots inside of him seemed to have loosened, relaxing both his body and mind. He still had all the problems of tomorrow to face—the fire, raising the water, the empire—but for tonight, it felt good to feel like himself again.

29

The sky was dark as night, but with no stars. Flames reached across the forest like fingers, grabbing hold of the ancient trees and clutching them in a fiery grasp. The rim above the forest appeared like a thin line of molten rock, obscured here and there by dark clouds of smoke. The small river in front of Damien reflected the approaching fire, a mirror of horror.

As the water lapped across his boots, a sound began to spread across the forest, slight at first, then growing like a roar. Moments later, the hellish sound burst across the area, filling the air with smoke, bellows, and flames. The hair along Damien's arms stood on end as he breathed through the soaked cloth across his face.

Dear Light, could he really put out this fire? Certainly not with this small river. He turned back to Taegis. "I'll do what I can here, but we're going to need to be ready to head to the stream over the next hill."

"I'll let Reidin and Finn know." Taegis's reply came out muffled from the wet cloth wrapped around his face. He turned and headed back toward the wyverns and men to convey Damien's message.

A fear unlike any other he had felt before

seeped into his limbs, spreading until it filled his body with a deadly chill. The heat from the inferno filled the air. Beads of sweat formed along his upper lip, and his heart thrashed inside his chest until he could hear his own heartbeat inside his ears.

A hand came to rest on his shoulder moments later. "You can do this," Taegis said.

Damien nodded. That reassuring touch was all he needed to push back his emotions. He crouched down and held his arms out, palms up. He closed his eyes, ignoring everything around him—the heat, the sound, the flames—and concentrated on the river in front of him. His fingers tingled with power, ready to raise the water.

Focus. He breathed in. *Just focus on the river.* He breathed out and imagined the water shooting into the air, then directing the water over the burning forest.

He could do this. He *had* to do this.

He took in a deep breath. One. Two—

Something moved out of the corner of his eye, and a gasp sounded behind him.

Damien held his arms in place and glanced back.

Taegis stared at him, his eyes wide in surprise. His hand reached for the narrow shaft sticking out of his chest.

More arrows came flying from the forest,

ricocheting off the rocks that lined the stream and hitting the water with a splash. One whizzed by Damien's head, leaving a heated trail of pain along his cheek.

Reidin let out a yell in the old tongue as he raised his spear and ran for the forest. Finn followed with his bow. The wyverns lifted off the ground with a roar and took to the sky.

There was another thud. Taegis shuddered and fell to one knee. An arrow protruded from his arm. "My . . . lord," he said as he pulled down the cloth from across his mouth. A trickle of blood appeared in the corner of his lips.

Damien blinked, his body feeling as though it had turned to stone. He knew he needed to run, find shelter from the arrows, but he was unable to move.

This can't be happening.

He had to get them away from the stream and this open area before they were shot at again. The fire lit up Taegis's face, the sweat along his skin glistening in the orange light. Damien came around and brought his hands beneath Taegis's arms, then pulled. Taegis screamed, his voice blending in with the fire's roar.

Light, help me, Damien cried. Panic laced his senses, but he held it back with a firm grip. If he lost control now, he would be no good.

"I'm sorry, my friend, I need to move you."

Taegis gave his head a hard jerk as another

moan escaped his lips. Damien dragged him opposite of the fire and past the tree line, then leaned him against a large fir. The surrounding trees would provide cover from the archers until Reidin and Finn could find them.

"D-Damien."

Damien turned toward Taegis, and his heart stopped. He fell to his knees beside his guardian. Taegis stared at him with shiny eyes. "You need to get . . . to safety."

"I'm not leaving you behind," Damien said, his voice muffled by the cloth.

"You need to li—" Taegis sucked in a pained breath. The red had spread across his entire tunic beneath his leather jerkin. Each heartbeat spilled more blood, and the other arrow still stuck out of his forearm. Even as Damien watched, Taegis paled, and the life in his eyes began to go out.

Damien pulled the cloth away from his mouth so he could speak, and grabbed Taegis's hand. "Taegis, you need to stay with me. We will get away from here and find a healer for you."

"No." His eyes fluttered for a moment, then focused on Damien. "You need . . . to finish. These people need you. You need to survive so you can . . . stop the fires."

"No! I won't lose you." Damien lifted his head, looking for Reidin or Finn so they could leave this place.

Taegis placed his hand over Damien's. "Let . . . me go."

Damien scrunched up his face. "I can't. I can't let go of people."

"You have to. Or . . . you will never . . . heal." Taegis breathed his last, and his body went limp.

"Taegis? No, Taegis!" He gripped Taegis's jerkin in his fists and yelled up at the sky. Smoke swirled around him, growing thicker by the minute.

Finn appeared through the brush. "Lord Damien, we need to leave!"

Damien shook his head, tears prickling his eyes, his lungs burning from the smoke and the grief. *I can't leave him,* his mind screamed. His fingers curled at the thought, and a snarl spread across his lips. "I'm not going without him."

Finn bent down beside Taegis, then shook his head. "He's gone." He ran his hand across Taegis's face and closed the older man's eyes before looking over at Damien. "He wouldn't want you to stay here and die."

Damien lifted his hands, now covered in Taegis's blood. He couldn't think, he couldn't breathe. Taegis couldn't be dead. He was just standing here a moment ago, watching over him, telling him he could do this. They'd laughed together last night as he told stories of the past. It wasn't supposed to end, not like this, not so fast. Taegis was supposed to be around for many years to come and watch House Maris grow, as his father had been unable to do.

Damien stumbled to his feet, his body alternating between hot and cold. Out of the corner of his eye, he could see the flames approaching the stream. "I need to stop the fire," he said in a daze.

"I don't think we have enough time."

You need to finish. Taegis's last words.

"I have to, or else all of this was for nothing."

Damien staggered across the meadow back toward the stream. He felt like he was drunk. His body didn't seem to be able to do what he wanted it to. And his head was filled with cotton. He blinked at the burning tree line in front of him, shook his head, then lifted his hands again before hunching down and preparing to lift the stream. *I need to finish this. For Taegis.*

One. Two. Three.

He shot to his feet and raised his hands, but nothing happened.

What . . . ?

He stared at his palms. What was going on? He couldn't feel the weight of the water, and his fingers weren't tingling with power.

Damien settled back into position and tried to raise the water once more, but nothing happened, not even a wave. The fire was closer, and the smoke was beginning to choke him.

He stared down at his hands through blurry

eyes and clenched them into two tight fists. Why wasn't his power working? It was only a small river! Even if he couldn't manipulate the water, he could at least raise it, even with what little power still remained inside of him.

Reidin appeared at his side and gripped his shoulder. "The fire is too close. We need to retreat."

Somewhere in the back of his mind, he knew Reidin was right. They were out of time and needed to get out of here before the flames caught them. But a stubborn part of him wanted to stay, to do something, *anything,* to keep his mind off of—

No, don't think about it.

A darkness spread across his heart. Somewhere deep inside, a part of him welcomed the idea of the flames taking him so he would no longer feel this piercing emptiness. Everyone he cared about was gone, so why keep on going?

Selene.

He still had Selene.

And he had a future he needed to uphold for his people. But who was he without his power? How could he lead his house if he had lost his gift?

My son, go now.

He knew that voice, the one that had guided him since he was a boy. It broke through his mind, allowing him to take control again of his body. "All right. Let's go."

Damien turned and started for the other side of the clearing. In the shadows, he could see Finn standing where he had left Taegis. An intense wave of heartache washed over him, but he pressed on.

The trees behind them began to burn as the fire jumped the stream. They only had minutes to leave this place. A blast of wind swept across the area, shooting red embers and blazing sticks directly at them.

Fire erupted across his right side, the flames so hot it felt like his skin was melting. Then he smelled it: burning flesh and hair.

Before he could react, Reidin grabbed him and threw him to the ground, smothering out the flames with his cloak.

Damien stared up at him in agony. It felt like someone was skinning him with a white-hot dagger. Darkness filled his vision as Reidin lifted him up and heaved him over the wyvern. He screamed before slumping forward, his right side searing, his lungs burning, his mind numb.

The last thing he saw were trees flashing past him and the fire coming to devour them all.

30

Damien's vision went in and out of darkness. When he was awake, he burned. And when he slept, his mind passed through the painful memories of his past. Ghosts of loved ones and enemies alike haunted him, reminding him that he lived and they did not.

A hand held him securely across the chest as his body moved up and down in a rhythmic pattern. A low whistle blew near his ear, followed by unintelligible words. Then he went down, down, down, until minutes later, there was a thud, and his body became motionless.

There were shouts and words.

"You are not welcome here, wyvern rider."

"I come bearing Lord Damien Maris. He is badly hurt."

"And what is that to us?"

Damien slowly turned his head and tried to open his eyes. Instead, the shifting of his body sent spasms across his back and side, and he let out a sharp cry. Everything hurt: his body, his thoughts, his soul.

There were more words. He wasn't sure how long he lay there or where he even was. Part of him wanted to give in to the darkness that kept beckoning him, but there was a small flickering light inside of him that refused to be extinguished.

Then a low, musical voice spoke. "I will heal him."

"But Lady Ayaka—"

"Take him to the healer's ward."

"Your father will not be pleased."

"I was not given this gift to let people die. Let Father do as he wishes. As for me, I will heal Lord Damien."

More words.

"Yes, my lady."

Damien's body was jostled again, sending him crashing under a barrage of agony, and all went black.

"Such wounds," said a soft feminine voice. A stark breeze blew across his body. He'd barely registered the removal of his clothing. "I've not seen such terrible burns before. Why was he in the forest?"

"The wyvern rider says he was putting out the fires," replied a hoarse voice.

There was a moment of silence. "So House Maris came to our rescue." There was a sigh. "Father, why are we not joining them?"

Cool, gentle hands moved along his skin, soothing the fire burning along his body like a stream of water. Something cold and wet pressed against the inferno across his skin. More words

311

were spoken, but he could barely make them out before he went back under.

More gentle touches. More comforting words. But neither were enough to help his mind. His body embraced the healing touch, but it could not reach his dreams where a fire still burned, memories haunted his mind, and a dark figure hovered. The only thing he could do was curl up inside himself against the pain.

"It's been days. Why hasn't he woken yet?"

"He was burned badly. His body has only just begun to heal," that familiar musical voice replied.

"But would that affect his consciousness?" said another feminine voice.

"It could. We will have to wait and see."

"What about the fires approaching Surao?"

A hand rested on his forehead. "From what I have heard, Lord Damien has already done much for the war against the empire. We are fortunate that he has chosen to help us, despite our stance toward the alliance."

"Do you think he will still help us when he wakes up?" another female voice asked.

There was a pause. "I don't know. What I do know is we don't deserve his help. However, no matter what, I will do what I can to save his life."

Damien slipped back under, back into the cocoon he had created in his mind, away from death, away from memories, away from the dark one who stood in the shadows of his dreams.

"I don't understand," a woman murmured near him. Hands pressed against his side and his middle. "I was able to heal his body. Why isn't he waking up?"

"It is his mind," said a gruff, aged voice.

"What do you mean, Father?"

The cool touch was replaced with papery-thin fingers with a lingering smell of mint. The fingers felt along his cheekbones, then his temples. "It seems Lord Damien is trapped inside his mind. I've seen this before in people who have experienced terrifying events or carry difficult memories."

"What can we do?" the low feminine voice asked.

"Nothing. We can only heal the body, not the mind."

"Then he is gone?"

"Maybe. That is why I didn't want him here. This is not our war."

"But it is our war. Our land is burning, and our people are in danger."

"We have safeguards against the forest fire," said the gruff voice. Damien recognized it now. Lord Haruk Rafel.

"Not according to our scouts," continued the woman. "And refugees arrive in Surao every

313

day. Where will they live if the entire forest burns down? And what happens when the empire arrives at our doorstep?"

"Enough, Ayaka. I let you heal Lord Damien's body. There is nothing more we can do for him. I have already sent a message to the alliance letting them know he is here and for them to retrieve him."

"But what of our gift? What good does it do if we are not healing those who need it?"

"You know our family's position on this matter. Now I need to go."

A minute later, the door shut, and there was a long sigh. "I'm sorry, Father, but I don't agree with you." He heard a rustle of fabric. "I want to use these hands to heal all people—not just our own."

31

Selene emerged from the hatch within the highest tower of Rook Castle and stood with a torch in hand. Smoke and clouds hid the stars and moon above, leaving the area pitch black, save for the light from her torch. A cold wind blew, and the flame flickered for a moment.

She pulled her cloak closed with her free hand and hung the torch in an iron bracket set within the low wall, then knelt down in her usual spot beneath the night sky. With her eyes closed, she let herself submerge into the dreamscape.

Moments later, she spread her black wings across a blue sky. Those beneath her within Rook Castle slept peacefully. She lightly touched their minds, letting her heart flow from within her, checking on their dreams one more time, before soaring along the mountain dreamscape. Fear hung along the southern edge, where the fires burned the forest around Surao.

Help is coming. The Light has not forgotten you.

She wasn't sure if the people of House Rafel could hear the words inside her mind or just sensed her assurance, but she felt their dreams settle. Tomorrow, the people would have to run again, but at least they could sleep tonight.

Then she turned toward the alliance camp. Once again, a hungering darkness shadowed the camp. She spread her wings and surged across the mountain peaks, letting the wind of the dreamscape direct her. She hadn't actually seen the Dark Lady, just hints that she had been there in the dreamscape, leaving behind more victims of the death sleep.

Even now, exhaustion spread across her body. Waking those caught in the death sleep took almost everything out of her, and with each sleeper that was added to the count, she wasn't sure how much longer she could do this.

She shook her head and dove down toward the camp. *I have no choice. They need me. No one else can do this.*

Like the other nights, Selene landed between those caught in the unending dream and drew on the light from within, coaxing the sleepers back to reality.

As the last one returned, she struggled to her feet and looked up to the sky. Beyond the dreamscape, she could feel dawn coming.

She still had one more dream to visit.

Her body trembled as she went into her raven form. It took two tries to finally get back into the air, but once she was up, the cool wind and the thought of seeing Damien brought strength back into her weary body.

To the west she flew, over the dream forest

of Surao. At first, all she could sense were thousands of slumbering minds. She closed her eyes in order to find Damien's dreams apart from those below her. Around and around she soared, a restless feeling settling over her body. She couldn't find Taegis either. Where were they? Why couldn't she reach either of them?

She halted, her eyes wide. Amongst the nebulous dreamscapes was a dark and brooding structure. She flew down and circled the fortress-like tower. What in the lands? She had never seen this before. Her heart sped up. Was this the Dark Lady's doing?

No. As she drew closer, she could feel the soul within. This . . . this was Damien's dreamscape.

House Maris was known for their powerful minds, difficult for her ancestors to penetrate. But from the moment she first touched Damien's dreams, she had always been pulled in as if a door had been flung open only to her.

Until now.

Unlike the rest of the dreams around her, his was a fortress of stone. She flew around the image, searching for a window or a door into his dreamscape. But there was nothing. Damien had trapped his entire being inside himself, and there was no getting in.

Selene transformed into her human form as she landed and placed her hand on the stone.

It was freezing to the touch. She looked up at the fortress of his dreamscape. "Damien, what happened? Why aren't you letting me in?"

She closed her eyes and pressed against the dreamscape. Nothing. She pressed even harder, until both her body and the dreamscape began to shake from the exertion. Finally, she stepped back and dropped her hand. The dreamscape settled back.

Someone laughed nearby, cold and sinister. Selene spun around. The sky grew dark overhead as a chill swept across her body and a familiar ghastly smell filled her nostrils.

She stared out across the dark forest and balled her hands into fists. "You can't have him!" she shouted.

The voice laughed again.

Selene turned back toward Damien's dream and pounded on the wall with her fist. "Damien! Can you hear me?"

Pain. Fear.

The words echoed around the dreamscape.

Trapped.

If Damien was trapped in pain and fear, then this didn't seem like the work of the Dark Lady. The Dark Lady wove nightmares.

Was he doing this to himself?

She was answered only by another laugh. Panic squeezed her heart until every beat ached. "What do I do?" she whispered as she splayed her hand across the wall of Damien's mind. "Light, what do I do?"

Go to him.

How? She didn't even know where he was. He could be anywhere in the forest to the south.

Go to him.

She bowed her head. "All right. I will."

Selene stepped back and spread her arms out. A minute later, she was soaring back toward the dreamscape Rook Castle and toward the barrier between dreams and reality. She could still feel the lingering presence of the Dark Lady, but she wasn't pursuing her. Right now, Damien needed her, wherever he was. And she would go to him, even to the ends of the lands.

A half hour later, Selene was making her way through Rook Castle. Word had reached her that Lady Bryren had arrived at Rook Castle during the night on her journey south to meet with her people.

Selene gathered her skirts up and walked faster. She had to see if Lady Bryren could fly her as far as Surao when she took off again. Surely someone in Surao had seen Damien raise the water and might know where he was.

That is, if he had been able to.

Her stomach clenched tightly, and she placed a hand on her middle. No, he wasn't dead. If he was, his dreamscape would be gone. But why was it locked up?

She dropped her hand. *Focus on what you can do now.*

She found Lady Bryren in the meeting hall with her father. Her hair was a wild mess of copper braids, and there were travel stains along her leather clothing.

Lady Bryren turned. Dark circles matched the kohl beneath her eyes. "Lady Selene, it's a pleasure to see you. Please forgive my appearance. I flew all night to reach here and hope to fly again in a couple of hours. The rest of my forces are currently marching along the southern coast, and I plan to meet up with them. Your father has been telling me about what has happened recently."

Caiaphas narrowed his eyes as he studied Selene's face. "You've seen something in the dreamscape, haven't you?"

"Yes. And I'm glad you're both here."

As she told them what she'd seen, her father's lips tightened more and more. Lady Bryren blinked, her eyes widening as her fatigue vanished. "Wait, you can dreamwalk in anyone's dreams, near or far, without touching them?"

"Yes."

"Have you been able to wake those affected by the death sleep?"

"Yes, we sent a raven to let you know. Did you not receive it?"

Lady Bryren shook her head. "I might have

passed it during my flight here. Then it's true that your gift has grown. I've never heard of a house gift evolving. Fading, yes. But not growing stronger. Such power . . ." Lady Bryren murmured. She looked at Selene with the most serious look she had ever seen. "Be careful, Lady Selene. There is a saying amongst my people: the most powerful wyverns can also be the deadliest, depending on how they are trained. Take care in how you are using your gift."

Selene bowed her head. "You are correct, Lady Bryren. But I have you, my husband, and others to remind me of the Light." However, her mother didn't have such restrictions. The very thought sent a shiver down her spine.

"So you believe Damien is in danger?" Caiaphas asked, leading their conversation back to her dream.

Selene swallowed and turned toward her father. "Yes. Something has happened to him."

"Was he able to put out the fires?"

"I'm not sure."

Lady Bryren spoke up. "Given the amount of smoke, I think the fires are still burning."

"Then it is imperative we find out what happened to Lord Damien. He may be the only one who can stop the fires before they reach Surao."

Her father was right. Damien came first. She wasn't sure yet if and how her mother was spreading the death sleep, but so far, those that succumbed to it only slept. In the real world, people were dying. "Yes. Lady Bryren, will you take me to Surao?"

Her face darkened. "I'm not sure what Lord Haruk will think of our visit. Surao is usually not open to visitors, and especially now I would imagine he has tightened down the borders. That's why my people are crossing the continent along the sea border."

"I could go as an envoy of the alliance. Perhaps House Rafel will join us now that the empire has turned on them."

Lady Bryren raised one eyebrow. "That's a possibility. I would also like to know if my consort is there as well. After all, he was escorting Lord Damien. I suspect if we find Reidin, we will know Lord Damien's whereabouts."

Caiaphas crossed his arms. "If nothing else, this is Lord Haruk's last chance for him and his people. If the fires aren't stopped, his land will be destroyed, and his people will be wiped out by the empire, if they haven't already been wiped out by the fires."

"Then we need to go," Selene said, remembering Damien had once said the same thing. No matter what, they were of the same mind: to save people first and foremost.

"All right." A flame came back into Lady Bryren's eyes. "Be prepared to leave this afternoon. Shannu and the other wyverns are hunting, but when they come back, we'll take off."

"Thank you, Lady Bryren. I'll be ready."

Shortly after the room cleared, Caiaphas joined Selene in the hallway. "Are you going to say good-bye to Opheliana?" he asked as they walked along the cool, dark corridor.

"Yes. I don't know when I'll be back at Rook Castle. I suspect this journey will take me farther than just the forest around Surao."

"It will. We are at war now. Nothing is certain. You came here to free Rook Castle and the mountain people. Now you are being called to free others."

They walked along in silence. The window to the left held a breathtaking view of the Magyr Mountains, despite the haze of smoke clinging to the mountainsides. She would miss this place. Her home.

"Selene . . ." her father said, breaking the stillness between them. She glanced over to find her father had stopped in the middle of the hallway.

A hint of a smile crossed his tired and haggard face. "My dear daughter, you have become what I always believed House Ravenwood could be: dreamwalkers of old. Yes, I wanted to groom you to join the coalition, but more than that, I wanted you to embrace who your ancestors once were:

the protectors and inspirers of these lands. I . . . I'm proud of you."

Tears pricked Selene's eyes. "Thank you, Father," she said, her throat and chest tight with sudden emotion.

He leaned forward and kissed her forehead. "By the way, I think Opheliana is in the gardens with Petur."

Selene laughed, letting out a shaky breath as she started for the gardens. Caiaphas accompanied her down the stairs and out into the warm, dry summer air.

It didn't take long to find the little girl. Her auburn curls hung across her shoulders as she bent down to watch a white butterfly flit amongst the lavender. The innocence and light of her little sister was a sight that would forever remain in Selene's mind.

"Opheliana," her father called out softly.

Ophie raised her head, spotted the two of them, and came running with her arms wide. She hugged Caiaphas first, then Selene. When Selene looked up, she was sure she could see a tear in her father's eye. It seemed that even though Opheliana was not his daughter by blood, she was his daughter by heart.

"Don't worry about Opheliana, I'll watch over her and keep her safe," he said, confirming her thoughts. "And I will keep watch over Rook Castle."

Ophie raised her head, her brow furrowed.

Selene ran her hand along the top of her sister's head, tears once again pricking her eyes. "That's right, Ophie. I need to go. There are people who need my help."

She paused, then nodded, as if she understood more than what Selene was saying. Maybe she did. There was something special about Ophie behind those big amber eyes and lips that never spoke.

She hugged Ophie again, lingering for a moment before pulling away. "The Light will watch over you, Ophie."

Ophie smiled again with a strange, knowing smile, and for one heartbeat, Selene wondered if her little sister already knew the Light.

Petur came walking up with his hat in his hand, his boots covered in dirt. He bowed to Caiaphas and Selene.

Selene smiled at him. "Petur, the garden looks lovely."

"Thank you, my lady. You always loved this place when you were little. Looks like Lady Opheliana is taking after you."

Selene laughed. "I'm not surprised. She's always loved flowers."

"I'm watching her this morning so Maura could have a break. Not that it's hard to look after her; she's the prettiest and sweetest thing here."

Ophie looked over her shoulder and beamed at Petur. The grizzled old gardener smiled back.

"It's almost noon, and I'm sure you still need to pack a few things before you leave," Caiaphas gently reminded her.

"You're right."

She said good-bye one more time to Ophie, then watched Petur take her hand into his own and lead her back into the garden.

While she would always regret manipulating Petur's nightmares during her first dreamwalk, Selene felt an overwhelming calmness spread across her heart. There was a lot of pain from her past here, but in this moment it felt like those cracks across her heart were mending together. It felt like forgiveness.

Thank you, Light.

32

Thousands of tents stretched across the dry wasteland grass, each one housing the combined forces of the Dominia Empire and House Friere. For the last several weeks, the empire continued to move south and west, stopping at Friere villages and towns, demanding food and supplies for their military, and taking it by force when necessary.

Exactly what Raoul and the Friere leaders suspected the empire would do.

And each time Raoul or the generals spoke to Lord Ivulf about it, his father would say it was for everyone's benefit. When the war was won, there would be spoils enough to go around.

Raoul spat on the ground in disgust at the thought, then wiped his mouth. When he'd talked to his father about it again last night, his father had lost his temper. On one hand, it was good to see the fire back in his father. On the other hand, his father only burned for the empire and not for their land or people, proving again why his father should no longer lead House Friere. And why he should.

Raoul headed along the narrow path toward the meeting tent ahead. Another assembly, another display of the empire's power. He had yet to figure out a way to meet with the other Great Houses. So far nothing had presented itself. He would have to try harder.

Raoul slipped into the enormous tent, headed to the left near the guards, and leaned against the canvas wall. There was a hush as Commander Orion scowled at Lady Ragna across the table, his menacing look accentuated by the scar that ran along the left side of his face. From his position, Raoul could see Commander Orion, Lady Ragna, and his father. He had been expecting to hear about their recent victories in battle, but instead it seemed a fight was brewing. He folded his arms and waited to hear why.

"It appears you've failed again, Lady Ragna."

Raoul peered at the grand lady. The only sign that Commander Orion's words troubled her was the tightening of her lips. "The duplicity of my consort is a shock to me as well. If I had known, I would have had Captain Stanton—"

Commander Orion slashed the air with his hand. "Enough. We know now that your husband has ties with this secret coalition—and is perhaps even the leader. In any case, we have lost Rook Castle and the interior of the western continent. Yes, we have secured Shanalona. But we have lost the rest of the north."

Raoul bit back a smile. Lady Ragna was one of the most arrogant women he knew, and while he admired her power and charisma, there was something delicious about seeing her taken down a notch. It also reinforced his decision to accelerate his plans. He had no desire to find House Friere in Ravenwood's place and his future as grand lord swept up further in the empire's campaign.

Lord Ivulf spoke up. "I have received word from one of my messengers from the keep at the Drihst River that most of the eastern forest has burned away. We should be able to march on Surao soon."

"Very good," Commander Orion said. "We will ready our troops and continue our way westward." The talks turned toward the campaign and upcoming march toward Surao. Subtle glances were sent in Lady Ragna's direction, but she ignored them. Raoul wondered why Commander Orion had called out Lady Ragna in front of his men. Was it to put pressure on her? Stir up fear? Use her as an example to remind everyone that as the commander of the imperial army, he knew everything and was in absolute control?

A trickle of fear snaked down Raoul's spine. If that was the case, how long did he and the other collaborators have until their uprising was discovered?

The air grew warmer inside the tent as those gathered continued to plan out the next course of action. Just when Raoul thought the heat and buzz of conversation would put him to sleep, Commander Orion lifted his hand and dismissed the generals. Raoul stepped away from the canvas wall and stretched his body.

"Lady Ragna, I would like to have a word with you."

Raoul lifted his head, curious as to what Commander Orion wanted with Lady Ragna after reprimanding her in front of all of his generals.

Lady Ragna bowed her head. "Of course, Commander Orion."

The other generals were slowly making their way out of the tent, but his father remained. Raoul narrowed his eyes. If his father was staying, then he would stay as well. He sank back against the canvas again.

After the last man left, Commander Orion turned toward Lady Ragna, seeming to ignore him and his father. "How far have you been able to expand your dreamwalking power?"

Dreamwalking? They were discussing House Ravenwood's ability?

"I've been able to expand my distance from the sleepers. But I can only touch up to about twenty sleepers at a time. And it only seems to last a night."

"Or," Commander Orion began, "has someone been waking them?"

The blood drained from Lady Ragna's face. "I-I don't know what you are talking about."

"One of my men has informed me of something interesting. They've heard rumors of a raven woman visiting the dreams of all people across all lands."

Raoul leaned forward, waiting to hear more.

"You gave me the impression that only you were able to use the dreamwalking gift on more than one person and without touch. Only you could do it, with the help of the Dark Lady."

Raoul glanced at Lady Ragna, his eyebrows raised. A silent exchange occurred between Commander Orion and Lady Ragna. His father watched, an intense look on his face.

Raoul knew of the power of House Ravenwood, and how they had been using their dreamwalking gift, but this was completely new. If a dreamwalker could enter multiple minds without touch, that kind of power could be used to steal secrets or even obliterate the empire just with the use of her mind.

"I-I have not heard from my daughter Amara," Lady Ragna said finally.

Raoul scoffed. Lady Ragna didn't really think Amara had that power, did she? Or that she was even alive? If Amara had been caught trying to assassinate Lord Damien, then she was most likely dead. In any case, there was only one Ravenwood who could possibly do such a thing.

Selene Ravenwood.

His fingers twitched at the thought of the eldest

Ravenwood. Her dark beauty, her power. This news only confirmed his belief that his house had allied with the wrong Ravenwood.

"The look on your face says you know who this dreamwalker is," Commander Orion said in a dangerously soft voice. "And it is not Amara, is it?"

Lady Ragna paled even further. "No, it is not," she said in a strangled voice. Raoul couldn't decide if it was from fear or anger.

"Then it seems you have a new mission, Lady Ragna. We need to take out this dreamwalker. If your daughter Selene should choose to use her gift on my soldiers, then we lose. And if we lose"—he stared at her with cold eyes—"you lose."

Lord Ivulf stared at Lady Ragna. In that moment, Raoul could see the wolf in his father's eyes, hungering for blood, ready to turn on his partner.

Lady Ragna lifted her chin, her eyes as cold and dark as those around her. Given Lady Ragna's ability, perhaps Commander Orion should be more careful with his words.

"At the moment, I do not know where Selene is," she said. "But I will consult the Dark Lady. Together, we will hunt for her. And if she can do what you say she can do, perhaps we can use her ability for our own benefit."

"How?"

"I can only enter the mind of a handful of sleepers. But if I can enter Selene's dreamscape, I may be able to access the minds she is connected to. If she is truly capable of what you are saying, then her dreamscape is the gateway to the dreams of the alliance."

A chill went through Raoul's body at the thought of such power, and of the Dark Lady. It was one thing to fight flesh and blood, and another to go against an incorporeal being.

"Make it so, Lady Ragna. Everything, including my most elite men, will be at your disposal to find Lady Selene. Hunt her down, kill her, whatever you need to do to make sure that threat is eliminated."

Lady Ragna bowed her head. "Thank you, Commander Orion."

Raoul's mind spun. He needed to find a way to meet with the alliance—the sooner, the better. Perhaps he could volunteer to lead the capture of Lady Selene or scout for information. If he was able to find Lady Selene, he could share his own secret plans and the desires of his people. And she in turn could convey the request of his house to join the alliance.

Raoul leaned back against the wall, his arms crossed. He needed to be careful. If Lady Ragna's mistakes could be discovered, so could his duplicity.

However, he would much rather be aligned

with Lady Selene than with Lady Ragna. Perhaps this was their destiny. After all, each generation of House Friere and House Ravenwood came together in one way or another. It was about time he made his own alliance with Ravenwood.

33

The southern forest was a landscape of charred trees, burnt land, and death. Barely anything had survived the inferno. In the distance, orange and red flames licked the dark sky as the fire continued its path of destruction toward Surao.

"How much longer?" Selene asked over the beating of Shannu's powerful wings.

"A couple more hours," Lady Bryren yelled back.

For the last few days, Damien was all Selene could think about. Every night, she tried to visit his dreamscape, but it was closed off to her. It was closed off to everything. And his life essence grew dimmer by the day.

"Hold on, Damien," Selene whispered as she clung to the riding horn of her saddle. "I'm coming."

The smoke grew thicker the farther they flew until they finally landed to take a short break. Karl and the other two riders accompanying Lady Bryren landed nearby.

"I can't believe the empire really did this," Lady Bryren said, a fierce scowl across her face. "I flew over this forest countless times while training. It was beautiful, green, and ancient. Now . . ." She shook her head. "Centuries of beauty and growth reduced to ashes. And House Friere and Ravenwood condoned it." She sent a slightly apologetic look toward Selene. "Forgive me for implicating your house."

"No, you are correct. My mother allowed this—or at least she did not try to stop it." Selene looked around at the carnage and burnt grass with a pang in her heart. What if the empire had set the Magyr Mountains on fire? She couldn't imagine her lands being burned down to nothing. And yet that was exactly what happened four hundred years ago, when Rook Castle and House Ravenwood were razed—a razing that the other houses condoned.

She shook her head and spun around to find a place to take care of her personal needs. The past didn't give her house the right to hurt others. Hurt begat hurt. Hatred only begat more hatred. She wouldn't be a part of that.

When Selene returned, the others were eating hard, round biscuits and sharing waterskins. She took her portion while long pieces of cloth were soaked, wrung out, and handed around.

"Try not to breathe in too much smoke," the rider told her as he handed her the cloth. She nodded and tied the scarf around her face. Karl did likewise, then nodded to her.

Back on the wyverns they went and flew up into the air. Flying on a wyvern was similar but different from soaring in her raven form in the dreamscape. As cold, smoky wind blasted across her face, Selene decided she enjoyed her own flying more.

They turned southward, away from the fire, and headed for the city of Surao. As the sun began to set, she spotted tiny lights in the distance. As they drew closer, more and more lights appeared, until it looked like thousands of fireflies dancing in the trees. Right in front of the twinkling forest was a wide grassy meadow filled with tall green grass and hundreds of wildflowers.

A canopy of branches and leaves covered the city of Surao. As they dipped lower, buildings made of smooth wood with oval windows appeared below the natural roof. Greenery of every kind grew along the buildings and streets. Lamps hung on every corner, casting a calm light over the city. Lady Bryren led Shannu to the heart of Surao, where a palace was built into the largest tree she had ever seen. Branches had been carved into stairways and floors, and ivy twisted around the great trunk.

Down below stood a great door leading into the tree-palace, and guards dressed in emerald green converged with spears raised toward the sky.

"Hmph, some welcoming," Lady Bryren said as she directed Shannu to circle in front of the door. The moment they landed, Lady Bryren jumped from her mount and marched toward the guards. They held their spears up threateningly.

"I am Grand Lady Bryren of House Merek. Since when does House Rafel greet us in such a way?"

"You are not the first wyvern to venture into our city," said one of the guards. "And Lord Haruk does not wish for any more."

Not the first wyvern? Selene's hands trembled as she began to undo the clasps along the leather chaps that secured her legs to the wyvern's back. Did that mean Damien was here?

"Who is the wyvern rider? Give me his name."

"Reidin of House Ral," the guard replied.

Lady Bryren crossed her arms. "He is my consort, and I *will* see him. I have also brought Lady Selene of House Ravenwood and Maris."

"Ravenwood?" Whispers swept along the guards, and a few faces paled. Selene narrowed her eyes. What exactly had been shared about her house that would spark such a reaction?

The guard who spoke for the others took a step forward, his spear still raised. "I will let Lord Haruk know that someone has come to retrieve Lord Damien."

Retrieve? Then he was here. Selene came to stand beside Lady Bryren. "I am also here as an envoy of both the alliance of the Great Houses and the coalition. I will speak to Lord Haruk Rafel."

"He doesn't want to meet with you—"

"But I do." Lady Ayaka stepped out from the

ivy archway that covered the main door into the palace. "Lady Bryren, Lady Selene, you are most welcome to Surao."

These were more words than Selene had ever heard Lady Ayaka speak. Back at Rook Castle during the Assembly, the young woman had stood silently beside her father the entire time.

Now, a confidence seemed to fill her as she held her head tall, her dark hair pulled up and held in place with two ornate hair sticks. Her robes were deep green with wide sleeves and white flowers embroidered along the seams.

Lady Bryren smiled. "Lady Ayaka. It is good to see you."

"And you as well, my friend." Lady Ayaka turned her attention to Lady Selene. "Lady Selene, your husband has been in my care. We have been able to heal his body, but he has not yet woken up."

"You mean he sleeps?"

"No." Lady Ayaka shook her head. "It seems he is trapped inside his mind."

"Could you take me to him?"

Lady Ayaka bowed. "I will, but I'm not sure if there is anything you can do for him."

Lady Bryren stepped forward. "There is more to Lady Selene than you know. Take her to Lord Damien, then I will share with you news from the alliance and the coalition. And I wouldn't mind seeing Reidin as well."

Lady Ayaka paused, her emerald eyes studying Selene intensely before she raised her hand and beckoned them forward.

The first guard who had spoken to them looked up. "My lady, your father . . ."

"I will speak to Father, Lin. Thank you for your concern."

He bowed his head and stepped back, finally lowering his spear. The other guards followed suit. "Yes, my lady."

After giving a command to the other riders, Lady Bryren and Selene walked across the circle made of smooth stone to the front entrance. One of the guards opened the door and stood back, his head bowed.

The inside of the tree-palace was even more spectacular than the outside. The interior was carved within the massive tree. The walls were smooth, showing the rings and grains of the wood, while ivy and moss grew naturally along the walls. There were no doors. Rather, curtains of leaves and flowers covered the doorways, allowing light from the outside into the tree-palace. Small alcoves were carved into the sides of the walls and covered with a sheer protective coating to protect the tree from the candles lit inside. The air smelled like a forest: a combination of wood, water, and vegetation.

The center of the tree opened up into a wide area with a circular staircase rising up at least five stories. A grand chandelier made of thin woven metal and leaves hung from the very top, scattering light and shadows along the floors below.

"This way," Lady Ayaka said, moving toward the circular staircase. Up and around they went, past the first two floors, until they reached the third, where Lady Ayaka stepped off and headed back into the tree. Candles twinkled within the tiny alcoves. At the end of the hall, a round window had been carved into the tree.

Two guards were stationed beside an archway covered by hanging ivy. Both men bowed to Lady Ayaka but looked warily at Lady Bryren and Selene.

"They are with me," Lady Ayaka said, then moved the ivy aside. Selene and Lady Bryren followed her in. The room was large, with a port window on the other side of the room, a high ceiling with supporting wooden beams, and a bed against the wall, made of what looked like woven aspen branches. And on the bed . . .

"Damien," Selene whispered, her heart stopping in her chest.

His face was pale, almost matching the aspen bark, his dark hair plastered to his face. Dark stubble graced his jaw, indicating how much time had passed since he had last taken care of his personal needs.

"The wyvern rider Reidin brought Lord Damien here almost a week ago. His back and right side were badly burned. I was able to heal his burns, although they left scars across his body. But his mind . . ."

Selene stepped toward the bed, drawn there by the tether between her and Damien. She touched the top of the blanket covering his body, then his cheek. His skin was cold, so different from his usually warm self. "I don't mind scars. Damien is alive; that's all that matters to me." She longed to draw him into her arms, but there were others around her, and she wasn't sure if she should jostle him.

"Yes, he is alive, but if his mind is shattered, that may be all he is."

His mind . . . shattered . . .

Her whole body froze, her fingers lingering just above his face. What if this was just like Renata? What if something had damaged his mind beyond her ability? Had that dark shadow lingering around his soul finally consumed him entirely?

Selene turned around. "I need to enter his mind and see what is causing him to be like this."

Lady Ayaka frowned. "Enter his mind?"

"Yes, through the dreamscape."

"Wait . . ." Her eyes widened as comprehension dawned on her. "Do you mean . . . ?"

Lady Bryren laid a hand on Lady Ayaka's

arm. "Yes. Lady Selene possesses the ancient Ravenwood gift of dreamwalking. It is a long story, and one I will share with you soon. But for now, let us leave Lady Selene here to use her gift and see if she can awaken Lord Damien."

"A dreamwalker," Lady Ayaka murmured.

"Yes," Lady Bryren said as she slowly turned Lady Ayaka around. "And I would like to see my consort, Reidin."

The ivy fell back across the archway, leaving the room silent except for the soft breathing coming from the bed.

Selene turned back around. "Damien," she whispered, her heart swelling, her hands clasped by her side. Her stomach clenched again as she remembered the nothingness of Renata's mind. Was that what she would find within Damien's dreamscape?

She stepped toward the bed again and carefully lay down on her side close to Damien and stretched her arm across his chest. She could feel his pain even without entering his dreamscape. Ayaka had healed his physical wounds, but there were even deeper ones below the surface and a shadow that haunted his soul.

She took a deep breath, banishing the fear pulsing inside her chest. Fear would only interfere with her gift.

It was time to find out what that shadow was.

She spread her fingers along his arm, curled in close to his body, and closed her eyes. The moment she opened herself up to her power, she was pulled into Damien's dreams.

34

A storm raged across the beach of Damien's mind. The sea crashed against the sand in frothy waves, and a grey sky churned overhead. The dune grass bent back as a gust of wind swept across the area. Moments later, torrential rain fell across the coastline.

Selene shifted into her raven form. She flew upward, searching for his soul. The rain made it almost impossible to see, and each gust of wind slapped her small feathered body like a giant hand.

She righted herself, then swooped down toward the sand and began her search again. Where was he? Where was his soulsphere? The shadow inside of him always appeared near his soul.

She stayed near the dunes, following the curves of the hills. There was no bright light to be seen, no luminescence. Perhaps only his dreams were here, and not him.

Wait.

Selene spotted a small orb resting just beyond the next dune. She stretched out her wings and hastened toward the soul. As she drew closer, a clawing sensation filled her gut. The soulsphere looked nothing like she had remembered. It appeared cold and dull, as if the light had gone out of it.

A tendril of fear coiled around her heart. Could that happen?

Dear Light, please help me, she prayed as she swooped down and changed into her human form. The storm continued to rage around her, but the rain had tapered off to a drizzle. She was drenched; the blue gown she wore clung to her body, while her hair hung in long, wet strands down her back.

"Damien," she whispered as she approached his soul. "What happened to you?"

She knelt down in the sand and brushed her fingers along the orb. There was no warmth, no swirls of life. She reached out her hands and placed them on either side of the soulsphere and drew it to her lap.

She bowed her head. *What do I do? How can I help?*

Remind him.

Remind him of who he is.

She closed her eyes. The soulsphere shuddered. It stretched and extended until moments later a ghost image of Damien lay across her lap. He didn't seem to notice her. He didn't seem to notice anything.

Selene pressed her cheek to his own wet one and brushed his dark hair back with one hand as she wrapped her arm around his middle and held him against herself.

The shadow was here, she could feel it. Like a

gaping hole deep within him. She saw him blink, but he continued to stare into the distance.

"Show me," she whispered. "What is this darkness inside of you?"

"It hurts," he whispered back.

"I'm here. And the Light is here too. You are not alone."

She felt his chest expand with breath, then the dreamscape changed around them, memories and images appearing and disappearing like a kaleidoscope. Selene watched as Damien relived the time of the plague and his parents' deaths. Then Quinn's. Loneliness as icy as a glacier-filled river rushed over her, causing her to shiver from the cold. Pain, questions, and dark thoughts filled the air around them. She tightened her hold on Damien.

An image of an older man appeared, a full beard across his face and Damien's bright blue eyes.

A young Damien held out a ball of fur, motionless in his hand. There were no tears in his eyes, but Selene could see a slight quiver to his lips. "Why do I care so much, Father?"

The man reached over and placed his hand on Damien's shoulder. "Because you want to save everyone, my son. You have a big heart. And it hurts to see the pain in this world. But that's not a weakness. It is your hidden strength. Never forget that."

"But it *is* my weakness," the adult Damien mumbled, his voice rumbling in his chest beneath Selene's hand. "I can't let go."

The dreamscape changed. The sky darkened to a deep black, marked only by the light of a thousand burning trees. Another Damien knelt before a body nearby, his face twisted in anguish and lit orange by the surrounding fire.

Outside the dreamscape, Damien jerked inside her embrace and tried to sit up. "No, no, no, no."

But Selene could feel a connection here, one to the shadow consuming him, so she pressed against his mind and allowed the dream to continue.

"No! I won't lose you!" Damien yelled.

When Selene recognized the body next to Damien, the air left her lungs.

Taegis.

Blood covered the front of his tunic, and the shaft of an arrow pierced his leather jerkin, angled in such a way that there was no question the projectile had gone right through his heart.

Selene's own grief began to pour into the dreamscape, and a flash of lightning lit up the sky. She ducked her head and clutched Damien's spirit form close to her. *No, I can't lose it, not here, not in Damien's dreamscape.*

The memory continued to play out in front of

her. Taegis raised a shaky hand and placed it over Damien's. "Let . . . me go."

Damien collapsed, tears coursing down his face. "I can't. I can't let go of people."

On the bed in Surao, Damien squirmed inside Selene's hold like a wild animal. "Take me from this place, for Light's sake!"

Tears filled her eyes and a deep ache settled in her chest. But she remained, and she held him there too, in the dreamscape. The truth was here, and she needed to hear it if she was going to help her husband.

Taegis blinked, his face filled with tender love even as his soul began to slip away. "You have to. Or . . . you will never . . . heal." He breathed out his last words, and his body went limp.

Inside and outside the dreamscape, both Damiens screamed at the same time.

Selene closed her eyes and placed her head into the crook of his neck. *I understand what I must do now.* With a wave of her free hand, the darkness, the fire, and Taegis disappeared.

Damien panted in her arms, his soul trembling in the dreamscape. His father was right: Damien's greatest gift—far more than his ability to raise water—was his heart. He loved people and had compassion for all. But the strings that connected his heart to people kept him bound to them when they died, tying him down, drowning him.

He had yet to learn how to give those he loved over to the Light.

"Damien," she whispered.

His spirit form turned his head toward her voice.

"Let me show you what I've learned." She brought her hand up and placed her palm across his forehead, then closed her eyes.

From the depths of her soul, she brought forth the night her sister died, the night she encountered the Light. All the pain, the tears, and her fears filled her. A part of Damien connected with her emotions.

"Now let me share what the Light told me." Instead of speaking the words, she let the memory fill her being, the gentle tenor of the Light reaching past her and into Damien's mind.

All things are in my hands. Even your sister. Let them remain there. I will take care of them.

Then she showed him the day when she finally released Amara's ashes into the wind, along with those who died in taking the Magyr Mountains.

The memory faded away.

Selene pulled his soul tight against her chest, both arms wrapped around his ethereal body. "Letting go is not forgetting, and it is not a weakness to love people. But their lives are not yours to carry. They are yours to share. And when they pass on, they remain in the hands of the Light."

"I can't. I miss them too much."

"My dear husband, you are strong. But no one is strong enough. For too long you've been carrying everything by yourself. And even as you've sought the help of the other houses and led the coalition, you've been standing by yourself, depending upon your own strength. It is time for you to let others in to help you, as much as you have helped them."

His body tensed under her hand.

Selene closed her eyes, feeling his struggle. She could provide the words and images, but only the Light could truly reach his heart.

She pressed her palm against his chest as she held him. "You've been trying to do this alone. You need others to fill the hole inside of you, to help you love and teach you to let go. The Light made people to be together, to help each other, to hold each other. Please, let me in." She kissed the nape of his neck. "Let me be the first one to stand with you."

"Selene," he gasped in a tight voice. He raised his hand and placed it over hers, gripping her fingers in a death hold.

Selene didn't answer. She simply held him, letting him wrestle with her words, and with the Light. Sometimes his body would convulse, then he would lay as still as the dead. Selene held on to him as if she were the only thing keeping him from drowning, all the while praying for him.

She wasn't sure how long they sat there in the dreamscape, with nothing but grey around them. It felt like hours. Maybe it was even days. All she knew was she would stay here with him until he was ready.

Finally, she felt something change. Damien sagged against her body, and his head fell to the side, resting on her collarbone. His easy, unlabored breathing reminded her of a person waking up from a broken fever.

"Selene?" he said again, his voice tired.

"I'm still here."

He slowly turned in her arms and reached a hand up to her face. "Thank you . . . for staying with me."

Tears filled her eyes as she gazed into his face. Then Damien lay his head down on her chest, and she felt sleep—true sleep—overtake him, both here in the dreamscape and in the real world.

His fight was over. Whatever had transpired between him and the Light, she knew he had found peace. Another battle might arise; in fact, she knew more battles would arise as the war continued on and death befell more people. But he had a victory now, and that victory would give him the strength to win again. He would always have his heart. But now he wasn't alone. And there was someone greater to whom he could entrust the lives he loved.

"Sleep well, my love." Then Selene closed her own eyes and let herself drift into the dreamscape, still holding Damien in her arms.

35

Light spread across Damien's vision, moving him toward a state of wakefulness. He opened his eyes, feeling more rested than he could remember. Above him, thick wooden beams crisscrossed, holding up the high ceiling. Sunlight poured through a port window to his right, spreading soft rays across the bed on which he lay.

He blinked. The bedframe was made of woven slender aspen branches and logs. A rich woodsy smell hung in the air, coupled with smoke from a fireplace. Something warm moved beside him, and a hand came to rest on his chest.

He glanced over. Selene. Her fingers spread across his bare skin, and she let out a sigh, her eyes tightly closed.

He turned his head back and stared at the aspen branches above him. He remembered everything: the darkness, the pain, and Selene's voice and presence, beckoning him back toward the Light.

And the Light . . .

A blazing light had filled him, burning within him with a purifying fire. Every death, every person he'd held dear, stood before him. And each time the Light asked for them, it hurt. It hurt to let go. Especially Quinn and Taegis.

Damien swallowed. He still missed them. But the aching hole was gone. "Taegis, I did it," he whispered. "I was finally able to let go. I-I'm healing now."

He could almost picture Taegis smiling at him. *It's about time, my friend.*

"Damien?"

Damien looked over to find Selene stirring. She pushed up on her elbow and blinked. Her hair hung around her head in disarray, looking as if it had been tossed by the wind. "Are you awake?"

"Yes."

She ran a hand across her face and pulled back the errant black strands. "How long were we out?"

He frowned. "I'm not sure." He carefully disengaged himself from Selene and sat up. "I don't even know where we are."

"Surao, in the palace of House Rafel."

"House Rafel? When did I get here? *How* did I get here?" Memories came surging back: the forest fire, Taegis being hit by an arrow, his power—

Selene chuckled, her voice like the soft patter of rain.

He glanced over at her with a quizzical look.

She smiled. "It's good to see you awake and speaking. We were so worried."

"Worried?"

"Lady Ayaka said you were in bad shape when

355

Reidin brought you in from the forest. Your whole right side was burned. Lady Ayaka spent days healing you."

Damien looked down at his body. His chest was bare, exposing jagged red lines along the right side of his body from his arm to the lower part of his torso. The three white wave marks along his upper hip were distorted now along the ragged skin. Gone were the smooth lines. His right side was hideously marked.

Feeling exposed, he reached for the blanket, but Selene stopped him. "Don't."

"Don't what?" he said, fighting to pull the blanket from her grasp.

"Don't cover them up. Your scars are proof that you lived." She hesitated, then reached across his lap and gently placed her fingers across the scarred skin. "They are proof that you are still with me."

He sighed, then let go of the blanket. "You're right. I'm still alive." He had that to be grateful for, thanks apparently to Lady Ayaka. And if Selene was fine with the scars, then he would be too. He was alive. And . . .

He took a deep breath and focused on the center of his consciousness, the place where his power resided. It was flowing again, like a river free from a dam.

He looked over at Selene. "Is the forest still on fire?"

Her face sobered. "Yes. At least it was still burning when I came here to help you."

"And how did you get here?"

"I couldn't reach you in the dreamscape. Your mind . . . it was like a fortress, impenetrable. I knew something was wrong, and the Light told me to go to you. Lady Bryren arrived at Rook Castle and brought me here on her way to meet with the rest of the forces from House Merek."

"So you were watching over me."

Selene gave him a soft smile. "Yes. And I'm glad the Light told me to come." She leaned over and kissed him.

That fierce desire to protect came over Damien, causing his power to surge inside of him. Yes, he was whole again. And not just because of his wife, but also because of the Light. And now that his power was his again . . .

Damien drew away. "I have to go. If the fires still burn, I need to stop them." He turned toward his side of the bed, swung his legs around, and stood up. He glanced around the room, searching for his clothes.

"Over there," Selene said, the bed rustling with the sound of her movement. "On the wooden chest in the corner. Your old clothes were burned, so Lady Ayaka had new attire delivered to you."

Damien walked over to the chest to the right of the port window and lifted up the dark blue cloth. The shirt was like a tunic but longer, reaching to his midthigh. There was also a hooded cloak made from the same material but in a darker color, as well as a wide cloth belt, pants, and boots.

He'd seen some of the men of House Rafel wear this clothing and had a partial idea of how to put it on. After donning the pants and tunic, he pulled on the cloak, then took the dark cloth belt and began to wrap it around his middle.

"Here, let me help you," Selene said. After a moment, he felt her secure the cloth in the back.

"There," she said as he turned around. "It looks nice on you."

It was then that Damien realized Selene was still wearing her travel attire.

She must have sensed his perusal and blushed. "I came straight to your room the moment I arrived."

He placed his hands on her shoulders, his heart bursting with love for this woman. "Thank you," he said in a choked voice.

"Of course," she whispered as she placed her hand on his cheek. "You were all I could think about."

He kissed her again and took a step back. "I hate to go."

"No, you must. Go and use your gift."

He let out a long breath and smiled. "I love you." Then he turned and went through the ivy-covered doorway.

The guard standing outside the door led him down two hallways and into what looked like the center of a massive tree with a circular staircase inside. The moment he walked into the meeting hall on the first floor, Lady Bryren and Lady Ayaka stood.

"Lord Damien," Lady Bryren said with wide eyes. "You're awake."

"I am, and I need to leave." He turned toward Lady Ayaka and bowed. "Lady Ayaka, thank you for healing my body. In return, I want to go back to the forest and finish putting out the fires."

She bowed before him. "Lord Damien, it is a small thing I did for you. What you are doing for my people . . . we cannot thank you enough for coming in our time of need. Especially now. Ash is already falling across the city of Surao, and evacuation is underway." She looked up. "We have a defensible space with no trees around the city, but it won't stop a fire like this one; it will only slow it down. If you can stop it, we will be in your debt."

Lady Bryren spoke up. "Reidin is ready to go. He insisted on being the one to take you back out if you went again; that is, if Lady Selene was able to help you. And it appears she has."

"Yes." He touched his temple with his fingers. "She did more than that. Thank you, Lady Bryren, for bringing her to me. Now"—he dropped his hand—"there is no time to waste. Please take me to Reidin."

Lady Bryren led the way out of the room and down the corridor toward a massive door. Outside, where the courtyard would be, was a massive circle of smooth stone with plants, bushes, and tall trees surrounding it. Paths of dirt emerged from the stone and led through the forest city. Small bits of grey fell from an equally grey sky, coating everything in ash.

Lady Bryren stood in the middle of the circle and let out a sharp whistle. A minute went by, then a vast body appeared above and began its descent. The red wyvern lit down on the edge of the stone courtyard, gave a hard shake, and let out a snort.

Reidin dismounted and walked over. "Lord Damien," he said with a dip of his head. "It is good to see you."

Damien clapped him on the shoulder. "And you. Thank you for saving me, and for volunteering to take me out again."

"Anything for a man willing to risk his life for another."

Damien caught a hint of respect on Reidin's face before the man turned and whispered to Lady Bryren, then headed back to his wyvern. Damien followed. After securing himself into the saddle, Reidin shouted in the old tongue, and the wyvern lifted up on its powerful haunches, spread its wings, and took off into the sky.

Up they flew, above the canopy of branches and leaves that covered the city of Surao, past the meadow that surrounded the city, and toward the inferno ahead.

A narrow river appeared down below an hour into their flight, and Reidin started their descent toward it. Damien suspected Reidin had been prepared for this moment, charting out the streams and rivers, believing Damien would wake up. It was humbling to see such faith in this quiet man.

They checked the area for signs of the empire, then touched down when everything looked clear. There was no fear this time as Damien dismounted from the wyvern and came to stand before the river's edge. A confidence beyond anything he had ever experienced filled him, and even the roar of the fire, the heat, and the smoke could not shake him. He had been born for a time like this. He had been gifted to save others. He was a guardian, and by his power, he would do just that. Even for a house that chose to remain outside of the alliance. Light did not shy away from darkness.

Damien took in a deep breath and crouched down. He held his arms out in front of him, palms up, and stared at the fire ahead. The forest glowed with a red intensity under the grey sky.

He could already feel the heat across his face and skin. It was coming for him, a line of destruction and death, less than forty feet away.

He thought of Taegis as he readied his power. "This is for you, my friend." With a shout, he stood, lifting his hands. At his movement, the river shot up. It was as if he had never lost his power.

Strength flowed through his limbs like cool water as he held the river in place. "Light, please aid me. Guide my power. Extinguish these fires."

He imagined the trajectory of the water, then he slowly brought his right palm back. He would use the same motion he used when he moved the waves along the cliffs of Nor Esen.

He pushed his palm forward.

The water bowed, then burst forward across the land. The moment it hit the front wave of flames, a hiss spread across the line, and thick steam rose into the air. Damien kept the flow of water moving, putting all his energy into the movement until the river ran dry.

The fire still burned, but there was a patch gone now.

Reidin was at his side seconds later with a waterskin and a hard biscuit. "I have the next stream marked out," he said as he handed the nourishment to Damien.

Damien simply nodded as he drank deeply from the skin and tore into the biscuit. He was right; Reidin had been prepared the moment he awoke. Perhaps Lady Bryren's belief in him had seeped into her husband.

The two took off minutes later, soaring toward the western side of the fires. With every river, they cautiously checked the area before landing. Not a soldier or scout in sight. Maybe the empire believed they had taken Damien out. If so, that was in their favor.

Damien took his position in front of the water source. He lifted the water and scattered it across the nearest burning trees, putting out what he could before the water ran dry. Then they did it again and again. Days passed and time became a blur between flights, food, and raising the water. He pushed his body and power beyond anything he had done before. In the back of his mind, he knew he would crash, but until that time came, he would give all he had.

The last fire shrank as night fell, and only a small patch of red remained. They landed near a small lake, and Damien took up his place near the water's edge. His vision blurred for a moment. Yes, his energy was almost spent. He forged on, raising his hands and sending the water forward across the fire. Great plumes of steam rose into the night sky.

Everything darkened around him. There was nothing left inside of him. He was completely drained.

As he stumbled back, hands caught him below his arms. Taegis? No. Not Taegis. Taegis was gone.

"Well done, Lord Damien," Reidin said. "Now to head back to Surao."

Damien simply nodded, then his head lolled to the side. He couldn't even walk.

When the darkness took him again, it was different this time. His power was no longer bound inside of him, held back by his past and regrets. This time he had spent it all, every last drop of what he had, and he had finished his mission.

The fires were gone. Surao was saved. Another victory over the empire.

36

L ord Haruk's face was more haggard and aged since the Assembly less than a year ago. The only thing still young about him were his bright green eyes, gazing out from beneath his cowl. Selene sat next to Damien on one side of a small table. Lady Ayaka and her father sat on the other. Lady Bryren had already started her journey south to meet up with the rest of her people. Smoke still hung in the air, but sunlight was beginning to penetrate through the smog.

"Yes, I knew about the betrayal of the Great Houses during the first razing," Lord Haruk said after Selene and Damien shared everything that had happened so far. "It's been passed down to each generation of the Rafel family as a reminder of what we did and a warning to never sign another treaty with the other houses."

Bile filled Selene's mouth, and she clenched her hands beneath the table. He knew? When no one else did until Lord Renlar discovered those hidden records in Shanalona?

Lady Ayaka stared at her father, who avoided her gaze. "Why wasn't I told about this?" she asked in her soft, musical voice.

"It wasn't your time yet."

"Why didn't you speak of this to the other houses?" Damien asked.

"Because each house has their own choice to make in how they hand down their history. Your house"—Lord Haruk looked at Damien—"chose to hide what they had done. Same with House Luceras. House Vivek, never wanting knowledge to die away, wrote down their part and then hid it away. But my house, we would remember, and never repeat the same mistake."

"So you will still remain neutral, even after what the empire has done to your land?"

Lord Haruk sighed, the cowl of his green robe shading his eyes. The room was silent, save for a bird that began to sing outside the open window.

So many ripples from that one choice their houses made hundreds of years ago: her own house's hatred, distrust amongst the other houses, and House Rafel's burden and fears. Did their ancestors ever realize what they put in motion to save themselves from the empire? Had it been worth it?

Lady Ayaka reached a hand over to her father. "Father, if I may, perhaps it is time to put the past in the past and allow for the possibility that each house has changed. And that we need to change as well. We cannot fight the empire alone. Commander Orion is determined to wipe out our house. He has not honored our vow to remain neutral, and now he is killing our people."

Lord Haruk lifted his head. "And how can I trust all of you not to do the same thing? It is this stance that has kept House Rafel safe ever since the first war with the empire. Why would I want to align with houses that backstab and bite one another?"

"I wondered the same thing." Selene lifted her chin. "I have only just come into the knowledge of what happened four hundred years ago. The betrayal of my house and our near annihilation made me wonder if I can truly trust any of you here." She looked around the room, first at Lady Ayaka, then at Damien.

Damien gave her a knowing look and a small nod to continue.

Selene let out a long breath. "But what I do know is that I don't want the empire to win. I don't want to see the mountains I love taken from me. I don't want to see the people I've sworn to protect die. But I also will not sacrifice lives without them knowing what they are giving their lives for."

Her thoughts went back to all those she watched over and held in the dreamscape as their souls moved on. They knew what they were fighting for. And they were willing to pay the price. "I make that promise to all of you as well. My ancestors were given to the empire so the war could be won. They were never asked, never informed. I will not do that to any of you here.

We must all know what we are facing and what it will cost us."

"And what will you do, Lady Selene? Will you refuse to use your power like your ancestor did?"

Selene stiffened. "What do you mean?"

"There was another dreamwalker, one who could walk in the dreams of many. And with her gift, she inspired the Great Houses to push on. But when it was proposed that she use her gift against the empire, she refused. Every house is asked to use their gifts in order to win this war. But what if it takes using your gift contrary to your beliefs? Will you bloody your hands like others have?"

"Lord Haruk, are you proposing that I murder the soldiers of the empire in their sleep?"

He stared back. "If you did, we would win this war tomorrow."

She could finish this war with her gift. Selene steeled herself against her next words. There was a temptation now, a small one, to do just what Lord Haruk was proposing. But it wasn't right. It was twisted and wrong. Such an action would truly make her like her mother. "I will never use my gift in such a way. Even if my house is wiped out again. It might save us now, but in the end it would destroy us—all of us."

"Lady Roswitha Ravenwood believed the same thing. And your house was razed."

"Lady Roswitha Ravenwood?"

"She was grand lady of House Ravenwood during the first war with the empire, and she perished during the razing. I believed, along with everyone else, that House Ravenwood had died out at that time. But evidently her daughter Rabanna survived, carrying on your gift, but twisting it. And it is that corrupted gift that has been passed down since, as we can see by your mother."

She shook her head, still hardly believing that Lord Haruk would propose such a thing. It would start her down the path she had fought so hard to remove herself from and saddle her progeny with the same burden she had carried. "No, I could never do that. It is contrary to the ways of the Light." She held a fist over her heart. "It is against the very reason I have this gift."

For the first time, a shadow of a smile slipped across his lips. "It is good to hear you say such things, Lady Selene."

Selene drew her eyebrows together. Had Lord Haruk been testing her? "Then will you join us?"

Lord Haruk slowly stood. "Lady Selene, you have given me much to think about. Out of all the houses, yours was the one most harmed years ago. I know of your mother's hatred, and your grandmother's. But I can see now it does not run in you. That gives me hope. Still, I need more time."

Damien stood as well. "But we are running out

369

of time. Even now, the empire could be marching on your land."

"I will not make a hasty or emotional decision. Now, please excuse me."

Lord Haruk shuffled toward the doorway, his green robes trailing behind him. The other three watched him leave, no one moving or speaking until the ivy vines had fallen back in place.

"I'm sorry," Lady Ayaka finally said, breaking the silence in the room.

Damien sat back down and placed his hands on top of the table. Selene could tell what he was thinking. It was the very thing he believed in with all his heart: that it would take all seven houses to defeat the empire. But so far, they only had five. And now it appeared House Rafel would not be joining them, even though the empire had clearly turned against them and the alliance had come to their aid.

Selene sighed. She didn't even want to think about how impossible it would be for House Friere to join them as well.

After a moment, Damien looked up. "It is time we left Surao and met up with Lord Renlar and House Luceras. The empire may already be marching west."

Selene's throat tightened as she turned to look at her husband. "But what can we do? The rest of House Merek's forces won't arrive for at least another week, maybe even longer. That leaves only House Luceras, House Vivek, and House Maris to stop the empire's advancement." She shook her head. "That won't be enough."

"It'll have to be. We can at least hold the empire back until reinforcements arrive. And if we are driven as far as the Drihst River, I can try raising it."

"But you're already holding up the Hyr. And you spent so much of your power putting out the forest fires. Can you really raise another river?"

Damien sighed. "I don't know. I'm not sure if any of my ancestors have ever had to use our gift this much, except for Lord Tor Maris, who raised the wall alongside House Friere after the first razing."

"I'm going with you."

Both Selene and Damien turned and stared at Lady Ayaka.

She lifted her hands—palms up—toward them. "It's not much compared to all my house has to offer, but I will not stay back when I could be saving others with my gift."

"But what about your father?" Damien asked.

She shook her head. "I love my father, but this is one area where we do not agree. I hate going against him, and I will not try to convince anyone else to go. But I cannot stand by and let others die in my place."

"I understand," Selene said quietly. "I had to make the same decision: I could adhere to my house and our ways, or I could break away and find out the reason for dreamwalking and use it to help others."

Lady Ayaka sighed. "I hope my father will come to see that there is no peace in standing back while everyone else dies. For too long we have hidden away in our forest. It has made us immune to the sufferings of those outside of our lands—which is sadly ironic, since our gift is to ease the afflictions of others."

Damien spoke up. "I hate going against your father. Are you sure?"

"Yes. He has not forbidden me from leaving. And he hasn't necessarily turned down the alliance. But he can be slow to act and slow to come to a decision. I hope that by going, I can show my father and my people that we need to unite with the other houses and end this war."

Damien smiled. "Then we welcome you, Lady Ayaka, and appreciate the gift you bring."

Lady Ayaka returned his smile. "I hope I can bring healing to many, by the power of the Light."

37

A few hours later, the small group left Surao on horseback. Lady Ayaka rode silently beside Selene. Damien and Karl led the way, while two guards from House Rafel brought up the rear. Lady Ayaka didn't say a word about her meeting with her father, but the strain on her face said it all: He wouldn't stop her, but he didn't approve.

Selene could almost imagine how Lady Ayaka was feeling; she had felt the same way last harvest when she was making her way to Nor Esen. Alone, questioning her decision, but still having a deep conviction that this was the right path.

They traveled eastward through a patch of the great forest that hadn't been touched by the fires. But the subtle smell of smoke and a hazy blue sky above were reminders that the forest had burned, and soon there would be evidence of such. And as night drew near, the first signs of the recent fires began to appear: charred trees, blackened grass and bushes, and a lack of life.

If Lady Ayaka had been quiet before, she was now deathly silent as she took in the destruction. Having recently flown over the burnt forest, Selene knew it only got worse and felt for Lady

Ayaka. Very few words were spoken as they made camp and settled down for the night.

The next morning, they started out again. The destruction of the forest grew even more apparent. Hardly anything green or brown remained, just naked trees over a landscape of black. Selene spotted a tear trickle down Lady Ayaka's face. The day grew warmer as they progressed, and eventually they shed their cloaks and stowed them away. A light breeze pulled at Selene's hair and cooled her heated face. Once again, as night neared, a campsite was made, and blankets were laid out.

Under a starry sky, with her hand in Damien's, Selene walked the dreamscape. She brought peace to those suffering, starting with Lady Ayaka. She touched upon her mind, doing what she could for the young woman, before moving across the lands of her dreamscape. But this time, there was a shadow in the back of her mind.

You could win the war tomorrow if you used your power.

In her raven form, she turned toward the east, where more souls slumbered outside the dreamscape, dreams she had never touched. How easy would it be to cross over to the other side and visit the imperial forces?

Even as she thought on this, an apparition passed by her, a dark image that vaguely looked like another raven. Selene brought her wings up, but the shadow was gone.

Her stomach tensed while her feathers rose across her neck. Was she seeing things?

It appeared again, just outside the corner of her eye.

Selene dove for the ground, and with a twist of her body and feathers, she landed, both of her swords out and ready. She scanned the trees and hills around her, then looked up. Nothing.

She drew in a deep breath and let it out slowly, closing her eyes and spreading her senses throughout the dreamscape. Yes, something—or someone—was definitely here. Its presence felt cold and foreign in her dreamscape. And . . .

Her eyes flew open. It was not the Dark Lady.

Before she could change back into her raven form and fly toward the shadow, the presence vanished.

Selene stood there, pressing against her dreamscape, searching out every corner of the lands her dreams were made of. Nothing. The shadowy raven was gone.

Who could it be if not the Dark Lady? She slowly put her swords away and transformed back into her raven form. Could it be . . . her mother?

A whooshing sensation filled her as if she were falling, even though she was gliding along the wind. If it was her mother, did that mean her mother's gift was more powerful now too? Was the Dark Lady assisting her?

Selene flew toward the edge of the dreamscape. As she approached the thin line in the sky, the shadow appeared again, just outside her vision.

Selene hovered before the barrier and spread out her wings. With a loud *caw,* she pressed against the dreamscape with all her power. The shadowy apparition melted away.

She hovered there a moment more, waiting, searching, before racing toward the barrier and collapsing her dream world behind her.

Selene woke up and stared at the orange and red sky above as day broke across the dead forest. She brought a cold hand to her forehead and ran it down her face.

She reviewed the dreamscape over and over in her mind as they packed up camp and rode eastward, her lips pressed tight, her eyebrows drawn together. Finally Damien drew back and came to ride by her side.

"Something is disturbing you," he said quietly.

"Yes," Selene said just as quietly.

"What is it?"

At first, she wanted to dismiss the shadow as a trick of her mind. Her mother couldn't possibly possess that kind of power. But the more she thought about it, the more she knew she had seen something in the dreamscape, and it scared her. So far, she had avoided the Dark Lady. But now . . .

"There was someone in my dreamscape last night."

Damien turned to look at her. "Last night?"

"Yes. I've felt the Dark Lady before, hovering just at the edge of my dreamscape, but this time, it wasn't her."

"The Dark Lady has been visiting you again?"

"Yes."

"Why didn't you say anything?"

Selene gripped her reins tightly. "At first I wasn't sure it was her. Then it seemed like she was only watching me. And there were so many other things going on that I pushed it to the back of my mind."

"Selene, this is dangerous."

"I know." She looked down as her body swayed gently with the horse's movement. "I knew it wasn't over between us. She is powerful, and I am the first Ravenwood to turn her away. But it wasn't the Dark Lady in my dreamscape last night." Selene caught his gaze. "It was someone else."

"Who else could be in the dreamscape?"

But even before he finished the question, she could see the comprehension dawning on his face. "But why would your mother be in your dreamscape? If Lady Ragna is the one who has been spreading the death sleep, then she can already enter the dreams of our soldiers without touching them. Why would she enter yours?"

Why indeed? Unless . . . Selene paled. "Maybe she's trying to reach more sleepers. So far, the death sleep has only affected twenty or so soldiers. But I can reach almost every mind around me. What if . . ." She could hardly say the words. "What if . . ."

"What if she is trying to tap into your power?"

Selene could hardly breathe. By entering her dreamscape, her mother would have access to every mind she brought into her dreamscape.

"Is that possible?"

She shook her head, dazed. "I don't know. But if it is, then my dreamwalking could open up the alliance to both the Dark Lady and my mother." The very thought made her shudder. "I keep thinking about what Lord Haruk said, that I could win this war tomorrow if I just—"

"No."

She looked over at Damien. "But what if my mother and the Dark Lady are able to destroy the alliance because of my connection to the dreamscape? What if we lose because I wasn't willing to use my power to its full potential?"

"You would lose before you even started." He glanced at her. "Every house gift has a dark side, not just dreamwalking. I could use my power over water to drown people. House Merek could attack anyone from the sky with their connection to the wyverns through their gift of courage. House Vivek could use their wisdom to manipulate all the houses. House Rafel could kill rather than heal. Do you understand? Our gifts have the capacity for both good and evil. We could win the war and still lose everything." He let out a long breath. "That's what happened during the first war. Our ancestors decided it was more important to win than to have integrity. Even my house. And look at where we are now because of that."

Damien was right. Her mother's hatred of what had happened in the past had partially brought on this new war with the empire. And some of the other houses were distrustful and opposed to unity because of it. "You're right." She pressed a hand against her heart. "And yet I feel this tug inside of me to end all of this. Now. Before anything more devastating happens."

"I know. I feel the same way. I'm tired. I'm tired of all the death. I'm tired of fighting. And there is no guarantee we will win. When the empire starts marching westward, there is only House Luceras, a handful of my forces, and Lord Renlar's men to stop them until the rest of House Merek arrives. And even then . . ."

"Should I stop dreamwalking?"

Damien rode on silently. Just when she thought he wasn't going to answer, he spoke. "No. We need your gift."

"But is it worth the risk? What if they are able to take over my dreamscape?"

He looked at her again, his brilliant blue eyes piercing her. "You are strong, Selene Ravenwood Maris. Stronger than the Dark Lady. Stronger than your mother. With your gift, you give us strength and the ability to persevere each night. We will need that in the upcoming battle. It might be all we have."

Selene squeezed her fingers tight around the reins, then dropped them. They needed her. They needed her gift.

But would it be enough?

So far the alliance had seen victories, but they were small, and the alliance had yet to go against the full might of the empire. She lowered her chin, her heart thudding dully inside her chest. Despair washed over her like a frigid wave, leaving her feeling exposed and numb. She wanted to hope, to believe there was light at the end, but all she could see in her mind was a vast sea of imperial forces and the Dark Lady staring at her from beneath her shadowed cowl.

For the first time, she understood the desperate measures the Great Houses took four hundred years ago to drive back the empire. The willingness to sacrifice one house for the many. And yet . . .

She lifted her head. Lady Roswitha Ravenwood never gave in. She refused to use her powers in such a way, even though her daughter, Rabanna, eventually changed House Ravenwood into what it was today.

Could she change it back? Could she stand firm to her convictions like Lady Roswitha and continue on the path of the Light? Even if it might cost her everything and everyone else around her?

Selene stared ahead and took up the reins again. *Light, help us all.*

38

Lady Ragna sat up, a smile upon her lips. Red light spread across the canvas tent as morning dawned upon the imperial camp outside of Boldor.

"Finally," she whispered.

She did it. She passed her own dreamscape and entered Selene's, all without touching her daughter. Thanks to the Dark Lady. It was only a step. So far, Selene's dreamscape was the only one she could enter. But judging by how many minds she sensed within her daughter's dreamscape, what she had heard about Selene's power was true: Selene could reach into other dreams or bring the sleepers into her own dreamscape, all without touching them. And if she could enter Selene's dreamscape, then she could have access to those other dreamers as well.

After dressing and exiting the tent, she found the camp already tearing down and preparing to march again. Those around her gave her a wide berth as they collapsed tents and stored away the supplies needed for the journey.

Lady Ragna ignored them. She knew the rumors they spread about her, that she could kill a man with one touch. It wasn't quite true, but she enjoyed the fear and respect it brought toward her person.

The air was warming up, promising to be another hot day. Not for the first time she wished she were heading back to Rook Castle. She was tired of the brown landscape, sage grass, and prickly bushes. Once the empire took control of the southern lands, they would head into the mountains and take back what rightfully belonged to her.

Her lip curled. And then she would personally deal with her consort, Caiaphas.

A short walk brought her to Ivulf's tent. Already the men nearby were disassembling the tent poles and preparing to stow away his belongings. On the other side, she spotted Ivulf speaking with his son.

Raoul was as tall as Ivulf but thinner, with his thick hair pulled into a topknot at the crown of his head. His face looked like his deceased mother's: full lips and narrow eyes with a shady glint.

Lady Ragna drew near Ivulf. Raoul's eyes darted from his father to her and back again without his father realizing it.

She narrowed her eyes. Raoul had changed over the last few months. The heir to House Friere had always been a brash, headstrong young man, but she had seen the cunning of a serpent in him. Even now, he reminded her of a sand viper watching its prey, calculating, waiting for the right time to strike. A look she was seeing more and more often.

She moved in closer until she could pick out their voices above the commotion around her.

"I will lead a small party along the northern edge of the Omega Wastelands," Raoul said. "I know that area better than anyone, including you, Father."

"I don't think Commander Orion will approve of a scouting party made up of only our men."

Raoul's face grew dark. "Since when does House Friere bow to others?"

"We are not bowing to anyone. The Dominia Empire is our ally."

Raoul's look said otherwise. "Then, as our ally, the empire should be happy to employ our knowledge of these lands." His voice held an undertone of sarcasm.

"I will ask Commander Orion. But be prepared if the commander wishes to send his own men with you and your scouts."

"You know the dangers of the Omega Wastelands. We would lose days teaching imperial scouts how to avoid the sandpits and mirages. That is, if they don't succumb to them first, or any of the other dangers. We wouldn't have to worry about running into any alliance spies or parties in the wastelands. It's the best way to scout out the alliance without being caught."

Ivulf crossed his arms. "You're right. But I still need to speak to Commander Orion. The man is in a foul mood because of the setbacks we have experienced so far."

"I would wager that is more Lady Ragna's fault than our own. Am I right, Lady Ragna?" Raoul's eyes were now pinned on her.

Ivulf turned. "Ragna, I didn't hear you approach."

"I didn't want to interrupt." She chose to ignore Raoul's barb. He might be a viper, but he was young and still naïve in the ways of twisting words.

"Since you already overheard my plan," Raoul said, "maybe I can help you."

Lady Ragna frowned. "How?"

"I might run into your daughter during my surveillance. I seem to remember Commander Orion wanted something done about Lady Selene."

"I didn't realize you were privy to that conversation." Dart'an, she should have been watching her surroundings. She lifted her chin and glared at Raoul. "There is no need. I'm already taking care of my daughter."

"Really?" He lifted an eyebrow.

"Yes. But that is not your concern."

Raoul gave her a mocking bow. "Well then." His head came up. "My father is all yours." He turned with a smirk on his face and walked away.

Yes, Raoul was definitely a viper. Was Ivulf ever like that? Lady Ragna shook her head and turned back to Ivulf. "Raoul is scouting for the empire?"

Lord Ivulf let out a sigh, still watching the departing figure of his son. "Yes. Only a few know their way through the Omega Wastelands, and he's one of them. He will be able to scout out any movement of the alliance along the south."

"Do you think House Rafel has changed their stance?"

Lord Ivulf snickered. "No. Lord Haruk is a stubborn old man who wants to hide inside his trees."

"Perhaps," Lady Ragna murmured. But if threatened enough, Lord Haruk could be pushed into the arms of the alliance. They should have let the forest be and marched along the seacoast.

"So what brought you here this morning?"

Lady Ragna turned back. "We might have a breakthrough with the war."

Lord Ivulf lifted one eyebrow. "Why are you telling me this instead of Commander Orion?"

A flash of anger sparked through her body. "Because we were partners long before we allied with the empire." Had Ivulf really lost his fire? She scanned the area, careful for any listening ears, then leaned forward. "I was able to enter Selene's dreamscape last night."

Lord Ivulf leaned back and blinked. "Without touching her?"

"Yes, the same way it is rumored Selene can as well." A sandy breeze swept across her face. "But I was only able to enter Selene's dreamscape by combining my gift with the Dark Lady's power, just like with the death sleep for the soldiers."

"You think you can trust this being?"

"She's watched over my family for centuries. And she needs me to survive. Belief is what gives the Dark Lady her power. Just as much as she is a patron to my house, we are also her benefactors. Without House Ravenwood, she wouldn't survive."

"Well, taking out Lady Selene would be a boost to the empire. Who knows when she will turn her power on us?"

Lady Ragna twitched. Something had changed with her daughter. What she had witnessed in the dreamscape was Selene comforting the people she brought into her dreamscape, bringing peace and inspiring them. There was no hint of bloodlust or hatred. It reminded her of something her own mother said a long time ago, something about an ancestor before Rabanna. . . .

An hour later, the empire started westward. The efficiency and precision of thousands of soldiers following one command brought a sense of serenity to Lady Ragna. Even with the might and gifts of the Great Houses, the empire couldn't lose. They had more soldiers, more training, more structure.

How could a few gifts and an army of different peoples and cultures stand against the war machine of the Dominia Empire?

39

A red sun rose the morning of the first day of summer as Selene, Damien, Lady Ayaka, and their guards approached the sprawling camp of the alliance along the plains near the Drihst River. Makeshift tents and campsites were scattered across the green hills, while in the distance rose the Magyr Mountains. Banners of blue and white fluttered in the wind, indicating the collection of houses gathered. At the edge of the camp they were greeted by guards from House Luceras and escorted into the base.

Spirals of smoke slipped into the air from campfires, and voices echoed across the hills. A handful of soldiers sat around each fire, preparing food or cleaning their weapons. As the group passed, the soldiers bowed their heads to the lord and ladies.

Near the middle of the camp stood a large tent clearly marked with the sun sigil of House Luceras. One of the guards near the tent flaps lifted the covering and allowed them to enter.

Inside, the tent was spacious enough to house ten men, with a large table in the middle and two beds at the end. Around the table stood Lord Leo, Lord Elric, Caiaphas, and Lord Renlar. All four men looked up at their entrance, then bowed.

Lord Renlar raised his head. "Lord Damien, Lady Selene, you made it—"

"Lady Ayaka?" Lord Elric's eyes widened as he straightened. "We were not expecting you."

Lord Leo's head shot up at the mention of Lady Ayaka, and Selene didn't miss the quick, silent exchange between the two. "Does this mean House Rafel has decided to join us?" he asked, his gaze still on Lady Ayaka.

"No," Lady Ayaka said quietly. "I have come of my own volition to help where I can."

Lord Renlar's face fell. "That is unfortunate."

"Indeed," said Caiaphas. "But your presence is most welcome, Lady Ayaka. Thank you for coming."

As they settled around the table and each house provided updates, Selene chose to remain quiet about her own revelation in the dreamscape. There was no need to stir up fear at the moment.

Just as they turned their attention to battle plans, a messenger rushed in, panting as he leaned forward to catch his breath. "Came . . . as soon . . . as I could." He gulped and stood. "A small party was spotted to the south . . . near the Omega Wastelands . . . wearing the colors of House Friere."

Lord Leo's nostrils flared. "An imperial scouting party?"

"We're not sure," the messenger said, finally catching his breath.

Lord Renlar narrowed his eyes. "Why would a scouting party let themselves be seen?"

"It doesn't matter." Lord Leo slashed the air with his hand. "Send out a company of soldiers and capture them. Scouts, spies, whatever they are, we won't let them go back and report to Commander Orion."

The messenger pressed a fist to his chest and bowed. "Yes, my lord." He spun around and left the tent.

"It seems odd," Lord Renlar said, shaking his head.

"Which part?" Lord Leo asked.

"It's a group wearing the colors of House Friere."

"And?"

"The Omega Wastelands are part of House Friere's territory and very treacherous to cross."

"So? Perhaps they followed the border, or the empire specifically sent those men since they know the land."

"Yes," Lord Renlar said. "Which means they would also know how to hide their appearance amongst the mirages the wastelands are known for. In other words, a Friere scouting party should've never been seen."

Damien tapped his chin with his finger. "Lord Renlar is right."

"It could be a message," Caiaphas said, speaking up for the first time.

"And what message would that be?" Lord Leo crossed his arms.

"Who knows? But it's worth finding out."

"Possible defection?" Damien said.

Lord Leo scowled. "Not possible. Not House Friere. They are not known for covert dealings."

Damien shrugged. "Perhaps things have changed."

Selene detected a hint of optimism in his voice. But for once, she agreed with Lord Leo. Lord Ivulf would never defect, not without her mother, and her mother would rather die than align with the other houses.

Lord Renlar spoke up. "I say we find out more before making any assumptions."

The meeting adjourned, and Selene and Damien left to find Admiral Gerault so Damien could speak to his own people. Selene's stomach continued to twist as she thought about House Friere and her mother. There was no way House Friere would align with them. Not now, not when there was a chance of the empire winning.

So what could possibly be the reason for this scouting party? She shook her head. Perhaps their own scouts had made a mistake. But it still seemed too convenient. She would have to wait until the group was captured and questioned before she had answers.

Dusk had settled across the hills when the company Lord Leo sent arrived with five men in tow, all dressed in the colors of House Friere. One held a stick aloft, a strip of white linen tied to the top. Voices muttered as the men marched through the camp toward the meeting tent.

Selene watched the procession next to a tent with the hood of her cloak over her head. At the whisper of Raoul's presence, her hands clenched. The last time they had spoken, at the Assembly nearly a year ago, Raoul had revealed to her the lurid history of their houses and how she would be his someday.

The thought still made her blood boil.

After the group passed, she silently followed them, like a shadow along the tents. None of the soldiers noticed her movement as twilight spread.

At the meeting tent, the Friere men were ushered in, along with the guards. If the Luceras guards remained, the tent was going to be crowded, making a sudden attack hard to deflect. Maybe that was the opportunity Raoul was looking for.

Selene brushed her hands along the hilts of her swords beneath her cloak. He would find her ready.

She nodded to the guards outside the tent before ducking beneath the flaps and sliding along the canvas siding. On the right side stood Lords Leo, Elric, Renlar, and Damien. On the left were the Friere men and guards. Even with his hood on, Selene spotted Raoul.

His hood fell back, letting his long black hair hang from the topknot at the crown of his head. His usual ostentatious jewelry was gone, save for the gold skull pendant peeking out of his cloak.

"Lord Raoul Friere," Lord Leo said, taking a step forward. His presence seemed to grow as he spoke. Was this another of House Luceras's gifts?

Raoul smirked. "Lord Leo. And little Leo," he said, addressing Elric. If Raoul thought he could get a rise from Elric, he obviously didn't know him.

"Lord Renlar, I presume?" he said, shifting his gaze from Elric to the dark-skinned man in the blue of House Vivek. "Shame what happened to your father and aunt."

Lord Renlar's features hardened at the mention of his family.

Raoul's eyes stopped on the small figure partially hidden behind Lord Leo. "Ah, Lady Ayaka. Is your father here too, or does he know you have left your tree?"

He smirked at the defiant lift of her chin and continued looking around the tent. "Ah, and Lord Damien." He tilted his head to look around Damien, then settled his gaze back on him. "Where is your wife?"

Selene watched the exchange, her hood still hiding her face, the shadows hiding the rest of her.

"She's here."

A smile lit across her face. Of course Damien would know she was here.

Raoul gazed around again, but she melded within the darkness. She would step forward when she decided to. Right now, his very presence made her nauseous.

"I'm here to speak to the alliance," Lord Raoul said, bringing his attention back to those at the table.

"Is that what the white flag means? You're surrendering to us?" Lord Leo asked.

Raoul chuckled softly. "Not quite. I'm here on behalf of my generals and the lesser lords of my people. We wish to join the alliance."

Elric sputtered a laugh while Lord Leo scowled.

"What brought about this change?" Lord Renlar asked, his face guarded.

"There is no change. The people of House Friere never wanted to be part of the empire in the first place. If you recall, many of the skirmishes along the wall occurred on our land, with our people. It was my father's desire to be part of the empire, and no one else's."

"You're only now realizing this?" Lord Leo asked.

Lord Raoul's face darkened. "Perhaps there was a moment where I hoped we might be equal allies. Only a moment."

"Does your father still believe in his alliance with the empire?"

Lord Raoul worked his jaw. "He is drunk on the idea and promises of power."

Damien leaned forward. "And what makes you think the empire isn't going to fulfill their side of the bargain?"

"Because they have already taken from us. Our villages have been pillaged, our men sent to the front lines. We won't have anything left once the empire is finished."

Damien pointed a finger at his own chest. "And what if we lose? What if the empire beats us and takes over all the lands?"

Lord Raoul shrugged. "Even if the empire wins, we still lose. We lose our autonomy, we lose our lands, we lose our freedom. That is why we have chosen to seek out your alliance before it's too late."

"And why should we trust you?" Selene stepped away from the tent wall and passed between the guards as she pulled her hood back.

"Ah, and the dreamwalker finally appears," Lord Raoul murmured, his eyes turning to slits as he studied her.

"Why should we trust you?" she asked again. "I know our two houses better than anyone else here. For years our houses have deceived others. We have bartered in money, blood, and deceit. It was your house that would negotiate the deals for our skills as dreamkillers. And together, House Ravenwood and House Friere conspired to bring the empire to our lands."

"By your own argument, why should those here trust you?" Lord Raoul asked.

"Because I walked away from that life at the cost of exile and accusations of treason, and I revealed the secrets my family had harbored. I have earned the trust of the other houses by my sacrifices and honesty. What do you bring us to earn our trust?"

Lord Raoul glanced around as the other lords and lady nodded. "I bring information," he said finally, his gaze settling back on Selene. "The empire's plans and troop movements."

"Do you plan on publicly coming forward with your alliance with us, or will you and your men work in the shadows?" Lord Renlar asked.

"I believe that we can do the most by working covertly."

Selene snorted. "Of course you do. And if we lose, you can go back to the empire and deny any connections. No, it's not enough. We need something more. An official treaty with us. And"—she drew up level with him and stared into his dark eyes— "if I suspect you are double-crossing us, I will access your mind through your dreams."

A quiet hush fell over the tent.

"Lady Selene," Lady Ayaka began, "I'm not sure if that's necessary . . ."

"I think it wise," Lord Renlar said quietly. "But only if we all agree to it."

"I agree," Damien said next to her. "But we won't do it unless everyone here believes we need to see inside your mind."

Lady Ayaka pressed her lips together, while Lord Leo and Elric affirmed the idea.

"Fine," Raoul said heatedly, his eyes flashing. "And what about my protection? How do I know you won't use the treaty to reveal my defection to the empire?"

"Because it wouldn't be in our best interests," Lord Renlar said. "If the empire doesn't know your house is working with us, then we can use that to our advantage. What can you tell us about the empire's next move?"

Lord Raoul narrowed his eyes as he looked around the tent, first at Selene, then back at Lord Renlar. "Treaty first. Then I'll speak."

Lord Renlar glanced at the others gathered.

"Trust goes both ways," Lady Ayaka said softly. "Lord Raoul just showed he's willing to go first by agreeing to our terms. In turn, we will have to trust that the information he gives us is true."

Lord Leo leaned toward Lord Raoul. "If you turn against us, I will personally present the treaty to your father, even if I have to cut a swath across the entire imperial army to reach him."

Lord Raoul raised an eyebrow. "Then I guess I better fulfill my word." Once again, his eyes darted toward Selene, and she didn't miss the hint of unease. Perhaps that was a sign that he was telling the truth. Or he was just a really good liar.

As the parchment and witnesses were gathered, Selene crossed her arms. She didn't like this at all. She didn't want her name anywhere near Lord Raoul's. But if he truly wanted to align with them, then not only would they have the hidden might of House Friere on their side, they would have House Friere's gift. If they succeeded, Damien and Lord Raoul could raise the wall and seal back the empire.

But if he turned out to be a traitor . . .

Her fingers twitched.

He could still be working for the empire by doing this very thing. Breaking treaties between houses was akin to highest treason, but that didn't stop the other houses from doing that very thing to House Ravenwood during the last imperial war.

But things were different now. And Lord Leo wouldn't be alone. She would be right there with him, making sure Lord Raoul rued the day he turned against the Great Houses.

40

As Selene reached for the flap to the tent she shared with Damien that evening, Lord Leo's voice rang out behind her. "Lord Raoul Friere has asked to see you."

Selene stopped and slowly turned around. She could barely make out Lord Leo's face in the darkness.

"Why?"

"I don't know, other than he said he had private information he would only share with you."

Selene shrugged. "I see no reason to meet with him." She'd had enough of Raoul already.

"I agree. But he was insistent. He says he has a warning for you."

"Why couldn't he tell you? Or the men you've placed around him?"

"He refused."

Selene snorted and turned back to her tent. She already had a lot on her mind between watching over those in the dreamscape and staying alert for the Dark Lady.

"Perhaps you should meet with him."

Selene sighed and dropped the flap. Lord Leo didn't know the history between House Friere and House Ravenwood. If Raoul thought he could kindle any kind of partnership between himself and her, he was sorely mistaken.

On the other hand, Raoul had spent time with her mother recently and might know something about what she'd been seeing in her dreams. Selene pressed her lips together. Any knowledge could help her in the dreamscape.

She turned around again. "Fine, I'll see him."

"I'll go with you."

"Only to the tent. Then I'll speak to him alone."

Lord Leo nodded. "Agreed."

Selene pulled the hood of her cloak up over her head and pressed her hands to the swords strapped to her side, ready for any threat. Then she headed toward Lord Leo.

The two made their way between the tents to the northern side of the base, where House Luceras was in charge of guarding Raoul and his men until they left in the morning. Part of her wished Damien was with her, but he was meeting with Lord Renlar. That, and she wanted to confront Lord Raoul on her own strength, to put clear boundaries between them.

"I've been a bit harsh toward you since the war began."

Lord Leo's abrupt words caught her by surprise, and she didn't know how to respond.

"I'm a man of conviction and honor. Sometimes that can blind me. You are not like the rest of your family."

Again, words escaped her. She opened, then closed her mouth, then opened it again. "Thank you," she finally said. "I've only wished to be assessed by my own merits."

"I understand. But we are also part of our families."

"We are. And so my goal has been to change my family, to redeem our past and return to who we were made to be: dreamwalkers, not dreamkillers."

Lord Leo nodded. "A very noble purpose. And one I didn't see until recently. I know what you've been doing, not just for my men but for all of our forces during the night. Your words about how powerful our dreams can be have haunted my mind ever since you revealed what your family could do back in Lux Casta. Right now, you are keeping the fear of war at bay in the minds of our soldiers. You are giving them strength and a clear mind. That might save many of them on the battlefield."

He glanced over at her with none of his usual mistrust. "I also heard that you comfort those passing through the veil. I thought my gift was powerful, but now I understand the true power of House Ravenwood." His look was sincere. "Lady Selene, I'm glad you're on our side."

His affirmation bolstered her spirit in such a way that it sent her heart soaring. "Thank you, Lord Leo. Your words mean a lot to me. I will continue to help our alliance in any way I can. After all, that is why the Great Houses were given these gifts."

"Indeed. And here we are." He stopped near the edge of the camp. The hills and the Magyr Mountains rose up in the distance beneath a star-studded sky. There were at least twenty guards in House Luceras's colors standing guard along the perimeter. "House Friere's men are housed in the three tents ahead," he said quietly so as not to be overheard. "Raoul is in the one on the right. Be careful, Lady Selene. He is a snake. And if you need help, yell. My men and I are here."

"Thank you. But I don't think you need to worry." She drew back her cloak to reveal her set of twin swords.

He raised his eyebrows. "So I see. Still, we are here if you need anything." He nodded, folded his arms, and took his watch.

Selene stared at the third tent before silently making her way toward the entrance. She blended in with the night, walking along the shadows so as not to be seen or heard. This would be more than a talk between her and Lord Raoul; it would be a positioning of power and respect. And she would start by taking the upper hand.

She reached his tent and slipped between the folds of canvas like a night breeze. A single desk stood against the far wall with a bed on the right. The oil lamp on the desk was lit, spreading warm light around the area, but not quite reaching where Selene stood. Lord Raoul lay on the bed, his hands behind his head, staring at the canvas roof.

Selene studied him, wondering what was going on inside his mind. Why did he approach the alliance? Was he really afraid of the empire? Or was it for more selfish reasons, such as retaining his rights as the leader of House Friere? That made more sense. But was it enough to make him take such a risk?

Perhaps she would ask him. She took a step in his direction, then another, gauging how long it would take him to discover she was here.

He finally turned his head in her direction. "I see you."

Selene stepped out the rest of the way from the shadows. "You only see me because I let you see me. What do you want, Lord Raoul?"

He grinned as he turned and sat up on his bed. "It's good to see you too, Selene."

"It's Lady Selene. Or have you forgotten how to address a member of a Great House?"

He ignored her reprimand. "I summoned you here, but I'm wondering if there is more to your presence. Are you here to find out my true intentions? Reveal my secrets? Kill me with my own fears?" He snickered at his last sentence.

"If I were, you would've never known. But that is not the case. I came because you said you had information. So don't waste my time. Start talking."

Lord Raoul laughed again and stood. "Very well. Rumors of your power have even reached Commander Orion. To be able to walk in the dreams of so many people, and without a single touch. Even your mother was impressed when she heard." He sauntered toward her. "I have information about her I think you'd be interested in. Very interested."

Selene gazed at him with a cold, unflinching stare. "And what would that be?"

"This is one of the reasons I always liked you, Selene. You're strong and unwavering." He lifted his hand and ran a finger along the side of her face.

She slapped his hand away, a snarl spreading across her lips. "You seem to have also forgotten that I am married. And unlike the previous women of House Ravenwood, I love the man I married. I will not betray him with you or anyone else."

Lord Raoul let out a chuckle and dropped his hand. "There is no need to worry, Selene. I'm not here for that." But the spark in his eyes said otherwise.

"Lady Selene," she said through bared teeth. "And if you can't address me as such, I'm leaving."

"Fine, fine. I'll get right to the point. I brought

you here to warn you about your mother. Commander Orion fears you'll use your power on his army. Lady Ragna has been tasked to take you out personally."

"Really?" Selene crossed her arms. "Is that why you're here? At my mother's bidding?" Beneath her elbow, her hand slowly reached toward her sword.

Lord Raoul's demeanor changed. He drew his lips back, and his eyes darkened. "I'm not your mother's lapdog—or anyone else's. Not like my father." He turned and spit on the ground.

Selene was taken aback by Raoul's sudden anger.

"I bow to no one. You want to know why I'm here? My father has forgotten the pride of House Friere. He sold us to the empire and obeys every whim of Commander Orion. I refuse to be that way. We don't need the empire. We are strong enough on our own."

There was no pretense in Raoul's heated words. House Friere's fiery pride was well known throughout the lands. She could see it now, burning in his eyes.

"I know what happened to Amara."

Selene's heart lurched at her sister's name.

"I know that she was sacrificed for the empire. I will not die the same way. That is why I will join your alliance. I will live and die on my own terms, not for anyone else."

Raoul spun away from her and ran a hand along his head to his topknot, then down the long tail. "Enough about me." He turned back around. "We're here to talk about your mother. She's working with the Dark Lady. Right before I left, I heard she was able to enter your dreams."

So it *was* her mother she sensed in her dreamscape. Selene ran her fingers along her temple.

"I can see the truth on your face. You've seen her already. Do you fear your mother and the Dark Lady?"

Selene turned her attention back on Raoul. "They are more formidable than you know—than Commander Orion knows. The Dominia Empire has no idea who they have aligned with."

"We both know the power of your family. What I don't understand is why you haven't used your gift on the empire, especially with what you are capable of now. With that kind of power, you could have already wiped them out."

"And become a monster."

Raoul shrugged, his posture relaxing again. "We're all monsters in the end."

"We don't have to be. And I won't be."

He narrowed his eyes. "Anyway," he said a moment later, "your mother is hoping to use your power in the dreamscape to access the alliance soldiers you harbor in your dreams, with the help of the Dark Lady."

"And how do you know this?"

Raoul laughed. "Because I know Lady Ragna. And you know her as well. You know she'll find a way to do it."

Yes, she would. Her mother would burn the entire world to the ground if she could. But what if there was more? Did her mother have greater ambitions than just tapping into her dreamscape? Maybe this went beyond the alliance, beyond the war. Maybe her mother wanted the same power she possessed. *Light, help us.*

Raoul turned toward his bed. "I wanted to let you know how far your mother has come. And for you to be prepared." He sat down and looked at her. "I believe you're still the stronger Ravenwood, or I wouldn't be here. But you must be ready to fight, Lady Selene. It won't matter if the alliance wins the upcoming battle if you don't defeat your mother and the Dark Lady. If they win, we all lose."

Selene's middle tightened at Raoul's words. He was right. A familiar weight settled across her body. The weight of the future, of her destiny, of everyone's fate. She already knew how strong her mother and the Dark Lady were individually. How could she face them together? "I will think over what you have shared."

He gave her a dismissive wave as he lay back down and stared at the canvas roof. "I want to win. You're the better bet."

Selene turned and left the tent. She already suspected her mother had entered her dreamscape, but to hear it plainly from Raoul made it real. The question was, what should she do next?

No, she already had her answer. She would continue to guard the dreams of those in her care. The threat of her mother and the Dark Lady wouldn't stop her from using her gift. The alliance needed her just as much as they needed Lady Ayaka's healing, Lord Leo's light, or Lord Renlar's wisdom. It would take every house's gift, alongside the thousands here ready to fight and die for their lands and families, to win this war.

No, she would not hide. While they fought in the real world, she would take the fight to the dreamscape.

41

The Dominia Empire was coming.

A couple of days after Lord Raoul left, the first scout arrived with the news. Instead of weeks, they had less than a fortnight before the empire arrived and the battle started.

The camp turned into a frenzy of preparation, and Selene's nights were filled with doing what she could to calm those around her. But between the mingling fears and dread of the dreamers around her, her constant watch for her mother and the Dark Lady, and the subtle temptation to reach across her dreams toward the oncoming empire and end the war permanently left her drained each morning.

Damien hardly visited their tent. And when he did, he fell fast asleep, hardly leaving time for them to talk. He worked tirelessly with the soldiers, including his own forces that had arrived a week before under Admiral Gerault's command.

Selene stared up at the canvas roof of their tent, her hands tightly gripping the wool blanket across her body. Damien slept next to her, wrapped in his own blanket, and so exhausted that she could almost feel the fatigue drifting from his slumbering body.

It was real now, this battle they would soon face. The empire was only days away, maybe less. And for the first time, she keenly felt the mortality of those around her, including herself. Her mind lingered on Amara's death, how cold and chilling it was. How utterly unstoppable. How her grief afterward had shaken her to the core.

She swallowed hard, her chest tightening at her next thought. What if Damien died? There was a great possibility he would. More than almost anyone, the empire wanted him dead so the water-walls would fall. They would go for him and take him out if the chance presented itself.

But it wasn't like he could hide. In fact, she knew he wouldn't. He would do everything he could to save as many as possible. That was one of the countless things she loved about him.

She turned her head and stared at his sleeping face in the dim light. His hair had grown longer, and now a lock of it hung down his forehead, slightly curling at the end. She lifted her hand and brushed it gently to the side. She imagined his eyes, bright blue like the sea on a clear day. His smile, full of laughter. His strength tempered by uncommon tenderness.

What if all of that disappeared in a moment? How would she survive?

Selene dropped her hand and turned back until she was staring at the canvas roof again. "Light," she whispered, "I want my husband to live. I want to see him again when all this is finished. I want the alliance to win, so that we can live in peace. I want to see our children. I want to see our lands living in unity the way you first created them to be."

She swallowed and squeezed her eyes shut, willing the sudden rush of tears to disappear. "But I don't know if that's going to happen. Perhaps I will be the downfall and the last of my house. The empire might win. And Damien might die. So I ask one thing"—she gripped the blanket so tight her fingers hurt—"don't leave me. Even if everything else falls away. Please be with me. Help me be strong. Comfort me if my loved ones die. My life and my gift are yours to do with as you please. Be the light of my path."

Two tears trickled down the sides of her face before she slowly let go of the blanket. No matter how hard it was to walk the dreamscape and face all those fears and the possibility of meeting her mother and the Dark Lady, she would not stop using her gift to inspire and protect the alliance. She would be the Nightwatcher of their dreams and memories. She would guard the people in her care during the hours of darkness against the Dark Lady, against her mother, against death itself.

This was who she was. This was who the Light

had created her to be. And she would serve until her last breath, for as long as she lived.

She reached over and felt for Damien's hand. She found his wrist and made her way to his fingers and gripped his hand. His skin was always warmer than hers, his touch reassuring.

She let out a sigh and closed her eyes as a feeling of peace came over her. It was her turn to take watch.

Moments later, she entered the dream world. Unlike Damien's dreamscape, which appeared as the coast of the Northern Shores, hers always assumed the form of the highest tower of Rook Castle, with an overview of all the lands: from Tereth Bay to the wall, from the Northern Shores to the Rasa Gulf. These lands and these people were hers to protect.

Selene spread out her arms, then transformed into her raven form and began her vigilance over the dream world. The sky was clear and dark, with a full moon to the northeast. She soared beneath the pale light, feeling the sleeping souls around her slowly enter her dream.

Fear followed many of the sleepers. Fear of death, of pain, of the upcoming war. Given her thoughts minutes ago, she understood this fear all too well.

You're not alone.

She impressed this thought upon their minds as she soared along the sky.

The Light is here. He's always here. He's been here since the beginning of time.

She landed on a cliff that overlooked the valley where in the real world the alliance was currently based. She closed her eyes and focused on the Festival of Light, when the monks entered Nor Esen, chanting about the darkness and the Light that broke through.

The sound of her memory melded with the sounds of the night, creating a beautiful harmony that washed over those within her dreamscape. She could feel them, one by one, let go of their fears and fall into a deep sleep.

Rest, my friends. Rest so you will be ready for the upcoming battle.

A frigid chill swept across her back, causing her feathers to rise. She opened her eyes and looked down.

A shadow, darker than night, moved along the valley below.

She focused her power on the shadow but couldn't penetrate the smoke-like figure. Her eyes went wide. She rose off the cliff and dove, her beak tightly shut, slicing through the air with her wings tucked close to her sides.

This was her dreamscape, her people.

She would not let the darkness have them.

42

As Selene reached the tree line along the base of the dreamscape valley, the shadow disappeared.

Where are you? Her muscles quivered beneath her feathers. She scanned the area near the alliance camp as she hovered above the trees but could neither see nor feel the shadow.

Perhaps if she went a little higher . . .

Selene soared upward until she was thirty feet above the trees. There. That strong feeling of darkness, like a stain upon the dreamscape. There was no doubt about it. She knew this presence all too well.

The Dark Lady.

Wait.

There was another with the Dark Lady. Two presences, one overlapping the other.

Her mother.

In a flash, Selene dove for the ground. A second before landing, she changed into her human form and landed with her swords in her hands. Slowly she twisted around, searching the area. Already the presence of both had disappeared, all but for a lingering sense, left behind like perfume.

Selene brought her gaze back to the alliance camp where thousands of soldiers slept along the plains near the Drihst River. Raoul said her mother had been tasked to take her out. So was her mother here for her or for the soldiers?

And how did her mother become so powerful? Did she get here by the Dark Lady's power or on her own? What were they capable of together?

And can I stop them?

There, that presence again.

Selene took flight and headed straight for the alliance base. As she approached the camp, the dark feeling grew stronger, along with a subtle but distinct smell of rot and decay wafting between the tents and sleeping souls.

Selene touched down in the middle of the base near where she shared a tent with Damien and turned back into her human form, her swords out again. "I know you're here," she said, her voice echoing across the dreamscape.

A cold wind sprang up, whipping the hem of her cloak behind her.

A terrified cry went up nearby as the sleeper's fear rippled across the dreamscape. Selene turned and ran to the source.

A cold laugh cackled between the tents as she approached the frightened sleeper. Another cry, and another. She could feel it, the twisting of her dreamscape as the Dark Lady tapped into the dreams of those here, spreading the death sleep.

Selene gripped her swords tighter and looked around. How could she stop them? There wasn't time to release all the minds here. What else could she do?

Wait. What if she morphed the dreamscape and somehow hid the people here? It just might work, even for a little bit. At least it would buy her time.

Selene looked up and held her swords out. She still couldn't see her mother or the Dark Lady, but she could feel them moving amongst the tents. "This is *my* dreamscape!" she cried. "And these people are under *my* protection." She raised her swords. "You will not touch them!"

She swept her weapons across her body. At her motion, a blast of wind tore through the camp. The tents shook under her power, then disappeared, leaving an empty grassy plain beneath a night sky and moon.

Her knees buckled, but she remained standing. Her hands shook as she straightened her back. She did it. She was able to conceal the alliance within her dreamscape, but she wasn't sure how long she could keep them hidden from her mother or the Dark Lady.

A moment later, she spotted two figures standing thirty feet away beneath the moonlight. One wore a long black robe and cowl, the other a dark tunic, cloak, and boots.

Both turned toward her.

It had been almost a year since Selene had last seen her mother, and seeing her now brought a quiver to her stomach. Her mother was just as strong and fearsome as she remembered. Selene fought the desire to lay down her swords and fall to her knees.

No. I am a different person. I do not follow her or the Dark Lady. Selene gripped her swords tighter. *I am Selene Ravenwood, and I follow the Light.*

Selene raised her chin, her dark eyes set as both figures walked toward her.

"It is as I predicted," her mother began. "You have become the most powerful Ravenwood in history, Selene. You can draw people into your dreamscape or visit others all without touching them. It is a power I never thought possible, even for someone as gifted as you. Even now, you've hidden them from our sight. Most impressive."

"How are you here?" she asked, her gaze shifting to the Dark Lady. Pinpricks of light stared out from beneath the dark hood, and those familiar black lips crept upward into a smile as the two continued toward Selene.

"I, too, have been training, my daughter. Only I have a power on my side that you do not. The Dark Lady has made it possible for me to visit you in the dream world." They both stopped near Selene.

Selene pointed her right sword at the Dark Lady. "So it's her power that allowed you to come here. I've heard that you can also visit dreams without touching the sleeper. Why did you come here?"

"You are the heart of the dream world. You are able to gather many sleepers into your dreamscape. Why visit one mind when we can visit them all?"

Selene's heart fell. They were here for the alliance.

"You can't have them. These people are under my protection."

Her mother's eyes darted toward the swords in her hands. "You plan on fighting us? With mere swords? You don't actually believe you can take on both me *and* the Dark Lady, do you?"

"I'll do what I have to."

"Then let us see how long you can hold out."

The Dark Lady vanished in a flutter of black fabric as her mother held her hand out and her own sword appeared. "Interesting," she said as she held up her sword and gazed at the blade. "I have never held a weapon in the dreamscape. I didn't even know I could do this." Then she lifted her head and lunged, closing the space between them within seconds.

Selene met her mother's blade with her own while feverishly thinking of a plan. Even though she was hiding the alliance within her dreamscape, it wouldn't take her mother or the Dark Lady long to find them. And she couldn't free them, not yet. She wasn't sure what an abrupt departure would do to their minds. Somehow she had to protect the sleepers here until she found a chance to release them back into the real world.

Her mother came at her again. Her fighting style was similar to Amara's, but much more powerful. Rarely did she ever spar with her mother, but the few times she had, she won only once. Selene met her mother's blade with her left one, swept it away, and thrust with her right.

With each second that went by, Selene sank deeper inside herself, her blades becoming an extension of her body, while with her mind she scoured the dreamscape for the frigid presence of the Dark Lady.

There.

Before she could move, her mother came in with another blow. Selene dove forward, transformed into her raven form, and swept beneath the point of her mother's sword, past her body, and toward the mountains ahead. She understood now. Her mother was here to distract her while the Dark Lady moved about freely.

Then she felt it, the frigid touch of the Dark Lady as she peeled back Selene's illusion and went for the sleeping minds in the dreamscape.

Selene stopped in midair, her wings spread. A blast of power exploded inside her, spreading from wingtip to wingtip. Her lungs filled with air and a scream emerged, fueled by her power, racing along her throat until it exploded in a cry that echoed across the dreamscape.

An invisible wave swept across the grass and trees below her, bending the trunks toward the ground in reaction to her voice. The robed figure of the Dark Lady was tossed into the sky, caught by the sound, and hovered in the air, dazed.

Selene shot forward. Her talons spread, ready to catch the Dark Lady. Perhaps she could fling the dark one from her dreamscape if she could just get ahold of her.

The Dark Lady glanced back, then turned and flew toward Rook Castle.

Selene stretched her neck and wings and pressed forward.

A shadow appeared on her right.

A second later, another raven swerved around and dove for her. The raven brought her talons up, going for her eyes and throat.

Mother.

Selene let out a short, shrill call. Her left talon raked along her mother's neck, pulling out some feathers.

Her mother screamed and went for her again, her wings wide.

Selene had no time for this. She snapped her beak and brought her claws up again, pushed off of her mother, then dove downward.

Drawing on the dreamscape, Selene scanned for the Dark Lady while boosting her speed. The

Dark Lady moved from one sleeper to the next along the mountainside, almost as if she were luring Selene.

She dove for her, ready to attack with her claws, only to be caught again by her mother, giving the Dark Lady a chance to get away.

Her wings burned, and each breath of air she drew in felt like glass shards in her lungs. *I can't keep doing this. I can't defend against my mother while trying to protect everyone from the Dark Lady. But if I land and try to release the sleepers, I can't stop Mother's attacks.*

She dove again, aiming for the Dark Lady. The Dark Lady seemed to almost laugh at her as she rose into the air and flew away.

Then it hit her. *They're delaying me so I don't release the alliance.*

Selene plunged toward a cliff amongst the evergreen trees. *I've lost too much time. No matter what, I need to free everyone.*

At the last moment, she transformed and landed in a crouch. She only had seconds before her mother arrived.

Selene rose to her feet and brought her hands together. Sweat trickled down the sides of her face, and her blood burned within her body. Only seconds.

She closed her eyes. She would give the alliance one last gift before releasing them.

Remember what we're fighting for.

The dreamscape began to swirl around her, changing form. Using every bit of power she had left, Selene opened herself to the dreams of everyone around her. Faces of loved ones, children, homes and land, laughter, and friendship appeared and disappeared in a dizzying wave of images.

You must protect this.

Like a pebble tossed into a lake, her thoughts rippled across the dreamscape until she felt a thousand souls light up like stars in the sky.

Be strong. Take courage.

Remember, the Light is with you.

Always.

Then she let go.

She could feel the sleepers leaving her dreamscape like paper lanterns let loose into the sky. A small smile lit her face. She wasn't able to give them much, but maybe it would be enough during the darkest moments of the upcoming battle.

She felt the presence of her mother and the Dark Lady close in.

A hand clutched her throat, fingers so cold they burned against her skin. Selene didn't open her eyes. She needed to hang on for a moment more until everyone was gone.

That was the only thing that mattered now.

The fingers tightened around her throat, cutting off her airway.

"What have you done?" her mother shouted nearby.

Almost there. Colors shot across her eyelids as she struggled to breathe. Come one, just one more.

Seconds later, the last dreamer left the barrier.

She did it.

There was a hiss, and Selene opened her eyes to see the Dark Lady in front of her, her pale arm stretched out, her fingers a vise around her throat.

Their plan had failed. They were here to tap in to her ability to link the alliance together. Only now, the alliance was gone. She was the last one left in the dreamscape.

"What are you going to do now?" Selene rasped, her vision blurring into blackness.

The Dark Lady pulled her forward until she was inches from her dark hood. Even this close, there was no face within the cowl. Just her mouth and unending blackness. "We'll take you instead."

43

Damien sat up, Selene's words ringing in his ears.

Remember what we're fighting for.

He turned toward her side of the sleeping mat and placed a hand on her shoulder. "Selene," he said, giving her a shake. Her eyes remained closed. "Selene!" he said again, shaking her harder as the dream came back, of ravens and shadows and a cry that shook the entire dreamscape.

The flap lifted behind him, bright light streaming into the tent. "My lord," said Karl, out of breath. "The whole camp is in an uproar."

Damien looked behind him. "Karl, what's going on?"

"The empire is almost here."

Damien stood to his feet, the blanket falling from his legs. "How did that happen?" he asked as he grabbed his tunic and pulled it on. "Why weren't we notified? Why wasn't I woken up?"

"Half of our forces were caught in the death sleep and could not be awakened. Including myself."

Damien glanced again at the sleeping form of his wife. Was that what happened? Had there been a battle in the dreamscape? "How much time do we have before the empire arrives?"

"Less than half a day."

"Dear Light," he whispered as he moved across the tent and reached into the chest that held his leather armor. "Karl, help me. We don't have much time."

Karl moved across the tent and assisted him with the grey leather chest plate and pieces.

"What time is it?" Damien asked as he fastened the buckles in the front.

"Almost noon."

Damien choked. "And we were asleep for over a day? Was there anyone awake to notice?"

"Yes." Karl cinched the back belt. "Both Lady Ayaka and Healer Sildaern, along with a handful of others, never fell asleep and tried to rouse the camp."

Damien reached for his sword and scabbard as horns began to blow across the camp.

Karl's gaze was caught on the still-sleeping figure on the mat. "My lord, were those words I heard in my dream from Lady Selene?"

"Yes. She freed us from the death sleep—at great cost to herself, I fear."

After securing his sword, Damien went over to Selene's side of the sleeping mat and knelt down on one knee. Her eyes were still closed. "Selene," he said and brushed her hair back. "Where are you?"

The thought of his wife struggling alone against the Dark Lady and Lady Ragna made his stomach twist. But what could he do? No one else could enter the dreamscape. He bowed his head and gripped her hand. *Light, please help her. Help her fight. Protect her.* He prayed for a minute more before he opened his eyes.

"Karl, I can't wake Lady Selene. I believe whatever she did in the dreamscape to free us might have left her trapped inside. But just in case I'm wrong, please let Healer Sildaern know of her condition." He glanced over his shoulder. "And Karl, since Taegis isn't here . . ." Saying those words brought a pang of grief to his heart, but he pressed on. "I need you to stand in his stead. Stay here and watch over Selene. Watch over my wife."

"My lord—"

He clenched his hands to keep them from trembling. "As Lord of House Maris, I need to lead our people to war. Knowing Selene is safe will free me to use all of my strength against the enemy. Guard her, Karl. She is the most precious thing in my life."

"I . . . I understand, my lord."

"Thank you." Damien leaned down and kissed Selene's lips. "I will see you again," he whispered before standing up and backing away. "You are strong, Selene. And you are not alone. Remember that."

It took every bit of strength he had to turn away from Selene. The thought of leaving her behind filled his throat with bile. Leaving Selene in this condition was the same as leaving his heart behind.

The thunderous sound of thousands of soldiers hurrying past his tent and the continual blaring of horns finally pulled Damien toward the exit. It was time. Karl bowed in his direction and held up the canvas flap so Damien could pass through. His heart thudded dully inside his chest as he joined the multitude marching toward battle.

Light, please watch over my wife. He spoke those words over and over in his mind. Every time he imagined what she could be facing in the dreamscape, it made him want to turn around and run back. *No.* He had to leave her in the Light's hands. There was nothing he could do for her. She had her battle to fight, and he had his.

The alliance and the coalition gathered at the edge of camp, a mighty host of soldiers from Houses Luceras, Vivek, and his own, along with those who answered the coalition's call. There were thousands of men—and even a number of women. Some looked no older than fifteen or sixteen seasons, while others were entering the glory of their years. Alongside the foot soldiers, the cavalry gathered. And beyond them, a handful of wyverns were ready to take flight.

An attendant brought Damien his horse and handed him the reins. Damien nodded his thanks as he took the leather straps and made his way through the troops, leading his mount. The sun beat down on the forces, adding heat to the heavy stench of sweat and leather already permeating the air. Damien's sword softly hit his thigh with every step, but his real weapon—his power over the waters—he carried within him. One he hoped he would not need to use. Not yet.

"Remember what we're fighting for."

The words were whispered amongst the soldiers as Damien reached the front. Hearing Selene's words coming from the men around him made his heart swell. Whatever she faced inside the dreamscape, she had given them one last gift before they marched to war.

Damien joined the Luceras brothers and Lord Renlar, who was waiting to the left with his generals. Admiral Gerault made his way to Damien, along with the captains from his own forces. Damien checked his saddle one more time before mounting up.

"Do you hear what the soldiers are whispering?" Elric asked, awe in his voice. "The men might have been shaken by how abruptly they were called to arms, except for the rallying cry I keep hearing."

"It would seem Lady Selene has come fully into her power as a dreamwalker," Lord Renlar said, bringing his horse beside the other lords. "Just like the texts of old spoke of House Ravenwood.

If only my father could have lived to see this happen."

"If it wasn't for Lady Selene, the empire would have murdered us in our tents." Lord Leo tightened his hold on the reins. "Instead, we are ready to face Commander Orion and his forces." He let out a sigh. "I'm glad Lady Selene is on our side."

Damien's heart was both full and pained at the same time. Selene was redeeming the darkness of her family's past, and now the other houses were starting to see the power in her gift. There was no other person he wanted to be with for the rest of his life. *Please wake up, Selene.*

"Is she coming with us?"

Damien glanced over when he realized Lord Leo was talking to him. "No. She—she hasn't woken up yet."

Elric looked stricken. "She is still caught in the death sleep?"

Damien swallowed past the lump in his throat. "Yes, I believe so."

"Then we shall fight for her, as she did for us." Lord Leo brought his horse around. Elric nodded in agreement. "It is time to depart. I would like to address the men before we leave." His gaze settled on Damien. "And I would like to use Lady Selene's words."

Damien nodded. "She would be honored."

Lord Leo broke away on his steed and faced

the alliance. He held out his hand, and a moment later, a broadsword made of light appeared in his grasp. He raised the sword and looked over the troops. A quiet descended upon the soldiers. "Today will be the battle that determines the course of our lives. Will we be victorious, or will we be forced to live in the shadow of the Dominia Empire? I know the answer we all hold in our hearts. Remember your loved ones. Remember your homes." He brought his sword down in a sweeping motion. "Remember what we're fighting for."

"Remember what we're fighting for!" Weapons were raised in the air. "Remember what we're fighting for!" The chant took hold of the troops until the words echoed across the valley.

Damien knew what he was fighting for. For his people of the Northern Shores. For his friends and comrades. For his wife. And for the future he hoped they would have together.

For peace and freedom.

The four lords turned and started eastward. A loud roar echoed behind them as the wyverns took flight, soaring above the troops like living banners.

Chain mail and armor gleamed beneath tabards in the bright sun. The pounding of boots echoed across the hills. Those dressed in the colors of House Luceras broke out in song.

Damien sang with them, his tenor voice joining

the others. The song, combined with hope and determination, spurred the troops on toward the east.

They were ready to fight. And they knew *why* they were fighting. There would be pain. And death. Only the Light knew how much. But they would face it with the strength that came with protecting something they loved with all their might.

44

Hours later, Damien sat upon his mount, his shoulders tight, his stomach even tighter as the Dominia Empire appeared in the distance, an overwhelming mass of burnt orange and green on the horizon.

So this was war. He clutched the reins between his hands. The fear he had only heard about until now held him in its frigid claws, causing his whole body to tremble. It was as if death itself was marching toward him, and this time there was no river, no sea, between him and the enemy. His power would not work here. Only his skill and leadership.

His horse pawed nervously at the ground, and from the corner of his eye, he spotted the whites in the men's eyes nearest to him and beads of sweat dripping down their foreheads.

If only Lady Bryren were here. Even he could use a dose of her courage now. They hadn't received any word from her since she left Surao to join her remaining forces. He hoped to slow the empire down until House Merek arrived.

He readjusted his grip on the reins and looked over at Lord Leo and Lord Elric. The brothers seemed composed, even eager for the fight, given the look on Elric's face. Was it just a façade, or were they really not afraid?

Lord Leo turned his horse around. He lifted his hand, and his sword of light appeared once again. He held his weapon aloft and began to ride across the front line, shouting encouragements as he went. The sight of House Luceras's gift seemed to strengthen the men.

Damien took a deep breath as Admiral Gerault came to his side.

"Are you ready?" the older man said.

He let out his breath. "Yes." He wasn't at full strength, not with the Hyr River still raised and with having to put out the fires around Surao, but he was fit enough to fight today. If they were forced back to the Drihst River, he would raise it, but it would cost him much.

A shout went up and a horn blew. The empire drew closer.

"We will defend this land!" Lord Leo shouted as he made his way back along the line.

Lord Elric placed his hand out, his polearm of light appearing. He looked over at Damien. "Ready to fight?"

His heart pounded inside his chest, but the fear spreading across his body had been replaced by a deadly calm. Damien drew out his sword and looked back at Lord Elric. "I am."

"Then let us meet the enemy."

The cavalry units on either side pulled away to

start their flank of the empire while the archers moved forward. The wyverns circled above, the spears of their riders glinting in the sunlight.

Then the empire arrived.

The first volley of arrows were shot into the air while the wyvern riders and cavalry went for the outskirts.

Another volley was shot, then a third, then imperial soldiers broke through. The first clash came like the crashing of a typhoon across the sea cliffs.

Damien shouted out commands as he watched the fight burst forth. The air filled with shouts, swords clanging, screams of horses, and roars from the wyverns. Sweat soaked through his undershirt; his hair clung to his head as the sun beat down on him.

Lord Elric had already lost his horse and was now fighting three soldiers with his polearm, while Lord Leo continued to form light spheres and hit those in front of them. Any who made it past his first defense met the sharp edge of his broadsword.

Blood spilled across the ground, its metallic smell mixing with the stench of sweat as the long prairie grass was trampled beneath hoof and boot. Wave after wave of imperial soldiers filled in where their comrades fell. In the distance, there was a loud groan, then a snap. A black blot appeared against the blue sky as a boulder came hurtling over Damien and crashed behind him.

He turned back to find a handful of men trapped beneath the enormous rock. Another boulder took flight. The smoldering rock flew past and hit more men in the back.

In the distance, a wyvern faltered, one wing hanging useless. It flapped with its good wing as it tried to turn, only to be caught by a spear-like arrow. The shaft entered the beast's chest, and the wyvern fell to the ground in a great cloud of dust.

Men collapsed on both sides, their screams of agony echoing across the battlefield. The sound made Damien's stomach clench as he slashed at an imperial soldier, catching him across his upper arm. One of the coalition soldiers near him finished off the man.

A young alliance soldier nearby watching the whole thing went pale, then bent over and vomited. Damien knew how he felt as he turned his horse and moved forward, continuing to shout commands as the battle unfolded.

No, this wasn't war. This was hell.

Hours later, sweat-soaked and bloody, Damien scanned the horizon as he mistakenly thought he saw the red tabards of House Friere. Lord Raoul had vowed he would be here.

He turned away and ground his teeth. Had they

been fools to believe Lord Raoul? Had it all been a ruse?

Vultures flew high above, ready to feast when the battle ended. And what a feast it would be. Hundreds of bodies littered the field. Some dead, others close to it. How much longer could they hold out?

Damien cut his way through a group of imperial soldiers. Bile filled his throat, but he reminded himself that in order for his men to live, others had to die. He was simply making that choice.

But deep inside, his heart cried for the lives lost, no matter whose they were.

His horse stumbled over a body just as a spear went through its chest, held up by an imperial soldier who lay a couple of feet away.

The horse screamed and fell forward. Damien scrambled from his saddle and finished off the imperial soldier before falling to his knees, sick. *I hate this, I hate this, I hate this!* He gripped his sword tighter. *Light, how can I keep doing this?*

As darkness fell, the fighting slowly subsided. The alliance held one hill while the empire spread out across the other. Each side sent another volley of arrows and boulders, then set up a line of guards. Shifts were established, rotating the soldiers between watching the front line and letting others sleep, if they could. It was a stalemate until morning.

The injured were hauled back to camp by

torchlight. The dead were left where they had fallen. Damien's thoughts lingered on Selene as the fires from the empire burned in the distance.

Was she still asleep? Were they in danger from the Dark Lady or Lady Ragna if the alliance closed their eyes? Even now, absolute exhaustion was pulling him toward the oblivion, and he was helpless against it. As he fell into a restless sleep, he prayed for the people around him, and for his wife.

All too soon, Damien awoke. Sleep had brought back a small measure of energy, but not much. A handful of stars still hung in the sky as he stood and stretched, every muscle crying in agony, every bruise and cut a reminder of the many hits and near misses he had endured.

A healer from House Luceras shouted out orders to his left, and Damien could see the other healers' dim white robes as they knelt amongst the soldiers, still working to carry away the injured from the field. How many more men had passed on during the night?

If only they had House Rafel with them. They needed more healers.

Damien tightened the straps on his armor, then checked for his sword. Hard biscuits and water were passed around to those waking up. Dawn began to break across the eastern sky, past the valley between them, past the vast imperial army on the other side. The actions of man did not stop nature from running its cycle, nor the light from rising again.

Damien stood still for a moment and closed his eyes. The darkness could never extinguish the light, no matter how dark it became. He needed to remember that.

A cry went up along the front lines.

Damien lifted his head. Alliance soldiers around him struggled to their feet, and more shouts rang out across the hill.

The empire was on the move again.

Damien lifted his sword into the air. "Stand! Stand!" he yelled. He spotted the light-weapons of Lord Leo and Lord Elric rushing toward the front. "Remember what we're fighting for. Stand your ground!"

The two armies crashed at the base of the hills, the sound of the battle echoing across the plains.

Slowly, the empire pushed the alliance back to their hill, then up it.

Three boulders were launched into the air, red with fire, and hurled toward those at the top. They hit the back company and crushed the men beneath the weight. At the sight, the soldiers around Damien fled, parting around the boulders like a river.

Damien raised his voice and yelled, but his efforts were in vain. Soldiers ran past him like startled deer.

He spotted Lord Renlar and the tabards of House Vivek nearby. He couldn't hear what Lord Renlar was saying, but it seemed to bring sense back to the frightened soldiers. They stopped, then turned around.

The battle grew fierce again.

Minutes ticked by, the seconds counted by each body that fell to the ground. Damien and the Luceras brothers joined together in a short, fierce fight, leaving five imperial soldiers dead or gravely wounded.

Lord Leo sucked in a pained breath and brought his hand to his middle. His tabard, once white, was now covered in blood. "Where in all the lands is House Friere?" he said with bared teeth. "He's had over a day to join us."

Damien shook his head, too tired to speak.

"That traitor. Why did we think we could depend on the words of House Friere?"

"Those catapults combined with Lord Ivulf's power are devastating our rear line." Elric wiped his brow with his free hand. "I don't know how long we can fight and put out those fires at the same time."

"We don't have a choice, we have to hold out as long as we ca—"

"Look!" someone shouted nearby. More shouts erupted as fingers pointed toward the southwest sky.

Damien and the Luceras brothers turned.

In the distance, against the bright blue horizon, hundreds of figures appeared in the sky. Colors ranging from copper to red, black to blue-grey flew toward the battle.

"It's the wyvern riders!"

"House Merek!"

Lord Leo's shoulders sagged as a smirk replaced his glare from a minute ago. "About time, Lady Bryren."

The sight of the wyverns breathed new life into the alliance. A rally cry went up, and the battle became intense again. Damien bowed his head for a moment, his chest aching from exhaustion, but a renewing strength filling his body. *Thank you, Light.*

Then he brought his sword up and rejoined the fight. He assisted a group of his men fighting off a handful of imperial soldiers. His fingers began to tingle around the hilt of his sword, but he ignored the sensation. There was no time to waste. They had a chance now that House Merek had arrived.

Below the company of wyvern riders rode the rest of House Merek's forces on horseback, a banner of black and yellow leading the way. Minutes later, the wyverns arrived. Lady Bryren let out a shout in the old tongue, followed by a whistle as she flew overhead on Shannu. At her command, the first set of wyvern riders swooped down toward the imperial army. The wyvern riders let loose their arrows, hitting the first line of imperial soldiers. As they faltered, another group of wyverns swept down with long spears in hand and hit the next line, cresting back up into the sky after delivering their deadly blows.

For a moment, the imperial forces appeared stunned by the strange battle and the trancelike dance of the wyverns' flight. Then a cry went up, and the imperial soldiers took formation. A formidable line of burnt orange and green shot a volley of returning arrows. Most of the wyverns dodged the deadly rain, but a few arrows found their mark. One wyvern keeled to the side, and the rider pulled on the reins, guiding his mount toward the rear of the alliance.

Lady Bryren gave another shout in the old tongue. At once, the riders and wyverns spread out across the sky like a net spread out across the water. Then, with another whistle, the wyverns dove, once again raining down arrows. More imperial soldiers fell as the wyverns swerved and pumped their wings as they headed back toward the sky.

Lord Leo shouted nearby, reminding the alliance that there were imperial soldiers nearby and to be on guard. Damien shook his head, dazed at the fight he had just witnessed, and raised his sword, ready again. The combat savvy of the wyvern riders was remarkable. House Merek had trained them well.

One of the large javelins from the back of the imperial line shot into the air. It flew straight up and hit a small red wyvern in the chest. The wyvern let out a high-pitched scream before plummeting toward the ground.

Another javelin shot into the sky, this time catching a larger black wyvern and tearing a hole through the membrane of its wing. More javelins were launched skyward, most missing, but a few causing damage.

A sword came swinging, and Damien jumped back, catching his foot on a body behind him. He fell back, his sword up. The imperial soldier swung his own blade down.

Holding his blade up, Damien defended himself, but there was no time between blows to get back onto his feet.

Slash, deflect, parry.

His arm burned from holding his sword up and from the constant hits from the soldier. He gasped in great draughts of air as sweat dripped from the tip of his nose.

The next hit made his sword droop downward.

His arm shook as he braced for another hit when a piercing light appeared through the soldier's chest. A look of surprise covered the man's face as he dropped to his knees.

Elric stood behind the fallen soldier, his polearm of light in hand. "Need some help there?" he asked as he extended his other hand and helped Damien up.

"Thanks." Damien let out a ragged laugh as he wiped his face, then winced at the cut across his upper arm.

"Looks like the imperial got you."

"Yes, it's only a small cut, but it stings."

Two wyverns flew overhead.

Elric gazed over the battlefield. "You'd think with the arrival of House Merek that House Friere would finally step forward." He shook his head. "It would appear they might not be coming to our aid."

Damien looked around as well, his sword arm at his side. A small part of him had truly hoped that Lord Raoul had been telling the truth and House Friere would join in the fight. That same small part had held out hope since he had left Surao that Lord Haruk and House Rafel would follow Lady Ayaka's lead. He believed that with all seven houses working together, nothing could stop them.

But now . . .

"It doesn't matter." He wiped the blood from his hands along the side of his pants, then regripped his sword. "We can still win as long as we keep on fighting."

Elric nodded. "That was one thing Quinn always admired about you: your tenacity. You always seemed to have hope. You never gave up."

"Hmph." Maybe it was because he couldn't give up. Even if he wanted to.

The battle ebbed and flowed as the dead and gravely injured continued to fall across the battlefield. After a while, even the wyvern riders seemed exhausted. It appeared they were at another stalemate. Every time the alliance seemed to push through, the empire re-formed ranks.

The sun slowly made its way across the sky, and the air grew even hotter.

It was coming down to the end. Whichever side broke first would lose.

And the other side would win.

45

Selene couldn't breathe, couldn't feel, couldn't see. The moment the Dark Lady let go of her throat, darkness took hold of her. A primal scream filled her lungs, but her mouth refused to work, and so the scream thrashed inside of her. Her heart beat frantically, filling her ears with its desperate thuds.

Just when she thought she would pass out, the dream changed.

Selene gasped as her body dropped into a frigid sea. The cold hit her to her very core, freezing her heart for a moment. Above her, storm clouds rolled overhead and a violent gale swept across the surface as towering waves rushed toward her.

A moment later, the waves hit her.

She tumbled through the water, knocked end over end by the wave. Before she could get her bearings, the water sucked her under, pulling her beneath the surface with invisible hands. Down, down she went, one hand reaching for the sky. She kicked her legs and beat her arms, but the dark waters continued to pull her into the depths until all light disappeared.

A cry went up inside her chest. *Please, Light, help me.*

When she opened her eyes, she found herself

lying in an empty area devoid of everything except dim light. She rolled onto her side and vomited the water out of her stomach, then slowly sat up, wet strands of hair sticking to her cheeks.

"How do you like *my* dreams?" A cold laugh echoed throughout the empty space. "This is your future, little raven. Pain. Emptiness. Darkness. These are the dreams I give to people."

Selene coughed. "Why would people follow you . . . if this is all you can promise?"

The Dark Lady simply laughed that cold, cruel laugh.

Selene stood up on shaky legs. Her clothes clung to her shivering body. Where was her mother? Was she here, watching the Dark Lady? She hadn't heard her mother speak since the nightmares had first begun. "Mother, why are you doing this?" Her voice echoed within the empty space.

Her mother didn't answer.

Selene closed her eyes and took in a deep breath, drawing on her power. It rose inside of her, allowing her to touch every corner of this dreamscape. She could feel everything around her, every thread that wove the dream world together. This place the Dark Lady had brought her to felt like an empty room, but maybe if she pushed hard enough, she could break free of it.

She held out her hands, filled her lungs, then

pressed against the dreamscape until her arms shook from her exertion and every muscle strained. Cracks began to form along the walls, accompanied by the sound of splintering wood.

"You are indeed strong, little raven. But not strong enough."

The room vanished, along with the ground beneath her. Selene let out a scream as she fell into the darkness.

The Dark Lady's voice filled her mind. "You will live out the rest of your life here."

Selene clenched her jaw. *No, I won't.*

With a twist of her body, she changed into her raven form and caught the air beneath her wings, then hovered in the pitch black.

Pinpricks of light, the eyes of the Dark Lady, appeared before her. "You can't fly forever."

Selene pulled her wings toward her chest, then thrust them out with a loud cry. The power inside of her broke the inky blackness. Black pieces fell away like shards of broken glass, revealing Rook Castle beneath a night sky. Her dreamscape.

Selene dove for the tower and landed, changing into her human form. Her body shook from exhaustion. She was keeping up with the Dark Lady, but—like their previous encounter—just barely.

In a whirl of black cloth, the Dark Lady appeared on the other side of the tower. The sky above was a deep midnight with twinkling stars and a full moon, spilling pale light over the area. "How long do you think you can hold out against me, little raven?"

"As long as I have to."

The Dark Lady took a step forward, her black lips turned up in a sardonic smile. "Once we are done with you, we will control this dreamscape."

"Where is she? Where is my mother?"

Just as the words passed through her lips, a raven landed on the ramparts near the Dark Lady, the moonlight glancing off her black feathers.

Selene wanted to scream at her mother but held back. Still, a fire burned inside of her. For a moment, she imagined spreading out her hands and blasting the raven from the top of the tower in a gust of wind. Even now, her hands twitched at her sides, and she breathed heavily.

No. She closed her eyes. *I can't. I won't. I will remain true to who I am—a dreamwalker of the Light—no matter how much Mother has hurt me.*

She slowly opened her eyes again. "You may have me here, but just as much as I am trapped here, I will make sure you never leave either." She flicked her wrists and her swords appeared in her hands as she struggled to her feet. "I will fight both of you and bind you here in my dreams forever. You will not enter another person's dream. You will not hurt anyone else."

Those black lips curved upward again. "And what happens when your mind breaks? Who will save you?" She laughed and turned toward Mother. "Lady Ragna, it's your turn."

The raven fluttered from the rampart toward the middle of the tower and changed into her mother. Her long dark hair fluttered around her body as she pulled out her sword again. "You've always been stubborn, Selene. At least your sister had the sense to listen to me."

"Listen to what? You never talked to her and barely tolerated her. You know nothing of Amara."

"I know that she was a failure."

Selene shook her head. "She wasn't a failure. Not at the end. I held her as she died in my arms, and I showed her who we were meant to be. This—" she waved her swords—"this is not our destiny."

Lady Ragna held her sword up. "You were always fighting your fate, Selene." The air crackled above them, then lightning split across the sky.

Selene dove to the side as the flash of light hit the tower. Selene barely had time to raise her own swords when her mother's blade hit hers. She countered with her left, then reached out with her right sword.

Lady Ragna stepped to the side and swung again. The blade glanced off of Selene's as she bounced back. Her limbs felt like they would seize up at any moment, and her heart threatened to burst inside her chest. What would happen if she collapsed? What would happen to the alliance?

To Damien?

To their dreams?

I can't stop, she panted. *I have to keep going.*

The dreamscape fell away, and Selene found herself on a mountaintop. Below lay thousands of bodies along a grassy plain as a red sun rose in the east. A particular body caught her eye, dressed in blue, with dark hair and—

Her heart turned to stone inside her chest.

"You'll never see him again," the Dark Lady whispered.

She stared at the body as a chilling numbness stole over her. "This . . . isn't real."

"How do you know? This could be what's happening right now. And you'll never know because you are here."

The scene changed, and Selene was back at the top of the tower. She barely registered her mother racing toward her before she brought up her own blade.

They fought, Selene scarcely meeting each blow. Every muscle screamed, and sweat created a second skin across her body. Her hair stuck to her face and cheeks as she sucked in a lungful of air.

I can't give up. Don't give up.

Then the dreamscape and her mother disappeared.

Selene found herself inside the room she shared with Damien in Northwind Castle. Only it was cold, dark, and empty. One side of the bed was rumpled from sleep, the other pristinely made. As Selene turned, she caught her reflection in the window.

Staring back was a face creased with wrinkles and framed with silver hair. Selene raised her hand and touched her cheek. The reflection did the same.

It was her. An older her.

"This is your future in the real world." The Dark Lady's voice filled her mind. "Growing old, alone. Living in a foreign land. No friends. No family. . . ."

She was back on top of Rook Castle.

This time her mother caught her by surprise. Selene barely dodged the blade, but it still grazed her shoulder.

Selene gritted her teeth against the stinging pain and brought her swords up.

No. I won't die. Damien is waiting for me. And Ophie. And my father.

Selene focused on her mother and drew upon all her power. She reached for the threads of the dreamscape, took hold of them, then gave a hard yank with her mind.

The tower—and the Dark Lady—disappeared.

Seconds later, Selene and Lady Ragna appeared in her mother's rooms in Rook Castle. No, that wasn't quite right. It was the same room, but different furniture. Instead of crimson window hangings and coverlets, they were silver.

A ghostly figure entered the room. Her hair was long, black, and curly. Her face looked like Amara's, sporting that same determined look Amara always wore.

Selene could feel her mother tense in the dreamscape.

Another figure appeared. A young Lady Ragna, about Selene's own age. Her skin was smooth, her long hair pinned to the back of her head.

Her mother and grandmother, Lady Sunna. Selene looked between both women as she continued to pull threads of memories from her mother, weaving the dream.

Her grandmother narrowed her dark eyes. "What do you want, Ragna?"

Young Ragna raised her chin. "I want to talk about the marriage alliance."

"No."

"But—"

"There is nothing to talk about. You know our ways."

"But if you would just listen to me."

Lady Sunna turned and headed for her study.

Her mother followed. "There are reasons why Lord Ivulf would be a better match—"

Lady Sunna spun around. *Slap.*

The young Ragna recoiled, holding her cheek.

"You *will* marry a lesser lord of my choosing. You *will* go to Shanalona and meet with House Vivek. You will do *everything* I tell you to do. The legacy of our house means more than your life. Do you understand?"

Young Ragna's face grew hard, and she dropped her hand. "I understand."

"Then there will not be one more word about Lord Ivulf. Or I will make sure that you never see him again. Permanently."

"What are you doing, Selene?" her real mother whispered.

She glanced over to find her mother pale as she watched the scene before her.

"Is this what your life was like?" Selene asked quietly.

A vein pulsed along her mother's temple. "My mother was right. Our house is all that matters." With a sweep of her hand, the memory disappeared. But now it was engraved in Selene's mind. The way her mother had treated her and Amara was the same way she had been treated. And Selene was sure she would find the same cycles of hatred, bitterness, and cruelty with her grandmother and great-grandmother.

Each generation raising the next one to be just like it.

"We can change, Mother. You don't have to follow the Dark Lady anymore. I've found a reason to live, a reason to hope—"

"I've chosen my path. And I will not let you stop me."

They were back at the top of Rook Castle. Her mother stood before her, her sword out, anger almost visibly rising from her body like steam.

"My path is with the Dark Lady and the Dominia Empire. I will do what my mother and grandmother failed to do: regain our position and power as a Great House. The name *Ravenwood* means more than anything else, even our lives."

"No." Selene shook her head. "Nothing is more precious than life."

"If you truly believed that, then you would have joined us. The empire is nothing compared to what we can do with the Dark Lady's power. With one touch, we could subdue both the alliance and the imperial forces. No more war. No more deaths. No more fighting. There's still time, Selene. Every precious life you love could be saved."

Selene stared at her mother, her swords slightly lowering in her hands. Her mother was speaking the very words she longed to hear. No war. No fights. No death. Damien would be out of danger. And so would the others. They could have peace. Everyone. Except . . .

"Who would rule?" She brought her swords up again in a ready stance. "You?"

"Both of us. House Ravenwood would be the protector of all the lands."

"And what about the Dark Lady?" Selene asked, glancing at the silent figure near her mother.

"She would be the patroness of every house."

A chill went down Selene's spine. "Everyone would worship the Dark Lady?"

"Yes. But think about all those lives saved because of you, Selene."

Selene narrowed her eyes. She once bowed to the Dark Lady, and the Dark Lady had done nothing for her. And she didn't save Amara. She wasn't capable of anything. Her promises were a smoke in the wind, here for a moment, and whisked away with the slightest breeze. The Dark Lady had no power except what was given to her. Unlike the Light . . .

The Light came for her, even when she had never bowed a knee to him. His power was his own, he needed no worshipers, and yet he still used his power for others. He was there for her time and time again. And he was there for Amara.

Selene raised her head and stared boldly at the two. "Never."

"So you want war, Selene? You want to see everyone die?" Lady Ragna scoffed. "We see how precious life really is to you."

Selene leaned forward. "What kind of leader promises her people support and leaves them in poverty? What kind of leader preys on the weaknesses of others? What kind of leader practices her gift on those she should be protecting? No, Mother. I will not let House Ravenwood rule others. It is not why we were given the gift of dreamwalking. We were given this power to help others, not to rule others. I will never join you or the Dark Lady."

"Well, then. A Ravenwood has never taken the life of another Ravenwood, and I will not be the first to do so. But I've learned a few tricks over the past months. Remember your servant girl, Renata? The young woman whose mind you shattered? I will not take your life, Selene, but I will not have you using your gift to stop the empire."

Her mother took a step forward and pulled out her blade again. "It is time for me to show you what the Dark Lady and I can do together. And when we are done, there will be nothing left of you."

46

The Dominia Empire broke through the alliance line.

Damien watched from forty feet away, his heart going still inside his chest.

It . . . can't be.

Alliance soldiers scattered as they turned and ran west, the empire in pursuit. There was no stopping them now, not like the last time, before House Merek arrived. Fear and self-preservation had taken over, driving any reason or thought from their minds.

Damien lifted his sword toward the oncoming storm of imperial soldiers. If their army came through, then Selene . . . and the others behind them . . .

His hand shook, his eyes wide. He had to protect her. He had to protect all of them.

A hand grabbed his shoulder and pulled him back. "Don't throw your life away."

Damien looked back to find Lord Renlar behind him. "We can still win, but not if you stay here. We need to sound the horn for the retreat and regroup at the Drihst River."

Damien stared at Lord Renlar in a daze. He blinked and tried to focus on the man before him.

"Lord Damien, move now!"

Move . . . now . . .

The words finally penetrated the fog in his mind.

Damien blinked again and nodded. Then he began to run alongside Lord Renlar. A gash bled just above Renlar's eye, sending a red streak down his dark skin. There was another along his arm, that one appearing deeper.

Damien stared ahead. He could only imagine what his own body looked like at the moment. Above them, the wyvern riders covered their retreat, but it seemed to him that there were fewer beasts in the sky.

He shook his head, that feeling of despair threatening to devour him again. He clenched the sword in his hand and huffed as he ran. No time for that.

The Drihst River. Everyone needed to retreat beyond the river. Then he would raise it.

And he would have nothing more left to give.

His breath hitched as he stumbled forward. He caught himself and started running again.

It's a tactical retreat. We just need to get to the river and figure out what to do next.

Horns began to blare: two short blasts, followed by a long one. The sound for retreat. The sound of failure.

No, not failure. Just a setback. Reach the camp on the other side, raise the river, and regroup. He would raise the wall and protect the alliance.

Just a delay.

Two men tripped in front of him and fell to the ground. Damien stopped and reached out with his hand. One held out his hand in response, and Damien assisted him up.

The other crouched over and covered his head with his hands. He was young, with barely any facial hair along his jaw. "I'm going to die, I'm going to die," he said between his fingers.

Damien bent down. "No, you're going to live."

The man looked up between his hands as more soldiers ran around them. "How? The imperial army . . ." His eyes widened with fear, and his voice cracked.

"Because there is hope. There is always hope."

"We're dead men. The empire will wipe us all out."

"Not if we can make it to the river. I am the lord of House Maris. Do you know what that means?"

A spark came back into the man's eyes. "You control the waters."

"Yes. Now come. Not all is lost." Damien reached down again, and the soldier took his hand. As soon as the young man was standing, Damien looked around. They were near the tail end of the alliance soldiers. A sea of burnt orange and green was closing in.

"Go," he said, readying his sword. "Get to the river."

"What about you?"

"My real gift is to protect you. Now go."

The soldier hesitated, then started forward. Damien didn't expect him to stay. It took a certain kind of reckless courage to bring up the rear. He let out a tired laugh. Perhaps Quinn was right. He *was* stubborn. Right down to the end.

Damien started running again just as a familiar wyvern swooped down behind him. Shannu.

Lady Bryren let out a barbaric yell as she hoisted her spear up, then shoved it into the nearest imperial soldier. The spear came out, and she took to the sky before the body dropped.

Shannu swung around and dipped toward Damien.

"Keep running!" Lady Bryren yelled. "We'll cover you."

Damien waved his hand in the air as an acknowledgment and dragged in another breath through his lips.

Run. Run to the river.

A moment later, a range of shouts went up from the imperial army, followed by echoing bellows in the sky.

Damien glanced back again but couldn't see anything, only that the imperial army seemed to have slowed a bit.

He nodded to himself and kept on running. Maybe House Merek was buying them more time.

Shannu swept by again, turned, then brought

her great wings up as she reached down with her talons and landed in the trampled grass near Damien.

"I can't believe it," Lady Bryren shouted as she jumped from the back of Shannu, her spear in hand. "That back-end-of-a-wyvern is finally fighting for the right side."

"What?" Damien asked as the soldiers around him slowed, and more shouts filled the air.

"House Friere. I saw them suddenly raise their standards, and they just turned on the empire from the rear. They've already disabled the catapults that were hindering my riders."

Quickly, a shift in the alliance occurred. The soldiers had stopped running, and there were rumblings along the ranks. Then the soldiers began to turn and yell, fists and weapons in the air.

Lady Bryren's eyebrows drew together as she watched the change. "What in the lands is going on? There's no way they could know about House Friere's insurrection in the rear."

A chant went up, mingling with the pounding of boots, as streams of green-clad soldiers rushed past them.

House Rafel had joined the battle.

Lady Bryren and Damien stared at each other. "So that other stubborn house finally came." She hoisted her spear into the air and let out a shout in the old tongue. "Back to the battlefield!" she

462

yelled and ran for Shannu. A minute later, the great beast took to the sky with a roar.

Damien listened as the sound of the horns changed. One long blast, followed by another long one. The signal to fight once more. He turned with his sword hand as soldiers ran by him, ready to fight again.

They had a chance.

His whole body began to shake, and for a moment he felt like he would collapse right there on the ground. They had a chance. All seven houses were here, now, fighting together.

They could push back the empire.

They could win.

With a yell, Damien charged ahead. A moment later, the Luceras brothers joined him with their weapons of light. With his broadsword in one hand, Lord Leo used his other to launch light spheres at the oncoming enemy. "Lord Damien, it appears House Rafel has joined us."

Damien brought both hands around his sword and prepared for the next fight. "Yes. And so has House Friere."

Lord Leo shot him an incredulous look.

"I heard from Lady Bryren herself. She saw them raise their standards and start to fight back."

Lord Elric let out a whoop and swung his polearm.

Lord Leo nodded as the distance between the alliance and empire closed, his gaze alert and his lips pressed tight. "Then let's do this. Let's end this war."

The clash between the two armies was even stronger than when the fight first resumed, hours ago. The first line of both fell within minutes. Damien fought until he couldn't feel his arm anymore, and the sword became an extension of his body. There was no thought, no feeling. Only the powerful need to keep moving.

To win.

The smell of smoke, blood, and sweat filled the air as the sun began to sink in the west. What had started for the alliance as a retreat had turned into an iron wall of determination. The knowledge that both House Rafel and House Friere had joined the fight bolstered the alliance, filling their cries and shouts.

"Remember what we're fighting for!"

"We're fighting for all of us!"

The imperial line broke, the standard of House Friere leading the way. Damien spotted Lord Raoul's telltale topknot amongst the men in red, slashing through the imperial soldiers with his sword. The two men spotted each other across the field. They stared at each other for a moment, then Lord Raoul gave him a slight nod before fighting again.

The sun had begun to set in a brilliance of red when the empire finally broke away. Damien stood panting, holding his arm to his chest, his other hand at his side, gripping his sword. It felt like his left arm was broken, but he barely registered the pain as he watched the empire retreat.

The only thing keeping him standing was one thought: They were victorious.

He let out a long breath and dropped his head. With each breath, his emotions came rushing back into his body. They were victorious, but they had not won. The bodies piled up on both sides attested to who had really won.

Death.

Damien fell to one knee as the sun continued to sink behind him. Moments later, men and women in telltale green robes began to move amongst the dead and wounded. The healers of House Rafel.

A few spoke quietly with those groaning in pain as others brought makeshift stretchers to begin carrying the wounded from the battlefield.

Damien just knelt there with his left arm tucked next to his chest. He stayed there as the alliance slowly left the battlefield and the first star appeared in the distance.

Then he prayed.

Tears welled up behind his eyelids, but he forced them back and swallowed hard. Death, life, blood, sweat. It all mingled here on the ground around him. How much could have been saved if only the war had never started? If the wall had remained raised. If the houses had worked together in the first place?

He shook his head and stood. No, he would not replay the past. What was done was done. He lifted his head and turned around to face the dying sun. Shades of red and purple stretched across the sky. More stars came out like pinpricks of hope.

They were alive. They were free. They had won against the Dominia Empire. With all seven houses united, they would force the empire back across the wall and seal it.

But for now, he grieved for the lives lost on both sides.

47

*T*here will be nothing left of you.

Selene stared ahead, but her thoughts were trapped within her mother's words. Nothing left of her mind. A fate even crueler than death.

Before Selene could focus, she was yanked into another dreamscape. Her whole body shook from fatigue, and every breath burned inside her lungs. She slowly raised her head. She was in the main audience chamber of Rook Castle. Black standards hung from the ceiling, with a crescent moon sigil. The dreamscape swirled, and seconds later she found herself in the audience chamber of Northwind Castle. Then Palace Levellon, then Surao. In each place hung the crescent moon banner.

"You cannot stop me." The Dark Lady's voice filled the air as the dreamscape moved from one city to the next. "Even the Dominia Empire cannot stop me."

The fortress inside Ironmond faded away, and Selene was back on top of the tower of Rook Castle. Her mother stood before her, tall, proud, with her sword in her hand. "You thought you could stand against us?" she asked. "You were a fool to turn us down." Her mother raised her sword as the Dark Lady raised a pale, bony finger. They pointed at her. "Now we will break you," they said together.

Selene held out against her mother's next advance, but only barely. Her muscles screamed under the strain, and as much as she tried, the images the Dark Lady had brought forth were worming their way into her spirit.

Was there any future where the alliance won? Was it futile to fight back?

Someone has to stand against this.

Selene paused.

I need to be the one who stands. I can't give up.

She missed her mother's next thrust, and the tip of the sword went into her right shoulder, near her collarbone.

Selene fell to one knee. Intense pain blossomed from the wound, increasing with each breath until it was hard to breathe at all. Her heart pounded in response to the injury, and for a moment, she felt like she would collapse.

She placed her right sword point down and used it as a crutch. Two shadows appeared near her knees, framed by the pale light of the moon.

"You're wrong, Mother." Selene spit out the blood in her mouth and looked up. Just those few words brought a measure of strength and boldness back to her body. "The Dark Lady needs us."

She turned her attention to the tall figure beside her mother. "You can't do anything without us.

Our gift is the gateway into humankind's dreams. Without House Ravenwood, you would be trapped within the shadows."

The Dark Lady waved a pale hand. "I provide the power for your gift."

Selene bent her head down and laughed, which only made her chest hurt more. "Not mine. I *never* needed your power to reach into the dreams of those around me." She took in a labored breath. "I never needed your power to draw people into my dreamscape, to comfort the dying, or to inspire those still living. You only bring nightmares. The Light has taught me differently. A better way."

"And where is your precious Light now?" the Dark Lady rasped. "All I see is a naïve dreamwalker broken on the ground at my feet."

Selene stalled. She knew with all her heart he was here. But then why did it seem like she was facing the Dark Lady alone? Damien's words came back to her. *"Does the sun disappear when clouds come? Or is the sun still there? Just as the clouds cannot quench the sun, the darkness cannot quench the Light."*

Selene coughed, then winced and bent over with pain. She could barely draw in a breath. "The Light . . . is here. But even if he weren't"— she looked up one more time—"I will never follow you."

"We shall see."

Before Selene could react, the dreamscape changed. Painful memories flashed before her eyes.

The day when her gift came, and her mark burned along her back.

The moment when her mother shared what they really used their gift for.

Visiting servant after servant, barely controlling her emotions as she twisted their dreams into nightmares.

Shattering Renata's mind.

Her gut-wrenching doubts about if Damien loved her.

Amara's death.

A bleak, lonely future in Nor Esen.

On and on, every fear she had ever harbored played before her.

You will never be loved.

You will always be alone.

Never feel. Keep every emotion locked inside.

There is nothing redeeming about your gift.

A small voice whispered inside her mind, breaking through the haze of hurt and fear. *That's not true.*

It wasn't much, but it was enough for her to collect her thoughts and focus on the dreamscape. The bombardment of memories was more than she could handle, but she had enough power to pause it for a moment. Maybe that was all she needed.

She closed her eyes and sank deep inside herself until all she could sense was the burning ember of her power at the core of her being. She fanned it for a moment, bringing it to life, then opened her eyes. She took in a deep breath, spread out her hands, and pushed.

The last of her power exploded across the dreamscape. Her hands began to shake, but she continued to press against the dreamscape, molding it one last time to her will until spots of colors popped across her vision and she felt like she was going to pass out.

Seconds later, the dreamscape shattered. All the memories—and the Dark Lady's hideous voice—disappeared. She was no longer on top of Rook Castle. The sky and moon were gone. Everything went black.

Selene collapsed, panting. The only sound was her labored breathing. Her tongue tasted blood inside her mouth, and her chest ached from the wound her mother had given her.

Everything was gone now. Perhaps even her mind.

Her lips trembled, but she pressed them together. If she was able to trap her mother and the Dark Lady here, it was worth it. Everyone would be safe now.

"Tsk, little raven." The Dark Lady's voice echoed across the barren landscape.

Selene froze, her heart no longer beating.

"That was quite a display of your power. But don't you realize that the darkness is *my* domain? You've only trapped yourself here."

It . . . it couldn't be. She'd given everything she had, every ounce of strength and power—even her own mind—to stop them.

"But it was a good attempt."

Selene stared into the darkness. Then, slowly, the tears came, more and more until it felt like a dam had burst inside of her. She crouched over and wrapped her arms around her knees as every emotion poured from her.

She wept until her face felt raw and hot. Her heart was broken. So was the rest of her. Even if the alliance beat the empire, she would not be returning. Her mother would live and continue to use her gift to hurt others. The Dark Lady would roam the dreams of those she had protected, bringing nightmares in her wake.

She had not been enough.

Soon her sobs quieted. A stillness lay across the nothingness. As she lay there, words began to penetrate the fog of her mind. Words she heard the night of the Festival of Light, when the monks from Baris Abbey presented their gift to the people of Nor Esen.

Words of darkness, and the light that came when all was lost. A light that spread across the lands.

A light that darkness could not extinguish.

There is always hope.

It was small, but it was there. Hope. A thread of hope rising inside of her, like a flower struggling to break through the frozen ground. Right there, right where her heart was. Even as she thought this, something glowed beneath her.

Selene raised her head. A small orb of light appeared where her heart beat inside her chest.

It was her soul.

A soul full of light—the light she had longed for since the moment she first laid eyes on Damien's soul. That light now resided in her as well.

The Light was with her.

She closed her eyes. *Thank you, Light. Thank you for not giving up on me. For being with me, even here, now. For changing me. For showing me a new way.*

She opened her eyes and placed her hands over her chest, feeling the warmth of the light. The place where her mother had pierced her no longer throbbed, and she could fully draw in a breath.

"What's going on?" she heard her mother ask nearby.

There was a hiss.

"I cannot be trapped in the darkness," Selene said. By the dim light, she could see her mother standing with the Dark Lady. "I am a changed soul. The one I follow resides inside of me." A renewing vigor flowed through her veins. Her face and body felt weary and yet refreshed at the same time. "He banished the darkness and fills me with his own light. A beautiful, purifying, life-giving light. A light that can never be extinguished. Even in death." She smiled softly as she pictured Amara's soul at the end, soaring on wings beneath a bright sun.

The Dark Lady raised a pale hand and pointed her finger at Selene. "The darkness is *my* province."

"No." Feeling a bit of strength return to her body, she slowly stood to her feet. "Everywhere belongs to the Light." She looked around. "And he is here, even now."

Her gaze settled on the two figures that stood just beyond the light emitting from her soul. "I couldn't stop you by my power alone. I may be a dreamwalker, but I am still mortal. But the Light can and will stop you. Your power over my family ends today. I follow a new way. A path that will erase every remnant of you and your nightmares."

She could feel it, her connection with the Light, the spark of hope welling up inside of her. "The Light is coming, and when he does, he will burn away the darkness and those who choose to stay in it. Mother, if you stay with the Dark Lady, then you will experience the same sentence she does."

Her mother gripped the hem of her tunic. "Sentence? What do you mean?"

The Dark Lady let out another hiss.

"The time of the Dark Lady is over. She will no longer draw power from House Ravenwood." The light around Selene grew brighter and brighter. "From now on, I will lead our family toward the Light. It is he who gave us our gift, and we will give it back to him."

She held her hands out, palms up, just as she saw Damien do many times when he lifted up his people and home to the Light in prayer.

My gift is yours. This place is yours. These people are yours.

The light grew brighter and brighter until a brilliant white light banished the shadows and continued to grow in radiance and intensity.

Selene tilted her head back, her hands still held up.

The Light . . . was so beautiful.

And in that moment, she realized how each house gift was a reflection of the Light: courage, wisdom, protection, creation, healing, light, and dreams. He had given the gift of himself to each house in order to reflect who he was to the people. But they had forgotten.

Until now.

An eerie shriek echoed around her as the light continued to shine brighter and brighter.

"My eyes! My eyes!" her mother cried.

A piercing wail drowned out her mother's shouts, rising in pitch. Selene remained where she was, her hands held up, her eyes closed and her face turned toward the light. It was warm, like the sun, soaking into her skin and appearing as hazy red behind her eyelids. The age of the Dark Lady was over. It was time to burn away the hatred of House Ravenwood and to step into the Light.

Moments later, the high shrill faded into nothing. Silence fell across the dreamscape. Then the light began to fade as well.

Selene carefully opened one eye, then the other. Light still flooded the dreamscape with its iridescent glow, but now it was bearable to her sight. There was no darkness, no shadows, and no Dark Lady, only a small burnt circle where she had stood moments ago next to her mother.

Her mother was now on the ground, prostrate, with her hands to her face, shaking uncontrollably.

Selene lowered her arms and took a step forward. "Mother?"

At the sound of her voice, her mother dropped her hands and looked up. Her eyes were completely white, a stark contrast to the rich, dark color they had been before. "S-Selene?"

A sharp pain twisted inside her chest at the brokenness in her mother's voice. She had never heard her mother speak in fear before.

Lady Ragna lifted her hand hesitantly and looked around. "Selene, are you there?"

"Yes, Mother." Selene closed the distance between them, knelt down, and reached for her mother's hand. Her skin was cold and papery to the touch, and her fingers trembled.

"I can't see." Her voice cracked. "My eyes . . ."

Selene could barely speak past the tightness in her own throat. "I know."

"I can't feel . . . the dreamscape . . . anymore."

Selene's brow furrowed. She reached out with her senses, stretching across the dreamscape. Sure enough, the Dark Lady was gone, and the presence of her mother . . .

Felt like any other person she brought into the dreamscape. A simple dreamer and nothing more.

Selene brought her mother's hand between her own and bowed her head. The brilliance of the Light had not only burned away the Dark Lady, it had also burned away her mother's sight and her connection to the dream world.

Her mother continued to shake, and Selene could hear her rapid breaths. Witnessing her mother's humanity broke through the anger and bitterness inside her heart. She could no more turn away from her mother than she could from anyone else. They were both flawed human beings, caught in a cycle of darkness and hatred.

Perhaps now, with her connection and eyesight gone, her mother might finally see.

Maybe Selene could help her.

"It is time to go, Mother." Selene slowly stood

to her feet, her hand still wrapped around her mother's.

"I don't think I can. I—" She swallowed, and Selene barely caught her mother's next words. "I don't know the way out."

"I do. And I will help you."

Her mother hesitated, then lifted one knee and pushed off the ground. "What are you going to do with me?" she asked, her voice stronger as her sightless eyes stared past Selene.

"I'm going to take you home."

"What about the empire?"

"You don't belong to the empire. You belong to House Ravenwood."

"You will put me in a dungeon," her mother murmured.

"No, in a home. My home. And I will show you what I've learned over the last year."

Her mother didn't say a word. Selene wasn't sure if she was mulling over what she had said or was choosing to remain silent.

Now that a soft light filled the area, she could see the thin boundary that separated the dreamscape from the real world. With one hand in her mother's, she stretched out her other hand and spread her fingers. Using her power, she released her mother's mind from the dreamscape. Her mother faded away until Selene was alone in the light.

Now it was her turn.

Selene transformed into a raven and flew for the boundary. Just as she reached the top, she looked back one more time. She was free.

They were free. Her house. All of them, from this time onward.

48

Morning came in a blaze of sunlight as Selene woke and stared up at the canvas ceiling. She drew in a long breath, one without pain or tightness, and let it out slowly.

"It's done," she whispered. No more Dark Lady, no more shadows. She was free. Herself and her progeny. Four hundred years of service to the Dark Lady, to hatred, to living in the darkness, gone.

A smile crept across her face as the tent lit with the coming dawn. This was her gift to the future. A new start.

A shout sounded outside, then another.

Selene sat up, a frown on her face as she listened to the commotion. She rubbed her forehead, then brushed her hair back. The last she could remember was sleeping beside Damien and calming the soldiers of the alliance within the dreamscape. Then her mother and the Dark Lady had appeared, and she'd hidden the soldiers in the dreamscape before her last words to them and—

Her eyes widened, and she threw back the blanket. There was no sign of Damien. When did he leave? Had the empire arrived? Though the Dark Lady and her mother had contrived to keep the alliance locked away in the dreamscape, had she freed them in time to fight?

Selene stood and dressed quickly, not even bothering to do anything with her hair except run her fingers through it.

By now the camp was buzzing.

She double-checked her swords, then placed them in their scabbards and emerged from the tent, ready for whatever the real world brought.

Rays of gold and pink filled the sky above, and a warm wind blew across the camp. Several people ran past her with shouts and laughter.

Wait, laughter?

She glanced east. What did that mean?

"My lady!" Karl stood near the entrance to the tent, a relieved look on his face. "You're awake."

"Karl? Why are you here?"

"His lordship left you in my care." He bowed, then looked up. "Do you need to see a healer? You were asleep for three days."

Selene blinked. Three days? "No, I am fine." More than fine. "What happened while I was sleeping?"

"The empire arrived and the alliance left to meet them in battle."

She let out a deep breath. "Then they made it."

He gave her a puzzled look.

She brushed two fingertips along her temple and laughed. "Many things happened in the last three days, things I cannot talk about."

"I heard your voice in the dreamscape. Lord Damien said you freed us from the death sleep." His voice held a hint of awe.

"Yes. But it wasn't just me. The Light guided me."

"The Light," he murmured. "I've been thinking more about the Light." Then he looked at her. "Thank you, Lady Selene, on behalf of the Northern Shores. We are blessed to have you as our lady."

Our lady. A tender smile came over her face. "Thank you, Karl."

Selene glanced to the east, where a crowd was starting to gather.

Damien.

Was he with them? Or was he . . . ?

She turned and started running, her cloak whipping out behind her, her swords clapping against her thighs. One name, one face filled her mind. She had to know if he was still alive. She had to know if he was returning to her.

She ran past the edge of camp with Karl close behind. Ahead, beneath the rising sun, thousands of alliance soldiers came marching across the grassy plain. There was laughter and shouts, but also those clinging to their comrades as they supported each other. Selene scanned the soldiers, searching for one in blue, with dark hair and bright blue eyes.

The first line of people moved around her

like a river. The air filled with the smell of sweat and blood. It seemed only those injured were returning. Many of the men had bandages wrapped around their arms or legs, and there were even a few with linen around their heads. The dark green healing garb of House Rafel intermingled between the soldiers, some carrying stretchers.

House Rafel? When did they arrive?

Selene crushed her hands into two tight fists. Were those not returning healthy enough to continue the fight, or . . . ?

No, she would not go there. Not until she knew for sure if—

Her breath escaped her lungs as her eyes met blue ones of deep sapphire.

Damien.

She took one step, then another until she was running against the crowd, her gaze set on her husband.

He was alive.

A moment later, he caught sight of her. His eyes widened, and a smile came over his roughened face as he began making his way toward her. As she made her way around a stretcher, she noticed his arm bandaged and in a sling, a cut along his cheek, and dried blood all over his uniform.

She didn't care. He was alive, and that's all that mattered.

The second he drew near enough, she threw

her arms around him—careful of his sling—and kissed him fully on the lips. It didn't matter who was watching. And they were watching, given the hoots and laughter erupting around them.

"You're alive," she said, pulling back and looking at him with tears in her eyes.

Tears sparkled in his eyes as well. "You're alive too. When I left you, I wasn't sure . . ." He lifted his good hand and cupped her cheek. "But we did it, Selene, we won. The empire is on the run. House Luceras, House Friere, and the wyvern riders are rounding up the rest—"

"House Friere?"

Damien laughed, his eyes crinkling along the corners. "Yes, Lord Raoul came to our aid in the end. And so did House Rafel, just when we needed them the most."

"All seven houses were there?"

"Yes. And I believe that's why we won. We worked together and overcame in the end. Just like the Light gifted us to do."

They turned and started walking toward the camp, Damien's good arm over her shoulder while her own was wrapped around his waist.

"You have no idea how much your words impacted our troops."

Her brow furrowed as she hooked her arm more securely around him.

"*Remember what we're fighting for.* It was our rallying cry. You did what your forebearers did before you: You inspired the other houses as we slept, giving us one last bit of strength to fight." He leaned over and kissed her cheek. "It was not easy leaving you behind, knowing you were fighting your own battle somewhere in the dreamscape, far away from me. But I knew there was nothing I could do to help you. I could only do what I could do, and that was lead our people."

Selene let out a sigh. "The Dark Lady and my mother were there in the dreamscape." She shook her head. "It's a long story. But in the end, the Light was there. And together, we ended the dark legacy of my family."

"And the Dark Lady?"

"She is no more. House Ravenwood is free. My—our—future children are free."

"Children?"

Selene blushed. "Yes."

He chuckled. A moment later he asked in a more serious voice, "If the Dark Lady is gone, what happened to your mother?"

She sobered. "She's not a threat anymore. But she will need our help, Damien." She felt him tense beside her. "I know how you feel. She has hurt many people, us most of all. But I think the Light left her alive for a reason. So please help me find her. I hope to show her what we were really meant to be as dreamwalkers."

He was silent as they walked toward the camp

with the rest of the troops. It had to be hard to think about helping her mother on the heels of the war; it was hard for her. After all, her mother had killed many others and helped bring about this war in the first place. But now . . .

"If it is important to you, then I will do it."

Selene looked at him.

"My goal—and my father's goal—has always been to unite the Great Houses. Your mother is part of that."

A wave of warmth and pride spread across Selene, and she blinked back another set of tears. No other person she knew would give her mother a second chance. Only Damien and his strong, compassionate heart.

"Thank you. I know she doesn't deserve it, but I want to do what I can."

He gave her shoulder a squeeze. "I know."

49

The next few days were spent in a state of conflicting feelings. There was joy but also grief. Healing and pain. Fear and hope. Under the direction of Lady Ayaka, the healers from House Rafel worked all day and night with those who had survived the battle. More alliance troops trickled into the camp after burying the dead.

Word arrived that the empire had scattered. House Friere and those who remained from House Luceras and House Vivek pushed the empire toward the breach in the wall, while the wyvern riders cut off any chance the empire could regroup in Shanalona.

Selene spent the nights watching over those sleeping, easing their pain and driving away their nightmares. A little over a week later, Lady Bryren arrived. Her copper wyvern and a handful of others landed outside the camp with a cloud of dust that rose into the bright blue sky.

"Lord Damien, Lady Selene, Lady Ayaka, it is good to see you!" Lady Bryren shouted as she dismounted. Nothing had changed with the wyvern lady, other than a few cuts and bruises that were still healing. "We took back Shanalona, and the empire is heading toward the other side of the wall."

"And what of Commander Orion?"

"We have him."

"And his generals?"

"We also have them in custody."

"And my mother?"

Lady Bryren's face darkened. "We discovered your mother alone in a tent in the deserted imperial camp." Her eyes came to rest on Selene. "She . . . she won't be fighting anymore."

"I know what happened to her. I saw it in the dreamscape."

Lady Bryren gave her a respectful nod, then looked around. "Where is your father, Lady Ayaka?"

"He is not here. But I am glad that he sent our people to help at just the right time," she said softly.

Lady Bryren laughed. "Stubborn old man. I'm glad he saw the light in the end." Then she nodded to Damien. "I'm here to take you to the wall. We are hoping between your power and Lord Raoul's we can restore the boundary again."

Damien raised his good arm and stared at his palm. "It won't be easy with just one arm, but I'll try."

Lady Bryren snorted. "I've seen what you can do. A little thing like a broken arm won't stop you."

Selene stepped forward. "I would like to go as well."

"Actually, we would like all three of you to go. Lord Renlar and Lord Leo requested that all seven houses be present at the raising of the wall, both to hold council and to reaffirm the alliance of our houses."

"I believe I can stand in for my father," Lady Ayaka said quietly.

Lady Bryren's face lit up. "Of course you can. After all, you're his heir. And I know a certain lord is expecting to see you," she said with a wink.

A blush spread across Lady Ayaka's cheeks at the wyvern lady's bold words.

Selene hid her own smile. So it was true. There was something between Lord Leo and Lady Ayaka. The thought made her heart warm.

"My riders and I need a day to rest, then we can leave."

Damien nodded. "Then we will make sure we are ready."

The next morning found Selene high in the sky with the wind rushing past her face as she took to the air on the back of a wyvern. Down below lay those who had died in the battle, resting in the ground. Seeing the numerous large mounds of dirt brought a heaviness to her heart. So many died. And not just here but in Shanalona, along the Hyr

River, and in the Surao forest. So much grief. So many tears. All for power, greed, and hate.

Then she looked ahead at the blue sky and wispy clouds, her fingers tight around the saddle horn. Never again. No matter what, the Great Houses needed to work together to prevent this from happening in the future. They were gifted to help and protect their people, to bring peace—not war—to their lands. This would be their resolution.

After five days of flying, the small group approached the wall that divided their lands from the Dominia Empire. The clay-colored earth was barren, with only rocks and boulders scattered here and there. Just beyond the arid landscape, rising up from the ground toward the sky, stood the wall.

Selene had never seen it before, and to gaze on it now filled her with awe. It was at least a couple hundred feet tall and curved, like a wave in the sea at the height of its ascent. Along the top were jagged stone teeth to prevent anyone from scaling the wall—that is, if they could actually reach the top.

The wall spread from north to south as far as the eye could see, reaching from the Cliffs of Bora down to the Maelstrom. A jagged crack that marred the smooth surface of the wall drew her eye, the place where Lord Ivulf had split the wall and allowed the empire in.

A large camp was settled in front of the crack, with multiple banners representing the Great Houses flying in the wind.

A party consisting of Lord Renlar, Lord Leo and his brother Elric, Lord Raoul, and a handful of generals greeted them as the wyverns touched down at the edge of the camp. Selene smiled as she secretly watched Lord Leo assisting Lady Ayaka from her wyvern.

Then another sight caught her by surprise: near the banner and tents of Ravenwood stood her father and Ophie. The moment Ophie saw her, the little girl came running across the hard-packed earth, while her father smiled and slowly followed behind. Selene caught her sister up in her arms and twirled her around. Caiaphas came to stand beside Damien, and the two spoke for a moment while she savored this time with her sister.

Amara, if only you were here too.

That thought brought a tear to her eye. Ophie stilled as Selene held her, and she lifted her little fingers up and wiped the tear away.

"We both miss her, don't we?" Selene whispered. Ophie laid her head on Selene's chest in response.

Selene stood there, holding her sister as the others finished dismounting and retrieving their packs. Afterward, the wyverns were let loose to hunt and rest, and the lords and ladies were led to the main tent, where a long table and chairs were ready.

Selene placed Ophie down near the tent entrance and turned toward her father. "Thank you for coming, and for bringing Opheliana."

"Of course. This is a monumental occasion, one that will go down in history. It was important for both of us to be here. I will watch over Opheliana while you meet with the others."

"Thank you, Father."

He smiled as he took Ophie's hand, and both of them stood to the side as Selene followed Damien into the tent.

The rest of the afternoon was spent discussing what to do with Commander Orion and the imperial army.

"Most of the men have fled back into their own country," Lord Leo said. "As for Commander Orion, I would like to request that he be brought back to Lux Casta and imprisoned there."

Lord Raoul sat back with his arms folded. "Why not just put him to death?"

Lord Leo scowled. "That is not our way."

"I agree with Lord Leo," Selene said, glancing at Lord Raoul. "I can speak from experience that death only begets more death."

Lord Raoul shrugged. "But if he lives, it means there is always a chance of an uprising."

"Not in Lux Casta. He will be under the watch of my house and the Light for the rest of his life.

He will be secure and far from the border of his country."

"I also wish for a merciful sentencing," Lady Ayaka said. "Let us show the empire that we are different."

The other lords and ladies agreed, and the matter was put to rest, despite the scowl on Lord Raoul's face.

"And what about Lord Ivuf?" Lord Renlar asked.

"He was found dead on the battlefield," Lord Leo said. "I had his body recovered. He was a traitor, but he was also a lord of a Great House."

Lord Raoul's face darkened for a moment as he worked his jaw. "Thank you," he said finally. "His death gave my people the strength to turn away from the empire in the end."

"And it wasn't by your hand?" Lady Bryren asked.

Lord Raoul stared at her with such intensity that even Lady Bryren looked taken aback. "No. I didn't take my father's life. I might be many things, but I'm not a murderer."

"Wouldn't putting Commander Orion to death be murder?"

"No, it would be justice. After all, this is war. Or else all of us are murderers."

"Fair point," Lord Renlar murmured and turned toward Lady Selene. "And that leaves Lady Ragna."

All eyes turned toward Selene.

She let out a long breath, a mess of feelings rolling inside of her. For a split second, she was tempted to leave her mother in the hands of those gathered and forget about her. Maybe let her accompany Commander Orion to Lux Casta.

The moment passed. No. Deep down, she knew her next task was to share with her mother what had been given to her by the Light. Young Ragna's innocent face from her mother's memory flashed before Selene's eyes. Despite the pain, despite the hurt, it was time to bring reconciliation and redemption to House Ravenwood's past.

She looked up at the others. "If I may, I request that Lady Ragna be put under Lord Damien's and my care. As some of you know, she is now blind, and I can attest that she no longer has a connection to the dreamscape. I know she deserves prison, but I am asking for mercy on her behalf."

"Are you sure about this?" Lady Bryren asked. "Out of everyone, Lady Ragna hurt your own house the most."

"I agree." Lord Renlar folded his hands across the table. "It is a difficult request you make. Are you prepared to bring her into your home?"

Selene swallowed. "I am."

"Then"—Lord Renlar looked around for confirmation before answering her—"we release her into your care."

Selene bowed her head. "Thank you."

Damien gave her hand a hard squeeze under the table.

As the sun began to set later that day, the lords and ladies concluded their assembly and gathered outside. For the first time ever, the seven Great Houses were all in one accord.

"With the coalition aligned with the Great Houses, our people—all of our people—are finally united. Everyone working together." Damien sighed as he and Selene approached the wall. "I wish my father could have seen this."

"He would have been proud of you."

Word had spread across the camp that the wall would be raised, and crowds gathered at the base. Songs and laughter broke out as bonfires were lit, and food was prepared in celebration. The firelight danced across the smooth surface of the wall.

Damien left Selene's side and went to join Lord Raoul near the base. Seeing those two men together, one with dark hair and broad shoulders, the other with his hair pulled up in a topknot and his scarlet cloak rippling in the wind, was a wonder. They were as different as the gifts of water and fire they possessed. They didn't see eye to eye on many things. But they agreed on one thing: the preservation of their people and their lands.

They stood there alone, two small figures below the massive wall. For a moment, they spoke. Then Damien placed one foot back, the other forward, his left elbow back as far as his broken arm would allow, his right hand out in front of him. At the same time, Lord Raoul separated his feet and bent slightly forward, then held out two fists that were now burning with white fire.

Both gave out a great yell.

Water burst from the ground along with molten rock. Brilliant red and steaming water shot up like a geyser inside the crack. Up went the water and rock, hardening as it went. Both men shuddered with the intensity of their power, but still they continued.

The crowd watched in silence. Goose bumps spread along Selene's arms, and a shiver ran down her back. Once again she was in awe of the gifts the Light had given them. How powerful. How beautiful. How healing.

Sweat poured down both of their faces. When the water and rock reached the top, Damien changed his stance, his hands now moving synchronously with Lord Raoul's. Sharp, ragged teeth jutted out from the rock. Then Damien lifted his good arm high into the air. The water from within the ground responded to his movement and showered the wall with a spray of water, dousing the molten rock until the fiery red turned black.

Both men fell to their knees. It was done.

A shout went up, followed by another, until the voices of thousands echoed against the wall.

Selene, along with the other lords and ladies, rushed to the men.

Lady Bryren clapped Lord Raoul across the shoulder. "Well done, House Friere. That was a magnificent display of your gift."

Selene didn't say a word. Instead, she knelt beside Damien and reached for his hand. He looked up at her touch, his face haggard and slick with sweat. He appeared as if he was going to collapse any moment, but she held on tightly to him, and that seemed to give him the strength he needed to remain conscious. Behind them, the celebration began.

The others spoke their congratulations to Damien, then slowly made their way over to join their people gathered around the many bonfires.

"I didn't think it was possible," Raoul said, his voice sounding weak and in awe at the same time.

"All things are possible with the Light," Damien said.

"Perhaps." Lord Raoul slowly stood. "Well done, House Maris." He let out a laugh. "Perhaps we *can* work together."

A small figure emerged from amongst the crowd. It took Selene a moment in the dim light to realize it was Ophie. Instead of approaching

Selene, she walked toward Raoul. In her hand, she held a tiny white flower, which she offered to him. He stood there, staring down at her sister with a blank expression.

Selene's heart seized. What was Ophie doing? Did the little girl know the two were related? Did Raoul know? If he so much as said one word—

He took the flower from Ophie. "Thank you."

She nodded in response. As she turned and headed back toward Caiaphas in the distance, a small smile came over Raoul's face as he looked down at the flower in his hands. Selene let out her breath, and her shoulders relaxed. Maybe Raoul really had changed. If so, was there a chance her sister might find her rightful place within her true house?

With a final nod at Damien and Selene, Raoul turned and melted into the shadows.

They continued to kneel before the wall, hands held tight. It felt good to sit in the shadows outside the light of the bonfires and just rest. Darkness fell across the land, and songs filled the warm night air.

"I love you," Damien said softly, breaking the silence.

Selene turned and looked at him.

"I'm glad we were brought together, despite the circumstances. There is no greater gift than to spend a lifetime with the person you love until the day you die."

Tears pricked Selene's eyes. "I love you too. I look forward to our future together."

Then they leaned toward each other and met with a kiss.

Together. Always.

50

Selene knocked softly, then slowly opened the door to the small room where her mother lived on the western side of Northwind Castle. Summer had come and gone, along with harvest and winter. Spring was bringing new life to the Northern Shores, and recently to House Maris.

Her mother stirred slightly where she sat on the opposite side of the room and turned her head. "Who's there? You're not Elin."

Selene wasn't sure she would ever get used to the milky white of her mother's eyes. Or the grey streak that ran through her mother's ebony hair. "It's me, Mother. It's Selene."

Lady Ragna stiffened.

Selene stepped into the room and closed the door behind her. It was a simple room, with a four-poster bed made of grey wood, a wardrobe, a small stone fireplace, and a single chair next to the window, which was currently occupied by her mother. The window was open, letting in the fresh sea air. The wind pulled at her mother's hair, pushing the grey-and-black strands away from her aging face.

"Are you here to tell me about the child?"

Selene let out a long breath. "We had a son."

"A son?" Her mother tried to hide it, but Selene

caught the glimpse of curiosity on her mother's face.

"Yes. And . . ." She paused, still amazed herself by the miracle she and Damien had brought forth. "He carries the mark of Ravenwood on his back."

There was a quick intake of breath. "A boy?"

"Yes."

"A male dreamer," her mother murmured to herself.

Selene smiled as she pictured him, wrapped in blue linen, and the way Damien had glowed with love and pride as he held their son.

"There hasn't ever been a male dreamer," her mother said. "What did you name him?"

"Riven. Riven Maris."

"Riven . . . a severing. A name that means courage, strength, and beauty."

Selene approached her mother. "I believe he will be a new beginning for House Ravenwood. He will continue to lead our people along a different path, a new path."

Lady Ragna turned her head toward the window.

"Would you like to meet him?"

Her mother didn't answer.

Selene sighed and dropped her head. What had she been hoping for with this visit? That her mother had changed? That somewhere inside that broken woman was a regenerate soul? That the knowledge of a grandson and heir to House

Ravenwood would spark something inside of her? "If you decide you want to meet Riven, let Elin know, and I'll bring him to you."

Her mother never answered.

Selene balled her hands into fists at her sides. Why did her mother remain so bitter and cold when there was so much life and light around her?

A sound slowly drifted through the window. Selene paused and listened. Soft, serene, peaceful.

It was the chant from the abbey. But how was that possible? Usually the monks' chant did not carry this far. The wind blew in again through the window, carrying the sound.

Everything inside of her relaxed. Her fingers loosened, then her hands fell at her sides. The chant was an old one, the one that spoke of the Light at the beginning of creation. The voice of the monks blended with the gentle roll of the sea waves and the cool, salty wind. She took in a deep breath, savoring the feel and sound of the moment.

Her eyes came to rest on her mother. Lady Ragna's face was tilted to the side, toward the window.

Her breath caught in her chest.

For a moment she saw the same look of longing on her mother's face as she herself had experienced over a year ago.

Was it possible? Did a tiny flame burn inside her mother's heart?

If so, then perhaps there was hope after all.

Selene turned and headed for the door. Maybe she wouldn't wait for her mother to ask for Riven. Maybe she would bring her son to her mother and fan the small flame possibly starting to burn inside her heart. Riven would bring change, she was sure of it. And maybe it would start with her mother.

Selene stepped out into the hall and headed for the small room attached to the bedchambers she shared with Damien. Guards and servants greeted her with a smile, and she greeted them back in the same manner. When she reached the door, the sound of a low tenor voice reached her ears. Selene cracked the door open and peeked inside.

The room, which had once been her own when she first arrived in Northwind Castle, had been refurnished. Tall wooden bookshelves stood on either side of the window, stacked with colorful painted blocks, tiny toy ships, and an embroidered bunny. To the left stood a crib with a raven and three waves carved into the wooden side. And to the right . . .

There was Damien, half-turned toward the door, a gentle look on his face as he sang to their son in his arms, a song Selene recognized from the Festival of Light. It was a beautiful scene:

father and son, sunlight trickling in through the window. So full of love. So full of light.

The singing stopped as Damien looked up. "I didn't hear you enter."

Selene shut the door behind her. "I wasn't expecting you here. But then I didn't want to interrupt."

"He's incredible, isn't he?" Damien said, looking down at their son again.

"Yes, he is. A miracle."

"How is your mother?"

Selene paused and looked out the window at the sea. A collage of blues and greens stretched toward the horizon, glistening beneath a bright sun.

Then she glanced back at him with a smile. Even the fact that she could smile about her mother made her feel a deep sense of awe. It was small, but it was a start. "I think she is changing."

"Really? What makes you think that?"

"A look on her face before I left."

Damien shifted the babe in his arms. "And Riven? Did she want to see him?"

Selene couldn't help but notice how Damien pulled their son closer to his chest. She could understand that.

"No, she didn't. But I think Riven will live up to his name. I believe he will sever the Ravenwood past from the Ravenwood future. He will be the dreamwalker we were meant to be and bring hope to our people, starting perhaps with his grandmother."

Damien leaned down and kissed his son's forehead. "I hope so."

"I also received a letter this morning from my father."

"How is Caiaphas? And Rook Castle?"

"They've found a large vein of silver in the south and are planning on opening up a new mine. And he's been working with Opheliana. She finally spoke." Selene beamed. "He said from the moment she started speaking, it was as if she were never mute. He's personally overseeing her education and already teaching her how to read."

"Your sister is in good hands." Damien smiled as he bounced Riven in his arms. A tiny fist came up and waved in the air, catching Selene's heart. "That reminds me, a wedding has been announced between House Luceras and House Rafel, and we've been invited."

It took Selene a moment to look up from her son and register Damien's words. "Lord Leo and Lady Ayaka?"

"Yes. Next summer."

Her smile widened. "I'm glad."

A knock at the door interrupted their conversation. A servant peeked in. "Lord Damien, Steward Bertram is asking for you."

Damien looked down at Riven and sighed. "Let him know I'll be there soon."

"Yes, my lord."

As the door closed, Damien turned to Selene. "I let Emileigh have the morning off. Would you mind watching Riven?"

Damien didn't need to ask twice. Selene reached for her son, feeling the solid weight of his little body settle into her arms. Wispy dark hair covered the top of his head, and his cheeks were flushed with warmth.

Damien leaned over and kissed her cheek. "I'll see you tonight?"

"Yes," Selene said without taking her eyes off her son.

He kissed her again, then left, the door shutting behind him with a soft thud. Selene walked over to the window, letting the sunlight pour over Riven and herself. She quietly hummed as she rocked him in her arms. A moment later, Riven opened his eyes, as blue as the sea outside the window. Just like Damien's.

"Hello, little one."

He squinted as he looked up into her face.

She lifted him close and breathed in his soft scent. "My son," she whispered, "someday you will hold the hopes, dreams, and memories of humankind in your hands. Dreamwalking is the gift we have been given, and it is a heavy gift." She brushed her hand along his mark. "But there is another who will walk with you. He brings light to the darkness and hope to the weary."

Riven yawned, then closed his eyes.

Selene cupped his cheek and closed her eyes as well. She gently filled his little mind with sunlight and warmth, with love and light. The same way she filled the dreams of the people of these lands. The same way she would watch over them for the rest of her life.

As she drifted away from his mind, she spoke once more. "Remember, my little dreamwalker, you are never alone. The Light is always with you."

Morgan L. Busse is a writer by day and a mother by night. She is the author of the FOLLOWER OF THE WORD series and the steampunk series THE SOUL CHRONICLES. *Mark of the Raven*, the first book in THE RAVENWOOD SAGA, has won both a Carol Award and an Inspy Award. During her spare time she enjoys playing games, taking long walks, and dreaming about her next novel. Visit her online at www.morganlbusse.com.

Books are produced in the United States using U.S.-based materials

Books are printed using a revolutionary new process called THINKtech™ that lowers energy usage by 70% and increases overall quality

Books are durable and flexible because of Smyth-sewing

Paper is sourced using environmentally responsible foresting methods and the paper is acid-free

Center Point Large Print
600 Brooks Road / PO Box 1
Thorndike, ME 04986-0001 USA

(207) 568-3717

US & Canada:
1 800 929-9108
www.centerpointlargeprint.com